1968

SATANSTOE

SATANSTOE

JAMES FENIMORE COOPER

Introduction by

Robert L. Hough

UNIVERSITY OF NEBRASKA PRESS · Lincoln 1962

First Bison Book printing May, 1962
Second Bison Book printing March, 1965
Third Bison Book printing September, 1968

The text of the Bison Book edition is reproduced from
the 1937 American Book Company edition.

INTRODUCTION

In 1845 when James Fenimore Cooper wrote *Satanstoe*, the first book of the Littlepage trilogy—the other two are *The Chainbearer* (1845) and *The Redskins* (1846)—he was both angry and concerned, a man with an axe to grind. He felt strongly that unless America could be brought to recognize the implications of its democratic polity and to control its direction, the Western experiment in self-government was bound to deteriorate. Jacksonian democracy, with its emphasis on the common man, in Cooper's eyes lay very close to mob rule. Not that he thought Jackson was entirely to blame, but "Old Hickory's" presidency had brought to the surface dangers which had lurked in the shallows since 1787. Cooper saw—correctly—that only a short step separated political democracy, of which he heartily approved, from social and economic leveling, which he abhorred. If this disastrous leveling process was to be averted, the nation must face up to the threat and remain constantly and everlastingly on guard against it.

There was nothing new in these ideas—John Adams and other conservatives had been saying much the same things for forty years—but Cooper was a starchy old man and presented them with a bluntness and vigor that commanded attention. In 1838, seven years before the publication of *Satanstoe*, he had expounded his views in *The American Democrat*, a book in which his avowed aim was "correction" and which was "written more in the spirit of censure than of praise." Since the Littlepage trilogy is an expression in fictional form of the beliefs he sat forth in the earlier book, a brief summary of points stressed in *The American Democrat* may be useful.

It is demonstrably false, Cooper maintained, that all men

are created equal. Men should and—in the United States—do have equal political and civil rights: that is, equal rights before the law. But there never has been, nor should there be, what Cooper calls "equality of condition." That men should be born with different moral, physical, and intellectual endowments is a law of nature, and because these differences exist men will always strive to improve their condition by acquiring more of the world's goods. This is the beginning of property, a cornerstone of social well-being and advancement.

> As property is the base of all civilization, its existence and security are indispensable to social improvement . . . . The principle of individuality, or to use a less winning term, of selfishness, lies at the root of all voluntary human exertion. We toil for food, for clothes, for houses, lands, and for property in general. This is done, because we know the fruits of our labor will belong to ourselves, or to those who are most dear to us. It follows, that all which society enjoys beyond the mere supply of its first necessities is dependent of the right of property.

Because of its importance, the right to hold property must be rigorously defended by law and its benefits understood by everyone. That they be understood was, in Cooper's estimation, particularly important since in democracies there is a natural tendency to level downward, and such leveling often threatened property rights through higher taxes and other discrimination. "The maxim that one man is as good as another"—which today seems derived from a distortion of John Locke's views—meant for Cooper, not that the common man was raised from the mass, but that the superior man was pulled down to its level. Cooper does not conceal his distrust of the masses in certain situations; he believes that while men will usually decide aright when faced with a problem over a span of years, both large and small groups are likely to be irresponsible during a time of excitement or under the influence of demagogues. In these situations the substitution of public opinion for law—which Cooper calls "tyranny" and "a besetting vice of democracies"—opens the door to injustice and the destruction of legally held rights.

His hopes that such happenings can be prevented or minimized depend in great part on the gentleman, the man of position and wealth, and thus a strong current of *noblesse oblige* runs through both *The American Democrat* and the Littlepage trilogy. The gentleman has no more rights than the average man, but he usually has education and refinement, "the inevitable consequences of civilization"; because of these advantages he should be willing to lead, to speak out against abuses, "to be a guardian of the liberties of his fellow citizens." He should also display proper deportment, speak the language well, and persevere in his accomplishments, for all these things directly or indirectly advance the culture and civilization of society and are in themselves mitigators of evil. Thus, the gentry are capable of becoming leaders and worthy of trust if they assume their proper responsibility to others. And if they do, the populace would be well advised to look to such leadership. Cooper firmly believed

> that a nation is happy, in which the people, possessing the power to select their rulers, select the noble. . . [and] happy, indeed, is that nation, in which, power being the common property, there is sufficient discrimination and justice to admit the intelligent and refined to a just participation of its influence.

II

Satanstoe and the other Littlepage novels were born of Cooper's desire to comment on a specific episode in American history whose unfolding he witnessed—the Anti-Rent War (1839-1846) which climaxed a period of agrarian unrest in New York's upstate Hudson River counties. The fundamental issue—involving what tenant-farmers felt were inequities in perpetual or long-term leaseholds—was inherent in the patroon system, a holdover from the early days of Dutch settlement in the New World. To promote settlement the Dutch

West Indies Company had been empowered to grant patroon-
ships which bestowed on the grantees choicely located estates
and feudal rights over their property. In Cooper's day, some
two hundred years after the system was established, there
were descendants of the early Dutch settlers still holding land
which was leased, never sold, to tenant-farmers. In return,
the tenants paid an annual rent in the land's produce and
often were required to render certain services to the landowner. All the leases were long term and some were perpetual,
but the lessee could convert the yearly rent into a cash payment or, if he wished, could sell his lease to another party.
In the latter event he was required to pay the landlord an
alienation fine which might run as much as one-third of the
amount received.

Agitation for change in this leasing system began to mount
after 1828 when the completion of the Erie Canal brought a
flow of cheaper Western wheat into New York state. The
competition was felt keenly by both landowners and tenants:
the former reacted by trying to collect back rents, the latter
by seeking to evade payment altogether. The tenants formed
anti-rent societies, the landlords resorted to law, and both
sides sent lobbying groups to the state legislature. In some
counties practically no rents were paid after 1840, and sheriffs
attempting to evict tenants were intimidated or resisted by
defiant farmers. At one time early in the war Governor
William H. Seward called out the militia to suppress distur-
bances, but the state took no concerted legal action to enforce
payments. Public opinion strongly supported the tenants, and
at a constitutional convention summoned by Governor John
Young in 1846 new laws were passed which abolished feudal
tenures, outlawed alienation fines, restricted future leases to
twelve-year periods, and levied higher taxes on the landlords
—many of whom immediately began to sell their land.

As a wealthy landowner with holdings in Otsego and Westchester counties, Cooper had acquired an intimate knowledge
of the workings of the patroon system, but neither he nor
his father (the founder of Cooperstown, N.Y.) used it on

their own estates. They believed that ownership gave a farmer greater incentive and eventually resulted in greater benefit to the community, and preferred to sell parcels of land to individuals rather than to grant leases. (Similarly, in *Satanstoe*, the hero Corny Littlepage and his family intend to sell, not lease, sections of their land at Mooseridge.) But on the question of property rights Cooper's allegiance to the patroons was absolute, and he wrote the Littlepage trilogy primarily to present their side of the controversy.

A fictional exponent of his views in *Satanstoe* is Herman Mordaunt, a responsible Dutch landowner of the 1750's, who institutes the patroon system at Ravensnest, his recently acquired patent. Mordaunt's experiences demonstrate that "the settlement of new land was a slow and painful process, and was generally made at a great outlay to the proprietor." Land had to be cleared and settlers brought in, most of whom consented to come only on terms highly favorable to themselves.

> Not only was [Mordaunt] obliged to grant leases for three lives, or in some cases, for thirty or forty years, at rents that were merely nominal, but as a rule, the first six or eight years the tenants were to pay no rent at all. On the contrary he was obliged to extend to them many favors in various ways, that cost no inconsiderable sum in the course of the year.

While Mordaunt's sole purpose in settling Ravensnest is the nonaltruistic one of gaining material advantages for himself and his descendants (the natural motive "at the root of all human exertion"), Cooper makes it plain that the relationship between the landholder and his tenants was not simply that of exploiter to exploited. In the first place the roles could be reversed: in the beginning and for a long time thereafter it was the tenant, not the proprietor, who held the whip hand. And secondly, when the advantage did finally lie with the landlord the terms of most leases were not onerous.

The lease granted by Mordaunt to the New England school-teacher Jason Newcome stipulates that he pay no rent for the first ten years and only sixpence an acre for the ten after that, in the meantime having all the privileges of ownership of the mill and "the right to cut timber at pleasure." Jason was given these easy terms because of Mordaunt's desire to have as educated and civilized a community as possible, a concern for the cultural well-being of the tenants that Cooper found fairly typical of the patroon class. As he suggests in *Satanstoe* and dramatizes in *The Chainbearer* and *The Redskins,* building schools, opening commissaries, establishing churches, and constructing and maintaining roads were all burdens borne wholly or in part by the landlord, often at great expense and difficulty.

This appreciation of the proprietor's responsibilities coupled with his personal convictions as to the rights of property and the sanctity of contracts naturally predisposed Cooper to champion the cause of the landowner. As he saw it, the tenants were under no duress to sign the leases, and when they chose to do so, it was with the knowledge that they assumed certain obligations that were legal and binding. Cooper's indignation at the public sympathy given those who were evading their obligations and at the state's refusal to enforce its laws blazes out in the Preface to *Satanstoe*:

> In our view, New York is, at the moment, much the most disgraced State in the Union . . . and her disgrace arises from the fact that her laws are trampled underfoot, without any efforts, at all commensurate with the object, being made to enforce them. . . . if states, like individuals, are to be judged by their actions, and "the tree is to be known by its fruit," God help us!

The Anti-Rent War appeared to Cooper as an almost perfect example of the irresponsibility and tyranny of public opinion, and it drew from him the plaintive question that he asks in the Littlepage trilogy: Is this country one of men or of laws?

III

Turning from the novel's background to *Satanstoe* itself,
one is soon aware of an anomaly: the book is *not* about what
interested the author most. As a novelist Cooper never learned
the art of incorporating his social comment into the story's
action; thus despite his protestations in the Preface, the
book is not focused on anti-rentism and democracy. These
ideas are only discussed; and since no essential action ever
evolves from them, they remain peripheral, if not extraneous.
Although he was to do better by his thesis in the trilogy's
subsequent volumes, this first book centers on the romance
of Corny Littlepage and Anneke Mordaunt. Basically it is a
manners-adventure novel, an amalgam that Cooper created
from his reading of the eighteenth-century novelists (Fanny
Burney and Jane Austen, among others) and of Sir Walter
Scott, his most immediate influence. On this level it is one of
Cooper's most successful tales. The happenings are believable,
the characters engaging, and the pace (after a leisurely opening) lively. As much cannot be said for all Cooper's novels,
but this hardly compensates for the failure to integrate into
the story the important social ideas he intended to communicate. They remain the froth to Henry James' pudding rather
than the butter and eggs.

Perhaps the most perceptive and endearing aspect of the
book is the way in which it depicts colonial manners, and
it is to this evocation of an earlier time that *Satanstoe* owes
much of its unity. From childhood recollections and from his
reading of history, Cooper put together the best picture of
old New York to be found in American letters. His descriptions of the Negro saturnalia of Pinkster (Pentecost), of the
young gentleman in the city and at the rural manor, of
British soldiery, of American dress and dining customs, are
little masterpieces of genre painting. Cooper was perfectly
conscious that he was writing a social history of New York—
of early America, in some ways, and his flow of comment on
such subjects as Puritans, Negroes, Southerners, Dutchmen,

New Yorkers, and Englishmen shows a critical and discerning mind.

> It has always struck me as singular that the people of Jason's part of the provinces [that is, New England] should entertain so much profound respect for titles. No portion of the world is of simpler habits nor . . . [of] greater equality of actual condition. Notwithstanding these facts the love of title is so great, that even that of sergeant is often prefixed to the name of a man on his tombstone . . . and as for the militia ensigns and lieutenants, there is no end to them. Deacon is an important title . . . and woe betide the man who should forget to call a magistrate "esquire."

In a later passage Cooper makes the de Tocquevillian remark that the greater the equality, the greater the need to distinguish oneself.

Most of the social comment in the novel, of course, is made by or applied to one of the characters. The novel's narrator, Corny Littlepage, though sometimes treated in the warmly ironic way befitting a youth in love (and this gives him much of his charm), represents the responsible, educated young gentleman of English stock whose moderate middle-colony views coincide with Cooper's. By endowing him with a combination of courage, perceptiveness, and naïveté, the author has created a character capable of making pungent observations on the social scene as well as living an adventure story.

The opposite number of the responsible young gentleman is the virtuous young common man, Guert Ten Eyck: stouthearted, honest, and energetic, he exemplifies many of the qualities Cooper mentions favorably in *The American Democrat*. But he is uneducated; and, as Corny and the other *Satanstoe* people recognize, this one great lack interposes an insurmountable barrier between Guert and what might have been his eventual place in society. Nonetheless, his innate goodness and gaiety shine out, and in Guert Ten Eyck the author has projected an attractive picture of the Dutch and democratic character.

The antipathy that Cooper felt toward the typical New Englander manifests itself in his portrayal of the Connecticut schoolmaster, Jason Newcome. The Yankee characteristics of tenacity and perseverance, which can be admirable in a mettlesome man, in Jason are vitiated by the weakness which comes from too great a reliance on Puritanic and equalitarian principles. Materialistic, narrow, and conniving, he professes to live by a Puritan code, yet he sneaks drinks, plays cards, and does not hesitate to profit from another's misfortunes. Neither his background nor his beliefs have yielded him an understanding of what is meant by social responsibility, culture, tradition, "fitness." Jason's great lack, like Guert's, is education—but education in the broad sense; he simply has no way of recognizing, much less attaining, excellence. It becomes clear that Jason Newcome—perhaps the most successfully realized character in the book—represents one kind of democrat that Cooper feared.

Whereas such elements as character and plot may be timeless, the language of tale-telling is subject to change, and only a cursory inspection of *Satanstoe* suffices to place it as a work of the nineteenth century. Cooper was writing at a time when literary convention decreed that the language of the novel should be ornate and elevated in tone, and when elegance was often confused with eloquence. Since then, simplicity has become the touchstone, and in the United States particularly the democratic bias and the tradition inherited from the local colorists|and from Mark Twain have moved the language of the novel closer and closer to colloquial speech. Thus it is hardly surprising that Cooper's language (both in narration and dialogue), with its involved syntax and polysyllabic vocabulary, often seems pretentious and unnatural to present-day readers, and to some his style borders on inanity. There is, of course, a philosophic reason for Cooper's style—the necessity of a gentleman's speaking properly, which he discusses in *The American Democrat*. Since *Satanstoe* purports to be the narrative of Corny Littlepage, who is a gentleman, it follows that the account would be written in proper gentlemanly prose. (In recording the dialogue of Corny, Jason, and Guert, the author is careful to exhibit gradations of speech.) Yet even after making due allowance for the application of his philosophical theory and for outmoded literary conventions, it must be said that in places Cooper's style is inexcusably bad—clumsy, prolix, and imprecise—and that these faults are present in *Satanstoe* (though to a lesser degree than in many of his other works—than in *The Pioneers*, for example, or *The Deerslayer*). But we do not, after all, read Cooper for his faults. It is more to the point that he could shake off his cumbersome syntax and rise to spacious description:

> Far as the eye could reach, mountain behind mountain, the earth was covered with the green mantle of luxuriant leaves, such as vegetation bestows on a virgin soil beneath a beneficent sun. The rolling and variegated carpet of the earth resembled a firmament reversed, with clouds composed of foliage. . . . The sun had just tipped the mountain tops with gold, while the lake and the valleys, the hillsides even, and the entire world beneath, still reposed in shadow. It appeared to me like the awakening of created things from the sleep of nature.

IV

Although it is possible to gain a fairly comprehensive idea of Cooper's great strengths and characteristic weaknesses from a reading of *Satanstoe*, the novel is most important in what it tells us about his social thought. Because he was a great innovator—most notably, he introduced to American literature the frontier as an environment for the novel, the Indian, stories of physical adventure, and the pursuit-escape pattern of action—it is sometimes forgotten that Cooper, as time went on, devoted more and more of his energies to social reformation and to the presentation of such ideas in the novel. Increasingly, his own experience involved him in observation and comment on the American system of government. It is just this that gives Cooper's work its greatest value in the twentieth century and has made him, as one modern critic puts it, a writer of "enduring social criticism." For not only does Cooper deal with the American experience (and he was the first major writer to do so), but he is concerned with lasting aspects of our national existence and with problems that have recurred perennially in our history. Such questions as the proper role of public opinion in a democracy, liberty versus law, and the place of the extraordinary man (today perhaps the industrialist or the intellectual) in a democratic society are of continuing importance in the United States and perhaps inherent in any kind of democratic polity. That Cooper wrote of these matters perceptively is a major achievement, and it is regrettable that most of his social criticism is today out of print. Unfortunately, the Leatherstocking series has so dominated Cooper's modern reputation that his accomplishments in other areas are virtually unknown to the general reader. But Cooper's comments on democracy *are* important, and *Satanstoe*, as the best book in which he discusses American society, deservedly holds a high rank in the Cooper canon.

ROBERT L. HOUGH

BIOGRAPHICAL NOTE

JAMES FENIMORE COOPER was born on September 15, 1789, in Burlington, New Jersey. The following year the family moved to the settlement of Cooperstown, New York, where Cooper spent most of his boyhood on the family patent. In 1803 he entered Yale College but was dismissed in his junior year for disciplinary reasons. After serving in the merchant marine for two years (1806-1808), Cooper enlisted as a midshipman in the United States Navy. He married Susan De Lancey, the daughter of a wealthy Westchester County landowner, in 1811, and subsequently resigned from the Navy to become a country gentleman. After various ventures in business and house-building, Cooper took up writing, largely on a challenge from his wife. His first novel, *Precaution*, was published in 1820, and his first great success, *The Spy*, appeared the next year.

From 1826 to 1833 Cooper lived abroad, traveling widely in Italy, France, Switzerland, and England. While in Europe, he began to write social criticism, a practice he continued when he returned to America. The views expressed in his novels and essays published during the 1830's and 1840's and the violent disagreement over one section of his authoritative *History of the Navy of the United State*s involved him in constant controversy during the last two decades of his life. He died at Cooperstown on his sixty-second birthday, September 15, 1851.

BIBLIOGRAPHY

The best full-length biography of Cooper is still Thomas R. Lounsbury's *James Fenimore Cooper* (Boston, 1882). Two other judicious studies are Robert E. Spiller's *Fenimore Cooper, Critic of His Times* (New York, 1931), a biography with special attention to Cooper's social thought, and James Grossman's *James Fenimore Cooper* (New York, 1949), the most recent biography and one which emphasizes Cooper's personality and writing.

Briefer worthwhile studies are Yvor Winters' "Fenimore Cooper, or The Ruins of Time" in *In Defense of Reason* (New York, 1947); Marius Bewley's "Revaluations: James Fenimore Cooper," *Scrutiny*, XIX (1952-1953), 98-125; George Snell's "The Shaper of American Romance," *Yale Review*, XXXIX (1945), 482-494; and Dorothy Dondore's "The Debt of Two Dyed-in-the-Wool Americans to Mrs. Grant's *Memoirs*: Cooper's *Satanstoe* and Paulding's *The Dutchman's Fireside*," *American Literature*, XII (1940), 52-58.

(*Facsimile of title page of first American edition*)

SATANSTOE;

OR,

THE LITTLEPAGE MANUSCRIPTS.

A TALE OF THE COLONY.

BY

THE AUTHOR OF "MILES WALLINGFORD," "PATHFINDER," &c.

" The only amaranthine flower on earth
Is virtue ; the only treasure, truth."
SPENSER.

IN TWO VOLUMES,

VOL. I.

NEW YORK:
PUBLISHED BY BURGESS, STRINGER & CO.
1845.

NOTE ON THE TEXT

Satanstoe *was published first in America by Burgess, Stringer and Company in New York (1845) in paper wrappers. A month before its American appearance in July, it had been issued, for purposes of obtaining copyright in both countries, in England; and within the year it had been translated into French and German. There were comparatively few reprints in any of these countries during Cooper's lifetime; obviously the story was not popular. It was reissued by the original American publishers in a collection of Cooper's works, printed from the old plates, in 1852–54; and it took its place in the first new edition of the collected novels (32 volumes) in 1859–1861, published by W. A. Townsend and Company of New York, and illustrated by F. O. C. Darley. The text of the present reprint is taken from this last edition, which may for all of the novels be accepted as the standard.*

PREFACE

EVERY chronicle of manners has a certain value. When customs are connected with principles, in their origin, development, or end, such records have a double importance; and it is because we think we see such a connection between the facts and incidents of the Littlepage Manuscripts, and certain important theories of our own time, that we give the former to the world.

It is perhaps a fault of your professed historian, to refer too much to philosophical agencies, and too little to those that are humbler. The foundations of great events are often remotely laid in very capricious and uncalculated passions, motives, or impulses. Chance has usually as much to do with the fortunes of states, as with those of individuals; or, if there be calculations connected with them at all, they are the calculations of a power superior to any that exists in man.

We had been led to lay these manuscripts before the world, partly by considerations of the above nature, and partly on account of the manner in which the two works we have named, "Satanstoe" and the "Chainbearer," relate directly to the great New York question of the day, ANTI-RENTISM; which question will be found to be pretty fully laid bare, in the third and last book of the series. These three works, which contain all the Littlepage Manuscripts, do not form sequels to each other, in the sense of personal histories, or as narratives; while they do in that of principles. The reader will see that the early career, the attachment, the marriage, etc., of Mr. Cornelius Littlepage are completely related in the present book, for instance; while those of his son, Mr. Mordaunt Littlepage, will be just as fully given in the "Chainbearer," its successor. It is hoped that the connection, which certainly does exist between these three works, will have more tendency to increase the value of each, than to produce the ordinary effect of what are properly called sequels, which are known to lessen the interest a narrative might otherwise have with the reader. Each of these three books has its own hero, its own heroine, and its own picture of manners, complete; though the latter may be, and is, more or less thrown into relief by its *pendants*.

3

We conceive no apology is necessary for treating the subject of anti-rentism with the utmost frankness. Agreeably to our views of the matter, the existence of true liberty among us, the perpetuity of the institutions, and the safety of public morals, are all dependent on putting down, wholly, absolutely, and unqualifiedly, the false and dishonest theories and statements that have been boldly advanced in connection with this subject. In our view, New York is, at this moment, much the most disgraced state in the Union, notwithstanding she has never failed to pay the interest on her public debt; and her disgrace arises from the fact that her laws are trampled underfoot, without any efforts, at all commensurate with the object, being made to enforce them. If *words* and *professions* can save the character of a community, all may yet be well; but if states, like individuals, are to be judged by their actions, and the " tree is to be known by its fruit," God help us!

For ourselves, we conceive that true patriotism consists in laying bare every thing like public vice, and in calling such things by their right names. The great enemy of the race has made a deep inroad upon us, within the last ten or a dozen years, under cover of a spurious delicacy on the subject of exposing national ills; and it is time that they who have not been afraid to praise, when praise was merited, should not shrink from the office of censuring, when the want of timely warnings may be one cause of the most fatal evils. The great practical defect of institutions like ours, is the circumstance that " what is everybody's business, is nobody's business; " a neglect that gives to the activity of the rogue a very dangerous ascendency over the more dilatory correctives of the honest man.

CHAPTER I

"Look you,
"Who comes here; a young man, and an old, in solemn talk."

As You Like It.

It is easy to foresee that this country is destined to undergo great and rapid changes. Those that more properly belong to history, history will doubtless attempt to record, and probably with the questionable veracity and prejudice that are apt to influence the labors of that particular muse; but there is little hope that any traces of American society, in its more familiar aspects, will be preserved among us, through any of the agencies usually employed for such purposes. Without a stage, in a national point of view at least, with scarcely such a thing as a book of memoirs that relates to a life passed within our own limits, and totally without light literature, to give us simulated pictures of our manners and the opinions of the day, I see scarcely a mode by which the next generation can preserve any memorials of the distinctive usages and thoughts of this. It is true, they will have traditions of certain leading features of the colonial society, but scarcely any records; and, should the next twenty years do as much as the last, toward substituting an entirely new race for the descendants of our own immediate fathers, it is scarcely too much to predict that even these traditions will be lost in the whirl and excitement of a throng of strangers. Under all the circumstances, therefore, I have come to a determination to make an effort, however feeble it may prove, to preserve some vestiges of household life in New York, at least; while I have endeavored to stimulate certain friends in New Jersey, and farther south, to undertake similar tasks in those sections of the country. What success will attend these last applications, is more than I can say; but, in order that the little I may do myself shall not be lost for want of support, I have made a solemn request in my will, that those who come after me will consent to continue this narrative, committing to paper their own experience, as I have here committed mine, down as low at least as my grandson, if I ever have one. Perhaps, by the end of the latter's career, they will begin to

5

publish books in America, and the fruits of our joint family labors
may be thought sufficiently matured to be laid before the world.

It is possible that which I am now about to write will be
thought too homely, to relate to matters much too personal and
private, to have sufficient interest for the public eye; but it must
be remembered that the loftiest interests of man are made up of
a collection of those that are lowly; and, that he who makes a
faithful picture of only a single important scene in the events of
a single life, is doing something toward painting the greatest historical piece of his day. As I have said before, the leading events
of my time will find their way into the pages of far more pretending works than this of mine, in some form or other, with more
or less of fidelity to the truth, and real events, and real motives;
while the humbler matters it will be my office to record, will be
entirely overlooked by writers who aspire to enrol their names
among the Tacituses of former ages. It may be well to say here,
however, I shall not attempt the historical mood at all, but content myself with giving the feelings, incidents, and interests of
what is purely private life, connecting them no farther with things
that are of a more general nature, than is indispensable to render
the narrative intelligible and accurate. With these explanations,
which are made in order to prevent the person who may happen
first to commence the perusal of this manuscript from throwing
it into the fire, as a silly attempt to write a more silly fiction,
I shall proceed at once to the commencement of my proper task.

I was born on the 3d May, 1737, on a neck of land, called Satanstoe, in the county of Westchester, and in the colony of New
York; a part of the widely extended empire that then owned
the sway of His Sacred Majesty, George II., King of Great
Britain, Ireland, and France; Defender of the Faith; and, I may
add, the shield and panoply of the Protestant Succession; God
bless him! Before I say anything of my parentage, I will first
give the reader some idea of the *locus in quo*, and a more precise
notion of the spot on which I happened first to see the light.

A "neck," in Westchester and Long Island parlance, means
something that might be better termed a "head and shoulders,"
if mere shape and dimensions are kept in view. Peninsula would
be the true word, were we describing things on a geographical
scale; but, as they are, I find it necessary to adhere to the local
term, which is not altogether peculiar to our country, by the way.
The "neck" or peninsula to Satanstoe, contains just four hundred
and sixty-three acres and a half of excellent Westchester land; and

that, when the stone is hauled and laid into wall, is saying as much in its favor as need be said of any soil on earth. It has two miles of beach, and collects a proportionate quantity of sea-weed for manure, besides enjoying near a hundred acres of salt-meadow and sedges, that are not included in the solid ground of the neck proper. As my father, Major Evans Littlepage, was to inherit this estate from his father Captain Hugh Littlepage, it might, even at the time of my birth, be considered old family property, it having indeed, been acquired by my grandfather, through his wife, about thirty years after the final cession of the colony to the English by its original Dutch owners. Here we had lived, then, near half a century, when I was born, in the direct line, and considerably longer if we included maternal ancestors; here I now live, at the moment of writing these lines, and here I trust my only son is to live after me.

Before I enter into a more minute description of Satanstoe, it may be well, perhaps, to say a word concerning its somewhat peculiar name. The neck lies in the vicinity of a well-known pass that is to be found in the narrow arm of the sea that sepa-rates the island of Manhattan from its neighbor, Long Island, and which is called Hell Gate. Now, there is a tradition, that, I confess is somewhat confined to the blacks of the neighborhood, but which says that the Father of Lies, on a particular occasion, when he was violently expelled from certain roystering taverns in the New Netherlands, made his exit by this well-known danger-ous pass, and drawing his foot somewhat hastily from among the lobster-pots that abound in those waters, leaving behind him as a print of his passage by that route, the Hog's Back, the Pot, and all the whirlpools and rocks that render navigation so difficult in that celebrated strait, he placed it hurriedly upon the spot where there now spreads a large bay to the southward and eastward of the neck, just touching the latter with the ball of his great toe, as he passed Down-East; from which part of the country some of our people used to maintain he originally came. Some fancied resemblance to an inverted toe (the devil being supposed to turn every thing with which he meddles, upside-down) has been imagined to exist in the shape and swells of our paternal acres; a fact that has probably had its influence in perpetuating the name.

Satanstoe has the place been called, therefore, from time im-memorial; as time is immemorial in a country in which civilized time commenced not a century and a half ago; and Satanstoe it is called to-day. I confess I am not fond of unnecessary changes, and I sincerely hope this neck of land will continue to go by its old appellation, as long as the House of Hanover shall sit on the throne of these realms; or as long as water shall run and grass shall grow. There has been an attempt made to persuade the neighborhood, quite lately, that the name is irreligious and unworthy of an enlightened people, like this of Westchester; but it has met with no great success. It has come from a Connecticut man, whose father they say is a clergyman of the "standing order;" so called, I believe, because they stand up at prayer; and who came among us himself in the character of a schoolmaster. This young man, I understand, has endeavored to persuade the neighborhood that Satanstoe is a corruption introduced by the Dutch, from Devil's Town; which, in its turn, was a corruption from Dibbleston; the family from which my grandfather's father-in-law purchased having been, as he says, of the name of Dibblee. He has got half-a-dozen of the more sentimental part of our society to call the neck Dibbleton; but the attempt is not likely to succeed in the long run, as we are not a people much given to altering the language any more than the customs of our ancestors. Besides my Dutch ancestors did not purchase from any Dibblee, no such family ever owning the place, that being a bold assumption of the Yankee to make out his case the more readily.

Satanstoe, as it is little more than a good farm in extent, so it is little more than a particularly good farm in cultivation and embellishment. All the buildings are of stone, even to the hogsties and sheds, with well-pointed joints, and field walls that would do credit to a fortified place. The house is generally esteemed one of the best in the colony, with the exception of a few of the new school. It is of only a story and a half in elevation, I admit; but the rooms under the roof are as good as any of that description with which I am acquainted, and their finish is such as would do no discredit to the upper rooms of even a York dwelling. The building is in the shape of an L, or two sides of a parallelogram, one of which shows a front of seventy-five, and the other of fifty feet. Twenty-six feet make the depth, from outside to outside of the walls. The best room had a carpet, that covered two-thirds of the entire dimensions of the floor, even in my boyhood, and there were oil-cloths in most of the better passages. The buffet in the dining-room, or smallest parlor, was particularly admired; and I question if there be, at this hour, a handsomer in the county. The rooms were well-sized, and of fair dimensions, the larger parlors embracing the whole depth of the house, with proportionate widths, while the ceilings were higher than common, being eleven feet, if we except the places occupied by the larger beams of the chamber floors.

As there was money in the family, besides the Neck, and the Littlepages had held the king's commissions, my father having once been an ensign, and my grandfather a captain, in the regular army, each in the earlier portion of his life, we always ranked among the gentry of the county. We happened to be in a part of Westchester in which were none of the very large estates, and Satanstoe passed for property of a certain degree of importance. It is true, the Morrises were at Morrisania, and the Felipses, or Philipses, as these Bohemian counts were then called, had a manor on the Hudson, that extended within a dozen miles of us, and a younger branch of the De Lanceys had established itself even much nearer, while the Van Cortlandts, or a branch of them, too, dwelt near Kingsbridge; but these were all people who were at the head of the colony, and with whom none of the minor gentry attempted to vie. As it was, therefore, the Littlepages held a very respectable position between the higher class of the yeomanry and those who, by their estates, education, connections, official rank, and hereditary consideration, formed what might be justly called the aristocracy of the colony. Both my father and grandfather had sat in the Assembly, in their time, and, as I have heard elderly people say, with credit, too. As for my father, on one occasion, he made a speech that occupied eleven minutes in the delivery — a proof that he had something to say, and which was a source of great, but, I trust, humble felicitation in the family, down to the day of his death, and even afterward.

Then the military services of the family stood us in for a great deal. In that day it was something to be an ensign even in the militia, and a far greater thing to have the same rank in a regular regiment. It is true, neither of my predecessors served very long with the king's troops, my father in particular selling out at the end of the second campaign; but the military experience, and, I may add, the military glory each acquired in youth, did them good service for all the rest of their days. Both were commissioned in the militia, and my father actually rose as high as major in that branch of the service, that being the rank he held, and the title he bore, for the last fifteen years of his life.

My mother was of Dutch extraction on both sides, her father having been a Blauvelt, and her mother a Van Busser. I have

heard it said that there was even a relationship between the
Stuyvesants, and the Van Cortlandts, and the Van Bussers;
but I am not able to point out the actual degree and precise
nature of the affinity. I presume it was not very near, or my
information would have been more minute. I have always understood that my mother brought my father thirteen hundred
pounds for dowry (currency, not sterling), which, it must be confessed, was a very genteel fortune for a young woman in 1733.
Now, I very well know that six, eight, and ten thousand pounds
sometimes fall in, in this manner, and even much more in the
high families; but no one need be ashamed, who looks back fifty
years, and finds that his mother brought a thousand pounds to her
husband.

I was neither an only child, nor the eldest-born. There was
a son who preceded me, and two daughters succeeded, but they
all died in infancy, leaving me in effect the only offspring for my
parents to cherish and educate. My little brother monopolized
the name of Evans, and living for some time after I was christened,
I got the Dutch appellation of my maternal grandfather, for my
share of the family nomenclature, which happened to be Cornelius
— Corny was consequently the diminutive by which I was known
to all the whites of my acquaintance, for the first sixteen or
eighteen years of my life, and to my parents as long as they lived.
Corny Littlepage is not a bad name, in itself, and I trust they
who do me the favor to read this manuscript, will lay it down
with the feeling that the name is none the worse for the use I
have made of it.

I have said that both my father and grandfather, each in his
day, sat in the assembly; my father twice, and my grandfather
only once. Although we lived so near the borough of Westchester,
it was not for that place they sat, but for the county, the De
Lanceys and the Morrises contending for the control of the borough, in a way that left little chance for the smaller fishes to
swim in the troubled water they were so certain to create. Nevertheless, this political elevation brought my father out, as it might
be, before the world, and was the means of giving him a personal
consideration he might not have otherwise enjoyed. The benefits,
and possibly some of the evils, of thus being drawn out from the
more regular routine of our usually peaceable lives, may be made
to appear in the course of this narrative.

I have ever considered myself fortunate in not having been
born in the earlier and infant days of the colony, when the in-

terests at stake, and the events by which they were influenced, were not of a magnitude to give the mind and the hopes the excitement and enlargement that attend the periods of a more advanced civilization, and of more important incidents. In this respect, my own appearance in this world was most happily timed, as any one will see, who will consider the state and importance of the colony in the middle of the present century. New York could not have contained many less than seventy thousand souls, including both colors, at the time of my birth, for it is supposed to contain quite a hundred thousand this day on which I am now writing. In such a community, a man has not only the room, but the materials on which to figure; whereas, as I have often heard him say, my father, when he was born, was one of less than half of the smallest number I have just named. I have been grateful for this advantage, and I trust it will appear, by evidence that will be here afforded, that I have not lived in a quarter of the world, or in an age, when and where, and to which great events have been altogether strangers.

My earliest recollections, as a matter of course, are of Satanstoe and the domestic fireside. In my childhood and youth, I heard a great deal said of the Protestant Succession, the House of Hanover, and King George II.; all mixed up with such names as those of George Clinton, General Monckton, Sir Charles Hardy, James de Lancey, and Sir Danvers Osborne, his official representatives in the colony. Every age has its *old* and its *last* wars, and I can well remember that which occurred between the French in the Canadas and ourselves, in 1744. I was then seven years old, and it was an event to make an impression on a child of that tender age. My honored grandfather was then living, as he was long afterward, and he took a strong interest in the military movements of the period, as was natural for an old soldier. New York had no connection with the celebrated expedition that captured Louisbourg, then the Gibraltar of America, in 1745; but this could not prevent an old soldier, like Captain Littlepage, from entering into the affair with all his heart, though forbidden to use his hand. As the reader may not be aware of all the secret springs that set public events in motion, it may be well here to throw in a few words in the way of explanation.

There was and is little sympathy, in the way of national feeling, between the colonies of New England and those which lie farther south. We are all loyal, those of the east as well as those of the south-west and south; but there is, and ever has been, so wide a difference in our customs, origins, religious opinions, and histories, as to cause a broad moral line, in the way of feeling, to be drawn between the colony of New York and those that lie east of the Byram River. I have heard it said, that most of the emigrants to the New England states came from the west of England, where many of their social peculiarities and much of their language are still to be traced, while the colonies farther south have received their population from the more central counties, and those sections of the island that are supposed to be less provincial and peculiar. I do not affirm that such is literally the fact, though it is well known that we of New York have long been accustomed to regard our neighbors of New England as very different from ourselves, whilst, I dare say, our neighbors of New England have regarded us as different from themselves, and insomuch removed from perfection.

Let all this be as it may, it is certain New England is a portion of the empire that is set apart from the rest, for good or for evil. It got its name from the circumstance that the English possessions were met, on its western boundary, by those of the Dutch, who were thus separated from the other colonies of purely Anglo-Saxon origin, by a wide district that was much larger in surface than the mother country itself. I am afraid there is something in the character of these Anglo-Saxons that predisposes them to laugh and turn up their noses at other races; for I have remarked that the natives of the parent land itself, who come among us, show this disposition even as it respects us of New York and those of New England, while the people of the latter region manifest a feeling toward us, their neighbors, that partakes of any thing but the humility that is thought to grace that Christian character to which they are particularly fond of laying claim.

My grandfather was a native of the old country, however, and he entered but little into the colonial jealousies. He had lived from boyhood and had married in New York, and was not apt to betray any of the overweening notions of superiority that we sometimes encountered in native-born Englishmen, though I can remember instances in which he would point out the defects in our civilization, and others in which he dwelt with pleasure on the grandeur and power of his own island. I dare say this was all right, for few among us have ever been disposed to dispute the just supremacy of England in all things that are desirable, and which form the basis of human excellence.

I well remember a journey Captain Hugh Littlepage made to

Boston, in 1745, in order to look at the preparations that were making for the great expedition. Although his own colony had no connection with this enterprise, in a military point of view, his previous service rendered him an object of interest to the military men then assembled along the coast of New England. It has been said the expedition against Louisbourg, then the strongest place in America, was planned by a lawyer, led by a merchant, and executed by husbandmen and mechanics; but this, though true as a whole, was a rule that had its exceptions. There were many old soldiers who had seen the service of this continent in the previous wars, and among them were several of my grandfather's former acquaintances. With these he passed many a cheerful hour, previously to the day of sailing, and I have often thought since, that my presence alone prevented him from making one in the fleet. The reader will think I was young, perhaps, to be so far from home on such an occasion, but it happened in this wise: my excellent mother thought I had come out of the small-pox with some symptoms that might be benefited by a journey, and she prevailed on her father-in-law to let me be of the party when he left home to visit Boston in the winter of 1744-5. At that early day moving about was not always convenient in these colonies, and my grandfather travelling in a sleigh that was proceeding east with some private stores that had been collected for the expedition, it presented a favorable opportunity to send me along with my venerable progenitor, who very good-naturedly consented to let me commence my travels under his own immediate auspices.

The things I saw on this occasion have had a material influence on my future life. I got a love of adventure, and particularly of military parade and grandeur, that has since led me into more than one difficulty. Captain Hugh Littlepage, my grandfather, was delighted with all he saw until after the expedition had sailed, when he began to grumble on the subject of the religious observances that the piety of the Puritans blended with most of their other movements. On the score of religion there was a marked difference; I may say there *is* still a marked difference between New England and New York. The people of New England certainly did, and possibly may still, look upon us of New York as little better than heathens; while we of New York assuredly did, and for any thing I know to the contrary may yet, regard them as canters, and by necessary connection, hypocrites. I shall not take it on myself to say which party is right; though it has often occurred to my mind that it would be better had New England a little less self-righteousness, and New York a little more righteousness, without the self. Still, in the way of pounds, shillings and pence, we will not turn our backs upon them any day, being on the whole rather the most trustworthy of the two as respects money; more especially in all such cases in which our neighbor's goods can be appropriated without having recourse to absolutely direct means. Such, at any rate, is the New York opinion, let them think as they please about it on the other side of Byram.

My grandfather met an old fellow-campaigner, at Boston, of the name of Hight, Major Hight, as he was called, who had come to see the preparations, too; and the old soldiers passed most of the time together. The major was a Jerseyman, and had been somewhat of a free-liver in his time, retaining some of the propensities of his youth in old age, as is apt to be the case with those who cultivate a vice as if it were a hot-house plant. The major was fond of his bottle, drinking heavily of Madeira, of which there was then a good stock in Boston, for he brought some on himself; and I can remember various scenes that occurred between him and my grandfather, after dinner, as they sat discoursing in the tavern on the progress of things, and the prospects for the future. Had these two old soldiers been of the troops of the province in which they were, it would have been "major" and "captain" at every breath; for no part of the earth is fonder of titles than our eastern brethren; * whereas, I must think we had some claims to more true simplicity of character and habits, notwithstanding New York has ever been thought the most aristocratical of all the northern colonies. Having been intimate from early youth, my two old soldiers familiarly called each other Joey and Hodge, the latter being the abbreviation of one of my grandfather's names, Roger, when plain Hugh was not used, as sometimes happened between them. Hugh Roger Littlepage, I ought to have said, was my grandfather's name.

"I should like these Yankees better, if they prayed less, my old friend," said the major, one day, after they had been discussing the appearances of things, and speaking between the puffs of his pipe. "I can see no great use in losing so much time, by making these halts to pray, when the campaign is fairly opened."

---

* It will be remembered Mr. Littlepage wrote more than seventy years ago, when this distinction might exclusively belong to the *East;* but the *West* has now some claim to it, also.

"It was always their way, Joey," my grandfather answered, taking his time, as is customary with smokers. "I remember when we were out together, in the year '17, that the New England troops always had their parsons, who acted as a sort of second colonels. They tell me his excellency has ordered a weekly fast, for public prayers, during the whole of this campaign."

"Ay, Master Hodge, praying and plundering; so they go on," returned the major, knocking the ashes out of his pipe, preparatory to filling it anew; an employment that gave him an opportunity to give vent to his feelings, without pausing to puff. "Ay, Master Hodge, praying and plundering; so they go on. Now, do you remember old Watson, who was in the Massachusetts levies, in the year '12? — old Tom Watson; he that was a sub under Barnwell, in our Tuscarora expedition?"

My grandfather nodded his head in assent, that being the only reply the avocation of smoking rendered convenient, just at that moment, unless a sort of affirmatory grunt could be construed into an auxiliary.

"Well, he has a son going in this affair; and old Tom, or Colonel Watson, as he is now very particular to be called, is down here with his wife and two daughters, to see the ensign off. I went to pay the old fellow a visit, Hodge; and found him, and the mother and sisters, all as busy as bees in getting young Tom's baggage ready for a march. There lay his whole equipment before my eyes, and I had a favorable occasion to examine it at my leisure."

"Which you did with all your might, or you're not the Joe Hight of the year '10 " said my grandfather, taking his turn with the ashes and the tobacco-box.

Old Hight was now puffing away like a blacksmith who is striving to obtain a white heat, and it was some time before he could get out the proper reply to this half-assertion, half-interrogatory sort of remark.

"You may be sure of that," he at length ejaculated; when, certain of his light, he proceeded to tell the whole story, stopping occasionally to puff, lest he should lose the "vantage ground" he had just obtained. "What d'ye think of a half-a-dozen strings of red onions, for one item in a subaltern's stores! "

My grandfather grunted again, in a way that might very well pass for a laugh.

"You're certain they were red, Joey? " he finally asked.

"As red as his regimentals. Then there was a jug filled with

molasses, that is as big as yonder demijohn;" glancing at the
vessel which contained his own private stores. "But I should
have thought nothing of these, a large empty sack attracting
much of my attention. I could not imagine what young Tom
could want of such a sack; but, on broaching the subject to the
major, he very frankly gave me to understand that Louisbourg
was thought to be a rich town, and there was no telling what
luck, or Providence — yes, by George! — he called it *Providence!*
— might throw in his son Tommy's way. Now that the sack
was empty, and had an easy time of it, the girls would put his
Bible and hymn-book in it, as a place where the young man would
be likely to look for them. I dare say, Hodge, you never had
either Bible or hymn-book, in any of your numerous campaigns?"

"No, nor a plunder-sack, nor a molasses-jug, nor strings of red
onions," growled my grandfather in reply.

How well I remember that evening! A vast deal of colonial
prejudice and neighborly antipathy made themselves apparent
in the conversation of the two veterans; who seemed to entertain a strange sort of contemptuous respect for their fellow-sub-
jects of New England; who, in their turn, I make not the smallest
doubt, paid them off in kind — with all the superciliousness and
reproach, and with many grains less of the respect.

That night, Major Hight and Captain Hugh Roger Littlepage,
both got a little how-come-you-so, drinking bumpers to the success of what they called "the Yankee expedition," even at the
moment they were indulging in constant side-hits at the failings
and habits of the people. These marks of neighborly infirmity
are not peculiar to the people of the adjacent provinces of New
York and of New England. I have often remarked that the English think and talk very much of the French, as the Yankees
speak of us; while the French, so far as I have been able to
understand their somewhat unintelligible language — which seems
never to have a beginning nor an end — treat the English as the
Puritans of the old world. As I have already intimated, we were
not very remarkable for religion in New York, in my younger
days; while it would be just the word, were I to say that religion
was *conspicuous* among our eastern neighbors. I remember to
have heard my grandfather say, he was once acquainted with a
Colonel Heathcote, an Englishman like himself by birth, and a
brother of a certain Sir Gilbert Heathcote, who was formerly a
leading man in the Bank of England. This Colonel Heathcote
came among us young, and married here, leaving his posterity be-

hind him, and was lord of the manor of Scarsdale and Mamaroneck, in our county of Westchester. Well, this Colonel Heathcote told my grandfather, speaking on the subject of religion, that he had been much shocked, on arriving in this country, at discovering the neglected condition of religion in the colony; more especially on Long Island, where the people lived in a sort of heathenish condition. Being a man of mark, and connected with the government, the Society for the Propagation of the Gospel in Foreign Parts, applied to him to aid it in spreading the truths of the Bible in the colony. The colonel was glad enough to comply; and I remember my grandfather said, his friend told him of the answer he returned to these good persons in England. "I was so struck with the heathenish condition of the people, on my arriving here," he wrote to them, "that, commanding the militia of the colony, I ordered the captains of the different companies to call their men together, each Sunday at sunrise, and to drill them until sunset, unless they could consent to repair to some convenient place, and listen to morning and evening prayer, and to two wholesome sermons, read by some suitable person, in which case the men were to be excused from drill." * I do not think this would be found necessary in New England at least, where many of the people would be likely to prefer drilling to preaching.

But all this gossip about the moral condition of the adjacent colonies of New York and New England is leading me from the narrative, and does not promise much for the connection and interest of the remainder of the manuscript.

---

* On the subject of this story, the editor can say he has seen a published letter from Colonel Heathcote, who died more than a century since, at Mamaroneck, Westchester county, in which that gentleman gives the society for the propagation of the gospel an account of his proceedings, that agrees almost *verbatim* with the account of the matter that is here given by Mr. Cornelius Littlepage. The house in which Colonel Heathcote dwelt was destroyed by fire, a short time before the revolution; but the property on which it stood, and the present building, belong at this moment to his great-grandson, the Rt. Rev. Wm. *Heathcote* de Lancey, the bishop of Western New York.

On the subject of the *plunder*, the editor will remark, that a near connection, whose grandfather was a major at the taking of Louisbourg, and who was subsequently one of the first brigadiers appointed in 1775, has lately shown him a letter written to that officer, during the expedition, by *his* father; in which, blended with a great deal of pious counsel, and some really excellent religious exhortation, is an earnest inquiry after the *plunder*. — EDITOR.

CHAPTER II

"I would there were no age between ten and three-and-twenty: or that youth would sleep out the rest."

WINTER'S TALE.

IT is not necessary for me to say much of the first fourteen years of my life. They passed like the childhood and youth of the sons of most gentlemen in our colony, at that day, with this distinction, however. There was a class among us which educated its boys at home. This was not a very numerous class, certainly, nor was it always the highest in point of fortune and rank. Many of the large proprietors were of Dutch origin, as a matter of course; and these seldom, if ever, sent their children to England to be taught any thing, in my boyhood. I understand that a few are getting over their ancient prejudices in this particular, and begin to fancy Oxford or Cambridge may be quite as learned schools as that of Leyden; but no Van, in my boyhood, could have been made to believe this. Many of the Dutch proprietors gave their children very little education, in any way or form, though most of them imparted lessons of probity that were quite as useful as learning, had the two things been really inseparable. For my part, while I admit there is a great deal of knowledge going up and down the land, that is just of a degree to trick a fellow-creature out of his rights, I shall never subscribe to the opinion, which is so prevalent among the Dutch portion of our population, and which holds the doctrine that the schools of the New England provinces are the reason the descendants of the Puritans do not enjoy the best of reputations, in this respect. I believe a boy may be well taught, and made all the honester for it; though I admit there may be, and is, such a thing as training a lad into false notions, as well as training him in those that are true. But we had a class, principally of English extraction, that educated its sons well; usually sending them home to the great English schools, and finishing at the universities. These persons, however, lived principally in town, or, having estates on the Hudson, passed their winters there. To this class the Littlepages did not belong; neither their habits nor their fortunes tempting them

18

to so high a flight. For myself, I was taught enough Latin and Greek to enter college, by the Rev. Thomas Worden, an English divine, who was rector of St. Jude's, the parish to which our family properly belonged. This gentleman was esteemed a good scholar, and was very popular among the gentry of the county; attending all the dinners, clubs, races, balls, and other diversions that were given by them, within ten miles of his residence. His sermons were pithy and short; and he always spoke of your half-hour preachers as illiterate prosers, who did not understand how to condense their thoughts. Twenty minutes were his gauge, though I remember to have heard my father say, that he had known him preach all of twenty-two. When he compressed down to fourteen, my grandfather invariably protested he was delightful.

I remained with Mr. Worden until I could translate the two first Æneids, and the whole of the Gospel of St. Matthew, pretty readily; and then my father and grandfather, the last in particular, for the old gentleman had a great idea of learning, began to turn over in their minds, the subject of the college to which I ought to be sent. We had the choice of two, in both of which the learned languages and the sciences are taught, to a degree, and in a perfection, that is surprising for a new country. These colleges are Yale, at New Haven, in Connecticut, and Nassau Hall, which was then at Newark, New Jersey, after having been a short time at Elizabethtown, but which has since been established at Princeton. Mr. Worden laughed at both; said that neither had as much learning as a second-rate English grammar-school; and that a lower-form boy, at Eton or Westminster, could take a master's degree at either, and pass for a prodigy in the bargain. My father, who was born in the colonies, and had a good deal of the right colony feeling, was nettled at this, I remember; while my grandfather, being old-country born, but colony educated, was at a loss how to view the matter. The captain had a great respect for his native land, and evidently considered it the paradise of this earth, though his recollections of it were not very distinct; but, at the same time, he loved Old York, and Westchester in particular, where he had married and established himself at Satan's Toe; or, as he spelt it, and as we all have spelt it, now, this many a day, Satanstoe. I was present at the conversation which decided the question, as regarded my future education, and which took place in the common parlor, around a blazing fire, about a week before Christmas, the year I was fourteen. There were present Captain Hugh Roger, Major Evans, my mother, the Rev. M. Worden, and an old gentleman of Dutch designation and extraction, of the name of Abraham Van Valkenburgh, but who was familiarly called, by his friends, 'Brom Follock, or Colonel Follock, or Volleck, as the last happen to be more or less ceremonious, or more or less Dutch. Follock, I think, however, was the favorite pronunciation. This Colonel Van Valkenburgh was an old brother-soldier of my father's, and, indeed, a relation, a sort of cousin through my great-grandmother, besides being a man of much consideration and substance. He lived in Rockland, just across the Hudson, but never failed to pay a visit to Satanstoe at that season of the year. On the present occasion, he was accompanied by his son, Dirck, who was *my* friend, and just a year my junior.

"Vell, den," — the colonel commenced the discourse by saying, as he tapped the ashes out of his pipe for the second time that evening, having first taken a draught of hot flip, a beverage much in vogue then, as well as now, — "vell, den, Evans, vat is your intention as to ter poy? Vill he pe college-l'arnt, like as his grant-fa'ter, or only school-l'arnt, like as his own fa'ter?" The allusion to the grandfather being a pleasantry of the colonel's, who insisted that all the old-country born were " college-l'arnt " by instinct.

"To own the truth, 'Brom," my father answered, "this is a point that is not yet entirely settled, for there are different opinions as to the place to which he shall be sent, even admitting that he is to be sent at all."

The colonel fastened his full, projecting, blue eyes on my father, in a way that pretty plainly expressed surprise.

"Vat, den, is dere so many colleges, dat it is hart to choose?" he said.

"There are but two that can be of any use to us, for Cambridge is much too distant to think of sending the boy so far. Cambridge was in our thoughts at one time, but that is given up."

"Vhere, den, ist Cambridge?" demanded the Dutchman, removing his pipe to ask so important a question, a ceremony he usually thought unnecessary.

"It is a New England college — near Boston; not half a day's journey distant, I fancy."

"Don't sent Cornelius dere," ejaculated the colonel, contriving to get these words out alongside of the stem of the pipe.

"You think not, Colonel Follock," put in the anxious mother; "may I ask the reason for that opinion?"

"Too much Suntay, Matam Littlepage — the poy will be sp'ilt by ter ministers. He will go away an honest lat, and come pack a rogue. He will l'arn how to bray and to cheat."

"Hoity toity, my noble colonel!" exclaimed the Rev. Mr. Worden, affecting more resentment than he felt. "Then you fancy the clergy, and too much Sunday, will be apt to convert an honest youth into a knave!"

The colonel made no answer, continuing to smoke very philosophically, though he took occasion, while he drew the pipe out of his mouth, in one of its periodical removals, to make a significant gesture with it toward the rising sun, which all present understood to mean "down east," as it is usual to say, when we mean to designate the colonies of New England. That he was understood by the Rev. Mr. Worden is highly probable; since that gentleman continued to turn the flip of one vessel into another, by way of more intimately blending the ingredients of the mixture, quite as coolly as if there had been no reflection on his trade.

"What do you think of Yale, friend 'Brom?" asked my father, who understood the dumb-show as well as any of them.

"No tifference, Evans; dey all breaches and brays too much. *Goot* men have no neet of so much religion. Vhen a man is *really* goot, religion only does him harm. I mean Yankee religion."

"I have another objection to Yale," observed Captain Hugh Roger, "which is their English."

"Och!" exclaimed the colonel — "Deir English is horriple! Wuss dan ast to us Tutch."

"Well, I was not aware of that," observed my father. "They are English, sir, as well as ourselves, and why should they not speak the language as well as we!"

"Why toes not a Yorkshire man, or a Cornishman, speak as vell as a Lonnoner? I tell you what Evans, I'll pet the pest game-cock on ter Neck, against the veriest tunghill the parson hast, ter presitent of Yale calls p e e n, pen ant r o o f, ruff — and so on."

"My birds are all game," put in the divine; "I keep no other breed."

"Surely, Mr. Worden, you do not countenance cockfights by your presence!" my mother said, using as much of reproach in her manner as comported with the holy office of the party she addressed, and with her own gentle nature. The colonel winked

at my father, and laughed *through his pipe,* an exploit he might
have been said to perform almost hourly. My father smiled in
return; for, to own the truth, he *had* been present at such sports
on one or two occasions, when the parson's curiosity had tempted
him to peep in also; but my grandfather looked grave and much
in earnest. As for Mr. Worden himself, he met the imputation
like a man. To do him justice, if he were not an ascetic, neither
was he a whining hypocrite, as is the case with too many of those
who aspire to be disciples and ministers of our blessed Lord.

"Why not, Madam Littlepage?" Mr. Worden stoutly demanded.
"There are worse places than cock-pits; for, mark me, I never bet
— no, not on a horse-race even; and *that* is an occasion on which
any gentleman might venture a few guineas, in a liberal, frank
way. There are so few amusements for people of education in
this country, Madam Littlepage, that one is not to be too particular. If there were hounds and hunting, now, as there are at
home, you should never hear of me at a cock-fight, I can assure
you."

"I must say I do not approve of cockfights," rejoined my mother
meekly; "and I hope Corny will never be seen at one. No —
never — never."

"Dere you're wrong, Matam Littlepage," the colonel remarked,
"for ter sight of ter spirit of ter cocks wilt give ter boy spirit
himself. My Tirck, dere, goes to all in ter neighborhoot, and he
is a game-cock himself, let me tell you. Come, Tirck — come
— cock-a-doodle-do!"

This was true all round, as I very well knew, young as I was.
Dirck, who was as slow-moving, as dull-seeming, and as anti-
mercurial a boy to look at as one could find in a thousand, was
thorough game at the bottom, and he had been at many a main,
as he had told me himself. How much of his spirit was derived from witnessing such scenes I will not take on me to affirm;
for, in these later times, I have heard it questioned whether
such exhibitions do really improve the spectator's courage or
not. But Dirck had pluck, and plenty of it, and in that particular, at least, his father was not mistaken. The colonel's
opinion always carried weight with my mother, both on account
of his Dutch extraction, and on account of his well-established
probity; for, to own the truth, a text or a sentiment from him
had far more weight with her than the same from the clergyman. She was silenced on the subject of cockfighting for the
moment, therefore, which gave captain Hugh Roger further op-

portunity to pursue that of the English language. The grand-father, who was an inveterate lover of the sport, would have cut in to that branch of the discourse, but he had a great ten-derness for my mother, whom everybody loved by the way, and he commanded himself, glad to find that so important an interest had fallen into hands as good as those of the colonel. *He* would just as soon be absent from church as be absent from a cock-fight, and he was a very good observer of religion.

"I should have sent Evans to Yale, had it not been for the miserable manner of speaking English they have in New Eng-land," resumed my grandfather; "and I had no wish to have a son who might pass for a Cornish man. We shall have to send this boy to Newark, in New Jersey. The distance is not so great, and we shall be certain he will not get any of your Roundhead notions of religion, too. Colonel 'Brom, you Dutch are not alto-gether free from these distressing follies."

"Debble a pit?" growled the colonel, through his pipe; for no devotee of liberalism and latitudinarianism in religion could be more averse to extra-piety than he. The colonel, however, was not of the Dutch Reformed; he was an Episcopalian, like ourselves, his mother having brought this branch of the Follocks into the church; and, consequently, he entered into all our feel-ings on the subject of religion, heart and hand. Perhaps Mr. Worden was a greater favorite with no member of the four par-ishes over which he presided, than with Colonel Abraham Von Valkenburgh.

"I should think less of sending Corny to Newark," added my mother, "was it not for crossing the water."

"Crossing the water!" repeated Mr. Worden. "The New-ark we mean, Madam Littlepage, is not at home; the Jersey of which we speak is the adjoining colony of that name."

"I am aware of that, Mr. Worden; but it is not possible to get to Newark, without making that terrible voyage between New York and Powles' Hook. No, sir, it is impossible; and every time the child comes home, that risk will have to be run. It would cause me many a sleepless night!"

"He can go by Tobb's Ferry, Matam Littlepage," quietly ob-served the colonel.

"Dobb's Ferry can be very little better than that by Powles' Hook," rejoined the tender mother. "A ferry is a ferry; and the Hudson will be the Hudson, from Albany to New York. So water is water."

As these were all self-evident propositions, they produced a pause in the discourse; for men do not deal with new ideas as freely as they deal with the old.

"Dere is a way, Evans, as you and I know py experience," resumed the colonel, winking again at my father, "to go rount the Hudson altoget'er. To pe sure, it is a long way, and a pit in the woots; but petter to undertake dat, than to haf the poy lose his l'arnin'. Ter journey might be made in two mont's, and he none the wuss for ter exercise. Ter major and I were never heartier dan when we were operating on the he't waters of the Hutson. I will tell Corny the roat."

My mother saw that her apprehensions were laughed at, and she had the good sense to be silent. The discussion did not the less proceed, until it was decided, after an hour more of weighing the *pros* and the *cons*, that I was to be sent to Nassau Hall, Newark, New Jersey, and was to move from that place with the college, whenever that event might happen.

"You will send Dirck there, too," my father added, as soon as the affair in my case was finally determined. "It would be a pity to separate the boys, after they have been so long together, and have got to be so much used to each other. Their characters are so identical, too, that they are more like brothers than very distant relatives."

"Dey will like one anot'er all de petter for pein' a little tifferent, den," answered the colonel, dryly.

Dirck and I were no more alike than a horse resembles a mule.

"Ay, but Dirck is a lad who will do honor to an education — he is solid and thoughtful, and learning will not be thrown away on such a youth. Was he in England, that sedate lad might get to be a bishop."

"I want no pishops in my family, Major Evans, nor do I want any great l'arnin'. None of us ever saw a college, and we have got on fery vell. I am a colonel and a memper; my fat'er was a colonel and a memper; and my grandfat'er *woult* have peen a colonel and a memper, but dere vast no colonels and no mempers in his time; though Tirck yonter can be a colonel and a memper, wit'out crosting dat terriple ferry that frightens Matam Littlepage so much."

There was usually a little humor in all Colonel Follock said and did, though it must be owned it was humor after a very Dutch model; Dutch-built fun, as Mr. Worden used to call it. Nevertheless, it was humor; and there was enough of Holland in all

the junior generations of the Littlepages to enjoy it. My father
understood him, and my mother did not hear the last of the
" terriple ferry " until not only I, but the college itself, had quitted
Newark; for the institution made another remove to Princeton, the
place where it is now to be found, some time before I got my
degree.

" You have got on very well without a college education, as all
must admit, colonel," answered Mr. Worden; " but there is no
telling how much *better* you would have got on, had you been an
A.M. You might, in the last case, have been a general and a
member of the king's council."

" Dere ist no yeneral in ter colony, the commander-in-chief and
his majesty's representatif excepted," returned the colonel. " We
are no Yankees, to make yenerals of ploughmen."

Hereupon the colonel and my father knocked the ashes out of
their pipes at the same instant, and both laughed — a merriment
in which the parson, my grandfather, my dear mother, and I myself joined. Even a negro boy, who was about my own age, and
whose name was Jacob, or Jaap, but who was commonly called
Yaap, grinned at the remark, for he had a sovereign contempt for
Yankee-land, and all it contained; almost as sovereign a contempt
as that which Yankee-land entertained for York itself, and its
Dutch population. Dirck was the only person present who looked
grave; but Dirck was habitually as grave and sedate, as if he had
been born to become a burgomaster.

" Quite right, Brom," cried my father; " *colonels* are good
enough for us; and when we do make a man *that*, even, we are a
little particular about his being respectable and fit for the office.
Nevertheless learning will not hurt Corny, and to college he shall
go, let you do as you please with Dirck. So that matter is settled,
and no more need be said about it."

And it was settled, and to college I *did* go, and that by the
awful Powles' Hook Ferry, in the bargain. Near as we lived to
town, I paid my first visit to the island of Manhattan the day my
father and myself started for Newark. I had an aunt, who lived
in Queen street, not a very great distance from the fort, and she
had kindly invited me and my father to pass a day with her, on
our way to New Jersey, which invitation had been accepted. In
my youth, the world in general was not so much addicted to
gadding about as it is now getting to be, and neither my grandfather nor my father ordinarily went to town, their calls to the
legislature excepted, more than twice a year. My mother's visits

were still less frequent, although Mrs. Legge, my aunt, was her own sister. Mr. Legge was a lawyer of a good deal of reputation, but he was inclined to be in the opposition, or espoused the popular side in politics; and there could be no great cordiality between one of that frame of mind and our family. I remember we had not been in the house an hour, before a warm discussion took place between my uncle and my father, on the question of the right of the subject to canvass the acts of the government. We had left home immediately after an early breakfast, in order to reach town before dark; but a long detention at the Harlem Ferry, compelled us to dine in that village, and it was quite night before we stopped in Queen street. My aunt ordered supper early, in order that we might get early to bed, to recover from our fatigue, and be ready for sight-seeing next day. We sat down to supper, therefore, in less than an hour after our arrival; and it was while we were at table that the discussion I have mentioned took place. It would seem that a party had been got up in town among the disloyal, and I might almost say, the disaffected, which claimed for the subject the right to know in what manner every shilling of the money raised by taxation was expended. This very obviously improper interference with matters that did not belong to them, on the part of the ruled, was resisted by the rulers, and that with energy; inasmuch as such inquiries and investigations would naturally lead to results that might bring authority into discredit, make the governed presuming and prying in their dispositions, and cause much derangement and inconvenience to the regular and salutary action of government. My father took the negative of the proposition, while my uncle maintained its affirmative. I well remember that my poor aunt looked uneasy, and tried to divert the discourse by exciting our curiosity on a new subject.

" Corny has been particularly lucky in having come to town just as he has, since we shall have a sort of gala-day to-morrow, for the blacks and the children."

I was not in the least offended at being thus associated with the negroes, for they mingled in most of the amusements of us young people; but I did not quite so well like to be ranked with the children, now I was fourteen, and on my way to college. Notwithstanding this, I did not fail to betray an interest in what was to come next, by my countenance. As for my father, he did not hesitate about asking an explanation.

" The news came in this morning, by a fast-sailing sloop, that the Patroon of Albany is on his way to New York, in his coach-and-four, and with two outriders, and that he may be expected to reach town in the course of to-morrow. Several of my acquaintances have consented to let their children go out a little way into the country, to see him come in; and as for the blacks, you know, it is just as well to give them *permission* to be of the party, as half of them would otherwise go without asking it."

" This will be a capital opportunity to let Corny see a little of the world," cried my father, " and I would not have him miss it on any account. Besides, it is useful to teach young people early, the profitable lesson of honoring their superiors and seniors."

" In that sense it may do," growled my uncle, who, though so much of a latitudinarian in his political opinions, never failed to inculcate all useful and necessary maxims for private life; the Patroon of Albany being one of the most respectable and affluent of all our gentry. " I have no objection to Corny's going to see that sight; and I hope, my dear, you will let both Pompey and Cæsar be of the party. It won't hurt the fellows to see the manner in which the patroon has his carriage kept and horses groomed."

Pompey and Cæsar were of the party, though the latter did not join us until Pompey had taken me all round the town, to see the principal sights; it being understood that the patroon had slept at Kingsbridge, and would not be likely to reach town until near noon. New York was certainly not the place, in 1751, it is to-day; nevertheless, it was a large and important town, even when I went to college, containing not less than twelve thousand souls, blacks included. The Town Hall is a magnificent structure, standing at the head of Broad street; and thither Pompey led me, even before my aunt had come down to breakfast. I could scarcely admire that fine edifice sufficiently; which, for size, architecture and position, has scarcely now an equal in all the colonies. It is true, that the town has much improved, within the last twenty years; but York was a noble place, even in the middle of this century! After breakfast, Pompey and I proceeded up Broadway, commencing near the fort, at the Bowling Green, and walking some distance beyond the head of Wall street, or quite a quarter of a mile. Nor did the town stop here; though its principal extent is, or was then, along the margin of the East River. Trinity Church I could hardly admire enough either; for it appeared to me, that it was large enough to contain all the church people in the colony. It was a venerable structure, which had then felt the heats of summer and the snows of winter on its roofs and walls, near half a century, and it still stands a monument of pious zeal and cultivated

taste.* There were other churches, belonging to other denomina-
tions, of course, that were well worthy of being seen; to say nothing of the markets. I thought I never should tire of gazing at
the magnificence of the shops, particularly the silversmiths'; some
of which must have had a thousand dollars' worth of plate in their
windows, or otherwise in sight. I might say as much of the other
shops, too, which attracted a just portion of my admiration.

About eleven, the number of children and blacks that were seen
walking toward the Bowery road, gave us notice that it was time
to be moving in that direction. We were in the upper part of
Broadway at the time, and Pompey proceeded forthwith to fall
into the current, making all the haste he could, as it was thought
the traveller might pass down toward the East River, and get
into Queen street, before we could reach the point at which he
would diverge. It is true, the old town residence of Stephen de
Lancey, which stood at the head of Broadway, just above Trinity,†
had been converted into a tavern, and we did not know but the
patroon might choose to alight there, as it was then the principal
inn of the town; still, most people preferred Queen street; and the
new City Tavern was so much out of the way, that strangers in
particular were not fond of frequenting it. Cæsar came up, much
out of breath, just as we got into the country.

Quitting Broadway, we went along the country road that then
diverged to the east, but which is now getting to contain a sort
of suburb, and passing the road that leads into Queen street, we
felt more certain of meeting the traveller, whose carriage we soon
learned had not gone by. As there were and are several taverns
for country people in this quarter, most of us went quite into the

---

* The intelligent reader will, of course, properly appreciate the provincial admiration of Mr. Littlepage, who naturally fancied his own best was other people's best.
The Trinity of that day was burned in the great fire of 1776. The edifice that succeeded it at the peace of 1783, has already given place to a successor, that has more
claim to be placed on a level with modern English town-church architecture, than
any other building in the Union. When another shall succeed this, which shall be as
much larger and more elaborated than this is, compared to its predecessor, and still
another shall succeed, which shall bear the same relation to that, then the country
will possess an edifice that is on a level with the first-rate Gothic cathedral-architec-
ture of Europe. It would be idle to pretend that the new Trinity is without faults;
some of which are probably the result of circumstances and necessity; but, if the respectable architect who has built it, had no other merit, he would deserve the gratitude of every man of taste in the country, by placing church towers of a proper
comparative breadth, dignity and proportions, before the eyes of its population.
The diminutive meanness of American church-towers, has been an eyesore to every
intelligent, travelled American, since the country was settled. — Editor.

† The site of the present City Hotel. — Editor.

country, proceeding as far as the villas of the Bayards, De Lanceys, and other persons of mark; of which there are several along the Bowery road. Our party stopped under some cherry trees, that were not more than a mile from town, nearly opposite to Lieutenant-Governor de Lancey's country house; * but many boys, etc., went a long, long way into the country, finishing the day by nutting and gathering apples in the grounds of Petersfield and Rosehill, the country residences of the Stuyvesant and Watt, or, as the last is now called, the Watts families. I was desirous of going thus far myself, for I had heard much of both of those grand places; but Pompey told me it would be necessary to be back for dinner by half-past one, his mistress having consented to postpone the hour a little, in order to indulge my natural desire to see all I could while in town.

We were not altogether children and blacks who were out on the Bowery road that day — many tradesmen were among us, the leathern aprons making a goodly parade on the occasion. I saw one or two persons wearing swords, hovering round, in the lanes and in the woods — proof that even gentlemen had some desire to see so great a person as the Patroon of Albany pass. I shall not stop to say much of the *transit* of the *patroon*. He came by about noon, as was expected, and in his coach-and-four, with two outriders, coachman, etc., in liveries, as is usual in the families of the gentry, and with a team of heavy, black, Dutch-looking horses, that I remember Cæsar pronounced to be of the true Flemish breed. The patroon himself was a sightly, well-dressed gentleman, wearing a scarlet coat, flowing wig, and cocked hat; and I observed that the handle of his sword was of solid silver. But my father wore a sword with a solid silver handle, too, a present from my grandfather when the former first entered the army.† He bowed

---

* Now Delancey street. — EDITOR.

† This patroon must have been Jeremiah Van Rensselaer, who lived to be a bachelor of forty before he married. If there be no anachronism, this gentleman married Miss Van Cortlandt, one of the seven daughters of Stephanus Van Cortlandt, who was proprietor of the great manor of Cortlandt, Westchester county, and who, in his day, was the principal personage of the colony. The seven daughters of this Colonel Van Cortlandt, by marrying into the families of De Lancey, Bayard, Van Rensselaer, Beekman, M'Gregor — Skinner, etc., etc., brought together a connection that was long felt in the political affairs of New York. The Schuylers were related through a previous marriage, and many of the Long Island and other families of weight by other alliances. This connection formed the court party, which was resisted by an opposition led by the Livingstons, Morrises, and other names of *their* connection. This old bachelor, Jeremiah Van Rensselaer, believing he would never marry, alienated, in behalf of his next brother and anticipated heir, the Greenbush

to the salutations he received in passing, and I thought all the spectators were pleased with the noble sight of seeing such an equipage pass into the town. Such a sight does not occur every day in the colonies, and I felt exceedingly happy that it had been my privilege to witness it.

A little incident occurred to myself that rendered this day long memorable to me. Among the spectators assembled along the road on this occasion, were several groups of girls, who belonged to the better class, and who had been induced to come out into the country, either led by curiosity or by the management of the different sable nurses who had them in charge. In one of these groups was a girl of about ten, or possibly of eleven years of age, whose dress, air, and mien, early attracted my attention. I thought her large, bright, full, blue eye, particularly winning; and boys of fourteen are not altogether insensible to beauty in the other sex, though they are possibly induced oftener to regard it in those who are older than in those who are younger than themselves. Pompey happened to be acquainted with Silvy, the negress who had the care of my little beauty, to whom he bowed, and addressed as Miss Anneke (Anna Cornelia, abbreviated). Anneke I thought a very pretty name too, and some little advances were made toward an acquaintance by means of an offering of some fruit that I had gathered by the way-side. Things were making a considerable progress, and I had asked several questions, such as whether " Miss Anneke had ever seen a patroon," which " was the greatest personage, a patroon or a governor," whether " a nobleman who had lately been in the colony, as a military officer, or the patroon, would be likely to have the finest coach," when a butcher's boy, who was passing, rudely knocked an apple out of Anneke's hand, and caused her to shed a tear.

I took fire at this unprovoked outrage, and lent the fellow a dig in the ribs that gave him to understand the young lady had a protector. My chap was about my own age and weight, and he surveyed me a minute with a species of contempt, and then beckoned me to follow him into an orchard that was hard by, but a little out of sight. In spite of Anneke's entreaties I went, and Pompey and Cæsar followed. We had both stripped before the

---

and Claverack estates, portions of those vast possessions which, in our day, and principally through the culpable apathy, or miserable demagogueism of those who have been entrusted with the care of the public weal, have been the pretext for violating some of the plainest laws of morality that God has communicated to man. — EDITOR.

negroes got up, for they were in a hot discussion whether I was to be permitted to fight or not. Pompey maintained it would keep dinner waiting; but Cæsar, who had the most bottom, as became his name, insisted, as I had given a blow, I was bound to render satisfaction. Luckily, Mr. Worden was very skilful at boxing, and he had given both Dirck and myself many lessons, so that I soon found myself the best fellow. I gave the butcher's boy a bloody nose and a black eye, when he gave in, and I came off victor; not, however, without a facer or two, that sent me to college with a reputation I hardly merited, of that of a regular pugilist.

When I returned to the road, after this breathing, Anneke * had disappeared, and I was so shy and silly as not to ask her family name from Cæsar the Great, or Pompey the Little.

* Pronounced On-na-*kay*, I believe. — EDITOR.

CHAPTER III

"Believe me, thou talkest of an admirable conceited fellow. Has he any un-braided wares?"

"Pr'ythee, bring him in; and let him approach singing."   WINTER'S TALE.

I HAVE no intention of taking the reader with me through college, where I remained the usual term of four years. These four years were not idled away, as sometimes happens, but were fairly improved. I read all of the New Testament, in Greek; several of Cicero's Orations; every line of Horace, Satires and Odes; four books of the Iliad; Tully de Oratore, throughout; besides paying proper attention to geography, mathematics, and other of the usual branches. Moral philosophy, in particular, was closely attended to, senior year, as well as astronomy. We had a telescope that showed us all four of Jupiter's moons. In other respects, Nassau might be called the seat of learning. One of our class purchased a second-hand copy of Euripides, in town, and we had it in college all of six months; though it was never my good fortune to see it, as the young man who owned it was not much disposed to let profane eyes view his treasure. Nevertheless, I am certain the copy of the work was in college; and we took good care to let the Yale men hear of it more than once. I do not believe *they* ever saw even the outside of a Euripides. As for the telescope, I can testify of my own knowledge; having seen the moons of Jupiter as often as ten times, with my own eyes, aided by its magnifiers. We had a tutor who was expert among the stars, and who, it was generally believed, would have been able to see the ring of Saturn, could he have found the planet; which, as it turned out, he was unable to do.

My four college years were very happy years. The vacations came often, and I went home invariably; passing a day or two with my aunt Legge, in going or coming. The acquisition of knowledge was always agreeable to me; and I may say it without vanity, I trust, at this time of life, I got the third honor of my class. We should have graduated four, but one of our class was compelled to quit us at the end of junior year, on account of his health. He

was an unusually hard student, and it was generally admitted that
he would have taken the first honor had he remained. We were
thought to acquit ourselves with credit at the commencement;
although I afterward heard my grandfather tell Mr. Worden, that
he was of opinion the addresses would have been more masculine
and commendable, had less been said of the surprising growth,
prosperity, and power of the colonies. He had no objection to
the encouragement of a sound, healthful, patriotic feeling; but to
him it appeared that something more novel might have better
pleased the audience. This may have been true, as all three of
us had something to say on the subject; and it is a proof how
much we thought alike, that our language was almost as closely assimilated as our ideas.

As for the Powles' Hook Ferry, it was an unpleasant place I
will allow; though by the time I was junior I thought nothing of
it. My mother, however, was glad when it was passed for the
last time. I remember the very first words that escaped her, after
she had kissed me on my final return from college, were, " Well,
Heaven be praised, Corny! you will never again have any occasion
to cross that frightful ferry, now college is completely done with? "
My poor mother little knew how much greater dangers I was
subsequently called on to encounter, in another direction. Nor
was she minutely accurate in her anticipations, since I have
crossed the ferry in question, several times in later life; the distances not appearing to be as great of late years, as they certainly
seemed to be in my youth.

It was a feather in a young man's cap to have gone through
college, in 1755, which was the year I graduated. It is true the
university men, who had been home for their learning, were more
or less numerous; but they were of a class that held itself aloof
from the smaller gentry, and most of them were soon placed in
office, adding the dignity of public trusts to their acquisitions —
the former in a manner overshadowing the latter. But I was
nearer to the body of the community, and my position admitted
more of comparative excellence, as it might be. No one thinks of
certain habits, opinions, manners, and tastes, in the circle where
they are expected to be found; but, it is a different thing where
all, or any of these peculiarities form the exception. I am afraid
more was anticipated from my college education than has ever been
realized; but I will say this for my *Alma Mater*, that I am not
conscious my acquisitions at college have ever been of any disadvantage to me; and I rather think they have, in some degree at

least, contributed to the little success that has attended my humble
career.

I kept up my intimacy with Dirck Follock, during the whole
time I remained at college. He continued the classics with Mr.
Worden, for two years after I left the school; but I could not discover that his progress amounted to any thing worth mentioning.
The master used to tell the colonel that " Dirck's progress was
slow and sure; " and this did not fail to satisfy a man who had a
constitutional aversion to much of the head-over-heels rate of
doing things among the English population. Colonel Follock, as
we always called him, except when my father or grandfather asked
him to drink a glass of wine, or drank his health in the first glass
after the cloth was removed, when he was invariably styled Colonel
Van Valkenburgh, at full length; but Colonel Follock was quite
content that his son and heir should know no more than he knew
himself, after making proper allowances for the difference in years
and experience. By the time I returned home, however, a material
change had been made in the school. Mr. Worden fell heir to a
moderate competency at home, and he gave up teaching, a business
he had never liked, accordingly. It was even thought he was a
shade less zealous in his parochial duties, after the acquisition of
this fifty pounds sterling a-year, than he had previously been;
though I am far from insisting on the fact's being so. At any
rate, it was not in the power of fifty pounds per annum to render
Mr. Worden apathetic on the subject of the church; for he continued a most zealous churchman down to the hour of his death;
and this was something, even admitting that he was not quite so
zealous as a Christian. The church being the repository of the
faith, if not the faith itself, it follows that its friends are akin to
religion, though not absolutely religious. I have always liked a
man the better for being what I call a sound, warm-hearted churchman, though his habits may have been a little free.

It was necessary to supply the place left vacant by the emigra-
tion of Mr. Worden, or to abandon a school that had got to be the
nucleus of knowledge in Westchester. There was a natural desire,
at first, to obtain another scholar from home; but no such person
offering, a Yale College graduate was accepted, though not without sundry rebellions, and plenty of distrust. The moment he
appeared, Colonel Follock and Major Nicholas Oothout, another
respectable Dutch neighbor, withdrew their sons; and from that
hour Dirck never went to school again. It is true, Westchester
was not properly a Dutch county, like Rockland, and Albany,

and Orange, and several others along the river; but it had many respectable families in it, of that extraction, without alluding to such heavy people as the Van Cortlands, Felipses, Beekmans, and two or three others of that stamp. Most of our important county families had a different origin, as in the case of the Morrises, of Morrisania, and of the Manor of Fordham, the Pells, of Pelham, the Heathcotes, of Mamanneck, the branch of the De Lanceys at West Farms, the Jays, of Rye, etc., etc. All these came of the English or Huguenot stock. Among these last, more or less Dutch blood was to be found, however; though Dutch prejudices were a good deal weakened. Although few of these persons sent their boys to this school, they were consulted in the selection of a master; and I have always supposed that their indifference was the cause that the county finally obtained the services of a Yankee from Yale.

The name of the new pedagogue was Jason Newcome, or, as he pronounced the latter appellation himself, Noocome. As he affected a pedantic way of pronouncing the last syllable long, or as it was spelt, he rather called himself Noo-comb, instead of Newcum, as is the English mode, whence he soon got the nickname of Jason Old Comb among the boys; the lank, orderly arrangement of his jet-black, and somewhat greasy-looking locks, contributing their share toward procuring for him the *soubriquet,* as I believe the French call it. As this Mr. Newcome will have a material part to play in the succeeding portions of this narrative, it may be well to be a little more minute in his description.

I found Jason fully established in the school, on my return from college. I remember we met very much like two strange birds, that see each other for the first time on the same dunghill; or two quadrupeds, in their original interview in a common herd. It was New Haven against Newark; though the institution, after making as many migrations as the House of Loretto, finally settled down at Princeton, a short time before I took my degree. I was consequently entitled to call myself a graduate of Newark — a sort of scholar that is quite as great a curiosity in the country as a Queen Anne's farthing, or a book printed in the fifteenth century. I remember the first evening we two spent in company, as well as if the meeting occurred only last night. It was at Satanstoe, and Mr. Worden was present. Jason had a liberal supply of Puritanical notions, which were bred in-and-in in his moral, and I had almost said, in his physical system; nevertheless, he could unbend; and I did not fail to observe that very evening, a gleam of covert enjoyment on his sombre countenance, as the hot-stuff, the cards, and the pipes were produced, an hour or two before supper — a meal we always had hot and comfortable. This covert satisfaction, however, was not exhibited without certain misgiving looks, as if the neophyte in these innocent enjoyments distrusted his right to possess his share. I remember in particular, when my mother laid two or three new, clean packs of cards on the table, that Jason cast a stealthy glance over his shoulder, as if to make certain that the act was not noted by the minister, or the "neighbors." The neighbors! — what a contemptible being a man becomes, who lives in constant dread of the comments and judgments of these social supervisors! and what a wretch, the habit of deferring to no principle better than their decision has made many a being, who has had originally the materials of something better in him, than has been developed by the *surveillance* of ignorance, envy, vulgarity, gossiping and lying! In those cases in which education, social position, opportunities, and experience have made any material difference between the parties, the man who yields to such a government, exhibits the picture of a giant held in bondage by a pigmy. I have always remarked, too, that they who are best qualified to sit in this neighborhood-tribunal, generally keep most aloof from it, as repugnant to their tastes and habits, thus leaving its decisions to the portions of the community least qualified to make such as are either just or enlightened.

I felt a disposition to laugh outright, at the manner in which Jason betrayed a sneaking consciousness of crime, as he saw my meek, innocent, simple-minded, just and warm-hearted mother lay the cards on the table that evening. His sense of guilt was purely conventional, while my mother's sense of innocence existed in the absence of false instruction, and in the purity of her intentions. One had been taught no exaggerated and false notion of sin — nay, a notion that is impious, as it is clearly impious in man to torture acts that are perfectly innocent *per se*, into formal transgressions of the law of God — while the other had been educated under the narrow and exaggerated notions of a provincial sect, and had obtained a species of conscience that was purely dependent on his miserable schooling. I heard my grandfather say that Jason actually showed the white of his eyes the first time he saw Mr. Worden begin to deal, and he still looked, the whole time we were at whist, as if he expected some one might enter, and tell of his delinquency. I soon discovered that Jason had a much greater dread of being told of, than of doing such things as taking a hand at whist, or drinking a glass of punch, from which I inferred his true conscience drew perceptible distinctions between the acts and the penalties he had been accustomed to see inflicted on them. He was much disposed to a certain sort of frailty; but it was a sneaking disposition to the last.

But the amusing part of the exhibition, that first evening of our acquaintance, was Mr. Worden showing off his successor's familiarity with the classics. Jason had not the smallest notion of quantity; and he pronounced the Latin very much as one would read Mohawk, from a vocabulary made out by a hunter, or a savant of the French academy. As I had received the benefit of Mr. Worden's own instruction, I could do better, and, generally, my knowledge of the classics went beyond that of Jason. The latter's English, too, was long a source of amusement with us all, though my grandfather often expressed strong disgust at it. Even Colonel Follock did not scruple to laugh at Newcome's English, which, as he frequently took occasion to say, " hat a ferry remarkable sount to it." As this peculiarity of Jason's extended a good way into the Anglo-Saxon race, in the part of the country in which he was born, it may be well to explain what I mean a little more at large.

Jason was the son of an ordinary Connecticut farmer, of the usual associations, and with no other pretension to education than such as was obtained in a common school, or any reading which did not include the Scriptures, some half a dozen volumes of sermons and polemical works, all the latter of which were vigorously as well as narrowly one-sided, and a few books that had been expressly written to praise New England, and to undervalue all the rest of the earth. As the family knew nothing of the world beyond the limits of its own township, and an occasional visit to Hartford, on what is called "election-day," Jason's early life was necessarily of the most contracted experience. His English, as a matter of course, was just that of his neighborhood and class of life; which was far from being either very elegant or very Doric. But on this rustic, provincial, or rather, hamlet foundation, Jason had reared a superstructure of New Haven finish and proportions. As he kept school before he went to college, while he was in college, and after he left college, the whole energies of his nature became strangely directed to just such reforms of language as would be apt to strike the imagination of a pedagogue of his calibre. In the first place, he had brought from home with him a great number of sounds that were decidedly vulgar and vicious, and with these in full existence in himself, he had commenced his system of reform on other people. As is common with all tyros, he fancied a very little knowledge sufficient authority for very great theories. His first step was to improve the language, by adapting sound in spelling, and he insisted on calling angel, *an*-gel, because a-n spelt an; chamber, *cham*-ber, for the same reason; and so on through a long catalogue of similarly constructed words. "English," he did not pronounce as "*Ing*-lish," but as "*Eng*lish," for instance; and "nothing" (Anglice *nuth*ing), as *noth*-ing; or, perhaps, it were better to say "*naw*-thin'." While Jason showed himself so much of a purist with these and many other words, he was guilty of some of the grossest possible mistakes, that were directly in opposition to his own theory. Thus, while he affectedly pronounced "none," (nun), as "known," he did not scruple to call "stone," "stun," and "home," "hum." The idea of pronouncing "clerk," as it should be, or "clark," greatly shocked him, as it did to call "hearth," "h'arth;" though he did not hesitate to call this good earth of ours, the "'arth." "Been," he pronounced "ben," of course, and "roof," he called "ruff," in spite of all his purism.

From the foregoing specimens, half a dozen among a thousand, the reader will get an accurate notion of this weakness in Jason's character. It was heightened by the fact that the young man commenced his education, such as it was, late in life, and it is rare indeed that either knowledge or tastes thus acquired are entirely free from exaggeration. Though Jason was several years my senior, like myself he was a recent graduate, and it will be easy enough to imagine the numberless discussions that took place between us, on the subject of our respective acquisitions. I say "respective," instead of mutual acquisitions, because there was nothing mutual about it, or *them*. Neither our classics, our philosophy, nor our mathematics would seem to have been the same, but each man apparently had a science, or a language of his own, and which had been derived from the institution where he had been taught. In the classics I was much the strongest, particularly in the quantities, but Jason had the best of it in mathematics. In spite of his conceit, his vulgarity, his English, his provincialism, and the awkwardness with which he wore his tardily acquired information, this man had strong points about him, and a native shrewdness that would have told much more in his favor had it not been accompanied by a certain evasive manner, that caused one constantly to suspect his sincerity, and which often induced those who were accustomed to him, to imagine he had a sneaking propensity that rendered him habitually hypocritical. Jason held New York in great contempt, a feeling he was not always disposed to conceal, and of necessity his comparisons were usually made with the state of things in Connecticut, and much to the advantage of the latter. To one thing, however, he was much disposed to defer, and that was money. Connecticut had not then, or has it now, a single individual who would be termed rich in New York; and Jason, spite of his provincial conceit, spite of his overweening notions of moral and intellectual superiority, could no more prevent this profound deference for wealth, than he could substitute for a childhood of vulgarity and neglect, the grace, refinement and knowledge which the boys of the more fortunate classes in life obtain as it might be without knowing it. Yes, Jason bowed down to the golden calf, in spite of his Puritanism, his love of liberty, his pretension to equality and the general strut of his disposition and manner.

Such is an outline of the character and qualifications of the man whom I found, on my return from college, at the head of Mr. Worden's school. We soon became acquainted, and I do not know which got the most ideas from the other, in course of the first fortnight. Our conversation and arguments were free, almost to rudeness, and little mercy was shown to our respective prejudices. Jason was ultra levelling in his notions of social intercourse, while I had the opinions of my own colony, in which the distinctions of classes are far more strongly marked than is usual in New England, out of Boston, and its immediate association. Still Jason deferred to names, as well as money, though it was in a way very different from my own. New England was, and is, loyal to the crown; but having the right to name many of its own governors, and possessing many other political privileges through the charters that were granted to her people, in order to induce them to settle that portion of the continent, they do not always manifest the feeling in a way to be agreeable to those who have a proper reverence for the crown. Among other points, growing out of this difference in training, Jason and I had sundry arguments on the subject of professions, trades and callings. It was evident he fancied the occupation of a schoolmaster next in honor to that of a clergyman. The clergy formed a species of aristocracy, according to his notions; but no man could commence life under more favorable auspices, than by taking a school. The following dialogue occurred between us, on this subject; and I was so much struck with the novelty of my companion's notions, as to make a note of it, as soon as we parted.

"I wonder your folks don't think of giving you suthin' to do, Corny," commenced Jason, one day, after our acquaintance had ripened into a sort of belligerent intimacy. "You're near nineteen, now, and ought to begin to think of bringing suthin' in, to pay for all the outgoin's."

By "your folks," Jason meant the family of Littlepage; and the blood of that family quickened a little within me, at the idea of being profitably employed, in the manner intimated, because I had reached the mature and profitable age of nineteen.

"I do not understand you exactly, Mr. Newcome, by your bringing something in," answered I, with dignity enough to put a man of ordinary delicacy on his guard.

"Bringing suthin' in is good English, I hope, Mr. Littlepage. I mean that your edication has cost your folks enough to warrant them in calling on you for a little interest. How much do you suppose, now, has been spent on your edication, beginning at the time you first went to Mr. Worden, and leaving off the day you quitted Newark?"

"Really, I have not the smallest notion; the subject has never crossed my mind."

"Did the old folks never say any thing to you about it?— never foot up the total?"

"I am sure it is not easy to see how this could be done, for I could not help them in the least."

"But your father's books would tell that, as doubtless it all stands charged against you."

"Stands charged against me! How, sir! do you imagine my father makes a charge in a book against me, whenever he pays a few pounds for my education?"

"Certainly; how else could he tell how much you have had?— though, on reflection, as you are an only child, it does not make so much difference. You probably will get all, in the end."

"And had I a brother, or a sister, do you imagine, Mr. Newcome, each shilling we spent would be set down in a book, as charges against us?"

"How else, in natur', could it be known which had had the most, or any sort of justice be done between you?"

"Justice would be done, by our common father's giving to each just as much of his own money as he might see fit. What is it to me, if he chose to give my brother a few hundred pounds more than he chose to give me? The money is his, and he may do with it as he choose."

"An hunderd pounds is an awful sight of money!" exclaimed Jason, betraying by his countenance how deeply he felt the truth of this. "If you have had money in such large sums, so much the more reason why you should set about doing suthin' to repay the old gentleman. Why not set up a school!"

"Sir!"

"Why not set up a school, I say? You might have had this of mine, had you been a little older; but once in, fast in, with me. Still, schools are wanted, and you might get a tolerable good recommend. I dare say your tutor would furnish a certificate."

This word "recommend" was used by Jason for "recommendation;" the habit of putting verbs in the places of substantives, and *vice versa*, being much in vogue with him.

"And do you really think that one who is destined to inherit Satanstoe, would act advisedly to set up a school? Recollect, Mr. Newcome, that my father and grandfather have both borne the king's commission; and that the last bears it, at this very moment, through his representative, the governor."

"What of all that? What better business is there than keeping a good school? If you are high in your notions, get to be made a tutor in that New Jersey college. Recollect that a tutor in a college is somebody. I did hope for such a place, but having a governor's son against me, as a candidate, there was no chance."

"A governor's son a candidate for a tutorship in a college! You are pleased to trifle with me, Mr. Newcome."

"It's true as the gospel. You thought some smaller fish put me down, but he was the son of the governor. But, why do you give that vulgar name to your father's farm — Satanstoe is not decent; yet, Corny, I've heard you use it before your own mother!"

"That you may hear every day, and my mother use it too, before her own son. What fault do you find with the name of Satanstoe?"

"Fault! — In the first place it is irreligious and profane; then it is ungenteel and vulgar, and only fit to be used in low company. Moreover, it is opposed to history and revelation, the evil one having a huff, if you will, but no toes. Such a name couldn't stand a fortnight before public opinion in New England."

"Yes, that may be very true; but we do not care enough for

his Satanic majesty in the colony of New York, to treat him with so much deference. As for the ' huffs,' as you call them —— "

" Why, what do *you* call 'em, Mr. Littlepage? "

" Hoofs, Mr. Newcome; that is the New York pronunciation of the word."

" I care nothing for York pronunciation, which every body knows is Dutch and full of corruptions. You'll never do any thing worth speaking of in this colony, Corny, until you pay more attention to your schools."

" I do not know what you call attention, Mr. Jason, unless we have paid it already. Here, I have the caption, or rather preamble of a law, on that very subject, that I copied out of the statute-book on purpose to show you, and which I will now read in order to prove to you how things really stand in the colony."

" Read away," rejoined Jason, with an air of sufficient disdain.

Read I did, and in the following sententious and comprehensive language, viz.: — " Whereas the youth of this colony are found, by manifold experience, to be not inferior in their natural geniuses to the youth of any other country in the world, therefore be it enacted, etc." *

" There, sir," I said in exultation, " you have chapter and verse for the true character of the rising generation in the colony of New York."

" And what does that preamble lead to? " demanded Jason, a little staggered at finding the equality of our New York intellects established so clearly by legislative enactment.

" It is the preamble to an act establishing the free schools of New York, in which the learned languages have now been taught

---

* This quotation would seem to be accurate, and it is somewhat curious to trace the reason why a preamble so singular should have been prefixed to the law. Was it not owing to the oft-repeated and bold assertions of Europeans, that man deteriorated in this hemisphere? Any American who has been a near observer of European opinion even in our day, must have been frequently amused at the expression of surprise and doubt that so often escapes the residents of the old world, when they discover any thing that particularly denotes talent coming from the new. I make little question that this extraordinary preamble is a sort of indirect answer to an imputation that was known to be as general, in that age, as it was felt to be unjust. My own experience would lead me to think native capacity more abundant in America than in the midland countries of Europe, and quite as frequently met with as in Italy itself; and I have often heard teachers, both English and French, admit that their American and West India scholars were generally the readiest and cleverest in their schools. The great evil under which this country labors, in this respect, is the sway of numbers, which is constantly elevating mediocrity and spurious talent to high places. In America we have a *higher average* of intelligence, while we have far less of the *higher class;* and I attribute the latter fact to the control of those who have never enjoyed the means of appreciating excellence. — EDITOR.

these twenty years; and you will please to remember that another
law has not long been passed, establishing a college in town."

"Well, curious laws do sometimes get into the statute-books, and
a body must take them as he finds them. I dare say Connecticut
might have a word to say on the same subject, if you would give
her a chance. Have you heard the wonderful news from Phila-
delphia, Corny, that has just come among us?"

"I have heard nothing of late; for you know I have been over
in Rockland, with Dirck Follock, for the last two weeks, and news
never reaches that family, or indeed that county."

"No, that is true enough," answered Jason, dryly; "News and
a Dutchman have no affinity, or attraction, as we would say in
philosophy; though there is gravitation enough on one side, ha!
boy?"

Here Jason laughed outright, for he was always delighted whenever he could get a side-hit at the children of Holland, whom he
appeared to regard as a race occupying a position between the
human family and the highest class of the unintellectual animals.
But it is unnecessary to dwell longer on this dialogue, my object
being merely to show the general character of Jason's train of
thought, in order to be better understood when I come to connect
his opinions with his acts.

Dirck and myself were much together after my return from
college. I passed weeks at a time with him, and he returned my
visits with the utmost freedom and good will. Each of us had
now got his growth, and it would have done the heart of Frederick
of Prussia good, to have seen my young friend after he had ended
his nineteenth year. In stature he measured exactly six feet
three, and he gave every promise of filling up in proportion.
Dirck was none of your roundly-turned, Apollo-built fellows, but
he had shoulders that his little, short, solid, but dumpy-looking
mother, who was of the true stock, could scarcely span, when she
pulled his head down to give him a kiss; which she did regularly,
as Dirck told me himself, twice each year; that is to say, Christmas and New-Year. His complexion was fair, his limbs large
and well proportioned, his hair light, his eyes blue, and his face
would have been thought handsome by most persons. I will not
deny, however, that there was a certain ponderosity, both of mind
and body, about my friend, that did not very well accord with
the general notion of grace and animation. Nevertheless, Dirck
was a sterling fellow, as true as steel, as brave as a game-cock,
and as honest as noon-day light.

Jason was a very different sort of person, in many essentials.

In figure, he was also tall, but he was angular, loose-jointed and swinging — slouching would be the better word, perhaps. Still, he was not without strength, having worked on a farm until he was near twenty; and he was as active as a cat; a result that took the stranger a little by surprise, when he regarded only his loose, quavering sort of build. In the way of thought, Jason would think two feet to Dirck's one; but I am far from certain that it was always in so correct a direction. Give the Dutchman time, he was very apt to come out right; whereas Jason, I soon discovered, was quite liable to come to wrong conclusions, and particularly so in all matters that were a little adverse, and which affected his own apparent interests. Dirck, moreover, was one of the best-natured fellows that breathed; it being almost impossible to excite him to anger; when it did come, however, the earthquake was scarcely more terrific. I have seen him enraged, and would as soon encounter a wild-boar in an open field, as run against his course, while in the fit.

Modesty will hardly permit me to say much of myself. I was well-grown, active, strong, for my years; and, I am inclined to think, reasonably well-looking; though I would prefer that this much should be said by any one but myself. Dirck and I often tried our manhood together, when youngsters, and I was the better chap until my friend reached his eighteenth year, when the heavy metal of the young Dutch giant told in our struggles. After that period was past, I found Dirck too much for me, in a close gripe, though my extraordinary activity rendered the inequality less apparent than it might otherwise have proved. I ought not to apply the term of " extraordinary " to any thing about myself, but the word escaped me unconsciously, and I shall let it stand. One thing I will say, notwithstanding, let the reader think of it as he may: I was good-natured and well-disposed to my fellow-creatures, and had no greater love of money than was necessary to render me reasonably discreet.

Such is an outline of the characters and persons of three of the principal actors in the scenes I am about to relate; scenes that will possess some interest for those who love to read accounts of adventures in a new country, however much they may fail in interesting others, when I speak of the condition and events of the more civilized condition of society, that was enjoyed, even in my youth, in such old counties as Westchester, and such towns as York.

CHAPTER IV

THE spring of the year I was twenty, Dirck and myself paid
our first visit to town, in the characters of young men. Although
Satanstoe was not more than five-and-twenty miles from New
York, by the way of Kingsbridge, the road we always travelled
in order to avoid the ferry, it was by no means as common to visit
the capital as it has since got to be. I know gentlemen who pass
in and out from our neighborhood, now, as often as once a fortnight, or even once a week; but thirty years since this was a thing
very seldom done. My dear mother always went to town twice a
year; in the spring to pass Easter week, and in the autumn to
make her winter purchases. My father usually went down four
times, in the course of the twelve months, but he had the reputation of a gadabout, and was thought by many people to leave home
quite as much as he ought to do. As for my grandfather, old age
coming on, he seldom left home now, unless it were to pay stated
visits to certain old brother campaigners who lived within moderate
distances, and with whom he invariably passed weeks each
summer.

The visit I have mentioned occurred some time after Easter, a
season of the year that many of our country families were in the
habit of passing in town, to have the benefit of the daily services
of old Trinity, as the Hebrews resorted to Jerusalem to keep the
feast of the passover. My mother did not go to town this year, on
account of my father's gout, and I was sent to supply her place
with my aunt Legge, who had been so long accustomed to have one
of the family with her at that season, that I was substituted.
Dirck had relatives of his own, with whom he staid, and thus every
thing was rendered smooth. In order to make a fair start, my
friend crossed the Hudson the week before, and, after taking
breath at Satanstoe for three days, we left the Neck for the

capital, mounted on a pair of as good roadsters as were to be found in the country: and that is saying a good deal; for the Morrises, and De Lanceys, and Van Cortlandts all kept racers, and sometimes gave us good sport, in the autumn, over the county course. Westchester, to say no more than she deserved, was a county with a spirited gentry, and one of which no colony need be ashamed.

My mother was a tender-hearted parent, and full of anxiety in behalf of an only child. She knew that travelling always has more or less of hazard, and was desirous we should be off betimes, in order to make certain of our reaching town before the night set in. Highway robbers, Heaven be praised! were then, and are still, unknown to the colonies; but there were other dangers that gave my excellent parent much concern. All the bridges were not considered safe; the roads were, and are yet, very circuitous, and it was possible to lose one's way; while it was said persons had been known to pass the night on Harlem common, an uninhabited waste that lies some seven or eight miles on our side of the city. My mother's first care, therefore, was to get Dirck and myself off early in the morning; in order to do which she rose with the light, gave us our breakfasts immediately afterward, and thus enabled us to quit Satanstoe just as the sun had burnished the eastern sky with its tints of flame color.

Dirck was in high good-humor that morning, and, to own the truth, Corny did not feel the depression of spirits which, according to the laws of propriety, possibly ought to have attended the first really free departure of so youthful an adventurer from beneath the shadows of the paternal roof. We went our way laughing and chatting, like two girls just broke loose from boarding-school. I had never known Dirck more communicative, and I got certain new insights into his feelings, expectations, and prospects, as we rode along the colony's highway that morning, that afterward proved to be matters of much interest with us both. We had not got a mile from the chimney-tops of Satanstoe, ere my friend broke forth as follows: —

"I suppose you have heard, Corny, what the two old gentlemen have been at, lately?"

"Your father and mine? — I have not heard a syllable of any thing new."

"They have been suing out, before the governor and council, a joint claim to that tract of land they bought of the Mohawks, the last time they were out together on service, in the colony militia."

I ought to mention here, that though my predecessors had made but few campaigns in the regular army, each had made several in the more humble capacity of a militia officer.

"This is news to me, Dirck," I answered. "Why should the old gentlemen have been so sly about such a thing?"

"I cannot tell you, lest they thought silence the best way to keep off the Yankee. You know my father has a great dread of a Yankee's getting a finger into any of his bargains. He says the Yankees are the locusts of the west."

"But how came you to know any thing about it, Dirck?"

"I am no Yankee, Corny."

"And your father told *you*, on the strength of this recommendation?"

"He told me, as he tells me most things that he thinks it best I should know. We smoke together, and then we talk together."

"I would learn to smoke too, if I thought I should get any useful information by so doing."

"Dere is much to be l'arnt from ter pipe!" said Dirck, dropping into a slightly Dutch accent, as frequently happened with him, when his mind took a secret direction toward Holland, though in general he spoke English quite as well as I did myself, and vastly better than that miracle of taste, and learning, and virtue, and piety, Mr. Jason Newcome, A.B., of Yale, and prospective president of that, or some other institution.

"So it would seem, if your father is telling you secrets all the time you are smoking together. But where is this land, Dirck?"

"It is in the Mohawk country — or, rather, it is in the country near the Hampshire grants, and at no great distance from the Mohawk country."

"And how much may there be of it?"

"Forty thousand acres; and some of it of good, rich flats, they say; such as a Dutchman loves."

"And your father and mine have purchased all this land in company, you say — share and share alike, as the lawyers call it."

"Just so."

"Pray, how much did they pay for so large a tract of land!"

Dirck took time to answer this question. He first drew from his breast a pocket-book, which he opened as well as he could under the motion of his roadster, for neither of us abated his speed, it being indispensable to reach town before dark. My friend succeeded at length in putting his hand on the paper he wanted, which he gave to me.

"There," he said; "that is a list of the articles paid to the Indians, which I have copied, and then there have been several hundred pounds of fees paid to the governor and his officers."

I read from the list as follows; the words coming out by jerks, as the trotting of my horse permitted. "Fifty blankets, each with yellow strings and yellow trimmings; ten iron pots, four gallons each; forty pounds of gunpowder; seven muskets; twelve pounds of small beads; ten strings of wampum; fifty gallons of rum, pure Jamaica, and of high proof; a score of Jews-harps, and three dozen first quality English-made tomahawks."

"Well, Dirck," I cried, as soon as through reading, "this is no great matter to give for forty thousand acres of land, in the colony of New York. I dare say, a hundred pounds currency (two hundred and fifty dollars) would buy every thing here, even to the rum and the first quality of English-made tomahawks."

"Ninety-six pounds, thirteen shillings, sevenpence 't'ree fart'in's' was the footing of the whole bill," answered Dirck deliberately, preparing to light his pipe; for he could smoke very conveniently while trotting no faster than at the rate of six miles the hour.

"I do not find that dear for forty thousand acres; I suppose the muskets, and rum, and other things were manufactured expressly for the Indian trade."

"Not they, Corny; you know how it is with the old gentlemen — they are as honest as the day."

"So much the better for them, and so much the better for us! But what is to be done with this land, now they own it?"

Dirck did not answer until we had trotted twenty rods; for by this time the pipe was at work, and the moment the smoke was seen he kept his eye on it, until he saw a bright light in front of his nose.

"The first thing will be to find it, Corny. When a patent is signed and delivered, then you must send forth some proper person to find the land it covers. I have heard of a gentleman who got a grant of ten thousand acres, five years since; and though he has had a hunt for it every summer since, he has not been able to find it yet. To be sure, ten thousand acres is a small object to look for, in the woods."

"And our fathers intend to find this land as soon as the season opens?"

" Not so fast, Corny; not so fast! that was the scheme of your father's Welsh blood, but mine takes matters more deliberately. Let us wait until next year, he said, and then we can send the boys. By that time, too, the war will take some sort of a shape, and we shall know better how to care for the children. The subject has been fairly talked over between the two patentees, and we are to go early *next* spring, not this."

The idea of land-hunting was not in the least disagreeable to me; nor was it unpleasant to think that I stood in reversion, or as heir to twenty thousand acres of land, in addition to those of Satanstoe. Dirck and I talked the matter over, as we trotted on, until both of us began to regret that the expedition was so far in perspective.

The war to which Dirck alluded, had broken out a few months before our visit to town; a Mr. Washington, of Virginia — the same who has since become so celebrated as the Colonel Washington of Braddock's defeat, and other events at the south — having been captured, with a party of his men, in a small work thrown up in the neighborhood of the French, somewhere on the tributaries of the Ohio; a river that is known to run into the Mississippi, a vast distance to the west. I knew very little then, nor do I know much now, of these remote regions, beyond the fact that there are such places, and that they are sometimes visited by detachments, war-parties, hunters and other adventurers from the colonies. To me, it seems scarce worth fighting about such distant and wild territory; for ages and ages must elapse before it can be of any service for the purposes of civilization. Both Dirck and myself regretted that the summer would be likely to go by without our seeing the enemy; for we came of families that were commonly employed on such occasions. We thought both our fathers might be out; though even that was a point that still remained under discussion.

We dined and baited at Kingsbridge, intending to sup in town. While the dinner was cooking, Dirck and I walked out on the heights that overlook the Hudson; for I knew less of this noble river than I wished to know of it. We conversed as we walked; and my companion, who knew the river much better than myself, having many occasions to pass up and down it, between the village of Haverstraw and town, in his frequent visits to his relatives below, gave me some useful information.

" Look here, Corny," said Dirck, after betraying a good deal of desire to obtain a view of some object in the distance, along the river-side; "look here, Corny, do you see yonder house, in the little bay below us, with the lawn that extends down to the water, and that noble orchard behind it?"

I saw the object to which Dirck alluded. It was a house that stood near the river, but sheltered and secluded, with the lawn and orchard as described; though at the distance of some two or three miles, all the beauties of the spot could not be discovered, and many of them had to be received on the faith of my companion's admiration. Still, I saw very plainly, all the objects named; and, among others, the house, the orchard, and the lawn. The building was of stone — as is common with most of the better sort of houses in the country — was long, irregular, and had that air of solid comfort about it, which it is usual to see in buildings of that description. The walls were not whitewashed, according to the lively tastes of our Dutch fellow-colonists, who appear to expend all their vivacity in the pipe and the brush, but were left in their native gray; a circumstance that rendered the form and dimensions of the structure a little less distinct, at a first glance, than they might otherwise have proved. As I gazed at the spot, however, I began to fancy it a charm, to find the picture thus sobered down; and found a pleasure in drawing the different angles, and walls, and chimneys, and roofs, from this back-ground, by means of the organ of sight. On the whole, I thought the little sequestered bay, the wooded and rocky shores, the small but well-distributed lawn, the orchard, with all the other similar accessories, formed together one of the prettiest places of the sort I had ever seen. Thinking so, I was not slow in saying as much to my companion. I was thought to have some taste in these matters, and had been consulted on the subject of laying out grounds by one or two neighbors in the county.

"Whose house is it, Dirck?" I inquired; "and how came you to know any thing about it?"

"That is Lilacsbush," answered my friend; "and it belongs to my mother's cousin, Herman Mordaunt."

I had heard of Herman, or, as it is pronounced, Harman Mordaunt. He was a man of considerable note in the colony, having been the son of a Major Mordaunt, of the British army, who had married the heiress of a wealthy Dutch merchant, whence the name of Herman; which had descended to the son along with the money. The Dutch were so fond of their own blood, that they never failed to give this Mr. Mordaunt his Christian name, and he was usually known in the colony as Herman Mordaunt.

Further than this, I knew little of the gentleman, unless it might be that he was reputed rich, and was admitted to be in the best society, though not actually belonging to the territorial or political aristocracy of the colony.

"As Herman Mordaunt is your mother's cousin, I suppose, Dirck," I resumed, "that you have been at Lilacsbush, and ascertained whether the inside of the house is as pleasant and respectable as the outside."

"Often, Corny; while Madam Mordaunt lived, my mother and I used to go there every summer. The poor lady is now dead, but I go there still."

"Why did you not ride on as far as Lilacsbush, and levy a dinner on your relations? I should think Herman Mordaunt would feel hurt, were he to learn that an acquaintance, or a relation, had put up at an inn, within a couple of miles of his own house. I dare say he knows both Major and Captain Littlepage, and I protest I shall feel it necessary to send him a note of apology for not calling. These things ought not to be done, Dirck, among persons of a certain stamp, and who are supposed to know what is proper."

"This would be all right enough, Corny, had Herman Mordaunt, or his daughter, been at Lilacsbush; but they live in Crown street, in town, in winter, and never come out here until after the Pinkster holidays, let *them* come when they may."

"Oh! he is as great a man as that, is he? — a town and country house; after all, I do not know whether it would do to be quite so free with one of his standing, as to go to dine with him without sending notice."

"Nonsense, Corny. Who hesitates about stopping at a gentleman's door, when he is travelling? Herman Mordaunt would have given us a hearty welcome, and I should have gone on to Lilacsbush, did I not know that the family is certain to be in town at this season. Easter came early this year, and to-morrow will be the first day of the Pinkster holidays. As soon as they are over, Herman Mordaunt and Anneke will be out here to enjoy their lilacs and roses."

"Oh, ho! there is an Anneke, as well as the old gentleman. Pray, how old may Miss Anneke be, Master Dirck?"

As this question was asked, I turned to look my friend in the face, and I found that his handsome, smooth, fair, Dutch lineaments were covered with a glow of red, that it was not usual to see extended so far from his ruddy cheeks. Dirck was too much of a man, however, to turn away, or to try to hide blushes so ingenuous; but he answered stoutly: —

"My cousin, Anneke Mordaunt, is just turned of seventeen; and, I'll tell you what, Corny — "

"Well — I am listening with both ears, to hear your *what* — out with it, man; both ears are open."

"Why, Anneke (On-na-*kay*) is one of the very prettiest girls in the colony! What is more, she is as sweet and goot " — Dirck grew Dutch, as he grew animated — " as she is pretty."

I was quite astounded at the energy and feeling with which this was said. Dirck was such a matter-of-fact fellow, that I had never dreamed he could be sensible to the passion of love; nor had I ever paused to analyze the nature of our own friendship. We liked each other, in the first place, most probably from habit; then, we were of characters so essentially different, that our attachment was influenced by that species of excitement which is the child of opposition. As we grew older, Dirck's good qualities began to command my respect, and reason entered more into my affection for him. I was well convinced that my companion could and would prove to be a warm friend; but the possibility of his ever becoming a lover, had not before crossed my mind. Even then, the impression made was not very deep or lasting, though I well remember the sort of admiration and wonder with which I gazed at his flushed cheek, animated eye, and improved mien. For the moment, Dirck really had a commanding and animated air.

"Why, Anneke is one of the prettiest girls in the colony! " my friend had exclaimed.

"And your cousin? "

"My second cousin. Her mother's father and my mother's mother were brother and sister."

"In that case, I shall hope to have the honor of being introduced one of these days to Miss Anneke Mordaunt, who is just turned of seventeen, and is one of the prettiest girls in the colony, and is as good as she is pretty."

"I wish you to see her, Corny, and that before we go home," Dirck replied, all his philosophy, or phlegm, whichever the philosophy of other people may term it, returning; " come; let us go back to the inn; our dinner will be getting cold."

I mused on my friend's unusual manner, as we walked back toward the inn; but it was soon forgotten, in the satisfaction produced by eating a good, substantial meal of broiled ham, with hot potatoes, boiled eggs, a beefsteak done to a turn, with the accessions of pickles, cold-slaw, apple-pie, and cider. This is a common New York tavern dinner, for the wayfarer; and, I must say, I have got to like it. Often have I enjoyed such a repast, after a sharp forenoon's ride; ay, and enjoyed it more than I have relished entertainments at which have figured turkeys, oysters, hams, hashes, and other dishes that have higher reputations. Even turtle-soup, for which we are somewhat famous in New York, has failed to give me the same delight.

Dirck, to do him justice, ate heartily; for it is not an easy matter to take away his appetite. As usual, I did most of the talking; and that was with our landlady, who, hearing I was a son of her much-esteemed and constant customer, Major Littlepage, presented herself with the desert and cheese, and did me the honor to commence a discourse. Her name was Light; and light was she certain to cast on every thing she discussed; that is to say, innkeeper's light; which partakes somewhat of the darkness that is so apt to overshadow no small portion of the minds of her many customers.

" Pray, Mrs. Light," I asked, when there was an opening, which was not until the good woman had exhausted her breath in honor of the Littlepages, " do you happen to know any thing of a family, hereabouts, of the name of Mordaunt? "

" Do I *happen* to know, sir! — Why, Mr. Littlepage, you might almost as well have asked me, if I had ever heard of a Van Cortlandt, or a Philipse, or a Morris, or any other of the gentry hereabouts. Mr. Mordaunt has a country-place, and a very pretty one it is, within two miles and a half of us; and he and Madam Mordaunt never passed our door, when they went into the country to see Madam Van Cortlandt, without stopping to say a word, and leave a shilling. The poor lady is dead; but there is a young image of her virtues, that is coming a'ter her, that will be likely to do some damage in the colony. She is modesty itself, sir; so I thought it could do her no harm, the last time she was here, just to tell her, she ought to be locked up, for the thefts she was likely to commit, if not for them she had committed already. She blushed, sir, and looked for all the world like the shell of the most delicate boiled lobster you ever laid eyes on. She is truly a charming young lady! "

" Thefts of hearts, you mean of course, my good Mrs. Light? "

" Of nothing else, sir; young ladies are apt to steal hearts, you know. My word for it, Miss Anneke will turn out a great robber, after her own fashion, you know, sir."

"And whose hearts is she likely to run away with, pray? I should be pleased to hear the names of some of the sufferers."

"Lord, sir! — she is too young to have done much *yet*, but wait a twelvemonth, and I'll answer the question."

I could see all this time that Dirck was uneasy, and had some amusement in watching the workings of his countenance. My malicious intentions, however, were suddenly interrupted. As if to prevent further discourse, and, at the same time, further *espionage*, my young friend rose from table, ordering the horses and the bill.

During the ride to town, no more was said of Lilacsbush, Herman Mordaunt, or his daughter Anneke. Dirck was silent, but this was his habit after dinner, and I was kept a good deal on the alert in order to find the road which crossed the common, it being our desire to go in that direction. It is true, we might have gone into town by the way of Bloomingdale, Greenwich, the meadows and the Collect, and so down past the common upon the head of Broadway; but my mother had particularly desired we would fall into the Bowery lane, passing the seats that are to be found in that quarter, and getting into Queen street as soon as possible. By taking this course she thought we should be less likely to miss our way within the town itself, which is certainly full of narrow and intricate passages. My uncle Legge had removed into Duke street, in the vicinity of Hanover Square; and Queen street, I well knew, would lead us directly to his door. Queen street, indeed, is the great artery of New York, through which most of its blood circulates.

It was drawing toward night when we trotted up to the stable, where we left our horses, and obtaining a black to shoulder our portmanteaus, we began to thread the mazes of the capital on foot. New York was certainly, even in 1757, a wonderful place for commerce! Vessels began to be seen some distance east of Fly Market, and there could not have been fewer than twenty ships, brigs, and schooners, lying in the East River, as we walked down Queen street. Of course I include all descriptions of vessels that go to sea, in this estimate. At the present moment, it is probable twice that number would be seen. There Dirck and I stopped more than once, involuntarily, to gaze at the exhibitions of wealth and trade that offered themselves as we went deeper into the town. My mother had particularly cautioned me against falling into this evidence of country habits, and I felt much ashamed at each occurrence of the weakness; but I found it irresistible. At length my friend and I parted; he to go to the residence of his aunt, while I proceeded to that of mine. Before separating, however, we agreed to meet next morning in the fields at the head of Broadway, on the common, which, as it was understood, was to be the scene of the Pinkster sports.

My reception in Duke street was cordial, both on the part of my uncle and on the part of my aunt; the first being a good-hearted person, though a little too apt to run into extravagance on the subject of the rights of the rabble. I was pleased with the welcome I received, enjoyed an excellent hot supper, to which we sat down at half-past eight, my aunt being fond of town hours, both dining and supping a little later than my mother, as being more fashionable and genteel.* As I was compelled to confess fatigue, after so long a ride, as soon as we quitted the table I retired to my own room.

The next day was the first of the three that are devoted to Pinkster, the great Saturnalia of the New York blacks. Although this festival is always kept with more vivacity at Albany than in York, it is far from being neglected, even now, in the latter place. I had told my aunt, before I left her, I should not wait for

* The dinner of the last half-century is, in one sense, but a substitute for the *petits soupers* of the century or two that preceded. It is so entirely rational and natural, that the cultivated and refined should meet for the purposes of social enjoyment after the business of the day has terminated, that the supper has only given place to the same meal under another name, and at hours little varying from those of the past. The Parisian dines at half-past six, remaining at table until eight. The Englishman, later in all his hours, and more ponderous in all his habits, sits down to table about the time the Frenchman gets up; quitting it between nine and ten. The Italian pays a tribute to his climate, and has his early dinner and light supper, both usually alone, the habits of the country carrying him to the opera and the *conversazione* for social communion. But what is the American? A jumble of the same senseless contradictions in his social habits, as he is fast getting to be in his political creeds and political practices; being that is *in transitu*, pressed by circumstances on the one side, and by the habit of imitation on the other; unwilling, almost unable, to think and act for himself. The only American who is temporarily independent in such things, is the unfledged provincial, fresh from his village conceit and village practices, who, until, corrected by communion with the world, fancies the south-east corner of the north-west parish, in the town of Hebron, in the county of Jericho, and the state of Connecticut, to be the only portion of this globe that is perfection. If he should happen to keep a school, or conduct a newspaper, the community becomes in a small degree the participant of his rare advantages and vast experience! — EDITOR.

breakfast, but should be up with the sun, and off in quest of
Dirck, in order that we might enjoy a stroll along the wharves
before it was time to repair to the common, where the fun was to
be seen. Accordingly I got out of the house betimes, though it
was an hour later than I had intended; for I heard the rattling of
cups in the little parlor, the sign that the table was undergoing
the usual process of arrangement for breakfast. It then occurred
to me that most, if not all of the servants, seven in number, would
be permitted to enjoy the holiday; and that it might be well if
I took all my meals, that day, in the fields. Running back to the
room, I communicated this intention to Juno, the girl I found
doing Pompey's work, and left the house on a jump. There was
no great occasion for starving, I thought, in a town as large and
as full of eatables as New York; and the result fully justified this
reasonable opinion.

Just as I got into Hanover Square, I saw a gray-headed negro,
who was for turning a penny before he engaged in the amusements
of the day, carrying two pails that were scoured to the neatness
of Dutch fastidiousness, and which were suspended from the
yoke he had across his neck and shoulders. He cried "White
wine — white wine!" in a clear, sonorous voice; and I was at his
side in a moment. White wine was, and is still, my delight of a
morning; and I bought a delicious draught of the purest and
best of a Communipaw vintage, eating a cake at the same time.
Thus refreshed, I proceeded into the square, the beauty of which
had struck my fancy as I walked through it the previous evening.
To my surprise, whom should I find in the very centre of Queen
street, gaping about him with a most indomitable Connecticut air,
but Jason Newcome! A brief explanation let me into the secret
of his presence. His boys had all gone home to enjoy the
Pinkster holiday, with the black servants of their respective
families; and Jason had seized the opportunity to pay his first
visit to the great capital of the colony. He was on his travels,
like myself.

"And what has brought you down here!" I demanded, the
pedagogue having already informed me that he had put up at a
tavern in the suburbs, where horse-keeping and lodgings were
"reasonable." "The Pinkster fields are up near the head of
Broadway, on the common."

"So I hear," answered Jason; "but I want to see a ship and
all the sights this way, in the first place. It will be time enough
for Pinkster, two or three hours hence, if a Christian ought even

to look at such vanities. Can you tell me where I am to find Hanover Square, Corny?"

"You are in it now, Mr. Newcome; and to my fancy, a very noble area it is!"

"*This* Hanover Square!" repeated Jason. "Why, its shape is not that of a square at all; it is nearer a *triangle*."

"What of that, sir? By a square in a town, one does not necessarily understand an area with four equal sides and as many right angles, but an open space that is left for air and beauty. There are air and beauty enough to satisfy any reasonable man. A square may be a parallelogram, or a triangle, or any other shape one pleases."

"This, then, is Hanover Square! — a New York square, or a Nassau Hall square, Corny; but not a Yale College square, take my word for it. It is so small, moreover!"

"Small! — the width of the street at the widest end must be near a hundred feet; I grant you it is not half that at the other end, but that is owing to the proximity of the houses."

"Ay, it is all owing to the proximity of the houses, as you call it. Now, according to my notion, Hanover Square, of which a body hears so much talk in the country, ought to have had fifty or sixty acres in it, and statues of the whole house of Brunswick, besides. Why is that nest of houses left in the middle of your square?"

"It is not, sir. The square ceases when it reaches *them*. They are too valuable to be torn down, although there has been some talk of it. My uncle Legge told me, last evening, that those houses have been valued as high as twelve thousand dollars; and some persons put them as high as six thousand pounds."

This reconciled Jason to the houses; for he never failed to defer to money, come in what shape it would. It was the only source of human distinction that he could clearly comprehend, though he had some faint impressions touching the dignity of the crown, and the respect due to its representatives.

"Corny," said Jason, in an under tone, and taking me by the arm to lead me aside, though no one was near, like a man who has a great secret to ask, or to communicate, "what was that I saw you taking for your bitters, a little while ago?"

"Bitters! I do not understand you, Jason. Nothing bitter have I tasted to-day; nor can I say I have any great wish to put any thing bitter into my mouth."

"Why, the draught you got from the nigger who is now coming

back across the square, as you call it, and which you seemed to enj'y particularly. I am dry, myself, and should wonderfully like a drink."

" Oh! that fellow sells ' white wine,' and you will find it delicious. If you want your ' bitters,' as you call them, you cannot do better than stop him, and give him a penny."

" Will he let it go so desperate cheap as that? " demanded Jason, his eyes twinkling with a sort of " bitters " expectation.

" That is the stated price. Stop him boldly; there is no occasion for all this Connecticut modesty. Here, uncle, this gentleman wishes a cup of your white wine."

Jason turned away in alarm, to see who was looking on; and when the cup was put into his hand, he shut his eyes, determined to gulp its contents at a swallow, in the most approved " bitters " style. About half the liquor went down his throat, the rest being squirted back in a small white stream.

" Buttermilk, by Jingo! " exclaimed the disappointed pedagogue, who expected some delicious combination of spices with rum. St. Jingo was the only saint, and a " darnation " or " darn you," were the only oaths his Puritan education ever permitted him to use.

CHAPTER V

" Here's your fine clams!
As white as snow!
On Rockaway these clams do grow."
NEW YORK CRIES.

IT was some time before Jason's offended dignity and disappointment would permit him to smile at the mistake; and we had walked some distance toward Old Slip, where I was to meet Dirck, before the pedagogue even opened his lips. Then, the only allusion he made to the white wine, was to call it "a plaguy Dutch cheat;" for Jason had implicitly relied on having that peculiar beverage of his caste, known as "bitters." What he meant by a *Dutch* cheat, I do not know; unless he thought the buttermilk was particularly Dutch, and *this* buttermilk an imposition.

Dirck was waiting for me at the Old Slip; and, on inquiry, I found he had enjoyed his draught of white wine as well as myself, and was ready for immediate service. We proceeded along the wharves in a body, admiring the different vessels that lined them. About nine o'clock, all three of us passed up Wall street, on the stoops of which, no small portion of its tenants were already seated, enjoying the sight of the negroes, as, with happy "shining" faces they left the different dwellings, to hasten to the Pinkster field. Our passage through the street attracted a good deal of attention; for, being all three strangers, it was not to be supposed we could be thus seen in a body, without exciting a remark. Such a thing could hardly have been expected in London itself.

After showing Jason the City Hall, Trinity Church, and the City Tavern, we went out of town, taking the direction of a large common that the king's officers had long used for a parade ground, and which has since been called the Park, though it would be difficult to say why, since it is barely a paddock in size, and certainly has never been used to keep any animals wilder than the boys of the town. A park, I suppose, it will one day become, though it has little at present that comports with my ideas of such a thing. On this common, then, was the Pinkster ground, which was now quite full of people, as well as of animation.

There was nothing new in a Pinkster frolic, either to Dirck, or to myself; though Jason gazed at the whole procedure with wonder. He was born within seventy miles of that very spot, but had not the smallest notion before, of such a holiday as Pinkster. There are few blacks in Connecticut, I believe; and those that are there, are so ground down in the Puritan mill, that they are neither fish, flesh, nor red-herring, as we say of a nondescript. No man ever heard of a festival in New England that had not some immediate connection with the saints, or with politics.

Jason was at first confounded with the noises, dances, music, and games that were going on. By this time, nine-tenths of the blacks of the city, and of the whole country within thirty or forty miles, indeed, were collected in thousands in those fields, beating banjoes, singing African songs, drinking, and worst of all, laughing in a way that seemed to set their very hearts rattling within their ribs. Every thing wore the aspect of good-humor, though it was good-humor in its broadest and coarsest forms. Every sort of common game was in requisition, while drinking was far from being neglected. Still, not a man was drunk. A drunken negro, indeed, is by no means a common thing. The features that distinguish a Pinkster frolic from the usual scenes at fairs, and other merry-makings, however, were of African origin. It is true, there are not now, nor were there then, many blacks among us of African birth; but the traditions and usages of their original country were so far preserved as to produce a marked difference between this festival, and one of European origin. Among other things, some were making music, by beating on skins drawn over the ends of hollow logs, while others were dancing to it, in a manner to show that they felt infinite delight. This, in particular, was said to be a usage of their African progenitors.

Hundreds of whites were walking through the fields, amused spectators. Among these last were a great many children of the better class, who had come to look at the enjoyment of those who attended them, in their own ordinary amusements. Many a sable nurse did I see that day, chaperoning her young master, or young mistress, or both together, through the various groups; demanding of all, and receiving from all, the respect that one of these classes was accustomed to pay to the other.

A great many young ladies between the ages of fifteen and twenty were also in the field, either escorted by male companions, or, what was equally as certain of producing deference, under the care of old female nurses, who belonged to the race that kept the festival. We had been in the field ourselves two hours, and even Jason was beginning to condescend to be amused, when, unconsciously, I got separated from my companions, and was wandering through the groups by myself, as I came on a party of young girls, who were under the care of two or three wrinkled and gray-headed negresses, so respectably attired, as to show at once they were confidential servants in some of the better families. As for the young ladies themselves, most were still of the age of school-girls; though there were some of that equivocal age, when the bud is just breaking into the opening flower, and one or two that were even a little older; young women in forms and deportment, though scarcely so in years. One of a party of two of the last, appeared to me to possess all the graces of young womanhood, rendered radiant by the ingenuous laugh, the light-hearted playfulness, and the virgin innocence of sweet seventeen. She was simply, but very prettily dressed, and every thing about her attire, air carriage, and manner, denoted a young lady of the better class, who was just old enough to feel all the proprieties of her situation, while she was still sufficiently youthful to enjoy all the fun. As she came near me, it seemed as if I knew her; but it was not until I heard her sweet, mirthful voice, that I recollected the pretty little thing in whose behalf I had taken a round with the butcher's boy, on the Bowery road, near six years before. As her party came quite near the spot where I stood, what was only conjecture at first, was reduced to a certainty.

In the surprise of the moment, happening to catch the eye of the young creature, I was emboldened to make her a low bow. At first she smiled, like one who fancies she recognizes an acquaintance; then her face became scarlet, and she returned my bow with a very lady-like, but, at the same time, a very distant curtsey; upon which, bending her blue eyes to the ground, she turned away, seemingly to speak to her companion. After this, I could not advance to speak, though I was strongly in hopes the old black nurse who was with her would recognize me, for she had manifested much concern about me on the occasion of the quarrel with the young butcher.

This did not occur; and old Katrinke, as I heard the negress called, jabbered away, explaining the meaning of the different ceremonies of her race, to a cluster of very interested listeners, without paying any attention to me. The tongues of the pretty little things went, as girls' tongues will go, though my unknown fair one maintained all the reserve and quiet of manner that comported with her young womanhood, and apparent condition of life.

"Dere, Miss Anneke!" exclaimed Katrinke, suddenly; "dere come a gentleum dat will bring a pleasure, I know."

"*Anneke*," I repeated, mentally, and "gentleman that will cause pleasure by his appearance." "Can it be Dirck?" I thought. Sure enough, Dirck it proved to be, who advanced rapidly to the group, making a general salute, and finishing by shaking my beautiful young stranger's hands, and addressing her by the name of "cousin Anneke." This, then, was Annie Mordaunt, as the young lady was commonly called in the English circles, the only child and heiress of Herman Mordaunt, of Crown street and of Lilacsbush. Well, Dirck has more taste than I had ever given him credit for? Just as this thought glanced through my mind, my figure caught my friend's eye, and, with a look of pride and exultation, he signed to me to draw nearer, though I had managed to get pretty near as it was, already.

"Cousin Anneke," said Dirck, who never used circumlocution, when direct means were at all available, "this is Corny Littlepage, of whom you have heard me speak so often, and for whom I ask one of your best curtsies and sweetest smiles."

Miss Mordaunt was kind enough to comply literally, both curtseying and smiling, precisely as she had been desired to do, though I could see she was also slightly disposed to laugh. I was still making my bow, and mumbling some unintelligible compliment, when Katrinke gave a little exclamation, and using the freedom of an old and confidential servant, she eagerly pulled the sleeve of her young mistress, and hurriedly whispered something in her ear. Anneke colored, turned quickly toward me, bent her eyes more boldly and steadily on my face — and then it was that I fancied the sweetest smile which mortal had ever received, or that with which I had just before been received, was much surpassed.

"Mr. Littlepage, I believe, is not a total stranger, cousin Dirck," she said. "Katrinke remembers him, as a young gentleman, who once did me an important service, and now I think I can trace the resemblance myself. I allude to the boy who insulted me on the Bowery road, Mr. Littlepage, and your handsome interference in my behalf."

"Had there been twenty boys, Miss Mordaunt, an insult to *you* would have been resented by any man of ordinary spirit."

I do not know that any youth, who was suddenly put to his wits to be polite, or sentimental, or feeling, could have done a great deal better than *that!* So Anneke thought too, I fancy, for her color increased, rendering her ravishingly lovely, and she looked surprisingly pleased.

"Yes," put in Dirck, with energy — "let twenty, or a hundred try it if they please, Anneke, men or boys, and they'll find those that will protect you."

"You for one, of course, cousin Dirck," rejoined the charming girl, holding out her hand toward my friend, with a frankness I could have dispensed with in her; "but, you will remember, Mr. Littlepage, or *Master* Littlepage, as he then was, was a stranger, and I had no such claim on *him*, as I certainly have on you."

"Well, Corny, it is odd you never said a word of this to me! when I was showing him Lilacsbush, and talking of you and of your father, not a word did he say on the subject."

"I did not then know it was Miss Mordaunt I had been so fortunate as to serve; but here is Mr. Newcome at your elbow, Follock, and dying to be introduced, as he sees I have been."

Anneke turned to smile and curtsey again to Jason, who made his bow in a very schoolmaster sort of a fashion, while I could see that the circumstance I had not boasted of my exploit gave it new importance in the sweet creature's eyes. As for Jason, he had no sooner got along with the introduction — the first, I fancy, he had ever gone regularly through — than, profiting by some questions Miss Mordaunt was asking Dirck about his mother and the rest of the family, he came round to me, drew me aside by a jerk of the sleeve, and gave me to understand he had something for my private ear.

"I did not know before that you had ever kept school, Corny," he half whispered, earnestly.

"How do you know it now, Mr. Newcome, since the thing never happened?"

"How comes it, then, that this young woman called you *Master* Littlepage?"

"Bah! Jason, wait a year or two, and you will begin to get truer notions of us New Yorkers."

"But I heard her with my own ears — *Master* Littlepage; as plain as words were ever called?"

"Well, then, Miss Mordaunt must be right, and, and I have forgotten the affair. I must once have kept a woman's school, somewhere, in my younger days, but forgotten it."

"Now this is nothing (nawthin', as expressed) but your desperate York pride, Corny; but I think all the better of you for it. Why, as it could not have taken place after you went to college, you must have got the start of even me! But, the Rev. Worden is enough to start a youth with a large capital, if he be so minded. I admit he does understand the dead languages. It is a pity he is so very dead in religious matters."

"Well — well — I will tell you all about it another time; you perceive, now, that Miss Mordaunt wishes to move on, and does not like to quit us too abruptly. Let us follow."

Jason complied, and for an hour or two we had the pleasure of accompanying the young ladies, as they strolled among the booths and different groups of that singular assembly. As has been said, most of the blacks had been born in the colony, but there were some native Africans among them. New York never had slaves on the system of the southern planters, or in gangs of hundreds, to labor in the fields under overseers, and who lived apart in cabins of their own; but, our system of slavery was strictly domestic, the negro almost invariably living under the same roof with the master, or, if his habitation was detached, as certainly sometimes happened, it was still near at hand, leaving both races as parts of a common family. In the country, the negroes never toiled in the field, but it was as ordinary husbandmen; and, in the cases of those who labored on their own property, or as tenants of some extensive landlord, the black did his work at his master's side. Then all, or nearly all our household servants were, and still are, blacks, leaving that department of domestic economy almost exclusively in their hands, with the exception of those cases in which the white females busied themselves also in such occupations, united to the usual supervision of the mistresses. Among the Dutch, in particular, the treatment of the negro was of the kindest character, a trusty field-slave often having quite as much to say on the subject of the tillage and the crops, as the man who owned both the land he worked and himself.

A party of native Africans kept up for half an hour. The scene seemed to have revived their early associations, and they were carried away with their own representation of semi-savage sports. The American-born blacks gazed at this group with intense interest also, regarding them as so many ambassadors from the land of their ancestors, to enlighten them in usages and superstitious lore, that were more peculiarly suited to their race. The last even endeavored to imitate the acts of the first, and, though the attempt was often ludicrous, it never failed on the score of intention and gravity. Nothing was done in the way of caricature, but much in the way of respect and affection.

Lest the habits of this generation should pass away and be forgotten, of which I see some evidence, I will mention a usage that was quite common among the Dutch, and which has passed in some measure, into the English families that have formed connections with the children of Holland. Two of these inter-marriages had so far brought the Littlepages within the pale, that the usage to which I allude was practised in my own case. The custom was this: when a child of the family reached the age of six, or eight, a young slave of the same age and sex, was given to him, or her, with some little formality, and from that moment the fortunes of the two were considered to be, within the limits of their respective pursuits and positions, as those of man and wife. It is true, divorces do occur, but it is only in cases of gross misconduct, and quite as often the mis-conduct is on the side of the master, as on that of the slave. A drunkard may get in debt, and be compelled to part with his blacks; this one among the rest; but this particular negro re-mains with him as long as any thing remains. Slaves that seriously misbehave, are usually sent to the island, where the toil on the sugar plantations proves a very sufficient punish-ment.

The day I was six, a boy was given to me, in the manner I have mentioned; and he remained not only my property, but my factotum, to this moment. It was Yaap, or Jacob, the negro to whom I have already had occasion to allude. Anneke Mordaunt, whose grandmother was of a Dutch family, it will be remembered, had with her there, in the Pinkster field, a negress of just her own age, who was called Mari; not Mary, or Maria; but the last, as it would be pronounced without the final a. This Mari was a buxom, glistening, smooth-faced, laugh-ing, red-lipped, pearl-toothed, black-eyed hussy, that seemed

born for fun; and who was often kept in order by her more
sedate and well-mannered young mistress with a good deal of
difficulty. My fellow was on the ground, somewhere, too; for
I had given him permission to come to town to keep Pinkster;
and he was to leave Satanstoe, in a sloop, within an hour
after I left it myself. The wind had been fair, and I made no
question of his having arrived; though, as yet, I had not seen him.

I could have accompanied Anneke, and her party, all day,
through that scene of unsophisticated mirth, and felt no want
of interest. Her presence immediately produced an impression; even the native Africans moderating their manner, and
lowering their yells, as it might be, the better to suit her more
refined tastes. No one, in our set, was too dignified to laugh,
but Jason. The pedagogue, it is true, often expressed his disgust at the amusements and antics of the negroes, declaring
they were unbecoming human beings, and otherwise manifesting that disposition to hypercriticism, which is apt to distinguish one who is only a tyro in his own case.

Such was the state of things, when Mari came rushing up to
her young mistress, with distended eyes and uplifted hands, exclaiming, on a key that necessarily made us all sharers in the
communication —

"Oh! Miss Anneke! What you t'ink, Miss Anneke! Could
you ever s'pose sich a t'ing, Miss Anneke! "

"Tell me at once, Mari, what it is you have seen, or heard;
and leave off these silly exclamations; " said the gentle mistress, with a color that proved she was unused to her own girl's
manner.

"Who *could* t'ink it, Miss Anneke! Dese, here, werry niggers have sent all 'e way to deir own country, and have had a
lion cotched for Pinkster! "

This was news, indeed, if true. Not one of us all had ever
seen a lion; wild animals, then, being exceedingly scarce in the
colonies, with the exception of those that were taken in our
own woods. I had seen several of the small brown bears, and
many a wolf, and one stuffed panther, in my time; but never
supposed it within the range of possibilities, that I could be
brought so near a living lion. Inquiry showed, nevertheless,
that Mari was right, with the exception of the animal's having
been expressly caught for the occasion. It was the beast of a
showman, who was also the proprietor of a very active and
amusing monkey. The price of admission was a quarter of a

dollar, for adult whites; children and negroes going in for half price. These preliminaries understood, it was at once settled that all who could muster enough of money and courage, should go in a body, and gaze on the king of beasts. I say, of courage; for it required a good deal for a female novice to go near a living lion.

The lion was kept in a cage, of course, which was placed in a temporary building of boards, that had been erected for the Pinkster field. As we drew near the door, I saw that the cheeks of several of the pretty young creatures who belonged to the party of Anneke, began to turn pale; a sign of weakness that, singular as it may appear, very sensibly extended itself to most of their attendant negresses. Mari did not flinch, however; and, when it came to the trial, of that sex, she and her mistress were the only two who held out in the original resolution of entering. Some time was thrown away in endeavoring to persuade two or three of her older companions to go in with her; but, finding it useless, with a faint smile, Miss Mordaunt calmly said —

"Well, gentlemen, Mari and myself must compose the female portion of the party. I have never seen a lion, and would not, by any means, miss this opportunity. We shall find my friends waiting for such portions of us as shall not be eaten, on our return."

We were now near the door, where stood the man who received the money, and gave the tickets. It happened that Dirck had been stopped by a gentleman of his acquaintance, who had just left the building, and who was laughingly relating some incident that had occurred within. I stood on one side of Anneke, Jason on the other, while Mari was close in the rear.

"A quarter for each gentleman and the lady," said the doorkeeper, "and a shilling for the wench."

On this hint, Jason, to my great surprise (for usually he was very backward on such occasions), drew out a purse, and emptying some silver into his hand, he said with a flourish —

"Permit me, Miss — it is an honor I covet; a quarter for yourself, and a shilling for Mari."

I saw Anneke color, and her eye turn hastily towards Dirck. Before I had time to say any thing, or to do any thing in fact, she answered steadily —

"Give yourself no trouble, Mr. Newcome; Mr. Littlepage will do me the favor to obtain tickets for me."

Jason had the money in his fingers, and I passed him and bought the tickets, while he was protesting —

"It gave him pleasure — he was proud of the occasion — another time her brother could do the same for his sisters and he had six," and other matters of the sort.

I simply placed the tickets in Anneke's hand, who received them with an expression of thanks, and we all passed; Dirck inquiring of his cousin, as he came up, if he should get her tickets. I mention this little incident as showing the tact of woman, and will relate all that pertains to it, before I proceed to other things. Anneke said nothing on the subject of her tickets until we had left the booth, when she approached me, and with that grace and simplicity which a well-bred woman knows how to use on such an occasion, and quietly observed —

"I am under obligations to you, Mr. Littlepage, for having paid for my tickets; — they cost three shillings, I believe."

I bowed, and had the pleasure of almost touching Miss Mordaunt's beautiful little hand, as she gave me the money. At this instant, a jerk at my elbow came near causing me to drop the silver. It was Jason, who had taken this liberty, and who now led me aside with an earnestness of manner it was not usual for him to exhibit. I saw by the portentous look of the pedagogue's countenance, and his swelling manner, that something extraordinary was on his mind, and waited with some little curiosity to learn what it might be.

"Why, what in human natur', Corny, do you mean?" he cried, almost angrily. "Did ever mortal man hear of a gentleman's making a lady pay for a treat! Do you know you have made Miss Anneke pay for a treat?"

"A treat, Mr. Newcome!"

"Yes, a treat, Mr. Corny Littlepage! How often do you think young ladies will accompany you to shows, and balls, and other sights, if you make *them pay!*"

Then a laugh of derision added emphasis to Jason's words.

"Pay! — could I presume to think Miss Mordaunt would suffer me to pay money for her, or for her servant?"

"You almost make me think you a nat'ral! Young men *always* pay for young women, and no questions asked. Did you not remark how smartly I offered to pay for this Miss, and how well she took it, until you stepped forward and cut me out; — I bore it, for it saved me three ninepences."

"I observed how Miss Mordaunt shrunk from the familiarity

of being called Miss, and how unwilling she was to let you buy
the tickets; and that I suspect was solely because she saw you
had some notion of what you call a treat."

I cannot enter into the philosophy of the thing; but certainly
nothing is more vulgar in English, to address a young lady as
Miss, without affixing a name, whereas I know it is the height
of breeding to say Mademoiselle in French, and am told the
Spaniards, Italians, and Germans use its synonyme in the same
manner. I had been indignant at Jason's familiarity when he
called Anneke — the pretty Anneke! — Miss; and felt glad of an
occasion to let him understand how I felt on the subject.

"What a child you be, a'ter all, Corny!" exclaimed the
pedagogue, who was much too good-natured to take offence at
a trifle. "You, a bachelor of arts! But this matter *must* be
set right, if it be only for the honor of my school. Folks " —
Jason never blundered on the words "one" or "people" in this
sense — "Folks may think that you have been in the school
since it has been under my care, and I wouldn't for the world
have it get abroad that a youth from my school had neglected
to treat a lady under such circumstances."

Conceiving it useless to remonstrate with *me* any further,
Jason proceeded forthwith to Anneke, with whom he begged
permission to say a word in private. So eager was my companion to wipe out the stain, and so surprised was the young
lady, who gently declined moving more than a step, that the
conference took place immediately under my observation,
neither of the parties being aware that I necessarily heard or saw
all that passed.

"You must excuse Corny, Miss," Jason commenced, producing his purse again, and beginning to hunt anew for a quarter and a shilling; "he is quite young, and knows nawthin'
worth speaking of, of the ways of mankind. Ah! here is just
the money — three ninepennies, or three York shillings. Here
Miss, excuse Corny, and overlook it all; when he is older, he
will not make such blunders."

"I am not certain that I understand you, sir!" exclaimed
Anneke, who had shrunk back a little at the "Miss," and who
now saw Jason hold out the silver, with a surprise she took no
pains to conceal.

"This is the price of the tickets — yes, that's all. Nawthin'
else, on honor. Corny, you remember, was so awful dumb as
to let you pay, just as if you had been a gentleman."

Anneke now smiled, and, glancing at me at the same instant, a bright blush suffused her face, though the meaning of my eye, as I could easily see, strongly tempted her to laugh.

"It is very well as it is, Mr. Newcome, though I feel much indebted to your liberal intentions," she said, turning to rejoin her friends; "it is customary in New York for ladies to pay, themselves, for every thing of this nature. When I go to Connecticut, I shall feel infinitely indebted to you for another such offer."

Jason did not know what to make of it! He long after insisted that the young lady was "huffed," as he called it, and that she had refused to take the money merely because she was thus offended.

"There is a manner, you know, Corny," he said, "of doing even a genteel thing, and that is to do it genteelly. I much doubt if a genteel thing *can* be done ungenteelly. One thing I'm thankful for, and that is, that she don't know that you ever were at the 'Seminarian Institute' in your life;" such being the appellation Jason had given to that which Mr. Worden had simply called a "boy's school." To return to the booth.

The lion had many visitors, and we had some difficulty in finding places. As a matter of course, Anneke was put in front, most of the men who were in the booth giving way to her with respectful attention. Unfortunately, the young lady wore an exceedingly pretty shawl, in which scarlet was a predominant color; and that which occurred has been attributed to this circumstance, though I am far from affirming such to have been literally the case. Anneke, from the first, manifested no fear; but the circle pressing on her from without, she got so near the cage that the beast thrust a paw through, and actually got hold of the shawl, drawing the alarmed girl quite up to the bars. I was at Anneke's side, and with a presence of mind that now surprises me, I succeeded in throwing the shawl from the precious creature's shoulders, and of fairly lifting her from the ground and setting her down again at a safe distance from the beast. All this passed so soon that half the persons present were unconscious of what had occurred until it was all over; and what astonishes me most is, that I do not retain the least recollection of the pleasure I ought to have felt while my arm encircled Anneke Mordaunt's slender waist, and while she was altogether supported by me. The keeper interfered immediately, and the lion relinquished the shawl, looking like a disappointed beast when he found it did not contain its beautiful owner.

Anneke was rescued before she had time fully to comprehend the danger she had been in. Even Dirck could not advance to her aid, though he saw and comprehended the imminent risk ran by the being he loved best in the world; but Dirck was always so slow! I must do Jason the credit to say that he behaved well, though so situated as to be of no real use. He rushed forward to assist Anneke, and remained to draw away the shawl, as soon as the keeper had succeeded in making the lion relinquish his hold. But all this passed so rapidly, as to give little opportunity for noting incidents.

Anneke was certainly well frightened by the adventure with the lion, as was apparent by her changing color, and a few tears that succeeded. Still, a glass of water, and a minute or two, seated in a chair, were sufficient to restore her self-composure, and she remained with us, for half an hour, examining and admiring her terrible assailant.

And, here, let me add, for the benefit of those who have never had an opportunity of seeing the king of beasts, that he is a sight well worthy to behold? I have never viewed an elephant, which travelled gentlemen tell me is a still more extraordinary animal, though I find it difficult to imagine any thing finer, in its way, than the lion which came so near injuring "sweet Anne Mordaunt." I question if any of us were aware of the full extent of the danger she ran, until we began to reflect on it coolly, after time and leisure were afforded. As soon as the commotion naturally produced at first, had subsided, the incident seemed forgotten, and we left the booth, after a long visit, expatiating on the animal and its character, apparently in forgetfulness of that which, by one blow of his powerful paw, the lion might have rendered fatal to one of the very sweetest and happiest innocents of the whole province, but for the timely and merciful interposition of a kind Providence.

After the little affair of the tickets, I walked on with Anneke, who declared her intention of quitting the field, her escape beginning to affect her spirits, and she was afraid that some particularly kind friend might carry an exaggerated account of what had happened to her father. Dirck offered to accompany her home, for Mr. Mordaunt kept no carriage; or, at least, nothing that was habitually used as a town equipage. We had all gone as far as the verge of the Common with Anneke, when the sweet girl stopped, looked at me earnestly, and, while her color changed, and tears rose to her eyes, she said:

"Mr. Littlepage, I am just getting to be fully conscious of what I owe to you. The thing passed so suddenly, and I was so much alarmed, that I did not know how to express myself at the time, nor am I certain that I do now. Believe me, notwithstanding, that I never can forget this morning, and I beg of you, if you have a sister, to carry to her the proffered friendship of Anneke Mordaunt, and tell her that her own prayers in behalf of her brother will not be more sincere than mine."

Before I could recollect myself, so as to make a suitable answer, Anneke had curtsied and walked away, with her handkerchief to her eyes.

CHAPTER VI

"Nay, be brief;
I see into thy end, and am almost
A man already."
CYMBELINE.

As Dirck accompanied Miss Mordaunt to her father's house in Crown street,* I took an occasion to give Jason the slip, being in no humor to listen to his lectures on the proprieties of life, and left the Pinkster field as fast as I could. Notwithstanding the size and importance of New York, a holiday like this could not fail to draw great crowds of persons to witness the sports. In 1757, James de Lancey was at the head of the government of the province, as indeed he had been, in effect, for much of his life; and I remember to have met his chariot, carrying the younger children of the family to the field, on my way into the town. As the day advanced, carriages of one sort and another made their appearance in Broadway, principally conveying the children of their different owners. All these belonged to people of the first mark; and I saw the ship that denotes the arms of Livingston, the lance of the De Lanceys, the burning castle of the Morrises, and other armorial bearings that were well known in the province. Carriages, certainly, were not as common in 1757 as they have since become; but most of our distinguished people rode in their coaches, chariots, or phaetons, or conveyances of some sort or other, when there was occasion to go so far out of town as the Common, which is the site of the present "Park." The roads on the island of Manhattan were very pretty and picturesque, winding among rocks and through valleys, being lined with groves and copses in a way to render all the drives rural and retired. Here and there, one came to a country-house, the residence of some person of importance, which, by its comfort and snugness, gave all the indications of wealth and of a prudent taste. Mr. Speaker Nicoll †

---

* Now Liberty street.

† The person meant here was William Nicoll, Esquire, Patentee of Islip, a large estate on Long Island, that is still in the family, under a patent granted in 1683. This gentleman was a son of Mr. Secretary Nicoll, who is supposed to have been a

had occupied a dwelling of this sort for a long series of years, that was about a league from town, and which is still standing, as I pass it constantly travelling between Satanstoe and York. I never saw the patentee myself, as he died long before my birth; but his house near town still stands, as I have said, a memorial of past ages!

The whole town seemed alive, and every body had a desire to get a glance at the sports of the Pinkster field; though the more dignified and cultivated had self-denial enough to keep aloof, since it would hardly have comported with their years and stations to be seen in such a place. The war had brought many regiments into the province, however, and I met at least twenty young officers, strolling out to the scene of amusement, as I walked into town. I will confess I gazed at these youths with admiration, and not entirely without envy, as they passed me in pairs, laughing and diverting themselves with the grotesque groups of blacks that were occasionally met, coming in from their sports. These young men I knew had enjoyed the advantages of being educated at home, some of them, quite likely, in the universities, and all of them amid the high civilization and taste of England. I say all of them, too hastily; as there were young men of the colonies among them, who probably had not enjoyed these advantages. The easy air, self-possession, and quiet, what shall I call it? — insolence would be too strong a word, and a term that I, the son and grandson of old king's officers, would not like to apply, and yet it comes nearest to

---

relative of Colonel Nicoll, the first English governor. Mr. Speaker Nicoll, as the son was called, in consequence of having filled that office for nearly a generation, was the direct ancestor of the Nicolls of Islip and Shelter Island, as well as of a branch long settled at Stratford, Connecticut. The house alluded to by Mr. Littlepage, as a relic of antiquity in *his* day — American antiquity, be it remembered — was standing a few years since, if it be not still standing, at the point of junction between the Old Boston Road and the New Road, and nearly opposite to the termination of the long avenue that led to Rosehill, originally a seat of the Wattses. The house stood a short distance above the present Union Square, and not far from that of the present Gramercy. It was, or is, a brick house of one story, with a small court-yard in front; the House of Refuge being at a little distance on its right. If still standing, it must now be one of the oldest buildings of any sort, in a town of 400,000 souls! As Mr. Speaker Nicoll resigned the chair in 1718, this house must be at least a hundred and thirty or forty years old; and it may be questioned if a dozen as old, public or private, can be found on the whole island.

As the regular family residence of the Nicolls was in Suffolk, or on their estates, it is probable that the abode mentioned was, in a measure, owing to an intermarriage with the Wattses, as much as to the necessity of the Speaker's passing so much time at the seat of government. — EDITOR.

what I mean as applicable to the covert manner of these young men — but, whatever it was, that peculiar air of metropolitan superiority over provincial ignorance and provincial dependence, which certainly distinguished all the younger men of this class, had an effect on me, I find it difficult to describe. I was a loyal subject, loved the king — most particularly since he was so identified with the Protestant succession — loved all of the blood-royal, and wished for nothing more than the honor and lustre of the English crown. One thus disposed could not but feel amicably toward the king's officers; yet, I will confess, there were moments when this air of ill-concealed superiority, this manner that so much resembled that of the master toward the servant, the superior to the dependent, the patron to the client, gave me deep offence, and feelings so bitter, that I was obliged to struggle hard to suppress them. But this is anticipating, and is interrupting the course of my narrative. I am inclined to think there must always be a good deal of this feeling, where the relation of principal and dependent exists, as between distinct territories.

I was a good deal excited, and a little fatigued with the walk and the incidents of the morning, and determined to proceed at once to Duke street, and share the cold dinner of my aunt; for few private families in York, that depended on regular cooks for their food, had any thing served warm on their tables, for that and the two succeeding days. Here and there a white substitute was found, it is true, and we had the benefit of such an assistant at half-past one. It was the English servant of a Colonel Mosely, an officer of the army, who was intimate at my uncle's, and who had had the civility to offer a man for this occasion. I afterward ascertained, that many officers manifested the same kind spirit toward various other families in which they visited on terms of friendship.

Marriages between young English officers and our pretty, delicate York belles, were of frequent occurrence, and I had felt a twinge or two, on the subject of Anneke, that morning, as I passed the youths of the 55th, 60th, or Loyal Americans, 17th, and other regiments that were then in the province.

My aunt was descending from the drawing-room, in dinner dress — for that no lady ever neglects, even though she dines on a cold dumpling. As I opened the street-door, Mrs. Legge was not coming down alone to take her seat at table, but, having some extra duty to perform in consequence of the absence of most of her household, she was engaged in that service. Seeing me, however, she stopped on the landing of the stairs, and beckoned me to approach.

"Corny," she said, "what have you been doing, my child, to have drawn this honor upon you?"

"Honor! I am ignorant of having even received any. What can you mean, my dear aunt?"

"Here is Herman Mordaunt waiting to see you, in the drawing-room. He asked particularly for *you;* — wishes to *see* you — expresses his regrets that you are not in, and talks only of *you!*"

"In which case, I ought to hasten up stairs in order to receive him, as soon as possible. I will tell you all about it at dinner, aunt; excuse me now."

Away I went with a beating heart, to receive a visit from Anneke's father. I can scarcely give a reason why this gentleman was usually called, when he was spoken of, and sometimes when he was spoken to, *Herman* Mordaunt; unless, indeed, it were, that being in part of Dutch extraction, the name which denoted the circumstance (Hermanus — pronounced by the Hollanders, Her*maa*nus) was used by a portion of the population in token of the fact, and adopted by others in pure compliance. But *Herman* Mordaunt was he usually styled; and this, too, in the way of respect, and not as coarse-minded persons affect to speak of their superiors, or in a way to boast of their own familiarity. I should have thought it an honor, at my time of life, to receive a visit from Herman Mordaunt; but my heart fairly beat, as I have said, as I went hastily up stairs, to meet Anneke's father.

My uncle was not in, and I found my visitor waiting for me, alone, in the drawing-room. Aware of the state of the family, and of all families, indeed, during Pinkster, he had insisted on my aunt's quitting him, while he looked over some new books that had recently been received from home; among which was a new and very handsome edition of the Spectator, a work that enjoys a just celebrity throughout the colonies.

Mr. Mordaunt advanced to receive me with studied politeness, yet a warmth that could not well be counterfeited, the instant I approached. Nevertheless, his manner was easy and natural; and to me he appeared to be the highest-bred man I had ever seen.

" I am thankful that the debt of gratitude I owe you, my
young friend," he said, at once, and without preface of any
sort, unless that of manner be so received, " is due to the son
of a gentleman I so much esteem as Evans Littlepage. A loyal
subject, an honest man, and a well-connected and well-descended
gentleman, like him, may well be the parent of a brave youth,
who does not hesitate to face even lions, in defence of the weaker
sex."

" I cannot affect to misunderstand you, sir," I answered;
" and I sincerely congratulate you that matters are no worse;
though you greatly overrrate the danger. I doubt if even a
lion would have the heart to hurt Miss Mordaunt, were she in
his power."

I think this was a very pretty speech, for a youth of twenty;
and I confess I look back upon it, even now, with complacency.
If I occasionally betray weakness of this character, I beg the
reader to recollect that I am acting in the part of an honest
historian, and that it is my aim to conceal nothing that ought
to be known.

Herman Mordaunt did not resume his seat, on account of
the lateness of the hour (half-past one); but he made me professions of friendship, and named Friday, the first moment
when he could command the services of his domestics, when
I should dine with him. The army had introduced later hours
than was usual; and this invitation was given for three o'clock;
it being said, at the time, as I well remember, that persons of
fashion in London sat down to table even later than this.
After remaining with me five minutes, Herman Mordaunt took
his leave. Of course, I accompanied him to the door, where
we parted with many bows.

At dinner, I told my uncle and aunt all that had occurred,
and was glad to hear them both speak favorably of my new
acquaintances.

" Herman Mordaunt might be a much more considerable man
than he is," observed my uncle, " were he disposed to enter into
public life. He has talents, a good education, a very handsome
estate, and is well-connected in the colony, certainly; some say
at home, also."

" And Anneke is a sweet young thing," added my aunt;
" and, since Corny was to assist any young lady, I am heartily
glad it was Anneke. She is an excellent creature, and her
mother was one of our most intimate friends, as she was of my

sister Littlepage, too. You must go and inquire after her health this evening, Corny. Such an attention is due, after what has passed all round."

Did I wish to comply with this advice? Out of all question; and yet I was too young, and too little at my ease, to undertake this ceremony, without many misgivings. Luckily, Dirck came in, in the evening; and my aunt repeating her opinion before my friend, he at once declared it was altogether proper, and that he thought Anneke would have a right to expect it. As he offered to be my companion, we were soon on our way to Crown street, in which Mr. Mordaunt owned and inhabited a very excellent house. We were admitted by Mr. Mordaunt himself, not one of his blacks having yet returned from the Pinkster field.

Dirck appeared to be on the best terms, not only with Herman Mordaunt, but with his charming daughter. I had observed that the latter always called him "*cousin* Dirck," and I hardly knew whether to interpret this as a sign of particular or of family regard. That Dirck was fonder of Anneke Mordaunt than of any other human being, I could easily see, and I confess that the discovery already began to cause uneasiness. I loved Dirck, and wished he loved any one else but the very being I feared he did.

Herman Mordaunt showed me the way, up the noble, wide, mahogany-garnished staircase of his dwelling, and ushered us into a very handsome, though not very large, but well-lighted drawing-room. There sat Anneke, his daughter, in the loveliness of her maiden charms, a little more dressed than usual, perhaps, for she had three or four young and lovely girls with her, and five or six young men; among whom were no less than three scarlet coats.

I shall not attempt to conceal my weakness. Only twenty, inexperienced and unaccustomed to town society, I felt awkward and unpleasantly the instant I entered the room; nor did the feeling subside during the first half-hour. Anneke came forward, one or two steps, to meet me; and I could see she was almost as much confused as I was myself. She blushed, as she thanked me for the service I had rendered, and expressed her satisfaction that her father had been fortunate enough to find me at home, and had had an opportunity of saying a little of what he felt, on the occasion. She then invited me to be seated, naming me to the company, and telling me who two or three of the young ladies

were. From these last I received sundry approving smiles; which
I took as so many thanks for serving their friend; while I could
not help seeing that I was an object of examination to most of the
men present. The three officers, in particular, looked at me the
most intently, and the longest.

"I trust, your little accident, which could have been of no
great moment, in itself, since you escaped so well, did not have
the effect to prevent you from enjoying the rare fun of this
Pinkster affair?" said one of the scarlet coats, as soon as the
movement caused by my reception had subsided.

"You call it a 'little accident,' Mr. Bulstrode," returned
Anneke, with a reproachful shake of her pretty head, "but, I
can assure you, it is not a trifle, to a young lady, to find herself
in the paws of a lion."

"*Serious* accident, then; since I see you are resolved to consider yourself a victim;" rejoined the other; "but, not serious
enough, I trust, to deprive you of the fun?"

"Pinkster fields, and Pinkster frolic, are no novelties to us,
sir, as they occur every season; and I am just old enough not
to have missed one of them all, for the last twelve years."

"We heard you had been out," put in another red-coat,
whom I had heard called Billings, "accompanied by a little army,
of what Bulstrode called the light infantry."

Here three or four of the other young ladies joined in the
discourse, at once, protesting against Mr. Bulstrode's placing
their younger sisters in the army, in so cavalier a manner; an
accusation that Mr. Bulstrode endeavored to parry, by declaring
his hopes of having them all, not only in the army, but in his
own regiment, one day or other. At this, there was a certain
amount of mirth, and various protestations of an unwillingness
to enlist; in which, I was glad to see, that neither Anneke, nor
her most intimate friend, Mary Wallace, saw fit to join. I liked
their reserve of manner, far better than the girlish trifling of
their companions; and I could see that all the men respected
them the more for it. There was a good deal of general and
disjointed conversation that succeeded; which I shall not pretend to follow or relate, but confine myself to such observations as had a bearing on matters that were connected with
myself.

As none of the young soldiers were addressed by their military
titles, such things never occurring in the better circles, as I
now discovered, and, least of all, in those connected with the

army, I was not able, at the time, to ascertain the rank of the
three red-coats; though I afterward ascertained, that the youngest
was an ensign, of the name of Harris; a mere boy, and the
younger son of a member of Parliament. The next oldest,
Billings, was a captain, and was said to be a natural son of a
nobleman; while Bulstrode was actually the oldest son of a
baronet, of three or four thousand a year, and had already
bought his way up as high as a majority, though only four-and-
twenty. This last was a handsome fellow, too; nor had I been
an hour in his company, before I saw, plainly enough, that he
was a strong admirer of Anneke Mordaunt. The other two
evidently admired themselves too much, to have any very lively
feelings on the subject of other persons. As for Dirck, younger
than myself, and diffident, as well as slow by nature, he kept
himself altogether in the background, conversing, most of the time,
with Herman Mordaunt, on the subject of farming.

We had been together an hour, and I had acquired sufficient
ease to change my seat, and to look at a picture or two, which
adorned the walls, and which were said to be originals from
the old world; for, to own the truth, the art of painting has
not made much progress in the colonies. We *have* painters, it
is true, and one or two are said to be men of rare merit, the
ladies being very fond of sitting to them for their portraits; but
these are exceptions. At a future day, when critics shall have
immortalized the names of a Smybert, and a Watson, and a
Blackburn, the people of these provinces will become aware of
the talents they once possessed among them; and the grand-
children of those who neglected these men of genius, in their
day — ay, their descendants to the latest generations — will
revenge the wrongs of merit and talent, to the end of civilized
time. It is a failing of colonies to be diffident of their own
opinions; but I have heard gentlemen who were educated at
home, and who possessed cultivated and refined tastes, affirm
that the painters of Europe, when visiting this hemisphere, have
retained all their excellence; and have painted as freely and
as well, under an American, as under a European sun. As for
a sister art, the Thespian muse had actually made her appearance among us, five years before the time of my visit to town
in 1757, or in 1752; a theatre having actually been built and
opened in Nassau street in 1753, with a company under the
care of the celebrated Hallam, and his family. This theatre I
had been dying to visit, while it stood, for as yet I had never

witnessed a theatrical performance; but my mother's injunctions prevented me from entering it while at college. "When you are old enough, Corny," she used to say, "you shall have my permission to go as often as is proper; but you are now of an age when Shakspeare and Rowe might unsettle your Latin and Greek." My task of obedience had not been very difficult, inasmuch as the building in Nassau street, the second regular theatre ever erected in British America, was taken down, and a church erected in its place.* The comedians went to the islands, and had not reappeared on the continent down to the period of which I am now writing; nor did their return occur until the following year. That they were expected, however, and that a new house had been built for them, in another part of the town, I was aware, though month after month passed away, and the much-expected company did not appear. I had understood, however, that the large military force collecting in the colony, would be likely to bring them back soon; and the conversation soon took a turn, that proved how much interest the young, the gay, and the fair, felt in the result. I was still looking at a picture, when Mr. Bulstrode approached me, and entered into conversation. It will be remembered, that this gentleman was four years my senior; that he had been at one of the universities; was the heir to a baronetcy; knew the world; had risen to a majority in the army, and was by nature, as well as training, agreeable, when he had a mind to be, and genteel. These circumstances, I could not but feel, gave him a vast advantage over me; and I heartily wished that we stood anywhere but in the presence of Anneke Mordaunt, as he thus saw fit to single me out for invidious comparison, by a sort of *tête-à-tête*, or aside. Still, I could not complain of his manner, which was both polite and respectful; though I could scarce divest myself of the idea, that he was covertly amusing himself, the whole time.

"You are a fortunate man, Mr. Littlepage," he commenced, "in having had it in your power to do so important a service to Miss Mordaunt. We all envy you your luck, while we admire your spirit, and I feel certain the men of our regiment will take some proper notice of it. Miss Anneke is in possession of half our hearts, and we should be still more heartless to overlook such a service."

---

* The church is now (1845) being converted into a post-office.

I muttered some half-intelligible answer to this compliment, and my new acquaintance proceeded.

"I am almost surprised, Mr. Littlepage," he added, "that a man of your spirit does not come among us in times as stirring as these. They tell me both your father and grandfather served, and that you are quite at your ease. You will find a great many men of merit and fashion among us, and I make no doubt they would contribute to make your time pass agreeably enough. Large reinforcements are expected, and if you are inclined for a pair of colors, I think I know a battalion in which there are a vacancy or two, and which will certainly serve in the colonies. It would afford me great pleasure to help to further your views, should you be disposed to turn them toward the army."

Now all this was said with an air of great apparent frankness and sincerity, which I fancied was only the more visible from the circumstance that Anneke was so seated as unavoidably to hear every word of what was said. I observed that she even turned her eyes on me as I made my answer, though I did not dare so far to observe her in turn as to note their expression.

"I am very sensible, Mr. Bulstrode, of the liberality and kindness of your intentions," I answered steadily enough, for pride came to my assistance, "though I fear it will not be in my power to profit by it at once, if ever. My grandfather is still living, and he has much influence over me and my fortune, and I know it is his wish that I should remain at Satanstoe."

"Where?" demanded Bulstrode, with more quickness and curiosity than strictly comported with good-breeding perhaps.

"Satanstoe; I do not wonder you smile, for it has an odd sound, but it is the name my grandfather has given the family place in Westchester. Given, I have said, though translated would be better, as I understand the present appellation is pretty literally rendered into English from the Dutch."

"I like the name exceedingly, Mr. Littlepage, and I feel certain I should like your good, old, honest, Anglo-Saxon grandfather. But, pardon me, is it his wish you should remain at Satansfoot?"

"Satanstoe, sir; we do not aspire to the whole foot. It is my grandfather's wish that I remain at home until of age, which will not be now for some months."

"By way of keeping you out of Satan's footsteps, I suppose. Well, these old gentlemen are often right. Should you alter your views, however, my dear Littlepage, do not forget me,

but remember you can count on one who has some little influence, and who will ever be ready to exert it in the behalf of
one who has proved so serviceable to Miss Mordaunt. Sir
Harry is a martyr to the gout, and talks of letting me stand in
his place at the dissolution. In that case my wishes will naturally
carry more weight. I like that name of Satanstoe amazingly! "

"I am infinitely obliged to you, Mr. Bulstrode, though I
will confess I have never looked forward to rising in the world
by taxing my friends. One may own that he has had some
hopes founded on merit and honesty — "

"Poh! poh! — my dear Littlepage, honesty is a very pretty
thing to talk about, but I suppose you remember what Juvenal
says on that interesting subject — '*Probitas laudatur et alget.*'
I dare say you are fresh enough from college to remember that
comprehensive sentiment."

"I have never read Juvenal, Mr. Bulstrode, and never wish
to, if such be the tendency of what he teaches — "

"Juvenal was a satirist, you know," interrupted Bulstrode a
little hastily, for by this time he too had ascertained that Anneke
was listening, and he betrayed some eagerness to get rid of so
flagitious a sentiment; "and satirists speak of things as they
are, rather than as they ought to be. I dare say Rome deserved
all she got, for the moralists give a very sad account of her
condition. Of all the large capitals of which we have any
account, London is the only town of even tolerable manners."

What young Bulstrode would have ventured to say next, it
is out of my power to guess; for a certain Miss Warren, who
was of the company, and who particularly affected the youth,
luckily called out at this critical instant —

"Your attention one moment, if you please, Mr. Bulstrode;
is it true that the gentlemen of the army have been getting the
new theatre in preparation, and that they intend to favor us
with some representations? A secret something like this has
just leaked out, from Mr. Harris, who even goes so far as to add
that you can tell us all about it."

"Mr. Harris must be put under an arrest for this, though I
hear the colonel let the cat out of the bag, at the lieutenant-
governor's table, as early as last week."

"I can assure you, Mr. Bulstrode," Anneke observed calmly,
"that I have heard rumors to this effect for quite a fortnight.
You must not blame Mr. Harris solely, for your whole regiment
has been hinting to the same purpose far and near."

"Then the delinquent will escape, this time. I confess the charge; we have hired the new theatre, and do intend to solicit the honor of the ladies coming to hear me murder Cato, and Scrub; a pretty climax of characters, you will admit, Miss Mordaunt?"

"I know nothing of Scrub, though I have read Mr. Addison's play, and think you have no need of being ashamed of the character of Cato. When is the theatre to open?"

"We follow the sable gentry. As soon as St. Pinkster has received his proper share of attention, we shall introduce Dom-Cato and Mr. Scrub to your acquaintance."

All the young ladies, but Anneke and her friend Mary Wallace, laughed, two or three repeating the words "St. Pinkster," as if they contained something much cleverer than it was usual to hear. A general burst of exclamations, expressions of pleasure, and of questions and answers followed, in which two or three voices were heard at the same moment, during which time Anneke turned to me, who was standing near her, at the spot occupied by Bulstrode a minute before, and seemed anxious to say something.

"Do you seriously think of the army, Mr. Littlepage?" she asked, changing color at the freedom of her own question.

"In a war like this, no one can say when he may be called on to go out," I answered. "But only as a defender of the soil, if at all."

I thought Anneke Mordaunt seemed pleased with this answer. After a short pause, she resumed the dialogue.

"Of course you understand Latin, Mr. Littlepage, although you have not been at the universities?"

"As it is taught in our own colleges, Miss Mordaunt."

"And that is sufficient to tell me what Mr. Bulstrode's quotation means — if it be proper for me to hear."

"He would hardly presume to use even a Latin saying in your presence, that is unfit for your ear. The maxim which Mr. Bulstrode attributes to Juvenal, simply means 'that honesty is praised and starves.'"

I thought that something like displeasure settled on the fair, polished brow of Miss Mordaunt, who, I could soon see, possessed much character and high principles for one of her tender years. She said nothing, however, though she exchanged a very meaning glance with her friend Mary Wallace. Her lips were moved, and I fancied I could trace the formation of the sounds "honesty is praised and starves!"

"And *you* are to be Cato, I hear, Mr. Bulstrode," cried one of the young ladies, who thought more of a scarlet coat, I fancy, than was for her own good. "How very charming! Will you play the character in regimentals or in mohair — in a modern or in an ancient dress?"

"In my *robe de chambre*, a little altered for the occasion, unless St. Pinkster and his sports should suggest some more appropriate costume," answered the young man, lightly.

"Are you quite aware what feast Pinkster is?" asked Anneke, a little gravely.

Bulstrode actually changed color, for it had never crossed his mind to inquire into the character of the holiday, and, to own the truth, the manner in which it is kept by the negroes of New York, never would enlighten him much on the subject.

"That is information for which I perceive I am now about to be indebted to Miss Mordaunt."

"Then you shall not be disappointed, Mr. Bulstrode; Pinkster is neither more or less than the festival of Whitsunday, or the feast of Pentecost. I suppose we shall now hear no more of your saint."

Bulstrode took this little punishment, which was very sweetly but quite steadily uttered, with perfect good-humor, and with a manner so rebuked as to prove that Anneke possessed great control over him. He bowed in submission, and she smiled so kindly, that I wished the occasion for the little pantomime had not occurred.

"*Our* ancestors, Miss Mordaunt, never heard of any Pinkster, you will remember, and that must explain my ignorance," he said meekly.

"But some of *mine* have long understood it, and observed the festival," answered Anneke.

"Ay, on the side of Holland — but when I presume to speak of *our* ancestors, I mean those which I can claim the honor of boasting as belonging to me in common with yourself."

"Are you and Mr. Bulstrode then related?" I asked, as it might be involuntarily and almost too abruptly.

Anneke replied, however, in a way to show that she thought the question natural for the circumstances, and not in the least out of place.

" My grandfather's mother, and Mr. Bulstrode's grandfather, were brother and sister," was the quiet answer. " This makes us a sort of cousins, according to those Dutch notions which he so much despises, though I fancy it would not count for much at home."

Bulstrode protested to the contrary, stating that he knew his father valued his relationship to Mr. Mordaunt, by the earnest manner in which he had commanded him to cultivate the acquaintance of the family the instant he reached New York. I saw by this, the footing on which the formidable major was placed in the family, every body seeming to be related to Anneke Mordaunt but myself. I took an occasion that very evening, to question the dear girl on the subject of her Dutch connections, giving her a clue to mine; but with all our industry, and some assistance from Herman Mordaunt, who took an interest in such a subject, as it might be *ex officio*, we could make out no affinity worth mentioning.

CHAPTER VII

" Sir Valentine, I care not for her, I."

" I hold him but a fool, that will endanger
His body for a girl that loves him not."

" I claim her not, and therefore she is thine."

Two Gentlemen of Verona.

I saw Anne Mordaunt several times, either in the street or in
her own house, between that evening and the day I was to dine
with her father. The morning of the last-named day Mr. Bulstrode favored me with a call, and announced that he was to be
of the party in Crown street, and that the whole company were
to repair to the theatre, to see his own Cato and Scrub, in the
evening.

" By giving yourself the trouble to call at the Crown and Bible,
kept hard by here, in Hanover Square, or Queen street, by honest
Hugh Gaine, you will find a package of tickets for yourself, Mr.
and Mrs. Legge, and your relative Mr. Dirck Follock, as I believe
the gentleman is called. These Dutch have extraordinary pat-
ronymics, you must admit, Littlepage."

" It may appear so to an Englishman, though our names are
quite as odd to strangers. But Dirck Van Valkenburgh is not
a kinsman of mine, though he is related to the Mordaunts, *your*
relatives."

" Well, it's all the same! I knew he was related to somebody
that I knew, and I fancied it was to yourself. I am sure I never
see him but I wish he was in our grenadier company."

" Dirck would do honor to any corps, but you know how it
is with the Dutch families, Mr. Bulstrode. They still retain
much of their attachment for Holland, and do not as often take
service in the army, or navy, as we of English descent."

" I should have thought a century might have cooled them
off, a little, from their veneration of the meadows of Holland.
It is the opinion at home, that New York is a particularly well-
affected colony."

" So it is, as I hear from all sides. As respects the Dutch, among ourselves, I have heard my grandfather say that the reign of King William had a powerful influence in reconciling them to the new government, but since his day that they are less loyal than formerly. The Van Valkenburghs, notwithstanding, pass for as good subjects as any that the house of Hanover possesses. On no account would I injure them in your opinion."

"Good or bad, we shall hope to see your friend, who is a connection in some way, as you believe, of the Mordaunts. You will get but a faint idea of what one of the royal theatres is, Littlepage, by this representation of ours, though it may serve to kill time. But I must go to rehearsal; we shall meet at three."

Here my gay and gallant major made his bow, and took his leave. I proceeded on to the sign of the Crown and the Bible, where I found a large collection of people, coming in quest of tickets. As the *élite* of the town would not of themselves form an audience sufficiently large to meet the towering ambition of the players, more than half the tickets were sold, the money being appropriated to the sick families of soldiers — those who were not entitled to receive aid from government. It was deemed a high compliment to receive tickets gratis, though all who did, made it a point to leave a donation to the fund, with Mr. Gaine. Receiving my package, I quitted the shop, and it being the hour for the morning promenade, I went up Wall street, to the Mall, as Trinity Church walk was even then called. Here I expected to meet Dirck, and hoped to see Anneke, for the place was much frequented by the young and gay, both in the mornings and in the evenings. The bands of different regiments were stationed in the churchyard, and the company were often treated to much fine martial music. Some few of the more scrupulous objected to this desecration of the churchyard, but the army had every thing pretty much in its own way. As they were supposed to do nothing but what was approved of at home, the dissenters were little heeded, nor do I think the army would have greatly cared, had they been more numerous.

I dare say there were fifty young ladies promenading the church-walk when I reached it, and nearly as many young men in attendance on them; no small portion of the last being scarlet-coats, though the mohairs had their representatives there too. A few blue-jackets were among us also, there being two or three king's cruisers in port. As no one presumed to promenade the Mall, who was not of a certain stamp of respectability, the company were all gayly dressed; and I will confess that I was much struck with the air of the place, the first time I showed myself among the gay idlers. The impression made on me that morning was so vivid, that I will endeavor to describe the scene, as it now presents itself to my mind.

In the first place, there was the noble street, quite eighty feet in width in its narrowest part, and gradually expanding as you looked toward the bay, until it opened into an area of more than twice that width, at the place called the Bowling-Green.* Then came the fort, crowning a sharp eminence, and overlooking every thing in that quarter of the town. In the rear of the fort, or in its front, taking a water view, lay the batteries that had been built on the rocks which form the south-western termination of the island. Over these rocks, which were black and picturesque, and over the batteries they supported, was obtained a view of the noble bay, dotted here and there with some speck of a sail, or possibly with some vessel anchored on its placid bosom. Of the two rows of elegant houses, most of them brick, and, with very few exceptions, principally of two stories in height, it is scarcely necessary to speak, as there are few who have not heard of, and formed some notion of Broadway; a street that all agree is one day to be the pride of the western world.

In the other direction, I will admit that the view was not so remarkable, the houses being principally of wood, and of a somewhat ignoble appearance. Nevertheless the army were said to frequent those habitations quite as much as they did any other in the place. After reaching the Common, or present Park, where the great Boston road led off into the country, the view was just the reverse of that which was seen in the opposite quarter. Here, all was inland, and rural. It is true, the new Bridewell had been erected in that quarter, and there was also a new gaol, both facing the Common; and the king's troops had barracks in their rear; but high, abrupt, conical hills, with low marshy land, orchards and meadows, gave to all that portion of the island a peculiarly novel and somewhat picturesque character. Many of the hills in that quarter, and indeed all over the widest part of the island, are now surmounted by country-houses, as

* Mr. Cornelius Littlepage betrays not a little of provincial admiration, as the reader will see. I have not thought it necessary to prune these passages, their causes being too familiar to leave any danger of their insertion's being misunderstood. Admiration of Broadway, certainly not more than a third-class street, as streets go in the old world, is so very common among us as to need no apology. — EDITOR.

some were then, including Petersfield, the ancient abode of the
Stuyvesants, or that farm which, by being called after the old
Dutch governor's retreat, has given the name of Bowery, or
Bouerie, to the road that led to it; as well as the Bowery House,
as it was called, the country abode of the then lieutenant-governor, James De Lancey, Mount Bayard, a place belonging to
that respectable family; Mount Pitt, another that was the
property of Mrs. Jones, the wife of Mr. Justice Jones, a daughter
of James De Lancey, and various other mounts, houses, hills, and
places, that are familiar to the gentry and people of New
York.

But the reader can imagine for himself the effect produced
by such a street as Broadway, reaching very nearly half a mile
in length, terminating at one end, in an elevated, commanding
fort, with its background of batteries, rocks and bay, and, at
the other, with the Common, on which troops were now constantly parading, the Bridewell and gaol, and the novel scene I
have just mentioned. Nor is Trinity itself to be forgotten. This
edifice, one of the noblest, if not the most noble of its kind, in
all the colonies, with its Gothic architecture, statues in carved
stone, and flanking walls, was a close accessory of the view, giving to the whole grandeur, and a moral.*

As has been said, I found the Mall crowded with young persons of fashion and respectability. This Mall was near a hundred yards in length; and it follows that there must have been
a goodly show of youth and beauty. The fine weather had
commenced; spring had fairly opened; Pinkster blossoms
(the wild honeysuckle) had been seen in abundance throughout the week; and every thing and person appeared gay and
happy.

I could discover that my person in this crowd attracted attention as a stranger. I say as a stranger; for I am unwilling to
betray so much vanity as to ascribe the manner in which many
eyes followed me, to any vain notion that I was known or admired. Still, I will not so far disparage the gifts of a bountiful
Providence, as to leave the impression that my face, person, or
air was particularly disagreeable. This would not be the fact;

* The provincial admiration of Mr. Cornelius Littlepage was not quite as much in
fault, as respects the church, as the superciliousness of our more modern tastes and
opinions may lead us to suspect. The church that was burned in 1776, was a
larger edifice than that just pulled down, and, in many respects, was its superior. — EDITOR.

and I have now reached a time of life when something like the truth may be told, without the imputation of conceit. My mother often boasted to her intimates, " that Corny was one of the best-made, handsomest, most active, and genteelest youths in the colony." This I know, for such things will leak out; but mothers are known to have a remarkable weakness on the subject of their children. As I was the sole surviving offspring of my dear mother, who was one of the best-hearted women that ever breathed, it is highly probable that the notions she entertained of her son partook largely of the love she bore me. It is true, my aunt Legge, on more than one occasion, has been heard to express a very similar opinion; though nothing can be more natural than that sisters should think alike, on a family matter of this particular nature, more especially as my aunt Legge never had a child of her own to love and praise.

Let all this be as it may, well stared at was I, as I mingled among the idlers on Trinity Church walk, on the occasion named. As for myself, my own eyes were bent anxiously on the face of every pretty, delicate young creature that passed, in the hope of seeing Anneke. I both wished and dreaded to meet her; for, to own the truth, my mind was dwelling on her beauty, her conversation, her sentiments, her grace, her gentleness, and withal her spirit, a good deal more than half the time. I had some qualms on the subject of Dirck, I will confess; but Dirck was so young, that his feelings could not be much interested, after all; and then Anneke was a second cousin, and that was clearly too near to marry. My grandfather had always put his foot down firmly against any connection between relations that were nearer than *third* cousins; and I now saw how proper were his reasons. If they were even farther removed, so much the better, he said; and so much the better it was.

If the reader should ask me why I *dreaded* to meet Anne Mordaunt, under such circumstances, I might be at a loss to give him a very intelligible answer. I feared even to see the sweet face I sought; and oh! how soft, serene, and angel-like it was, at that budding age of seventeen! — but, though I almost feared to see it, when at last I saw her I had so anxiously sought approaching me, arm and arm with Mary Wallace, having Bulstrode next herself, and Harris next her friend, my eyes were instantly averted, as if they had unexpectedly lighted on something disagreeable. I should have passed without even the compliment of a bow, had not my friends been more at their ease, and more accustomed to the free ways of town life than I happened to be myself.

"How's this, Cornelius, *Cœur de Lion!*" exclaimed Bulstrode, stopping, thus causing the whole party to stop with him, or to appear to wish to avoid me; "will you not recognize us, though it is not an hour since you and I parted? I hope you found the tickets; and when you have answered 'yes,' I hope you will turn and do me the honor to bow to these ladies."

I apologized, I am afraid I blushed; for I detected Anneke looking at me, as I thought, with some little concern, as if she pitied my awkward country embarrassment. As for Bulstrode, I did not understand him at that time; it exceeding my observation to be certain whether he considered me of sufficient importance or not, to feel any concern on my account, in his very obvious suit with Anneke. Nevertheless, as he treated me with cordiality and respect, while he dealt with me so frankly, there was not room to take offence. Of course, I turned and walked back with the party, after I had properly saluted the ladies and Mr. Harris.

"*Cœur de Lion* is a better name for a soldier than for a civilian;" said Anneke, as we moved forward; "and, however much Mr. Littlepage may *deserve* the title, I am not certain, Mr. Bulstrode, he would not prefer leaving it among you gentlemen who serve the king."

"I am glad of this occasion, Mr. Littlepage, to enlist you on my side, in a warfare I am compelled to wage with Miss Anne Mordaunt," said the major gaily. "It is on the subject of the great merit of us poor fellows who have crossed the wide Atlantic in order to protect the colonies, New York among the number, and their people, Miss Mordaunt and Miss Wallace inclusively, from the grasp of their wicked enemies, the French. The former young lady has a way of reasoning on the matter to which I cannot assent, and I am willing to choose you as arbitrator between us."

"Before Mr. Littlepage accept the office, it is proper he should know its duties and responsibilities," said Anneke, smiling. "In the first place, he will find Mr. Bulstrode, with loud professions of attachment to the colonies, much disposed to think them provinces that owe their very existence to England; while I maintain it is English*men*, and that it is not England, that have done so much in America. As for New York, Mr. Littlepage, and especially as for you and me, we can also say a word in favor of Holland. I am very proud of my Dutch connections and Dutch descent."

I was much gratified with the "as for you and me;" though I believe I cared less for Holland than she did herself. I made an answer much in the vein of the moment; but the conversation soon changed to the subject of the military theatre that was about to open.

"I shall dread you as a critic, cousin Annie," so Bulstrode often termed Anneke, as I soon discovered; "I find you are not too well disposed to us of the cockade, and I think you have a particular spite to our regiment. I know that Billings and Harris, too, hold you in the greatest possible dread."

"They then feel apprehensive of a very ignorant critic; for I never was present at a theatrical entertainment in my life," Anneke answered with perfect simplicity. "So far as I can learn, there never has been but one season of any regular company, in this colony; and that was when I was a very little and a very young girl — as I am now neither very large, nor very old as a young woman."

"You see, Littlepage, with how much address my cousin avoids adding, and 'very uninteresting, and very ugly, and very disagreeable, and very much unsought,' and fifty other things she *might* add with such perfect truth and modesty! But is it true, that the theatre was open only one season, here?"

"So my father tells me, though I know very little of the facts themselves. To-night will be my first appearance in *front* of any stage, Mr. Bulstrode, as I understand it will be your first appearance on it."

"In one sense the last will be true, though not altogether in another. As a school-boy, I have often played, school-boy fashion; but this is quite a new thing with us, to be *amateur* players."

"It may seem ungrateful, when you are making so many efforts, principally to amuse us young ladies, I feel convinced, to inquire if it be quite as wise as it is novel. I must ask this, as a cousin, you know, Henry Bulstrode, to escape entirely from the imputation of impertinence."

"Really, Anneke Mordaunt, I am not absolutely certain that it is. Our manners are beginning to change in this respect, however, and I can assure you that various noblemen have permitted sports of this sort at their seats. The custom is French, as you probably know, and whatever is French has much vogue with us during times of peace. Sir Harry does not altogether approve of it, and as for my lady mother, she has actually dropped more than one discouraging hint on the subject in her letters."

"The certain proof that you are a most dutiful son. Perhaps when Sir Harry and Lady Bulstrode learn your great success, however, they will overlook the field on which your laurels have been won. But our hour has come, Mary; we have barely time to thank these gentlemen for their politeness, and to return in season to dress. I am to enact a part myself, at dinner, as I hope you will all remember."

Saying this, Anneke made her courtesies in a way to preclude any offer of seeing her home, and went her way with her silent but sensible-looking and pretty friend. Bulstrode took my arm with an air of easy superiority, and led the way toward his own lodgings, which happened to be in Duke street. Harris joined another party, making it a point to be always late at dinner.

"That is not only one of the handsomest, but she is one of the most charming girls in the colonies, Littlepage!" my companion exclaimed, as soon as we had departed, speaking at the same time with an earnestness and feeling I was far from expecting. "Were she in England, she would make one of the first women in it, by the aid of a little fashion and training; and very little would do too, for there is a charm in her *naïveté* that is worth the art of fifty women of fashion."

"Fashion is a thing that any one may want who does not happen to be in vogue," I answered, notwithstanding the great degree of surprise I felt. "As for training, I can see nothing but perfection in Miss Mordaunt as she is, and should deprecate the lessons that produced any change."

I believe it was now Bulstrode's turn to feel surprise, for I was conscious of his casting a keen look into my face, though I did not like to return it. My companion was silent for a minute; then, without again adverting to Anneke, he began to converse very sensibly on the subject of theatres and plays. I was both amused and instructed, for Mr. Bulstrode was an educated and a clever man; and a strange feeling came over the spirit of my dream, even then, as I listened to his conversation. This man, I thought, admires Anne Mordaunt, and he will probably carry her with him to England, and obtain for her that fashion and training of which he has just spoken. With his advantages of birth, air, fortune, education, and military rank, he can scarcely fail in his suit, should he seriously attempt one;

and it will be no more than prudent to command my own feelings, lest I become the hopeless victim of a serious passion. Young as I was, all this I saw, and thus I reasoned; and when I parted from my companion I fancied myself a much wiser man than when we had met. We separated in Duke street, with a promise on my part to call at the major's lodgings half an hour later, after dressing, and walk with him to Herman Mordaunt's door.

"It is fortunate that it is the fashion of New York to walk to a dinner party," said Bulstrode, as he again took my arm on our way to Crown street; "for these narrow streets must be excessively inconvenient for chariots, though I occasionally see one of them. As for sedan chairs, I detest them as things unfit for a man to ride in."

"Many of our leading families keep carriages, and *they* seem to get along well enough," I answered. "Nevertheless, it is quite in fashion even for ladies to walk. I understand that many, perhaps most of your auditors, will walk to the playhouse door this evening."

"They tell me as much," said Bulstrode, curling his lip a little, in a way I did not exactly like. "Notwithstanding, there will be many charming creatures among them, and they shall be welcome. Well, Littlepage, I do not despair of having you among us; for, to be candid, without wishing to boast, I think you will find the ——th as liberal a set of young men as there is in the service. There is a wish to have the mohairs among us, instead of shutting ourselves up altogether in scarlet. Then your father and grandfather have both served, and that will be a famous introduction."

I protested my unfitness for such an amusement, never having seen such an exhibition in my life; but to this my companion would not listen; and we picked our way, as well as we could, through William street, up Wall, and then by Nassau into Crown; Herman Mordaunt owning a new house, that stood not far from Broadway, in the latter street. This was rather in a remote part of the town; but the situation had the advantage of good air; and, as a place extends, it is necessary some persons should live on its skirts.

"I wish my good cousin did not live so much in the suburbs," said Bulstrode, as he knocked in a very patrician manner; "it is not altogether convenient to go quite so much out of one's ordinary haunts, in order to pay visits. I wonder Mr. Mordaunt came so far out of the world to build."

"Yet the distances of London must be much greater, though *there* you have coaches."

"True; but not a word more on *this* subject; I would not have Anneke fancy I ever find it far to visit *her.*"

We were the last but one; the tardy Mr. Harris making it a point always to be the last. We found Anneke Mordaunt supported by two or three ladies of her connection, and a party of quite a dozen assembled. As most of those present saw each other every day, and frequently two or three times a day, the salutations and compliments were soon over, and Herman Mordaunt began to look about him, to see who was wanting.

"I believe every body is here but Mr. Harris," the father observed to his daughter, interrupting some of Mr. Bulstrode's conversation, to let this fact be known. "Shall we wait for him, my dear; he is usually so uncertain and late?"

"Yet a very important man," put in Bulstrode, "as being entitled to lead the lady of the house to the table, in virtue of his birthright. So much for being the fourth son of an Irish baron! Do you know Harris's father has just been ennobled?"

This was news to the company; and it evidently much increased the doubts of the propriety of sitting down without the young man in question.

"Failing of this son of a new Irish baron, I suppose you fancy I shall be obliged to give my hand to the eldest son of an English baronet," said Anneke, smiling, so as to take off the edge of a little irony that I fancy just glimmered in her manner.

"I wish to heaven you *would*, Anne Mordaunt," whispered Bulstrode, loud enough for me to hear him, "so that the heart were its companion!"

I thought this both bold and decided; and I looked anxiously at Anneke, to note the effect; but she evidently received it as trifling, certainly betraying no emotion at a speech I thought so pointed. I wished she had manifested a little resentment. Then she was so very young to be thus importuned.

"Dinner had better be served, sir," she calmly observed to her father. "Mr. Harris is apt to think himself ill-treated if he do not find every body at table. It would be a sign his watch was wrong, and that he came half an hour too soon."

Herman Mordaunt nodded assent, and left his daughter's side to give the necessary order.

"I fancy Harris will regret this," said Bulstrode. "I wish I dared repeat what he had the temerity to say to me on this very subject, no later than yesterday."

"Of the propriety of so doing Mr. Bulstrode must judge for himself; though *repetitions* of this nature are usually best avoided."

"No, the fellow deserves it; so I will just tell you and Mr. Littlepage in confidence. You must know that as his senior in years, and his senior officer in the bargain, I was hinting to Harris the inexpediency of always being so late to dinner; and here is my gentleman's answer: — 'You know,' said he, 'that excepting my lord Loudon, the commander-in-chief, the governor, and a few public officers, I shall now take precedence of almost every man here; and I find, if I go early to dinner, I shall have to hand in all the elderly ladies, and to take my place at *their* sides; whereas, if I go a little late, I can steal in alongside of their daughters.' Now, on the present occasion, he will be altogether a loser, the lady of the house not yet being quite fifty."

"I had not given Mr. Harris credit for so much ingenuity," said Anneke, quietly. "But here he is, to claim his rights."

"Ay, the fellow has remembered *your* age, and quite likely your *attractions!*"

Dinner was announced at that instant, and all eyes were turned on Harris, in expectation that he would advance to lead Anneke down stairs. The young man, even more youthful than myself, had a good deal of *mauvaise honte;* for though the son of an Irish peer, of two months' creation, the family was not strictly Irish, and he had very little ambition to figure in this manner. From what I saw of him subsequently, I do believe that nothing but a sense of duty to his order made him respect these privileges of rank at all, and that he would really just as soon go to the dinner-table last, as first. In the present case, however, he was soon relieved by Herman Mordaunt, who had been educated at home, and understood the usages of the world very well.

"Gentlemen," he said, "I must ask you to waive the privileges of rank in favor of Mr. Cornelius Littlepage, to-day. This good company has met to do honor especially to his courage and devotion to his fellow-creatures, and he will do me the favor to hand Miss Mordaunt down stairs."

Herman Mordaunt then pointed out to the Hon. Mr. Harris the next lady of importance, and to Mr. Bulstrode a third; after which all the rest took care of themselves. As for myself, I felt my face in a glow, at this unexpected order, and scarcely dared

to look at Anneke as we led the way to the dining-room door.
So much abashed was I, that I scarce touched the tips of her
slender little fingers, and a tremor was in the limb that performed
this office, the whole time it was thus employed. Of course, my
seat was next to that of the young and lovely mistress of the
house, at this banquet.

What shall I say of the dinner? It was the very first entertainment of the sort at which I had ever been present; though I
had acquired some of the notions of town habits, on such occasions, at my aunt Legge's table. To my surprise, there was
soup; a dish that I never saw at Satanstoe, except in the most
familiar way; while here it was taken by every one, seemingly
as a matter of course. Every thing was elegant, and admirably
cooked. Abundance, however, was the great feature of the feast;
as I have heard it said, is apt to be the case with most New
York entertainments. Nevertheless, I have always understood
that, in the way of eating and drinking, the American colonies
have little reason to be ashamed.

"Could I have foreseen this dinner, Miss Mordaunt," I said,
when every body was employed, and I thought there was an opening to say something to my beautiful neighbor, "it would have
made my father very happy to have sent a sheepshead to town,
for the occasion."

Anneke thanked me, and then we began to converse about
the game. Westchester was, and is still, famous for partridges,
snipes, quails, ducks, and meadow-larks; and I understood expatiating on such a subject, as well as the best of them. All
the Littlepages were shots; and I have known my father bag ten
brace of woodcock, among the wet thickets of Satanstoe, of a
morning; and this with merely a second-class dog, and only one.
Both Bulstrode and Harris listened to what I said on this subject
with great attention, and it soon would have been the engrossing
discourse, had not Anneke pleasantly said —

"All very well, gentlemen; but you will remember that neither
Miss Wallace nor I shoot."

"Except with the arrows of Cupid," answered Bulstrode, gayly;
"with these you do so much execution *between you*," emphasiz-
ing the words, so as to make me look foolish, for I sat between
them, "that you ought to be condemned to hear nothing but
fowling conversation for the next year."

This proved a laugh, a little at my expense, I believe; though
I could see that Anneke blushed, while Mary Wallace smiled in-

differently; but as the healths now began, there was a truce to
trifling. And a serious thing it is, to drink to every body by
name, at a large table; serious I mean to a new beginner. Yet,
Herman Mordaunt went through it with a grace and dignity,
that I think would have been remarked at a royal banquet. The
ladies acquitted themselves admirably, omitting no one; and
even Harris felt the necessity of being particular with this indispensable part of good-breeding. So well done was this part
of the ceremony, that I declare, I believe every body had drunk
to every body, within five minutes after Herman Mordaunt commenced; and it was very apparent that there was more ease and
true gayety *after* all had got through, than there had previously
been.

But the happy period of every dinner-party, is after the cloth
is removed. With the dark, polished mahogany for a background, the sparkling decanters making their rounds, the fruit
and cake baskets, the very scene seems to inspire one with a
wish for gayety. Herman Mordaunt called for toasts, as soon as
the cloth disappeared, with a view I believe of putting every
body at ease, and to render the conversation more general. He
was desired to set the example, and immediately gave " Miss
Markham," who, as I was told, was a single lady of forty, with
whom he had carried on a little flirtation. Anneke's turn came
next, and she chose to give a sentiment, notwithstanding all
Bulstrode's remonstrances, who insisted on a gentleman. He
did not succeed, however; Anneke very steadily gave " The
Thespian corps of the ——th; may it prove as successful in the
arts of peace, as in its military character it has often proved
itself to be in the art of war." Much applause followed this
toast, and Harris was persuaded by Bulstrode to stand up, and
say a few words, for the credit of the regiment. Such a speech!
It reminded me of the horse that was advertised as a show, in
London, about this time, and which was said " to have its tail
where its head ought to be." But Bulstrode clapped his hands,
and cried " hear," at every other word, protesting that the regiment was honored as much in the thanks, as in the sentiment.
Harris did not seem displeased with his own effort, and, presuming on his rank, he drank, without being called on, " to the fair
of New York; eminent alike for beauty and wit, may they only
become as merciful as they are victorious."

" Bravo! " again cried Bulstrode — " Harris is fairly inspired,
and is growing better and better. Had he said imminent, in-

stead of eminent, it would be more accurate, as their frowns are as threatening as their smiles are bewitching."

"Is that to pass for *your* sentiment, Mr. Bulstrode, and are we to drink it?" demanded Herman Mordaunt.

"By no means, sir; I have the honor to give Lady Dolly Merton."

Who lady Dolly was, nobody knew, I believe, though we of the colonies always drank a titled person, who was known to be at home, with a great deal of respectful attention, not to say veneration. Other toasts followed, and then the ladies were asked to sing. Anneke complied, with very little urging, as became her position, and never did I hear sweeter strains than those she poured forth! The air was simple, but melody itself, and the sentiment had just enough of the engrossing feeling of woman in it, to render it interesting, without in the slightest degree impairing its fitness for the virgin lips from which it issued. Bulstrode, I could see, was almost entranced; and I heard him murmur, "An angel, by heaven!" He sang, himself, a love-song full of delicacy and feeling, and in a way to show that he had paid much attention to the art of music. Harris sang, too, as did Mary Wallace; the former, much as he spoke; the last plaintively, and decidedly well. Even Herman Mordaunt gave us a strain, and my turn followed. Singing was somewhat of a *forte* with me, and I have reason to think I made out quite as well as the best of them. I know that Anneke seemed pleased, and I saw tears in her eyes, as I concluded a song that was intended to produce just such an effect.

At length the youthful mistress of the house arose, reminding her father that he had at table the principal performer of the evening, by way of a caution, when three or four of us handed the ladies to the drawing-room door. Instead of returning to the table, I entered the room, and Bulstrode did the same, under the plea of its being necessary for him to drink no more on account of the work before him.

CHAPTER VIII

"Odds bodikins, man, much better: use
Every man after his desert, and who shall 'scape
Whipping? use them after your own honor
And dignity: the less they deserve, the more
Merit is in your bounty."
                                        HAMLET.

"HARRIS will be *hors de combat*," Bulstrode soon observed,
"unless I can manage to get him from the table. You know he is
to play Marcia this evening; and, though a *little* wine will give
him fire and spirit for the part, too much will impair its feminine
beauties. Addison never intended that 'the virtuous Marcia,' in
towering above her sex, was to be picked out of a kennel, or from
under a table. Harris is a true Irish peer, when claret is concerned."

All the ladies held up their hands, and protested against Mr.
Harris being permitted to act a travesty on their sex. As yet,
no one had known how the characters were to be cast, beyond
the fact that Bulstrode himself was to play Cato, for great care
had been taken to keep the bills of the night from being seen,
in order that the audience might have the satisfaction of finding
out who was who, for themselves. At the close of each piece
a bill was to be sent round, among the favored few, telling the
truth. As Anneke declared that her father never locked in his
guests, and had faithfully promised to bring up every body for
coffee in the course of half an hour, it was determined to let things
take their own way.

Sure enough, at the end of the time mentioned, Herman
Mordaunt appeared, with all the men, from the table. Harris was
not tipsy, as I found was very apt to be the case with him after
dinner, but neither was he sober. According to Bulstrode's notion,
he may have had just fire enough to play the "virtuous Marcia."
In a few minutes he hurried the ensign off, declaring that, like
Hamlet's ghost, their hour had come. At seven, the whole party
left the house in a body to walk to the theatre. Herman
Mordaunt did not keep a proper town equipage, and, if he had,

it would not have contained a fourth of our company. In this, however, we were not singular, as nine in ten of the audience that night, I mean nine in ten of the gentle sex, went to the theatre on foot.

Instead of going directly down Crown street, into Maiden Lane, which would have been the nearest way to the theatre, we went out into Broadway, and round by Wall street, the walking being better, and the gutters farther from the ladies; the centre of the street being at no great distance from the houses, in the narrower passages of the town. We found a great many well-dressed people moving in the same direction with ourselves. Herman Mordaunt remarked that he had never before seen so many hoops, cardinals, cocked hats and swords in the streets, at once, as he saw that evening. All the carriages in town rolled past us as we went down Wall street, and by the time we reached William street, the pavements resembled a procession, more than any thing else. As every one was in full dress the effect was pleasing, and the evening being fine, most of the gentlemen carried their hats in their hands, in order not to disturb their curls, thus giving to the whole the air of a sort of vast drawing-room. I never saw a more lovely creature than Anneke Mordaunt appeared, as she led our party, on this occasion. The powder had got a little out of her fine auburn hair, and on the part of the head that was not concealed by a cap, that shaded half her beautiful face, it seemed as if the rich covering bestowed by nature was about to break out of all restraint, and shade her bust with its exuberance. Her negligée was a rich satin, flounced in front, while the lace that dropped from her elbows seemed as if woven by fairies, expressly for a fairy to wear. She had paste buckles in her shoes, and I thought I had never beheld such a foot, as was occasionally seen peeping from beneath her dress, while she walked daintily, yet with the grace of a queen, at my side. I do not thus describe Anneke with a view of inducing the reader to fancy her stately and repulsive; on the contrary, winning ease and natural grace were just as striking in her manner, as were beauty, and sentiment, and feeling in her countenance. More than once, as we walked side by side, did I become painfully conscious how unworthy I was to fill the place I occupied. I believe this humility is one of the surest signs of sincere love.

At length, we reached the theatre, and were permitted to enter. All the front seats were occupied by blacks, principally in New York liveries; that is to say, with cuffs, collars and pocket-flaps

of a cloth different from the coat, though a few were in lace.
These last belonged to the topping families, several of which gave
colors and ornaments almost as rich as those that I understand
are constantly given at home. I well remember that two entire
boxes were retained by servants, in shoulder-knots, and much
richer dresses than common, one of whom belonged to the
lieutenant-governor, and the other to my lord Loudon, who was
then commander-in-chief. As the company entered, these domestics disappeared, as is usual, and we all took our seats on the
benches thus retained for us. Bulstrode's care was apparent in
the manner in which he had provided for Anneke, and her party,
which, I will take it on myself to say, was one of the most striking,
for youth and good looks, that entered the house that evening.

   Great was the curiosity, and deep the feeling, that prevailed
among the younger portion of the audience in particular, as party
after party was seated, that important evening. The house was
ornamented as a theatre, and I thought it vast in extent; though
Herman Mordaunt assured me it was no great thing, in that
point of view, as compared with most of the playhouses at home.
But the ornaments, and the lights, and the curtain, the pit, the
boxes, the gallery, were all so many objects of intense interest.
Few of us said any thing; but our eyes wandered over all with a
species of delight, that I am certain can be felt in a theatre only
once. Anneke's sweet face was a picture of youthful expectation; an expectation, however, in which intelligence and discretion had their full share. The orchestra was said to have an
undue portion of wind instruments in it; though I perceived ladies
all over the house, including those in our own box, returning the
bows of many of the musicians, who, I was told, were *amateurs*
from the army and the drawing-rooms of the town.

   At length the commander-in-chief and the lieutenant-governor
entered together, occupying the same box, though two had
been provided, their attendants having recourse to the second.
The commotion produced by these arrivals had hardly subsided,
when the curtain arose, and a new world was presented to our
view! Of the playing, I shall not venture to say much; though
to me it seemed perfection. Bulstrode gained great applause
that night; and I understand that divers gentlemen, who had
either been educated at home, or who had passed much time
there, declared that his Cato would have done credit to either
of the royal theatres. His dress appeared to me to be every thing
it should be; though I cannot describe it. I remember that

Syphax wore the uniform of a colonel of dragoons, and Juba that of a general officer; and that there was a good deal of criticism expended, and some offence taken, because the gentlemen who played these parts came out in wool, and with their faces blacked. It was said, in answer to these feelings, that the characters were Africans; and that any one might see, by casting his eyes at the gallery, that Africans are usually black, and that they have woolly hair; a sort of proof that, I imagine, only aggravated the offence.* Apart from this little mistake, every thing went off well, even to virtuous Marcia. It is true that some evil-inclined persons whispered that the "virtuous Marcia" was a little how-came-you-so; but Bulstrode afterward assured me that his condition helped him along amazingly, and that it added a liquid lustre to his eyes, that might otherwise have been wanting. The high-heeled shoes appeared to trouble him; but some persons fancied it gave him a pretty tottering in his walk, that added very much to the deception. On the whole, the piece went off surprisingly, as I could see by Lord Loudon and the lieutenant-governor, both of whom seemed infinitely diverted. Herman Mordaunt smiled once or twice, when he ought to have looked grave; but this I ascribed to a want of practice, of late years, in scenic representations. He certainly was a man of judgment, and must have known the proper moments to exhibit particular emotions.

During the interval between the play and the farce, the actors came among us, to receive the homage they merited, and loud were the plaudits that were bestowed on them. Anneke's bright eyes sparkled with pleasure as she admitted, without reserve, to Bulstrode the pleasure she had received, and confessed she had formed no idea, hitherto, of the beauty and power of a theatrical representation, aided as was this, by the auxiliaries of lights, dress and scenery. It is true, the women had been a little absurd, and the "virtuous Marcia" particularly so; but the fine sentiments of Addison, which, though as Herman Mordaunt observed, they had all the accuracy and all the stiffness of a pedantic age, were sufficiently beautiful and just, to cover the delinquencies of the honorable Mr. Harris. She hoped the after-piece would be of the same general character, that they might all enjoy it as much as they had the play itself.

---

* In England, Othello is usually played as a black, while in America he is played as a nondescript; or of no color that is ordinarily seen. It is not clear that England is nearer right than America, however; the Moor not being a negro, any more than he is of the color of a dried herring. — EDITOR.

The other young ladies were equally decided in their praise, through it struck me that Anneke *felt* the most, on the occasion. That the major had obtained a great advantage by his efforts, I could not but see; and the folly of my having any pretensions with one who was courted by such a rival, began to impress itself on my imagination with a force I found painful. But the bell soon summoned away the gallant actors, in order to dress for the farce.

The long interval that occurred between the two pieces, gave ample opportunity for visiting one's acquaintances, and to compare opinions. I went to my aunt's box, and found her well satisfied, though less animated than the younger ladies, in the expression of her pleasure. My uncle was altogether himself; good-natured, but not disposed to award any indiscreet amount of praise.

"Pretty well for boys, Corny," he said, "though the youngster who acted Marcia had better been at school. I do not know his name, but he completely took all the virtue out of Marcia. He must have studied her character from some of the ladies who follow the camp."

"My dear uncle, how differently you think from all in our box! That gentleman is the Honorable Mr. Harris, who is only eighteen, and has a pair of colors in the ——th, and is a son of Lord Ballybannon, or Bally-something else, and is said to have the softest voice in the army!"

"Ay, and the softest head, too, I'll answer for it. I tell you, Corny, the Honorable Mr. Ballybilly, who is only eighteen, and has a pair of colors in the ——th, and the softest voice in the army, had better been at school, instead of undermining the virtue of the "virtuous Marcia," as he has so obviously done. Bulstrode did well enough; capitally well, for an amateur, and must be a first-rate fellow. By the way, Jane " — that was my aunt's name — "they tell me, he is likely to marry that exceedingly pretty daughter of Herman Mordaunt, and make her Lady Bulstrode, one of these days."

"Why not, Mr. Legge? — Anne Mordaunt is as sweet a girl as there is in the colony, and is very respectably connected. They even say the Mordaunts are of a high family at home. Mary Wallace told me that Herman Mordaunt and Sir Henry Bulstrode are themselves related; and you know, my dear, how intimate the Mordaunts and the Wallaces are?"

"Not I; — I know nothing of their intimacies, though I dare say it may be all true. Mordaunt's father was an English gentleman of some family, I have always heard, though he was as poor as a church-mouse when he married one of our Dutch heiresses; and as for Herman Mordaunt himself, he proved he had not lost the instinct by marrying another, though she did not happen to be Dutch. Here comes Anneke to inherit it all, and I'll answer for it that care is had that she shall marry an heir."

"Well, Mr. Bulstrode is an heir, and the eldest son of a baronet. I am always pleased when one of our girls makes a good connection at home, for it does the colony credit. It is an excellent thing, Corny, to have our interest well sustained at home — especially before the Privy Council, they tell me."

"Well, I am not," answered my uncle. "I think it more to the credit of the colony for its young women to take up with its young men, and its young men with its young women. I wish Anne Mordaunt had been substituted for the Honorable Ballyshannon to-night. She would have made a thousand times better ' virtuous Marcia.' "

"You surely would not have had a young lady of respectability appear in public, in this way, Mr. Legge."

My uncle said something to this, for he seldom let " Jane " get the better of it for want of an answer; but as I left the box, I did not hear his reply. It seemed then to be settled, in the minds of most persons, that Bulstrode was to marry Anneke! I cannot describe the new shock this opinion gave me; but it seemed to make me more fully sensible of the depth of the impression that had been made on myself, in the intercourse of a single week. The effect was such as I did not return to the party I had left, but sought a seat in a distant part of the theatre, though one in which I could distinctly see those I had abandoned.

The Beau's Stratagem soon commenced, and Bulstrode was again seen in the character of Scrub. Those who were most familiar with the stage, pronounced his playing to be excellent — far better in the footman than in the Roman Senator. The play itself struck me as being as broad and coarse as could be tolerated; but as it had a reputation at home, where it had a great name, our matrons did not dare to object to it. I was glad to see the smiles soon disappear from Anneke's face, however, and to discover that she found no pleasure in scenes so unsuited to her sex and years. The short, quick glances that were exchanged between Anneke and Mary Wallace, did not escape me, and the manner in which they both rose, as soon as the curtain dropped, told quite plainly the haste they were in to quit the theatre. I reached their box-door in time to assist them through the crowd.

Not a word was said by any of us, until we reached the street, where two or three of Miss Mordaunt's female friends became loud in the expression of their satisfaction. Neither Anneke nor Mary Wallace said any thing, and so well did I understand the nature of their feelings, that I made no allusion whatever to the farce. As for the others, they did but chime in with what appeared to be the common opinion, and were to be pitied rather than condemned. It was perhaps the more excusable in them to imagine such a play right, inasmuch as they must have known it was much extolled at home, a fact that gave any custom a certain privilege in the colonies. A mother country has much of the same responsibility as a natural mother, herself, since its opinions and example are apt to be quoted in the one case by the dependent, in justification of its own opinions and conduct, as it is by the natural offspring in the other.

I fancy, notwithstanding, this sort of responsibility gives the ministers or people of England very little trouble, since I never could discover any sensitiveness to their duties on this score. We all went in at Herman Mordaunt's, after walking to the house as we had walked from it, and were made to take a light supper, including some delicious chocolate. Just as we sat down to table, Bulstrode joined us, to receive the praises he had earned, and to enjoy his triumph. He got a seat directly opposite to mine, on Anneke's left hand, and soon began to converse.

" In the first place," he cried, " you must all admit that Tom Harris did wonders to-night, as Miss Marcia Cato. I had my own trouble with the rogue, for there is no precedent for a tipsy Marcia; but we managed to keep him straight, and that was the nicest part of my management, let me assure you."

" Yes," observed Herman Mordaunt, dryly; " I should think keeping Tom Harris straight, after dinner, an exploit of no little difficulty, but a task that would demand a very judicious management, indeed."

" You were pleased to express your satisfaction with the performance of Cato, Miss Mordaunt," said Bulstrode, in a very deferential and solicitous manner; " but I question if the entertainment gave you as much pleasure? "

" It certainly did not. Had the representation ended with the first piece, I am afraid I should too much regret that we are without a regular stage; but the farce will take off much of the keenness of such regrets."

"I fear I understand you, cousin Anne, and greatly regret that we did not make another choice," returned Bulstrode, with a humility that was not usual in his manner, even when addressing Anneke Mordaunt; "but I can assure you the play has great vogue at home; and the character of Scrub, in particular, has usually been a prodigious favorite. I see by your look, however, that enough has been said; but after having done so much to amuse this good company to-night, I shall feel authorized to call on every lady present, at least for a song, as soon as the proper moment arrives. Perhaps I have a right to add, a sentiment, and a toast."

And songs, and toasts, and sentiments, we had as usual, the moment we had done eating. It was, and indeed *is*, rather more usual to indulge in this innocent gayety after supper than after dinner, with us; and that night every body entered into the feeling of the moment with spirit. Herman Mordaunt gave "Miss Markham," as he had done at dinner, and this with an air so determined, as to prove no one else would ever be got out of *him*.

"There is a compact between Miss Markham and myself, to toast each other for the remainder of our lives," cried the master of the house, laughing; "and we are each too honest ever to violate it."

"But Miss Mordaunt is under no such engagement," put in a certain Mr. Benson, who had manifested much interest in the beautiful young mistress of the house throughout the day; "and I trust we shall not be put off by any such excuse from her."

"It is not in rule to ask two of the same race for toasts in succession," answered Herman Mordaunt; "there is Mr. Bulstrode dying to give us another English belle."

"With all my heart," said Bulstrode, gayly. "This time it shall be Lady Betty Boddington."

"Married or single, Bulstrode?" inquired Billings, as I thought with some little point.

"No matter which, so long as she be a beauty and a toast. I believe it is now my privilege to call on a lady, and I beg a gentleman from Miss Wallace."

There had been an expression of pained surprise, at the trifling between Billings and Bulstrode, in Anneke's sweet countenance; for, in the simplicity of our provincial habits, we of the colonies did not think it exactly in rule for the single to toast the married, or *vice versa;* but the instant her friend was thus called on, it changed to a look of gentle concern. Mary Wallace manifested no concern, but gave " Mr. Francis Fordham."

" Ay, Frank Fordham with all my heart," cried Herman Mordaunt. " I hope he will return to his native country as straightforward, honest, and good as he left it."

" Mr. Fordham is then abroad? " inquired Bulstrode. " I thought the name new to me."

" If being at home can be called being abroad. He is reading law at the Temple."

This was the answer of Mary Wallace, who looked as if she felt a friendly interest in the young Templar, but no more. She now called on Dirck for his lady. Throughout the whole of that day, Dirck's voice had hardly been heard; a reserve that comported well enough with his age and established diffidence. This appeal, however, seemed suddenly to arouse all that there was of manhood in him; and that was not a little, I can tell the reader, when there was occasion to use it. Dirck's nature was honesty itself; and he felt the appeal too direct, and the occasion too serious, to admit of duplicity. He loved but one, esteemed but one, felt for one only; and it was not in his nature to cover his preference by any attempt at deception. After coloring to the ears, appearing distressed, he made an effort, and pronounced the name of — " Anneke Mordaunt."

A common laugh rewarded this blunder; common with all but the fair creature who had extorted this involuntary tribute, and myself, who knew Dirck's character too well not to understand how very much he must be in earnest thus to lay bare the most cherished secret of his heart. The mirth continued for some time, Herman Mordaunt appearing to be particularly pleased, and applauding his kinsman's directness with several " bravos " very distinctly uttered. As for Anneke, I saw she looked touched, while she looked concerned, and as if she would be glad to have the thing undone.

" After all, Dirck, much as I admire your spirit and plain dealing, boy," cried Herman Mordaunt, " Miss Wallace can never let such a toast pass. She will insist on having another."

" I! — I protest I am well pleased with it, and ask for no other," exclaimed the lady in question. " No toast can be more agreeable to me than Anneke Mordaunt, and I particularly like the quarter from which this comes."

" If friends can be trusted in a matter of this nature," put in

Bulstrode, with a little pique, " Mr. Follock has every reason to be contented. Had I known, however, that the customs of New York allowed a lady who is present to be toasted, that gentleman would not have had the merit of being the first to make this discovery."

" Nor is it," said Herman Mordaunt; " and Dirck must hunt up another to supply my daughter's place."

But no other was forthcoming from the stores of Dirck Follock's mind. Had he a dozen names in reserve, not one of them would he have produced under circumstances that might seem like denying his allegiance to the girl already given; but he *could* not name any other female. So, after some trifling, the company attributing Dirck's hesitation to his youth and ignorance of the world, abandoned the attempt, desiring him to call on Anneke herself for a toast in turn.

" *Cousin* Dirck Van Valkenburgh," said Anneke, with the greater self-possession and ease of her sex, though actually my friend's junior by more than two years; laying some emphasis, at the same time, on the word *cousin.*

" There! " exclaimed Dirck, looking exultingly at Bulstrode; " you see, gentlemen and ladies, that *it* is permitted to toast a person present, if you happen to respect and esteem that person! "

" By which, sir, we are to understand how much Miss Mordaunt respects and esteems Mr. Dirck Van Valkenburgh," answered Bulstrode gravely. " I am afraid there is only too much justice in an opinion that might, at the first blush, seem to savor of self-love."

" An imputation I am far from denying," returned Anneke, with a steadiness that showed wonderful self-command, did she really return any of Dirck's attachment. " My kinsman gives me as his toast, and I give him as mine. Is there any thing unnatural in that? "

Here there was an outbreak of raillery at Anneke's expense, which the young lady bore with a calmness and composure that at first astonished me. But when I came to reflect that she had been virtually at the head of her father's house for several years, and that she had always associated with persons older than herself, it appeared more natural; for it is certain we can either advance or retard the character by throwing a person into intimate association with those who, by their own conversation, manners, or acquirements, are most adapted for doing either. In a few minutes the interruption was forgotten by those who had no interest in the subject, and the singing commenced. I had obtained so much credit by my attempt at dinner, that I had the extreme gratification of being asked to sing another song by Anneke herself. Of course I complied, and I thought the company seemed pleased. As for my young hostess, I knew she looked more gratified with my song than with the afterpiece, and that I felt to be something. Dirck had an occasion to renew a little of the ground lost by the toast, for he sang a capital comic song in low Dutch. It is true, not half the party understood him, but the other half laughed until the tears rolled down their cheeks, and there was something so droll in my friend's manner, that every body was delighted. The clocks struck twelve before we broke up.

I staid in town but a day or two longer, meeting my new acquaintances every day, and sometimes twice a-day, however, on Trinity Church walk. I paid visits of leave-taking with a heavy heart, and most of all to Anneke and her father.

"I understood from Follock," said Herman Mordaunt, when I explained the object of my call, "that you are to leave town to-morrow. Miss Mordaunt and her friend, Miss Wallace, go to Lilacsbush this afternoon; for it is high time to look after the garden and the flowers, many of which are now in full bloom. I shall join them in the evening; and I propose that you young men take a late breakfast with us, on your way to Westchester. A cup of coffee before you start, and getting into your saddle at six, will bring all right. I promise you that you shall be on the road again by one, which will give you plenty of time to reach Satanstoe before dark."

I looked at Anneke, and fancied that the expression of her countenance was favorable. Dirck left every thing to me, and I accepted the invitation. This arrangement shortened my visit in Crown street, and I left the house with a lighter heart than that which I had entered it. It is always so agreeable to get an unpleasant duty deferred!

Next day Dirck and I were in the saddle at six precisely, and we rode through the streets just as the blacks were washing down their stoops and side-walks; though there were but very few of the last, in my youth. This is a commodious improvement, and one that it is not easy to see how the ladies could dispense with, and which is now getting to be pretty common; all the new streets, I see, being provided with the convenience.

It was a fine May morning, and the air was full of the sweet fragrance of the lilac, in particular, as we rode into the country.

Just as we got into the Bowery lane, a horseman was seen walking out of one of the by-streets, and coming our way. He no sooner caught sight of two travellers going in his own direction, than he spurred forward to join us; being alone, and probably wishing company. As it would have been churlish to refuse to travel in company with one thus situated, we pulled up, walking our horses until the stranger joined us; when, to our surprise, it turned out to be Jason Newcome. The pedagogue was as much astonished when he recognized us, as we were in recognizing him; and I believe he was a little disappointed; for Jason was so fond of making acquaintances, that it was always a pleasure to him to be thus employed. It appeared that he had been down on the island to visit a relative, who had married and settled in that quarter; and this was the reason we had not met since the morning of the affair of the lion. Of course we trotted on together, neither glad nor sorry at having this particular companion.

I never could explain the process by means of which Jason wound his way into every body's secrets. It is true he had no scruples about asking questions; putting those which most persons would think forbidden by the usages of society, with as little hesitation as those which are universally permitted. The people of New England have a reputation this way; and I remember to have heard Mr. Worden account for the practice in the following way: every thing and every body were brought under rigid church government among the Puritans; and, when a whole community gets the notion that it is to sit in judgment on every act of one of its members, it is quite natural that it should extend that right to an inquiry into all his affairs. One thing is certain; our neighbors of Connecticut do assume a control over the acts and opinions of individuals that is not dreamed of in New York; and I think it very likely that the practice of pushing inquiry into private things, has grown up under this custom.

As one might suppose, Jason, whenever baffled in an attempt to obtain knowledge by means of inquiries, more or less direct, sought to advance his ends through conjectures; taking those that were the most plausible, if any such could be found, but putting up with those that had not even this questionable recommendation, if nothing better offered. He was, consequently, forever falling into the grossest errors, for, necessarily making his conclusions on premises drawn from his own ignorance and inexperience, he was liable to fall into serious mistakes at the very

outset. Nor was this the worst; the tendency of human nature
not being very directly to charity, the harshest constructions were
sometimes blended with the most absurd blunders, in his mind, and
I have known him to be often guilty of assertions that had no
better foundation than these conjectures, which might have sub-
jected him to severe legal penalties.

On the present occasion, Jason was not long in ascertaining
where we were bound. This was done in a manner so characteristic and ingenious, that I will attempt to relate it.

"Why, you're out early, this morning, gentlemen!" exclaimed
Jason, affecting surprise. "What in natur' has started you off
before breakfast?"

"So as to be certain not to lose our suppers at Satanstoe, this
evening," I answered.

"Supper? why, you will almost reach home (Jason *would* call
this word *hum*) by dinner-time; that is, your York dinner-time.
Perhaps you mean to call by the way?"

"Perhaps we do, Mr. Newcome; there are many pleasant
families between this and Satanstoe."

"I know there be. There's the great Mr. Van Cortlandt's at
Yonkers; perhaps you mean to stop there?"

"No, sir; we have no such intention."

"Then there's the rich Count Philips's, on the river; that would
be no great matter out of the way?"

"It's farther than we intend to turn."

"Oh! so you do intend to turn a bit aside? Well, there's that
Mr. Mordaunt, whose daughter you pulled out of the lion's
paws; — he has a house near Kingsbridge, called Lilacsbush."

"And how did you ascertain that, Jason?"

"By asking. Do you think I would let such a thing happen,
and not inquire a little about the young lady? Nothing is ever
lost by putting a few questions, and inquiring round; and I did
not forget the rule in her case."

"And you ascertained that the young lady's father has a place
called Lilacsbush, in this neighborhood?"

"I did; and a queer York fashion it is to give a house a name,
just as you would a Christian being; that must be a Roman
Catholic custom, and some way connected with idolatry."

"Out of all doubt. It is far better to say, for instance, that
we are going to breakfast at Mr. Mordaunt's-es-es, than to say
we intend to stop at Lilacsbush."

"Oh! you be, be you? Well, I thought it would turn out

that some such place must have started you off so early. It will be a desperate late breakfast, Corny! "

" It will be at ten o'clock, Jason, and that is rather later than common; but our appetites will be so much the better."

To this Jason assented, and then commenced a series of manœuvres to be included in the party. This we did not dare to do, however, and all Jason's hints were disregarded, until, growing desperate by our evasions, he plumply proposed to go along, and we as plumply told him we would take no such liberty with a man of Herman Mordaunt's years, position and character. I do not know that we should have hesitated so much had we considered Jason a gentleman, but this was impossible. The custom of the colony admitted of great freedom in this respect, being very different from what it is at home, by all accounts, in these particulars; but there was always an understanding that the persons one brought with him should be of a certain stamp and class in life; recommendations to which Jason Newcome certainly had no claim.

This case was getting to be a little embarrassing when the appearance of Herman Mordaunt himself, fortunately removed the difficulty. Jason was not a man to be thrown off very easily; but here was one who had the power, and who showed the disposition to set things right. Herman Mordaunt had ridden down the road a mile or two to meet us, intending to lead us by a private and a shorter way to his residence, than that which was already known to us. He no sooner saw that Jason was of our company, than he asked that as a favor, which our companion would very gladly have accepted as a boon.

CHAPTER IX

"I question'd Love, whose early ray
So heavenly bright appears;
And Love, in answer, seem'd to say,
His light was dimm'd by tears."
HEBER.

IT was not long after the explanation occurred, as respects Jason, and the invitation was given to include him in our party, before Herman Mordaunt opened a gate, and led the way into the fields. A very tolerable road conducted us through some woods, to the heights, and we soon found ourselves on an eminence, that overlooked a long reach of the Hudson, extending from Haverstraw to the north, as far as Staten Island to the south; a distance of near forty miles. On the opposite shore, rose the wall-like barrier of the Palisadoes, lifting the tableland on their summits to an elevation of several hundred feet. The noble river itself, fully three-quarters of a mile in width, was unruffled by a breath of air, lying in one single, extended, placid sheet, under the rays of a bright sun, resembling molten silver. I scarce remember a lovelier morning; every thing appeared to harmonize with the glorious but tranquil grandeur of the view, and the rich promises of a bountiful nature. The trees were mostly covered with a beautiful clothing of a young verdure; the birds had mated, and were building in nearly every tree; the wild-flowers started up beneath the hoofs of our horses; and every object, far and near, seemed, to my young eyes, to be attuned to harmony and love.

"This is a favorite ride of mine, in which Anneke often accompanies me," said Herman Mordaunt, as we gained the commanding eminence I have mentioned. "My daughter is a spirited horsewoman, and is often my companion in these morning rides. She and Mary Wallace should be somewhere on the hills, at this moment, for they promised to follow me, as soon as they could dress for the saddle."

A cry of something like wild delight burst out of Dirck, and the next moment he was galloping away for an adjoining ridge, on the top of which the beautiful forms of the two girls were just then visible; embellished by neatly-fitting habits, and beavers with drooping feathers. I pointed out these charming objects to Herman Mordaunt, and followed my friend, at half-speed. In a minute or two the parties had joined.

Never had I seen Anneke Mordaunt so perfectly lovely as she appeared that morning. The exercise and air had deepened a bloom that was always rich; and her eyes received new lustre from the glow on her cheeks. Though expected, I thought she received us as particularly acceptable guests; while Mary Wallace manifested more than a usual degree of animation in her reception. Jason was not forgotten, but was acknowledged as an old acquaintance, and was properly introduced to the friend.

"You frequently take these rides, Mr. Mordaunt tells me," I said, reining my horse to the side of that of Anneke's as the whole party moved on; "and I regret that Satanstoe is so distant, as to prevent our oftener meeting of a morning. We have many noted horsewomen, in Westchester, who would be proud of such an acquisition."

"I know several ladies, on your side of Harlem River," Anneke answered, "and frequently ride in their company; but none so distant as any in your immediate neighborhood. My father tells me, he used often to shoot over the fields of Satanstoe, when a youth; and still speaks of your birds with great affection."

"I believe our fathers were once brother sportsmen. Mr. Bulstrode has promised to come and imitate their good example. Now you have had time to reflect on the plays you have seen, do you still feel the same interest in such representations as at first?"

"I only wish there was not so much to condemn. I think Mr. Bulstrode might have reached eminence as a player, had not fortune put it, in one sense, beyond his reach, as an elder son, and a man of family."

"Mr. Bulstrode, they tell me, is not only the heir of an old baronetcy, but of a large fortune?"

"Such are the facts, I believe. Do you not think it creditable to him, Mr. Littlepage, that one so situated, should come so far to serve his king and country, in a rude war like this of our colonies?"

I was obliged to assent, though I heartily wished that Anneke's manner had been less animated and sincere, as she put the question. Still, I hardly knew what to think of her feelings toward that gentleman; for, otherwise, she always heard him

named with a calmness and self-possession that I had observed
was not shared by all her young companions, when there was
occasion to allude to the gay and insinuating soldier. I need
scarcely say, it was no disadvantage to Mr. Bulstrode to be the
heir of a baronetcy, in an English colony. Somehow or other,
we are a little apt to magnify such accidental superiority, at a
distance from home; and I *have* heard Englishmen themselves
acknowledge that a baronet was a greater man in New York, than
a duke was in London. These were things that passed through
my mind as I rode along at Anneke's side, though I had the discretion not to give utterance to my thoughts.

Herman Mordaunt rode in advance, with Jason; and he led
the party, by pretty bridle-paths, along the heights for nearly
two miles, occasionally opening a gate, without dismounting, until
he reached a point that overlooked Lilacsbush, which was soon
seen, distant from us less than half a mile.

" Here we are, on my own domain," he said, as he pulled up to
let us join him; " that last gate separating me from my nearest
neighbor south. These hills are of no great use, except as early
pastures, though they afford many beautiful views."

" I have heard it predicted," I remarked, " that the time
would come, some day, when the banks of the Hudson would
contain many such seats as that of the Philipses, at Yonkers,
and one or two more like it, that I am told are now standing
above the Highlands."

" Quite possibly; it is not easy to foretell what may come
to pass in such a country. I dare say, that in time, both towns
and seats will be seen on the banks of the Hudson, and a powerful and numerous nobility to occupy the last. By the way, Mr.
Littlepage, your father and my friend Colonel Follock have
been making a valuable acquisition in lands, I hear; having
obtained a patent for an extensive estate, somewhere in the
neighborhood of Albany? "

" It is not so very extensive, sir, there being only some forty
thousand acres of it, altogether; nor is it very near Albany,
by what I can learn, since it must lie at a distance of some forty
miles, or more, from that town. Next winter, however, Dirck
and myself are to go in search of the land, when we shall learn
all about it."

" Then we may meet in that quarter of the country. I have
affairs of importance at Albany, which have been too long
neglected; and it has been my intention to pass some months

at the north, next season, and early in the season, too. We
may possibly meet in the woods."

"You have been at Albany, I suppose, Mr. Mordaunt?"

"Quite often, sir; the distance is so great, that one has not
much inducement to go there, unless carried by affairs, however, as has been my case. I was at Albany before my marriage, and have had various occasions to visit it since."

"My father was there, when a soldier; and he tells me it is
a part of the province well worth seeing. At all events, I shall
encounter the risk and fatigue next season; for it is useful to
young persons to see the world. Dirck and myself may make
the campaign, should there be one in that direction."

I fancied Anneke manifested some interest in this conversation; but we rode on, and soon alighted at the door of
Lilacsbush. Bulstrode was not in the way, and I had the su-
preme pleasure of helping Miss Mordaunt to alight, when we
paused a moment before entering the house, to examine the
view. I have given the reader some idea of the general appearance of the place; but it was necessary to approach it, in
order to form a just conception of its beauties. As its name
indicated, the lawn, house, and out-buildings were all garnished
or buried in lilacs, the whole of which were then in full blossom.
The flowers filled the air with a species of purple light, that cast
a warm and soft radiance even on the glowing face of Anneke,
as she pointed out to me the magical effect. I know no flower
that does so much to embellish a place as the lilac, on a large
scale, common as it is, and familiar as we have become with its
hues and its fragrance.

"We enjoy the month our lilacs are out, beyond any month
in the year," said Anneke, smiling at my surprise and delight;
"and we make it a point to pass most of it here. You will at
least own, Mr. Littlepage, that Lilacsbush is properly named."

"The effect is more like enchantment than any thing else!"
I cried. "I did not know that the simple, modest lilac could
render any thing so very beautiful!"

"Simplicity and modesty are such charms in themselves, sir,
as to be potent allies," observed the sensible but taciturn Mary
Wallace.

To this I assented, of course, and we all followed Mr. Mordaunt into the house. I was as much delighted with the appearance of things in the interior of Lilacsbush, as I had been
with the exterior. Everywhere, it seemed to me, I met with

the signs of Anneke's taste and skill. I do not wish the reader to suppose that the residence itself was of the very first character and class, for this it could not lay claim to be. Still, it was one of those staid, story-and-a-half dwellings, in which most of our first families were, and are content to dwell, in the country; very much resembling the good old habitation at Satanstoe in these particulars. The furniture, however, was of a higher town-finish than we found it necessary to use; and the little parlor in which we breakfasted was a model for an eating-room. The buffets in the corners were so well polished that one might see his face in them; the cellarets were ornamented with plated hinges, locks, etc., and the table itself shone like a mirror. I know not how it was, but the china appeared to me richer and neater than common under Anneke's pretty little hand; while the massive and highly-finished plate of the breakfast service, was such as could be wrought only in England. In a word, while every thing appeared rich and respectable, there was a certain indescribable air of comfort, gentility, and neatness about the whole, that impressed me in an unusual manner.

"Mr. Littlepage tells me, Anneke," observed Herman Mordaunt, while we were at breakfast, "that he intends to make a journey to the north, next winter, and it may be our good fortune to met him there. The ——th expects to be ordered up as high as Albany, this summer; and we may all renew our songs and jests, with Bulstrode and his gay companions, among the Dutchmen."

I was charmed with this prospect of meeting Anneke Mordaunt at the north, and took occasion to say as much; though I was afraid it was in an awkward and confused manner.

"I heard as much as this, sir, while we were riding," answered the daughter. "I hope cousin Dirck is to be of the party?"

Cousin Dirck assured her he was, and we discussed in anticipation the pleasure it must give to old acquaintances to meet so far from home. Not one of us, Herman Mordaunt excepted, had ever been one hundred miles from his or her birthplace, as was ascertained on comparing notes. I was the greatest traveller; Princeton lying between eighty and ninety miles from Satanstoe, as the road goes.

"Perhaps I come nearer to it than any of you," put in Jason, "for my late journey on the island must have carried me nearly that far from Danbury. But, ladies, I can assure you, a traveller has many opportunities for learning useful things, as I know by the difference there is between York and Connecticut."

"And which do you prefer, Mr. Newcome?" asked Anneke, with a somewhat comical expression about her laughing eyes.

"That is hardly a fair question, Miss;" no reproof could break Jason of this vulgarism, "since it might make enemies for a body to speak all of his mind in such matters. There are comparisons that should never be made, on account of circumstances that overrule all common efforts. New York is a great colony — a very great colony, Miss; but it was once Dutch, as every body knows, begging Mr. Follock's pardon; and it must be confessed Connecticut has, from the first, enjoyed almost unheard-of advantages, in the moral and religious character of her people, the excellence of her lands, and the purity " — Jason called this word " poority; " but that did not alter the sentiment — though I must say, once for all, it is out of my power to spell every word as this man saw fit to pronounce it — " of her people and church."

Herman Mordaunt looked up with surprise, at this speech, but Dirck and I had heard so many like it, that we saw nothing out of the way on this particular occasion. As for the ladies, they were too well-bred to glance at each other, as girls sometimes will; but I could see that each thought the speaker a very singular person.

"You find, then, a difference in customs between the two colonies, sir?" said Herman Mordaunt.

"A vast difference truly, sir. Now there was a little thing happened about your daughter, 'Squire Mordaunt, the very first time I saw her " — the present was the *second* interview — " that could no more have happened in Connecticut, than the whole of the province could be put into that teacup."

"To my daughter, Mr. Newcome! "

"Yes, sir, to your own daughter; Miss, that sits there looking as innocent as if it had never come to pass."

"This is so extraordinary, sir, that I must beg an explanation."

"You may well call it extr'ornary, for extr'ornary it would be called all over Connecticut; and I'll never give up that York, if this be a York usage, is or can be right in such a matter, at least."

"I entreat you to be more explicit, Mr. Newcome."

"Why, sir, you must know, Corny, here, and I, and Dirck

there, went in to see the lion, about which no doubt you've heard so much, and Corny paid for Miss's ticket. Well, *that* was all right enough, but — "

"Surely, Anneke, you have not forgotten to return to Mr. Littlepage the money! "

"Listen patiently, my dear sir, and you will get the whole story, my delinquencies and debts included, if any there are."

"That's just what she did, 'Squire Mordaunt, and I maintain there is not the man in all Connecticut that would have taken it. If the ladies can't be treated to sights, and other amusements, I should like to know who is to be so."

Herman Mordaunt, at first, looked gravely at the speaker, but catching the expression of our eyes he answered with the tact of a perfectly well-bred man, as he certainly was, on all occasions that put him to the proof —

"You must overlook Miss Mordaunt's adhering to her own customs, Mr. Newcome, on account of her youth, and her little knowledge of any world but that immediately around her. When she has enjoyed an opportunity of visiting Danbury, no doubt she will improve by the occasion."

"But, Corny, sir — think of Corny's falling into such a mistake! "

"As for Mr. Littlepage, I must suppose he labors under somewhat of the same disadvantage. We are less gallant here than you happen to be in Connecticut; hence our inferiority. At some future day, perhaps, when society shall have made a greater progress among us, our youths will come to see the impropriety of permitting the fair sex to pay for any thing, even their own ribbons. I have long known, sir, that you of New England claim to treat your women better than they are treated in any other portion of the inhabited world, and it must be owing to that circumstance that they enjoy the advantage of being ' treated ' for nothing."

With this concession Jason was apparently content. How much of this provincial feeling, arising from provincial ignorance, have I seen since that time! It is certain that our fellow subjects of the eastern provinces are not addicted to hiding their lights under bushels, but make the most of all their advantages. That they are superior to us of York, in some respects, I am willing enough to allow; but there are certainly points on which this superiority is far less apparent. As for Jason, he was entirely satisfied with the answer of Herman Mordaunt, and often alluded to the subject afterward, to my prejudice, and with great self-complacency. To be sure, it is a hard lesson to beat into the head of the self-sufficient colonist, that his own little corner of the earth does not contain all that is right, and just, and good, and refined.

I left Lilacsbush, that day, deeply in love. I hold it to be unmanly to attempt to conceal it. Anneke had made a lively impression on me from the very first, but that impression had now gone deeper than the imagination, and had very sensibly touched the heart. Perhaps it was necessary to see her in the retirement of the purely domestic circle, to give all her charms their just ascendency. While in town, I had usually met her in crowds, surrounded by admirers or other young persons of her own sex, and there was less opportunity for viewing the influence of nature and the affections on her manner. With Mary Wallace at her side, however, there was always one on whom she could exhibit just enough of these feelings to bring out the loveliness of her nature without effort or affectation. Anne Mordaunt never spoke to her friend without a change appearing in her manner. Affection thrilled in the tones of her voice, confidence beamed in her eye, and esteem and respect were to be gathered from the expectation and deference that shone in her countenance. Mary Wallace was two years the oldest, and these years taken in connection with her character, entitled her to receive this tribute from her nearest associate; but all these feelings flowed spontaneously from the heart, for never was an intercourse between two of the sex more thoroughly free from acting.

It was proof that passion was getting the mastery over me, that I now forgot Dirck, his obvious attachment, older claims, and possible success. I know not how it was, or why it was, but it was certain that Herman Mordaunt had a great regard for Dirck Van Valkenburgh. The affinity may have counted for something, and it was possible that the father was already weighing the advantages that might accrue from such a connection. Colonel Follock had the reputation of being rich, as riches were then counted among us; and the young fellow himself, in addition to a fine manly figure, that was fast developing itself into the frame of a youthful Hercules, had an excellent temper, and a good reputation. Still, this idea never troubled me. Of Dirck I had no fears, while Bulstrode gave me great uneasiness, from the first. I saw all his advantages, may have even magnified them; while those of my near and immediate friend, gave me no trouble whatever. It is possible, had Dirck presented himself oftener, or more distinctly to my mind, a feeling of magnanimity might have induced me to withdraw in time, and leave him a field to which he had the earliest claim. But after the morning at Lilacsbush, it was too late for any such sacrifice on my part; and I rode away from the house, at the side of my friend, as forgetful of his interest in Anneke, as if he had never felt any. Magnanimity and I had no further connection in relation to my pretensions to Anneke Mordaunt.

" Well," continued Jason, as soon as we were fairly in the saddle, " these Mordaunts are even a notch above your folks, Corny? There was more silver vessels in that room where we ate, than there is at this moment in all Danbury! The extravagance amounts to waste. The old gentleman must be desperate rich, Dirck? "

" Herman Mordaunt has a good estate, and very little of it has gone for plate, Jason; that which you saw is old, and came either from Holland, or England; one home, or the other."

" Oh! Holland is no home for me, boy. Depend on it, all that plate is not put there for nothing. If the truth could be come at, this Herman Mordaunt, as you call him, though I do not see why you cannot call him *Squire* Mordaunt, like other folks, but this Mr. Mordaunt has some notion, I conclude, to get his daughter off on one of these rich English officers, of whom there happen to be so many in the province, just at this time. I never saw the gentleman, but there was one Bulstrode named pretty often this forenoon " — Jason's morning always terminated at his usual breakfast-hour — " and I rather conclude he will turn out to be the chap, in the long run. Such is my calculation, and *they* don't often fail."

I saw a quick, surprised start in Dirck; but I felt such a twinge myself, that there was little opportunity to inquire into the state of my friend's feelings, at this coarse, but unexpected remark.

" Have you any particular reason, Mr. Newcome, for venturing such an opinion? " I asked, a little sternly.

" Come, don't let us, out here in the highway, begin to mister one another. You are Corny, Dirck is Dirck, and I am Jason. The shortest way is commonly the best way, and I like given-names among friends. Have I any particular reason? — Yes, plenty on 'em, and them that's good. In the first place, no man has a daughter "— darter à la Jason — "that he does not begin to think about setting her out in the world, accordin' to his abilities; then, as I said before, these folks from home " (hum) " are awful rich, and rich husbands are always satisfactory to parents, whatever they may be to children. Besides, some of these officers will fall heirs to titles, and that is a desperate temptation to a woman, all over the world. I hardly think there is a young woman in Danbury, that could hold out agin' a real title."

It has always struck me as singular, that the people of Jason's part of the provinces, should entertain so much profound respect for titles. No portion of the world is of simpler habits, nor is it easy to find any civilized people among whom there is a greater equality of actual condition, which, one would think, must necessarily induce equality of feeling, than in Connecticut, at this very moment. Notwithstanding these facts, the love of title is so great, that even that of sergeant is often prefixed to the name of a man on his tombstone, or in the announcement of his death or marriage; and as for the militia ensigns and lieutenants, there is no end to them. Deacon is an important title, which is rarely omitted; and woe betide the man who should forget to call a magistrate "esquire." No such usages prevail among us; or, if they do, it is among that portion of the people of this colony which is derived from New England, and still retains some of its customs. Then, in no part of the colonies is English rank more deferred to, than in New England, generally, notwithstanding most of those colonies possess the right to elect nearly every officer they have among them. I allow that we of New York defer greatly to men of birth and rank from home, and it is right we should so do; but I do not think our deference is as great, or by any means as general, as it is in New England.* It is possible the influence

* As respects the love of titles that are derived from the people, there is nothing opposed to strict republican, or if the reader will, democratic principles, since it is deferring to the power that appoints, and manifests a respect for that which the community chooses to elevate. But the deference to *English* rank, mentioned by Mr. Littlepage, is undeniably greater among the mass in New England, than it is anywhere else in this country, at this very moment. One leading New York paper, edited by New England men, during the last controversy about the indemnity to be paid by France, actually styled the Duc de Broglie " his grace," like a Grub street cockney, — a mode of address that would astonish that respectable statesman, quite as much as it must have amused every man of the world who saw it. I have been much puzzled to account for this peculiarity — unquestionably one that exists in the country — but have supposed it must be owing to the diffusion of information which

of the Dutch may have left an impression on our state of society, though I have been told that the colonies further south exhibit very much the same characteristics as we do ourselves on this head.

We reached Satanstoe a little late, in consequence of the delay at Lilacsbush, and were welcomed with affection and warmth. My excellent mother was delighted to see me at home again, after so long an absence, and one which she did not think altogether without peril, when it was remembered that I had passed a whole fortnight amid the temptations and fascinations of the capital. I saw the tears in her eyes as she kissed me again and again, and felt the gentle, warm embrace, as she pressed me to her bosom, in maternal thanksgiving.

Of course, I had to render an account of all I had seen and done, including Pinkster, the theatre, and the lion. I said nothing, however, of the Mordaunts, until questioned about them by my mother, quite a fortnight after Dirck had gone across to Rockland. One morning, as I sat endeavoring to write a sonnet in my own room, that excellent parent entered and took a seat near my table, with the familiarity the relation she bore me justified. She was knitting at the time, for never was she idle, except when asleep. I saw by the placid smile on her face, which, Heaven bless her! was still smooth and handsome, that something was on her mind, that was far from disagreeable; and I waited with some curiosity for the opening. That excellent mother! How completely did she live out of herself in all that had the most remote bearing on my future hopes and happiness!

"Finish your writing, my son," commenced my mother, for I had instinctively striven to conceal the sonnet; "finish your writing; until you have done, I will be silent."

"I have done, now, mother; 'twas only a copy of verses I was endeavoring to write out — you know — that is — write out, you know."

---

carries intelligence sufficiently far to acquaint the mass with leading social features, without going far enough to compensate for a provincial position and provincial habits. Perhaps the exclusively English origin of the people may have an influence. The writer has passed portions of two seasons in Switzerland, and excluding the small forest cantons, he has no hesitation in saying that the habits and general notions of Connecticut are more inherently democratical than those of any part of that country. Notwithstanding, he thinks a nobleman, particularly an English nobleman, is a far greater man in New England, than he is among the real middle-state families of New York. — EDITOR.

"I did not know you were a poet, Corny," returned my mother, smiling still more complacently, for it *is* something to be the parent of a poet.

"I! — I a poet, mother? — I'd sooner turn schoolmaster, than turn poet. Yes, I'd sooner be Jason Newcome himself, than even suspect it possible I *could* be a poet."

"Well, never mind; people never turn poets, I fancy, with their eyes open. But what is this I hear of your having saved a beautiful young lady from the jaws of a lion, while you were in town; and why was I left to learn all the particulars from Mr. Newcome?"

I believe my face was of the color of scarlet, for it felt as if it were on fire, and my mother smiled still more decidedly than ever. Speak! I could not have spoken to be thus smiled on by Anneke.

"There is nothing to be ashamed of, Corny, in rescuing a young lady from a lion, or in going to her father's to receive the thanks of the family. The Mordaunts are a family any one can visit with pleasure. Was the battle between you and the beast a very desperate conflict, my child?"

"Poh! mother: — Jason is a regular dealer in marvels, and he makes mountains of molehills. In the first place, for ' jaws,' you must substitute ' paws,' and for a ' young lady,' ' her shawl.' "

"Yes, I understand it was the shawl, but it was on her shoulders, and could not have been disengaged time enough to save her, had you not shown so much presence of mind and courage. As for the ' jaws,' I believe that was my mistake, for Mr. Newcome certainly said ' claws.' "

"Well, mother, have it your own way. I was of a little service to a very charming young woman, and she and her father were civil to me, as a matter of course. Herman Mordaunt is a name we all know, and, as you say, his is a family that any man may be proud of visiting, ay, and pleased too."

"How odd it is, Corny," added my mother, in a sort of musing, soliloquizing way — " you are an only child, and Anneke Mordaunt is also an only child, as Dirck Follock has often told me."

"Then Dirck has spoken to you frequently of Anneke, before this, mother?"

"Time and again; they are relations, you must have heard; as, indeed, you are yourself, if you did but know it."

"I? — related to Anneke Mordaunt, without being too *near?*"

My dear mother smiled again, while I felt sadly ashamed of myself at the next instant. I believe that a suspicion of the truth, as respects my infant passion, existed in that dear parent's mind from that moment.

"Certainly related, Corny, and I will tell you how. My great-great-grandmother, Alida van der Heyden, was a first cousin of Herman Mordaunt's great-great-grandmother, by his mother's side, who was a Van Kleeck. So, you see, you and Anneke are actually related."

"Just near enough, mother, to put one at ease in their house, and not so near as to make relationship troublesome."

"They tell me, my child, that Anneke is a sweet creature! "

"If beauty, and modesty, and grace, and gentleness, and spirit, and sense, and delicacy, and virtue, and piety, can make any young woman of seventeen a sweet creature, mother, then Anneke is sweet."

My dear mother seemed surprised at my warmth, but she smiled still more complacently than ever. Instead of pursuing the subject, however, she saw fit to change it, by speaking of the prospects of the season, and the many reasons we all had for thankfulness to God. I presume, with a woman's instinct, she had learned enough to satisfy her mind for the present.

The summer soon succeeded to the May that proved so momentous to me; and I sought occupation in the fields. Occupation, however, would not do. Anneke was with me, go where I would; and glad was I when Dirck, about mid-summer, in one of his periodical visits to Satanstoe, proposed that we should ride over, and make another visit to Lilacsbush. He had written a note, to say we should be glad to ask a dinner and beds, if it were convenient, for a day a short distance ahead; and he waited the answer at the Neck. This answer arrived duly by mail, and was every thing we could wish. Herman Mordaunt offered us a hearty welcome, and sent the grateful intelligence that his daughter and Mary Wallace would both be present to receive us. I envied Dirck the manly feeling which had induced him to take this plain and respectable course to his object.

We went across the country, accordingly, and reached Lilacsbush several hours before dinner. Anneke received us with a bright suffusion of the face, and kind smiles; though I could not detect the slightest difference in her manners to either.

To both was she gracious, gentle, attentive, and lady-like. No allusion was made to the past, except a few remarks that were given on the subject of the theatre. The officers had continued to play until the ——th had been ordered up the river, when Bulstrode, Billings, Harris, virtuous Marcia, and all, had proceeded to Albany in company. Anneke thought there was about as much to be displeased with, as there was to please, in these representations; though her removal to the country had prevented her seeing more than three of them all. It was admitted all round, however, that Bulstrode played admirably; and it was even regretted by certain persons, that he should not have been devoted to the stage.

We passed the night at Lilacsbush, and remained an hour or two after breakfast next morning. I had carried a warm invitation from both my parents to Herman Mordaunt, to ride over with the young ladies, and taste the fish of the Sound; and the visit was returned in the course of the month of September. My mother received Anneke as a relation; though I believe that both Herman Mordaunt and his daughter were surprised to learn that they came within even the wide embrace of Dutch kindred. They did not seem displeased, however, for the family name of my mother was good, and no one need to have been ashamed of affinity to *her*, on her own account. Our guests did not remain the night, but they left us in a sort of chaise that Herman Mordaunt kept for country use, about an hour before sunset. I mounted my horse, and rode five miles with the party, on its way back, and then took my leave of Anneke, as it turned out, for many, many weary months.

The year 1757 was memorable in the colonies, by the progress of the war, and as much so in New York as in any other province. Montcalm had advanced to the head of Lake George, had taken Fort William Henry, and a fearful massacre of the garrison had succeeded. This bold operation left the enemy in possession of Champlain; and the strong post of Ticonderoga was adequately garrisoned by a formidable force. A general gloom was cast over the political affairs of the colony; and it was understood that a great effort was to be made, the succeeding campaign, to repair the loss. Rumor spoke of large reinforcements from home, and of greater levies in the colonies themselves than had been hitherto attempted. Lord Loudon was to return home, and a veteran of the name of Abercrombie was to succeed him in the command of all the forces of the king. Regiments began to arrive from the West Indies; and, in the course of the winter of 1757–8, we heard at Satanstoe of the gayeties that these new forces had introduced into the town. Among other things, a regular corps of Thespians had arrived from the West Indies.

CHAPTER X

"Dear hasty-pudding, what unpromised joy,
Expands my heart to meet thee in Savoy!
Doomed o'er the world through devious paths to roam,
Each clime my country, and each house my home,
My soul is soothed, my cares have found an end:
I greet my long-lost, unforgotten friend."

                                    BARLOW.

THE winter was soon drawing to a close, and my twenty-first birthday was past. My father and Colonel Follock, who came over to smoke more than usual that winter with my father, began to talk of the journey Dirck and I were to take in quest of the patent. Maps were procured, calculations were made, and different modes of proceeding were proposed, by the various members of the family. I will acknowledge that the sight of the large, coarse, parchment map of the Mooseridge patent, as the new acquisition was called, from the circumstance of the surveyors having shot a moose on a particular ridge of land in its centre, excited certain feelings of avarice within my mind. There were streams meandering among hills and valleys; little lakes, or ponds, as they were erroneously called in the language of the country, dotted the surface; and there were all the artistical proofs of a valuable estate that a good map-maker could devise, to render the whole pleasing and promising.* If it were a good thing to be the heir of Satanstoe, it was far better to be the tenant in common, with my friend Dirck, of all these ample plains, rich bottoms, flowing streams and picturesque lakes. In a word, for the first time in the history of the colonies, the Littlepages had become the owners of what might be termed an estate. According to our New

* Forty years ago, a gentleman in New York purchased a considerable body of wild land, on the faith of the map. When he came to examine his new property, it was found to be particularly wanting in watercourses. The surveyor was sought, and rebuked for his deception, the map having numerous streams, etc. "Why did you lay down all these streams here, where none are to be found?" demanded the irritated purchaser, pointing to the document. "Why? — Why, who the d——l ever saw a map without rivers?" was the answer. — EDITOR.

York parlance, six or eight hundred acres are not an estate; nor two or three thousand, scarcely, but ten, or twenty, and much more, forty thousand acres of land, might be dignified with the name of an estate!

The first knotty point discussed, was to settle the manner in which Dirck and myself should reach Mooseridge. Two modes of going as far as Albany offered, and on one of these it was our first concern to decide. We might wait until the river opened, and go as far as Albany in a sloop, of which one or two left town each week when business was active, as it was certain to be in the spring of the year. It was thought, however, that the army would require most of the means of transportation of this nature that offered; and it might put us to both inconvenience and delay, to wait on the tardy movements of quarter-masters and contractors. My grandfather shook his head when the thing was named, and advised us to remain as independent as possible.

" Have as little as possible to do with such people, Corny," put in my grandfather, now a gray-headed, venerable-looking old gentleman, who did not wear his wig half the time, but was content to appear in a pointed nightcap and gown at all hours, until just before dinner was announced, when he invariably came forth dressed as a gentleman — " Have as little as possible to do with these gentry, Corny. Money, and not honor, is their game; and you will be treated like a barrel of beef, or a bag of potatoes, if you fall into their hands. If you move with the army at all, keep among the real soldiers, my boy, and, above all things, avoid the contractors."

It was consequently determined that there was too much uncertainty and delay in waiting for a passage to Albany by water; for it was known that the voyage itself often lasted ten days, or a fortnight, and it would be so late before we could sail, as to render this delay very inconvenient. The other mode of journeying, was to go before the snow had melted from the roads, by the aid of which it was quite possible to make the distance between Satanstoe and Albany in three days.

Certain considerations of economy next offered, and we settled down on the following plan; which, as it strikes me, is, even now, worthy of being mentioned on account of its prudence and judgment. It was well known that there would be a great demand for horses for the army, as well as for stores, provisions, etc., of various sorts. Now, we had on the Neck several stout horses, that were falling into years, though still serviceable and good for a campaign. Colonel Follock had others of the same description, and when the cavalry of the two farms were all assembled at Satanstoe, there were found to be no fewer than fourteen of the venerable animals. These made just three four-horse teams, besides leaving a pair for a lighter load. Old, stout lumber sleighs were bought, or found, and repaired; and Jaap, having two other blacks with him, was sent off at the head of what my father called a brigade of lumber sleighs, all of which were loaded with the spare pork and flour of the two families. The war had rendered these articles quite high; but the hogs that were slaughtered at Christmas had not yet been sold; and it was decided that Dirck and myself could not commence our career as men who had to buy and sell from the respective farms, in any manner more likely to be useful to us and to our parents, than this. As Yaap's movements were necessarily slow, he was permitted to precede Dirck and myself by two entire days, giving him time to clear the Highlands before we left Satanstoe. The negroes carried the provender for their horses, and no small portion of food, and all of the cider that was necessary for their own consumption. No one was ashamed of economizing with his slaves in this manner; the law of slavery itself existing principally as a money-making institution. I mention these little matters, that posterity may understand the conventional feeling of the colony on such points.

When every thing was ready, we had to listen to much good advice from our friends, previously to launching ourselves into the world. What Colonel Follock said to Dirck, the latter never told me; but the following was pretty much the form and substance of that which I received from my own father — the interview taking place in a little room he called his " office," or " study," as Jason used to term it.

" Here, Corny, are all the bills, or invoices, properly made out," my father commenced, handing me a small sheaf of papers; " and you will do well to consult them before you make any sales. Here are letters of introduction to several gentlemen in the army, whose acquaintance I could wish you to cultivate. This, in particular, is to my old captain, Charles Merrewether, who is now a lieutenant-colonel, and commands a battalion in the Royal Americans. You will find him of great service to you while you remain with the army, I make no doubt. Pork, they tell me, if of the quality of that you will have, ought to bring three half-joes the barrel — and you might ask that much. Should accident procure you an invitation to the table of the commander-in-chief, as may happen through Colonel Merrewether's friendship, I trust you will do full credit to the loyalty of the Littlepages. Ah! there's the flour, too; it ought to be worth two half-joes the barrel, in times like these. I have thrown in a letter or two to some of the Schuylers, with whom I served when of your age. They are firstrate people, remember, and rank among the highest families of the colonies; full of good old Van Cortlandt blood, and well crossed with the Rensselaers. Should any of them ask you about the barrel of tongues, that you will find marked T — "

"Any of whom, sir; the Schuylers, the Cortlandts, or the Rensselaers?"

"Poh! any of the sutlers, or contractors, I mean, of course. You can tell them that they were cured at home, and that you dare recommend them as fit for the commander-in-chief's own table."

Such was the character of my father's parting instructions. My mother held a different discourse.

"Corny, my beloved child," she said; "this will be an all-important journey to you. Not only are you going far from home, but you are going to a part of the country where much will be to be seen. I hope you will remember what was promised for you, by your sponsors in baptism, and also what is owing to your own good name, and that of your family. The letters you take with you, will probably introduce you to good company, and that is a great beginning to a youth. I wish you to cultivate the society of reputable females, Corny. My sex has great influence on the conduct of yours, at your time of life, and both your manners and principles will be aided by being as much with women of character as possible."

"But, mother, if we are to go any distance with the army, as both my father and Colonel Follock wish, it will not be in our power to be much in ladies' society."

"I speak of the time you will pass in and near Albany. I do not expect you will find accomplished women at Mooseridge, nor, should you really go any distance with the troops, though I see no occasion for your going with them a single foot, since you are not a soldier, nor do I suppose you will find many reputable women in the camp; but, avail yourself of every favorable opportunity to go into good company. I have procured a letter for you, from a lady of one of the great families of the country, to Madam Schuyler, who is above all other women, they tell me, in and around Albany. Her you must see, and I charge you, on your duty, to deliver this letter. It is possible, too, that Herman Mordaunt —— "

"What of Herman Mordaunt and Anneke, mother?"

"I spoke only of Herman Mordaunt himself, and did not mention Anneke, boy," answered my mother, smiling, "though I doubt not that the daughter is with the father. They left town for Albany, two months since, my sister Legge writes me, and intend to pass the summer north. I will not deceive you, Corny, so you shall hear all that your aunt has written on the subject. In the first place, she says Herman Mordaunt has gone on public service, having an especial appointment for some particular duty of importance, that is private, but which it is known will detain him near Albany, and among the northern posts, until the close of the season, though he gives out to the world he is absent on account of some land he has in Albany county. His daughter and Mary Wallace are with him, with several servants, and they have taken up with them a sleigh-load of conveniences; that looks like remaining. Now, you ought to hear the rest, my child, though I feel no apprehension when such a youth as yourself is put in competition with any other man in the colony. Yes, though your own mother, I think I may say *that!*"

"What is it, mother? — never mind me; I shall do well enough, depend on it — that is — but what is it, dear mother?"

"Why, your aunt says it is whispered among a few in town, a very few only, but whispered, that Herman Mordaunt got the appointment named, merely that he might have a pretence for taking Anneke near the ——th, in which regiment it seems there is a baronet's son, who is a sort of relative of his, and whom he wishes to marry to Anneke."

"I am sorry, then, that my aunt Legge listens to any such unworthy gossip!" I indignantly cried. "My life on it, Anneke Mordaunt never contemplated so indelicate a thing?"

"No one supposes Anneke does, or did. But fathers are not daughters, Corny; no, nor mothers neither, as I can freely say, seeing you are my only child. Herman Mordaunt may imagine all this in *his* heart, and Anneke be every thing that is innocent and delicate."

"And how can my aunt Legge's informants know what is in Herman Mordaunt's heart?"

"How?—I suppose they judge by what they find in their own, my son; a common means of coming at a neighbor's failings, though I believe virtues are rarely detected by the same process."

"Ay, and judge of others by themselves. The means may be common, mother, but they are not infallible."

"Certainly not, Corny, and that will be a ground of hope to you. Remember, my child, you can bring me no daughter I shall love half as well as I feel I can love Anneke Mordaunt. We are related too, her father's great-great-grandmother——"

"Never mind the great-great-grandmother, my dear, good, excellent, parent. After this I shall not attempt to have any secret from you. Unless Anneke Mordaunt consent to be your daughter, you will never have one."

"Do not say that, Corny, I beseech you," cried my mother, a good deal frightened. "Remember there is no accounting for tastes; the army is a formidable rival, and, after all, this Mr. Bulstrode, I think you call him, may prove as acceptable to Anneke as to her father. Do not say so cruel a thing, I entreat of you, dearest, dearest, Corny."

"It is not a minute, mother, since you said how little you apprehended for me, when opposed by any other man in the province!"

"Yes, child, but that is a very different thing from seeing you pass all your days as a heartless, comfortless old bachelor. There are fifty young women in this very colony, I could wish to see you united to, in preference to witnessing such a calamity."

"Well, mother, we will say no more about it. But is it true that Mr. Worden actually intends to be of our party?"

"Both Mr. Worden and Mr. Newcome, I believe. We shall scarcely know how to spare the first, but he conceives he has a call to accompany the army, in which there are so few chaplains; and souls are called to their last dread account so suddenly in war, that one does not know how to refuse to let him go."

My poor, confiding mother! When I look back at the past, and remember the manner in which the Reverend Mr. Worden discharged the duties of his sacred office during the campaign that succeeded, I cannot but smile at the manner in which con-

fidence manifests itself in woman. The sex have a natural
disposition to place their trust in priests, by a very simple process of transferring their own dispositions to the bosoms of
those they believe set apart for purely holy objects. Well, we
live and learn. I dare say that many are what they profess to
be, but I have lived long enough to know *all* are not. As for
Mr. Worden, he had one good point about him, at any rate.
His friends and his enemies saw the worst of him. He was no
hypocrite, but his associates saw the man very much as he was.
Still, I am far from wishing to hold up this imported minister
as a model of Christian graces for my descendants to admire.
No one can be more convinced than myself how much sectarians
are prone to substitute their own narrow notions of right and
wrong for the law of God, confounding acts that are perfectly innocent in themselves with sin; but, at the same time, I
am quite aware too, that appearances are ever to be consulted
in cases of morals, and that it is a minor virtue to be decent
in matters of manners. The Reverend Mr. Worden, whatever
might have been his position as to substantials, certainly carried the external of liberality to the verge of indiscretion.

A day or two after the conversation I have related, our party
left Satanstoe, with some *éclat*. The team belonged equally to
the Follocks and the Littlepages, one horse being the property
of my father, while the other belonged to Colonel Follock.
The sleigh, an old one new painted for the occasion, was the
sole property of the latter gentleman, and was consigned, in
mercantile phrase, to Dirck, in order to be disposed of as soon
as we should reach the end of our journey. On its exterior it
was painted a bright sky-blue, while its interior was of vermil-
lion, a color that was and is much in vogue for this species of
vehicle, inasmuch as it carries with it the idea of warmth; so,
at least, the old people say, though I will confess I never found
my toes any less cold in a sleigh thus painted, than in one
painted blue, which is usually thought a particularly cold color
to the feet.

We had three buffalo-skins, or rather two buffalo (bison) skins
and one bear-skin. The latter, being trimmed with scarlet cloth,
had a particularly warm and comfortable appearance. The
largest skin was placed on the hind-seat, and thrown over the
back of the sleigh, as a matter of course; and, though this back
was high enough to break off the wind from our heads and
necks, the skin not only covered it, but it hung two or three

feet down behind, as is becoming in a gentleman's sleigh. The other buffalo was spread in the bottom of the sleigh, as a carpet for all four, leaving an apron to come in front upon Dirck's and my lap, as a protection against the cold in that quarter. The bear-skin formed a cushion for us in front and an apron for Mr. Worden and Jason, who sat behind. Our trunks had gone on the lumber sleighs, that is, mine and Dirck's had thus been sent, while our two companions found room for theirs in the conveyance in which we went ourselves.

It was March 1st, 1758, the morning we left Satanstoe on this memorable excursion. The winter had proved as was common in our latitude, though there had been more snow along the coast than was usual. Salt air and snow do not agree well together; but I had driven in a sleigh over the Neck, most of the month of February, though there were symptoms of a thaw, and of a southerly wind the day we left home. My father observed this, and he advised me to take the road through the centre of the county, and get among the hills, as soon as possible. Not only was there always more snow in that part of the country, but it resisted the influence of a thaw much longer than that which had fallen near the sea or Sound. I got my mother's last kiss, my father's last shake of the hand, my grandfather's blessing, stepped into the sleigh, took the reins from Dirck, and drove off.

A party in a sleigh must be composed of a very sombre sort of persons, if it be not a merry one. In our case, every body was disposed to good humor; though Jason could not pass along the highway in York colony, without giving vent to his provincial, Connecticut hypercriticism. Every thing was Dutch, according to his view of matters; and when it failed of being Dutch, why, it was York colony. The doors were not in the right places; the windows were too large, when they were not too small; things had a cabbage-look; the people smelt of tobacco; and hasty-pudding was called "suppaan." But these were trifles; and being used to them, nobody paid much attention to what our Puritanical neighbor saw fit to pour out, in the humility and meekness of his soul. Mr. Worden chuckled, and urged Jason on, in the hope of irritating Dirck; but Dirck smoked through it all, with an indifference that proved how much he really despised the critic. I was the only one who resented this supercilious ignorance; but even I was often more disposed to laugh than to be angry.

The signs of a thaw increased, as we got a few miles from home; and by the time we reached White Plains, the "south wind" did not blow "softly," but freshly, and the snow in the road became sloppy, and rills of water were seen running down the hill-sides, in a way that menaced destruction to the sleighing. On we drove, however, and deeper and deeper we got among the hills, until we found not only more snow, but fewer symptoms of immediately losing it. Our first day's work carried us well into the manor of the Van Cortlandts, where we passed the night. Next morning the south wind was still blowing, sweeping over the fields of snow, charged with the salt air of the ocean; and bare spots began to show themselves on all the acclivities and hill-sides — an admonition for us to be stirring. We breakfasted in the Highlands, and in a wild and retired part of them, though in a part where snow and beaten roads were still to be found. We had escaped from the thaw, and no longer felt any uneasiness on the subject of reaching the end of our journey on runners.

The second day brought us fairly through the mountains, out on the plains of Dutchess, permitting us to sup at Fishkill. This was a thriving settlement, the people appearing to me to live in abundance, as certainly they did in peace and quiet. They made little of the war, and asked us many questions concerning the army, its commanders, its force and its objects. They were a simple, and, judging from appearances, an honest people, who troubled themselves very little with what was going on in the world.

After quitting Fishkill, we found a great change, not only in the country, but in the weather. The first was level as a whole, and was much better settled than I could have believed possible so far in the interior. As for the weather, it was quite a different climate from that we had left below the Highlands. Not only was the morning cold, cold as it had been a month earlier with us, but the snow still lay two or three feet deep on a level, and the sleighing was as good as heart could wish.

That afternoon we overtook Yaap and the brigade of lumber sleighs. Every thing had gone right, and after giving the fellow some fresh instructions, I passed him, proceeding on our route. This parting did not take place, however, until the following had been uttered between us:

"Well, Yaap," I inquired, as a sort of close to the previous discourse, "how do you like the upper counties?"

A loud negro laugh succeeded, and a repetition of the question was necessary to extort an answer.

"Lor', Masser Corny, how you t'ink I know, when dere not'in but snow to be seen!"

"There was plenty of snow in Westchester; yet, I dare say you could give some opinion of our own county!"

"'Cause I know him, sah; inside and out, and all over, Masser Corny."

"Well; but you can see the houses, and orchards, and barns, and fences, and other things of that sort."

"'Em pretty much like our'n, Masser Corny; why do you bother nigger with sich question?"

Here another burst of loud, hearty "yah — yah — yahs" succeeded; and Yaap had his laugh out before another word could be got out of him, when I put the question a third time.

"Well, den, Masser Corny, sin' you *will* know, dis is my mind. Dis country is oncomparable with our ole county, sah. De houses seem mean, de barns look empty, de fences be low, and de niggers, ebbery one of 'em, look cold, sah — yes, sah — 'ey look berry cold!"

As a "cold negro" was a most pitiable object in negro eyes, I saw by this summary that Yaap had commenced his travels in much the same temper of superciliousness as Jason Newcome. It struck me as odd at the time; but since that day, I have ascertained that this feeling is a very general travelling companion for those who set out on their first journey.

We passed our third night at a small hamlet called Rhinebeck, in a settlement in which many German names were to be found. Here we were travelling through the vast estates of the Livingstons, a name well known in our colonial history. We breakfasted at Claverack, and passed through a place called Kinderhook — a village of Low Dutch origin and some antiquity. That night we succeeded in coming near Albany, by making a very hard day's drive of it. There was no village at the place where we slept; but the house was a comfortable and exceedingly neat Dutch tavern. After quitting Fishkill we had seen more or less of the river, until we passed Claverack, where we took our leave of it. It was covered with ice, and sleighs were moving about it, with great apparent security; but we did not like to try it. Our whole party preferred a solid highway, in which there was no danger of the bottom dropping out.

As we were now about to enter Albany, the second largest

town in the colony, and one of the largest inland towns in the whole country, if such a word can properly be given to a place that lies on a navigable river, it was thought necessary to make some few arrangements, in order to do it decently. Instead of quitting the tavern at daylight, therefore, as had been our practice previously, we remained until after breakfast, having recourse to our trunks in the mean time. Dirck, Jason, and myself, had provided ourselves with fur caps for the journey, with ear-laps and other contrivances for keeping one's self warm. The cap of Dirck, and my own, were of very fine martens' skin, and as they were round and high, and each was surmounted with a handsome tail that fell down behind, they had both a smart and military air. I thought I had never seen Dirck look so nobly and well, as he did in his cap, and I got a few compliments on my own air in mine, though they were only from my mother, who, I think would feel disposed to praise me, even if I looked wretchedly. The cap of Jason was better suited to his purse, being lower, and of fox-skins, though it had a tail also. Mr. Worden had declined travelling in a cap, as unsuited to his holy office. Accordingly, he wore his clerical beaver, which differed a little from the ordinary cocked hats that we all wore, as a matter of course, though not so much as to be very striking.

All of us had overcoats well trimmed with furs, mine and Dirck's being really handsome, with trimmings of marten, while those of our companion were less showy and expensive. On a consultation, Dirck and I decided that it was better taste to enter the town in travellers' dresses, than to enter it in any other, and we merely smartened up a little, in order to appear as gentlemen. The case was very different with Jason. According to his idea a man should wear his best clothes on a journey, and I was surprised to see him appear at breakfast in black breeches, striped woollen stockings, large plated buckles in his shoes, and a coat that I well knew he religiously reserved for high-days and holidays. This coat was of a light pea-green color, and but little adapted to the season; but Jason had not much notion of the fitness of things, in general, in matters of taste. Dirck and myself wore our ordinary snuff-colored coats, under our furs; but Jason threw aside all the overcoats, when we came near Albany, in order to enter the place in his best. Fortunately for him, the day was mild, and there was a bright sun to send its warm rays through the pea-green covering, to

keep his blood from chilling. As for Mr. Worden, he wore a
cloak of black cloth, laying aside all the furs but a tippet and
muff, both of which he used habitually in cold weather.

In this guise, then, we left the tavern, about nine in the
morning, expecting to reach the banks of the river about ten.
Nor were we disappointed; the roads being excellent, a light
fall of snow having occurred in the night, to freshen the track.
It was an interesting moment to us all, when the spires and
roofs of that ancient town, Albany, first appeared in view!
We had journeyed from near the southern boundary of the
colony, to a place that stood at no great distance from its frontier
settlements on the north. The town itself formed a pleasing
object, as we approached it, on the opposite side of the Hudson.
There it lay, stretching along the low land on the margin of the
stream, and on its western bank, sheltered by high hills, up the
side of which the principal street extended, for the distance of
fully a quarter of a mile. Near the head of this street stood
the fort, and we saw a brigade paraded in the open ground near
it, wheeling and marching about. The spires of two churches
were visible, one, the oldest, being seated on the low land, in
the heart of the place, and the other on the height at no great
distance from the fort; or about half-way up the acclivity,
which forms the barrier to the inner country, on the side of the
river. Both these buildings were of stone, of course, shingle
tenements being of very rare occurrence in the colony of New
York, though common enough further east.*

I will own that not one of our party liked the idea of crossing the Hudson, in a loaded sleigh, on the ice, and that in the
month of March. There were no streams about us to be crossed
in this mode, nor was the cold exactly sufficient to render such

---

* In nothing was the difference of character between the people of New England
and those of the middle colonies more apparent, than in the nature of the dwellings.
In New York, for instance, men worth thousands dwelt in humble, low (usually one
story) dwellings of stone, having window-shutters, frequently within as well as without, and the other appliances of comfort; whereas the farmer farther east was seldom satisfied, though his means were limited, unless he lived in a house as good as
his neighbor's; and the strife dotted the whole of their colonies with wooden buildings, of great pretensions for the age, that rarely had even exterior shutters, and
which frequently stood for generations unfinished. The difference was not of Dutch
origin, for it was just as apparent in New Jersey or Pennsylvania as in New York and
I think it may be attributed to a very obvious consequence of a general equality of
condition, a state of society in which no one is content to wear even the semblance
of poverty, but those who cannot by any means prevent it; but in which all strive
to get as high as possible, in appearances at least. — EDITOR.

a transit safe, and we felt as the inexperienced would be apt to feel in circumstances so unpleasant. I must do Jason the credit to admit that he showed more plain, practical good sense than any of us determining our course in the end by his view of the matter. As for Mr. Worden, however, nothing could induce him to venture on the ice in a sleigh, or *near* a sleigh, though Jason remonstrated in the following terms —

"Now, look here, Rev. Mr. Worden" — Jason seldom omitted any body's *title* — "you've only to turn your eyes on the river to see it is dotted with sleighs, far and near. There are highways north and south, and if that be the place where the crossing is at the town, it is more like a thoroughfare than a spot that is risky. In my judgment, these people who live hereabouts ought to know whether there is any danger or not."

Obvious as was this truth, "Rev. Mr. Worden" made us stop on terra firma, and permit him to quit the sleigh, that he might cross the river on foot. Jason ventured a hint or two about faith and its virtues, as he stripped himself to the peagreen, in order to enter the town in proper guise, throwing aside every thing that concealed his finery. As for Dirck and myself, we kept our seats manfully, and trotted on the river at the point where we saw sleighs and foot-passengers going and coming in some numbers. The Rev. Mr. Worden, however, was not content to take the beaten path, for he knew there was no more security in being out on the ice, *near* a sleigh, than there was in being *in* it, so he diverged from the road, which crossed at the ferry, striking diagonally athwart the river toward the wharves of the place.

It seemed to me to be a sort of holiday among the young and idle, one sleigh passing us after another, filled with young men and maidens, all sparkling with the excitement of the moment, and gay with youth and spirits. We passed no less than four of these sleighs on the river, the jingling of the bells, the quick movement, the laughter and gayety, and the animation of the whole scene, far exceeding any thing of the sort I had ever before witnessed. We were nearly across the river, when a sleigh more handsomely equipped than any we had yet seen, dashed down the bank, and came whirling past us like a comet. It was full of ladies, with the exception of one gentleman, who stood erect in front, driving. I recognized Bulstrode, in furs like all of us, capped and *tailed*, if not plumed, while among the half-dozen pairs of brilliant eyes that were turned with their owners' smiling faces on us, I saw one which never could be forgotten by me, that belonged to Anneke Mordaunt. I question if we were recognized, for the passage was like that of a meteor; but I could not avoid turning to gaze after the gay party. This change of position enabled me to be a witness of a very amusing consequence of Mr. Worden's experiment. A sleigh was coming in our direction, and the party in it seeing one who was known for a clergyman, *walking* on the ice, turned aside and approached him on a gallop, in order to offer the courtesy of a seat to a man of his sacred profession. Our divine heard the bells, and fearful of having a sleigh so near him, he commenced a downright flight, pursued by the people in the sleigh, as fast as their horses could follow. Every body on the ice pulled up to gaze in wonder at this strange spectacle, until the whole party reached the shore, the Rev. Mr. Worden pretty well blown, as the reader may suppose.

CHAPTER XI

"Bid physicians talk our veins to temper.
And with an argument new-set a pulse,
Then think, my lord, of reasoning unto love."

YOUNG.

As the road from the ferry into the town ran along the bank
of the river, we reached the point where the Rev. Mr. Worden
had landed precisely at the same instant with his pursuers, who
had been obliged to make a little circuit, in order to get off the
ice. I do not know which party regarded the other in the
greatest astonishment — the hunted, or the hunters. The sleigh
had in it two fine-looking young fellows, that spoke English
with a slight Dutch accent, and three young women, whose
bright coal-black eyes betokened surprise a little mitigated by a
desire to laugh. Seeing that we were all strangers, I suppose,
and that we claimed the runaway as belonging to our party,
one of the young men raised his cap very respectfully, and
opened the discourse by asking in a very civil tone —

"What ails the reverent gentleman, to make him run so
fast?"

"Run!" exclaimed Mr. Worden, whose lungs had been
playing like a blacksmith's bellows — "Run! and who would
not run to save himself from being drowned?"

"Drowned!" repeated the young Dutchman, looking round
at the river, as if to ascertain whether the ice were actually
moving — "why, does the Dominie suppose there was any danger of *that?*"

As Mr. Worden's bellows were still hard at work, I explained
to the young Albanians that we were strangers just arrived from
the vicinity of New York; that we were unaccustomed to frozen
rivers, and had never crossed one on the ice before; that our
reverend companion had chosen to walk at a distance from the
road, in order to be in less danger should any team break in,
and that he had naturally run to avoid their sleigh when he
saw it approaching. The Albanians heard this account in respectful silence, though I could see the two young men casting

144

sly glances at each other, and that even the ladies had some
little difficulty in altogether suppressing their smiles. When it
was through, the oldest of the Dutchmen — a fine, dare-devil,
roystering-looking fellow of four or five-and-twenty, whose dress
and mien, however, denoted a person of the upper class — begged
a thousand pardons for his mistake, quitting his sleigh and insisting on having the honors of shaking hands with the whole
of us. His name was "Ten Eyck," he said; "Guert Ten
Eyck," and he asked permission, as we were strangers, of doing
the honor of Albany to us. Every body in the place knew him,
which, as we afterward ascertained, was true enough, for he
had just as much reputation for fun and frolic as at all comported with respectability; keeping along, as it were, on the
very verge of the pale of reputable people, without being thrown
entirely out of it. The young females with him were a shade
below his own natural position in society, tolerating his frolics
on account of this circumstance, aided as it was by a singularly
manly face and person, a hearty and ready laugh, a full purse,
and possibly by the secret hope of being the happy individual
who was designed by Providence to convert "a reformed rake
into the best of husbands." In a word, he was always welcome with them, when those a little above them felt more disposed to frown.

Of course, all this was unknown to us at the time, and we
accepted Guert Ten Eyck's proffers of civility in the spirit in
which they were offered. He inquired at what tavern we
intended to stop, and promised an early call. Then, shaking
us all round by the hand again with great cordiality, he took
his leave. His companion doffed a very dashing, high, wolf-
skin cap to us, and the black-eyed trio,\ on the hind seat, smiled
graciously, and away they drove at a furious rate, startling all
the echoes of Albany with their bells. By this time Mr. Worden was seated, and we followed more moderately, our team
having none of the Dutch courage of a pair of horses fresh from
the stable. Such were the circumstances under which we made
our entrance into the ancient city of Albany. We were all
in hopes the little affair of the chase would soon be forgotten,
for no one likes to be associated with a ridiculous circumstance,
but we counted without our host. Guert Ten Eyck was not
of a temperament to let such an affair sleep, but, as I afterward ascertained, he told it with the laughing embellishments
that belonged to his reckless character, until, in turn, the Rev.

Mr. Worden came to be known, throughout all that region, by
the nickname of the "Loping Dominie."

The reader may be assured our eyes were about us, as we
drove through the streets of the second town in the colony.
We were not unaccustomed to houses constructed in the Dutch
style, in New York, though the English mode of building had
been most in vogue there, for half a century. It was not so
with Albany, which remained, essentially, a Dutch town in 1758.*
We heard little beside Dutch, as we passed along. The women
scolded their children in Low Dutch, a use, by the way, for which
the language appears singularly well adapted; the negroes sang
Dutch songs; the men called to each other in Dutch, and Dutch
rang in our ears, as we walked our horses through the streets,
toward the tavern. There were many soldiers about, and other
proofs of the presence of a considerable military force were not
wanting; still the place struck me as very provincial and peculiar,
after New York. Nearly all the houses were built with their
gables to the streets, and each had heavy wooden Dutch stoops,
with seats, at its door. A few had small court-yards in front,
and here and there was a building of somewhat more pretension
than usual. I do not think, however, there were fifty houses in
the place that were built with their gables off the line of the
streets.

We were no sooner housed, than Dirck and I sallied forth to
look at the place. Here we were, in one of the oldest towns of
America; a place that could boast of much more than a century's
existence, and it was natural to feel curious to look about one.
Our inn was in the principal street — that which led up the hill
toward the fort. This street was a wide avenue, that quite put
Broadway out of countenance, so far as mere width was concerned. The streets that led out of it, however, were principally
little better than lanes, as if the space that had been given to
two or three of the main streets had been taken off of the remainder. The High street, as we English would call it, was oc-

---

* The population of Albany could not have reached four thousand in 1758. Its
Dutch character remained down to the close of this century, with gradual changes.
The writer can remember when quite as much Dutch as English was heard in the
streets of Albany, though it has now nearly disappeared. The present population
must be near forty thousand.

Mr. Littlepage's description was doubtless correct at the time he wrote; but
Albany would now be considered a first-class country town in Europe. It has much
better claims to compare with the towns of the old world, in this character, than
New York has to compare with their capitals. — EDITOR.

cupied by sleds filled with wood for sale; sleds loaded with geese, turkeys, tame and wild, and poultry of all sorts; sleds with venison, still in the skin, piled up in heaps, etc. — all these eatables being collected, in unusual quantities as we were told, to meet the extraordinary demand created by the different military messes. Deer were no strangers to us; for Long Island was full of all sorts of game, as were the upper counties of New Jersey. Even Westchester, old and well settled as it had become, was not yet altogether clear of deer, and nothing was easier than to knock over a buck in the Highlands. Nevertheless, I had never seen venison, wild turkeys and sturgeons, in such quantities as they were to be seen that day in the principal street of Albany.

The crowd collected in this street, the sleighs that were whirling past, filled with young men and maidens, the incessant jingling of bells, the spluttering and jawing in Low Dutch, the hearty English oaths of serjeants and sutlers'-men and cooks of messes, the loud laughs of the blacks, and the beauty of the cold, clear day, altogether produced some such effect on me, as I had experienced when I went to the theatre. Not the least striking picture of the scene, was Jason, in the middle of the street, gaping about him, in the cocked-hat, the pea-green coat, and the striped woollen stockings.

Dirck and myself naturally examined the churches. These were two, as has been said already — one for the Dutch, and the other for the English. The first was the oldest. It stood at the point where the two principal streets crossed each other, and in the centre of the street, leaving sufficient passages all round it. The building was square, with a high, pointed roof, having a belfry and weathercock on its apex; windows, with diamond panes and painted glass, and a porch that was well suited both to the climate and to appearances.*

We were examining this structure, when Guert Ten Eyck accosted us, in his frank, off-hand way —

" Your servant, Mr. Littlepage; your servant, Mr. Follock," he cried, again shaking each cordially by the hand. " I was on the way to the tavern to look you up, when I accidentally saw you here. A few gentlemen of my acquaintance, who are in the habit of supping together in the winter time, meet for the last

---

* There were two churches of this character built on this spot. The second, much larger than the first, but of the same form, was built *round* the other, in which service was held to the last, when it was literally thrown out of the windows of its successor. The last edifice disappeared about forty years since. — EDITOR.

jollification of the season to-night, and they have all express't a wish to have the pleasure of your company. I hope you will allow me to say you will come? We meet at nine, sup at ten, and break up at twelve, quite regularly, in a very sedate and prudent manner."

There was something so frank and cordial, so simple and straightforward in this invitation, that we did not know how to decline it. We both knew that the name of Ten Eyck was respectable in the colony; our new acquaintance was well dressed, he seemed to be in good company when we first met him, his sleigh and horses had been actually of a more dashing stamp than usual, and his own attire had all the peculiarities of a gentleman's, with the addition of something even more decided and knowing than was common. It is true, the style of these peculiarities was not exactly such as I had seen in the air, manners and personal decorations of those of Billings and Harris; but they were none the less striking, and none the less attractive; the two Englishmen being "macaronis" from London, and Ten Eyck being a "buck" of Albany.

"I thank you, very heartily, Mr. Ten Eyck," I answered, "both for myself and for my friend — "

"And will let me come for you at half-past eight, to show you the way?"

"Why, yes, sir; I was about to say as much, if it be not giving you too much trouble."

"Do not speak of tr-r-ouple" — this last word will give a very good notion of Guert's accent, which I cannot stop to imitate at all times in writing — "and do not say your *fre'nt*, but your *fre'ntz*."

"As to the two that are not here, I cannot positively answer; yonder, however, is one that can speak for himself."

"I see him, Mr. Littlepage, and will answer for *him*, on my own account. Depend on it, *he* will come. But the Dominie — he has a hearty look, and can help eat a turkey, and swallow a glass of goot Madeira — I think I can rely on. A man cannot take all that active exercise without food."

"Mr. Worden is a very companionable man, and is excellent company at a supper table. I will communicate your invitation, and hope to be able to prevail on him to be of the party."

"T'at is enough, sir," returned Ten Eyck, or Guert, as I shall henceforth call him, in general; "vere dere ist a vill, dere ist a vay." Guert frequently broke out, in such specimens of broken

English, while at other times he would speak almost as well as any of us. "So Got pless you, my dear Mr. Littlepage, and make us lasting friends. I like your countenance, and my eye never deceives me in these matters."

Here, Guert shook us both by the hand again, most cordially, and left us. Dirck and I next strolled up the hill, going as high as the English church, which stood also in the centre of the principal street, an imposing and massive edifice in stone. With the exception of Mother Trinity in New York, this was the largest, and altogether the most important edifice devoted to the worship of my own church I had ever seen. In Westchester, there were several of Queen Anne's churches, but none on a scale to compare with this. Our small edifices were usually without galleries, steeples, towers, or bells; while St. Peter's, Albany, if not actually St. Peter's, Rome, was a building of which a man might be proud. A little to our surprise, we found the Reverend Mr. Worden and Mr. Jason Newcome had met at the door of this edifice, having sent a boy to the sexton in quest of the key. In a minute or two, the urchin returned, bringing not only the key of the church, but the excuses of the sexton for not coming himself. The door was opened, and we went in.

I have always admired the decorous and spiritual manner in which the Rev. Mr. Worden entered a building that had been consecrated to the services of the Deity. I know not how to describe it; but it proved how completely he had been drilled in the decencies of his profession. Off came his hat, of course; and his manner, however facetious and easy it may have been the moment before, changed on the instant to gravity and decorum. Not so with Jason. He entered St. Peter's, Albany, with exactly the same indifferent and cynical air with which he had seemed to regard every thing but money, since he entered " York colony." Usually, he wore his cocked-hat on the back of his head, thereby lending himself a lolloping, negligent, and, at the same time, defying air; but I observed that, as we all uncovered, he brought his own beaver up over his eyebrows, in a species of military bravado. To uncover to a church, in his view of the matter, was a sort of idolatry; there might be images about, for any thing he knew; "and a man could never be enough on his guard ag'n being carried away by such evil deceptions," as he had once before answered to a remonstrance of mine, for wearing his hat in our own parish church.

I found the interior of St. Peter's quite as imposing as its exterior. Three of the pews were canopied, having coats-of-arms on their canopies. These, the boy told us, belonged to the Van Rensselaer and Schuyler families. All these were covered with black cloth, in mourning for some death in those ancient families, which were closely allied. I was very much struck with the dignified air that these patrician seats gave the house of God.* There were also several hatchments suspended against the walls; some being placed there in commemoration of officers of rank, from home, who had died in the king's service in the colony; and others to mark the deaths of some of the more distinguished of our own people.

Mr. Worden expressed himself well pleased with appearances of things, in and about this building; though Jason regarded all with ill-concealed disgust.

"What is the meaning of them pews with tops to them, Corny?" the pedagogue whispered me, afraid to encounter the parson's remarks, by his own criticism.

"They are the pews of families of distinction in this place, Mr. Newcome; and the canopies, or tops, as you call them, are honorable signs of their owners' conditions."

"Do you think their owners will sit under such coverings in paradise, Corny?" continued Jason, with a sneer.

"It is impossible for me to say, sir; it is probable, however, the just will not require any such mark to distinguish them from the unjust."

"Let me see," said Jason, looking round and affecting to count; "there are just three — bishop, priest, and deacon, I suppose. Waal, there's a seat for each, and they can be comfortable *here*, whatever may turn up *herea'ter*."

I turned away, unwilling to dispute the point, for I knew it was as hopeless to expect that a Danbury man would feel like a

---

* I cannot recollect one of these canopied pews that is now standing, in this part of the Union. The last, of my knowledge, were in St. Mark's, New York, and, I believe belonged to the Stuyvesants, the patron family of that church. They were taken down when that building was repaired, a few years since. This is one of the most innocent of all our innovations of this character. Distinctions in the house of God are opposed to the very spirit of the Christian religion; and it were far more fitting that pews should be altogether done away with, the true mode of assembling under the sacred roof, than that men should be classed even at the foot of the altar.

It may be questioned if a hatchment is now hung up, either on the dwelling, or in a church, in any part of America. They were to be seen, however, in the early part of the present century. Whenever any such traces of ancient usages are met with among us, by the traveller from the old world, he is apt to mistake them for the shadows "that coming events cast before," instead of those of the past. — EDITOR.

New Yorker, on such a subject, as it was to expect that a New York could be made to adopt Danbury sentiments. As for the *argument*, however, I have heard others of pretty much the same calibre often urged against the three orders of the ministry.

On quitting St. Peter's, I communicated the invitation of Guert Ten Eyck to Mr. Worden, and urged him to be of the party. I could see that the notion of a pleasant supper was any thing but unpleasant to the missionary. Still he had his scruples, inasmuch as he had not yet seen his reverend brother who had the charge of St. Peter's, did not know exactly the temper of his mind, and was particularly desirous of officiating for him, in the presence of the principal personages of the place, on the approaching Sunday. He had written a note to the chaplain; for the person who had the cure of the Episcopalians held that rank in the army, St. Peter's being as much of an official chapel as a parish church; and he must have an interview with that individual before he could decide. Fortunately, as we descended the street, toward our inn, we saw the very person in question. The marks of the common office that these two divines bore about their persons in their dress, sufficed to make them known to each other at a glance. In five minutes, they had shaken hands, heard each man's account of himself, had given and accepted the invitation to preach, and were otherwise on free and easy terms. Mr. Worden was to dine in the fort, with the chaplain. We then walked forward toward the tavern.

" By the way, Mr. ——," said Mr. Worden in a parenthesis of the discourse, " the family of Ten Eyck is quite respectable, here in Albany."

" Very much so, sir — a family that is held in much esteem. I shall count on your assisting me, morning and evening, my dear Mr. Worden."

It is surprising how the clergy do depend on each other for " assistance! "

" Make your arrangements accordingly, my good brother — I am quite fresh, and have brought a good stock of sermons; not knowing how much might remain to be done in the army. Corny," in a half-whisper, " you can let our new friends know that I will sup with them; and, harkee — just drop a hint to them, that I am none of your Puritans."

Here, then, we found every thing in a very fair way to bring us all out in society, within the first two hours of our arrival.

Mr. Worden was engaged to preach the next day but one; and he was engaged to supper that same day. All looked promising, and I hurried on in order to ascertain if Guert Ten Eyck had made his promised call. As before, he was met in the street, and the acceptance of the Dominie was duly communicated. Guert seemed highly pleased at this success; and he left me, promising to be punctual to his hour. In the mean time we had to dine.

The dinner proved a good one; and, as Mr. Worden remarked, it was quite lucky that the principal dish was venison, a meat that was so easy of digestion, as to promise no great obstacle to the accommodation of the supper. He should dine on venison, therefore; and he advised all three of us to follow his example. But certain Dutch dishes attracted the eye and taste of Dirck; while Jason had alighted on a hash, of some sort or other, that he did not quit until he had effectually disposed of it. As for myself, I confess, the venison was so much to my taste, that I stuck by the parson. We had our wine, too, and left the table early, in order not to interfere with the business of the night.

After dinner it was proposed to walk out in a body, to make a further examination of the place, and to see if we could not fall in with an army contractor, who might be disposed to relieve Dirck and myself of some portion of our charge. Luck again threw us in the way of Guert Ten Eyck, who seemed to live in the public street. In the course of a brief conversation that took place, as a passing compliment, I happened to mention a wish to ascertain where one might dispose of a few horses, and of two or three sleigh-loads of flour, pork, etc., etc.

"My dear Mr. Littlepage," said Guert, with a frank smile and a friendly shake of the hand, "I am delighted that you have mentioned these matters to me; I can take you to the very man you wish to see; a heavy army-contractor, who is buying up every thing of the sort he can lay his hands on."

Of course, I was as much delighted as Guert could very well be, and left my party to proceed at once to the contractor's office, with the greatest alacrity; Dirck accompanying me. As we went along, our new friend advised us not to be very backward in the way of price since the king paid in the long run.

"Rich dealers ought to pay well," he added; "and, I can tell you, as a useful thing to know, that orders came on, no later than yesterday, to buy up every thing of the sort that offered. Put sleigh and harness, at once, all in a heap, on the king's servants."

I thought the idea not a bad one, and promised to profit by it. Guert was as good as his word, and I was properly introduced to the contractor. My business was no sooner mentioned, than I was desired to send a messenger round to the stables, in order that my conveyance, team, etc., might make their appearance. As for the articles that were still on the road, I had very little trouble. The contractor knew my father, and he no sooner heard that Mr. Littlepage, of Satanstoe, was the owner of the provisions, than he purchased the whole on the guaranty of his name. For the pork I was to receive two half-joes the barrel, and for the flour one. This was a good sale. The horses would be taken, if serviceable, as the contractor did not question, as also the lumber sleighs, though the prices could not be set until the different animals and objects were seen and examined.

It is amazing what war will do for commerce, as well as what it does against it! The demand for every thing that the judgment of my father had anticipated, was so great, that the contractor told me very frankly the sleighs would not be unloaded at Albany at all, but would be sent on north, on the line of the expected route of the army, so as to anticipate the disappearance of the snow and the breaking up of the roads.

"You shall be paid liberally for your teams, harness and sleighs," he continued, "though no sum can be named until I see them. These are not times when operations are to be retarded on account of a few joes more or less, for the king's service must go on. I very well know that Major Littlepage and Colonel Follock both understand what they are about, and have sent us the right sort of things. The horses are very likely a little old, but are good for one campaign; better than if younger, perhaps, and were they colts, we could get no more than that out of them. These movements in the woods destroy man and beast, and cost mints of money. Ah! there comes your team."

Sure enough, the sleigh drove round from the tavern, and we all went out to look at the horses, etc. Guert now became an important person. On the subject of horses he was accounted an oracle, and he talked, moved, and acted like one in all respects. The first thing he did was to step up to the animal's head, and to look into the mouth of each in succession. The knowing way in which this was done, the coolness of the interference, and the fine manly form of the intruder, would have given him at once a certain importance and a connection with what was going on, had not his character for judgment in horse-flesh been well established, far and near, in that quarter of the country.

"Upon my word, wonderfully good mouths! " exclaimed Guert, when through. "You must have your grain ground, Mr. Littlepage, or the teeth never could have stood it so well! "

"What age do you call the animals, Guert?" demanded the contractor.

"That is not so easily told, sir. I admit that they are aged horses; but they may be eight, or nine, and even ten, as for what can be told by their teeth. By the looks of their limbs, I should judge they might be nine, coming grass."

"The near horse is eleven," I said, "and the off horse is supposed to be —— "

"Poh! poh! Littlepage," interruped Guert, making signs to me to be quiet, "you may *think* the off horse ten, but I should place him at about nine. His teeth are excellent, and there is not even a wind-gall on his legs. There is a cross of the Flemish in that beast."

"Well, and what do you say the pair are worth, Master Guert? " demanded the contractor, who seemed to have a certain confidence in his friend's judgment, notwithstanding the recklessness and freedom of his manner. "Twelve half-joes for them both? "

"That will never do, Mr. Contractor," answered Guert, shaking his head. "In times like these, such stout animals, and beasts too in such heart and condition, ought to bring fifteen."

"Fifteen let it be then, if Mr. Littlepage assents. Now for the sleigh, and harness, and skins. I suppose Mr. Littlepage will part with the skins too, as he can have no use for them without the sleigh? "

"Have *you*, Mr. Contractor? " asked Guert, a little abruptly. "That bear-skin fills my eye beautifully, and if Mr. Littlepage will take a guinea for it, here is his money."

As this was a fair price, it was accepted, though I pressed the skin on Guert as a gift, in remembrance of our accidental acquaintance. This offer, however, he respectfully, but firmly resisted. And here I will take occasion to say, lest the reader be misled by what is met with in works of fiction, and other light and vain productions, that in all my dealings, and future connection with Guert, I found him strictly honorable in money matters. It is true, I would not have purchased a horse on his recommendation, if he owned the beast; but we all know how the best men yield in their morals when they come to deal in horses. I should scarcely have expected Mr. Worden to be orthodox, in making such bargains. But on all other subjects connected with money, Guert Ten Eyck was one of the honestest fellows I ever dealt with.

The contractor took the sleigh, harness, and skins, at seven more half-joes; making twenty-three for the whole outfit. This was certainly receiving two half-joes more than my father had expected; and I owed the gain of sixteen dollars to Guert's friendly and bold interference. As soon as the prices were settled, the money was paid me in good Spanish gold; and I handed over to Dirck the portion that properly fell to his father's share. As it was understood that the remaining horses, sleighs, harness, provisions, etc., were to be taken at an appraisal, the instant they arrived, this hour's work relieved my friend and myself from any further trouble on the subject of the property entrusted to our care. And a relief it was to be so well rid of a responsibility that was as new as it was heavy to each of us.

The reader will get some idea of the pressure of affairs, and how necessary it was felt to be on the alert in the month of March — a time of the year when twenty-four hours might bring about a change in the season — by the circumstance that the contractor sent his new purchase to be loaded up from the door of his office, with orders to proceed on north, with supplies for a depôt that he was making as near to Lake George as was deemed prudent; the French being in force at Ticonderoga and Crown Point, two posts at the head of Champlain; a distance considerably less than a hundred miles from Albany. Whatever was forwarded as far as Lake George while the snow lasted could then be sent on with the army, in the contemplated operations of the approaching summer, by means of the two lakes, and their northern outlets.

"Well, Mr. Littlepage," cried Guert, heartily; "*that* affair is well disposed of. You got goot prices, and I hope the king has got goot horses. They are a little venerable, perhaps; but what of that? The army would knock up the best and youngest beast in the colony, in one campaign in the woots; and it can do no more with the oldest and worst. Shall we walk rount into the main street, gentlemen? This is about the hour when the young ladies are apt to start for their afternoon sleighing."

"I suppose the ladies of Albany are remarkable for their beauty, Mr. Ten Eyck," I rejoined, wishing to say something agreeable to a man who seemed so desirous of serving me. "The specimens I saw in crossing the river this morning, would induce a stranger to think so."

"Sir," replied Guert, walking toward the great avenue of the town, "we are content with our ladies, in general, for they are charming, warm-hearted and amiable; but there has been an arrival among us this winter, from your part of the colony, that has almost melted the ice on the Hudson! "

My heart beat quicker, for I could only think of one being of her sex, as likely to produce such a sensation. Still, I could not abstain from making a direct inquiry on the subject.

"From *our* part of the colony, Mr. Ten Eyck! — You mean from New York, probably? "

"Yes, sir, as a matter of course. There are several beautiful English women who have come up with the army; but no colonel, major, or captain, has brought such paragons with him as Herman Mordaunt, a gentleman who may be known to you by name? "

"Personally too, sir. Herman Mordaunt is even a kinsman of Dirck Follock, my friend here."

"Then is Mr. Follock to be envied, since he can call cousin with so charming a young lady as Anneke Mordaunt."

"True sir, most true! " I interrupted, eagerly; "Anne Mordaunt passes for the sweetest girl in York! "

"I do not know that I should go quite as far as that, Mr. Littlepage," returned Guert, moderating his warmth, in a manner that a little surprised me, though his handsome face still glowed with honest, natural admiration; "since there is a Miss Mary Wallace in her company, that is quite as much thought of, here in Albany, as her friend Miss Mordaunt."

Mary Wallace! The idea of comparing the silent, thoughtful, excellent though she were, Mary Wallace, with Anneke could never have crossed my mind. Still, Mary Wallace certainly *was* a very charming girl. She was even handsome; had a placid, saint-like character of countenance that had often struck me, singular beauty and development of form, and, in any other company than that of Anneke's, might well have attracted the first attention of the most fastidious beholder.

And Guert Ten Eyck admired — perhaps loved, Mary Wallace! Here, then, was fresh evidence how much we are all inclined to love our opposites; to form close friendships with those who resemble us least, principles excepted, for virtue can never cling to vice, and how much more interest novelty possesses in the human breast, than the repetition of things to which we are accustomed. No two beings could be less alike than Mary Wallace and Guert Ten Eyck; yet the last admired the first.

"Miss Wallace is a very charming young lady, Mr. Ten Eyck," I rejoined, as soon as wonder would allow me to answer, "and I am not surprised you speak of her in terms of so much admiration."

Guert stopped short in the street, looked me full in the face with an expression of truth that could not well be feigned, squeezed my hand fervently, and rejoined with a strange frankness, that I could not have imitated, to be master of all I saw —

"Admiration, Mr. Littlepage, is not a wort strong enough for what I feel for Mary! I would marry her in the next hour, and love and cherish her for all the rest of my life. I worship *her*, and love the earth she treads on."

"And you have told her this, Mr. Ten Eyck?"

"Fifty times, sir. She has now been two months in Albany, and my love was secured within the first week. I offered myself too soon, I fear; for Mary is a prutent, sensible young woman, and girls of that character are apt to distrust the youth who is too quick in his advances. They like to be served, sir, for seven years and seven years, as Joseph served for Potiphar."

"You mean, most likely, Mr. Ten Eyck, as Jacob served for Rachel."

"Well, sir, it may be as you say, dough I t'ink that in our Dutch Bibles, it stands as Joseph served for Potiphar — but you know what I mean, Mr. Littlepage. If you wish to see the ladies, and will come with me, I will go to a place where Herman Mordaunt's sleigh invariably passes at this hour, for the ladies almost live in the air. I never miss the occasion of seeing them."

I had now a clue to Guert's being so much in the street. He was as good as his word, however, for he took a stand near the Dutch church, where I soon had the happiness of seeing Anneke and her friend driving past, on their evening's excursion. How blooming and lovely the former looked! Mary Wallace's eye turned, I fancied understandingly, to the corner where Guert had placed himself, and her color deepened as she returned his bow. But, the start of surprise, the smile, and the lightening eye of Anneke, as she unexpectedly saw me, filled my soul with delight almost too great to be borne.

CHAPTER XII

"Then the wine it gets into their heads,
    And turns the wit out of its station;
Nonsense gets in, in its stead,
    And their puns are now all botheration."
                    THE PUNNING SOCIETY.

GUERT TEN EYCK looked at me expressively, as the sleigh whirled round an angle of the building and disappeared. He then proposed that we should proceed. On ascending the main street, I was not a little surprised at discovering the sort of amusement that was going on, and in which it seemed to me all the youths of the place were engaged. By youths, I do not mean lads of twelve and fourteen, but young men of eighteen and twenty, the amusement being that of sliding down hill, or "coasting," as I am told it is called in Boston. The acclivity was quite sharp, and of sufficient length to give an impetus to the sled, that was set in motion at a short distance above the English church; an impetus that would carry it past the Dutch church — a distance that was somewhat more than a quarter of a mile. The hand-sleds employed were of a size and construction suited to the dimensions of those that used them; and, as a matter of course, there was no New Yorker that had not learned how to govern the motion of one of these vehicles, even when gliding down the steepest descent, with the nicest delicacy and greatest ease. As children, or boys as late in life as fourteen even, every male in the colony, and not a few of the females, had acquired this art; but this was the first place in which I had ever known adults to engage in the sport. The accidental circumstance of a hill's belonging to the principal street, joined to the severity of the winters, had rendered an amusement suited to grown people, that, elsewhere, was monopolized by the children.

By the time we had ascended as high as the English church, a party of young officers came down from the fort, gay with the glass and the song of the regimental mess. No sooner did they reach the starting-point, than three or four of the more

158

youthful got possession of as many sleds, and off they went, like
the shot starting from its gun. Nobody seemed to think it
strange; but, on the contrary, I observed that the elderly people
looked on with a complacent gravity, that seemed to say how
vividly the sight recalled the days of their own youth. I cannot say, however, that the strangers succeeded very well in man-
aging their sleds, generally meeting with some stoppage before
they reached the bottom of the hill.

"Will you take a slide, Mr. Littlepage?" Guert demanded,
with a courteous gravity, that showed how serious a business he
fancied the sport. "Here is a large and strong sled that will
carry double, and you might trust yourself with me, though a
regiment of horse were paraded down below."

"But are we not a little too *old* for such amusement, in the
streets of a large town, Mr. Ten Eyck?" I answered, doubtingly,
looking round me in an uncertain manner, as one who did not
like to adventure, even while he hesitated to refuse. "Those
king's officers are privileged people, you know."

"No man has a higher privilege to use the streets of Albany,
than Mr. Cornelius Littlepage, sir, I can assure you. The young
ladies often honor me with their company, and no accident has
ever happened."

"Do the young ladies venture to ride down this street, Mr.
Ten Eyck?"

"Not often, sir, I grant you; though that *has* been done, too,
of a moonlight night. There is a more retired spot, at no great
distance from this street, however, to which the ladies are rather
more partial. Look, Mr. Littlepage! — There goes the Hon.
Captain Monson, of the ——th, and he will be down the hill
and up again before we are off, unless you hurry. Take your
seat, lady-fashion, and leave me to manage the sled."

What could I do! Guert had been so very civil, was so much
in earnest, every body seemed to expect it of me, and the Hon.
Captain Monson was already a hundred yards on his way to the
bottom, shooting ahead with the velocity of an arrow. I took
my seat, accordingly, placing my feet together on the front round,
"*lady-fashion,*" as directed. In an instant Guert's manly frame
was behind me, with a leg extended on each side of the sled, the
government of which, as every American who has been born
north of the Potomac well knows, is effected by delicate touches
of the heels. Guert called out to the boys for a shove, and away
we went, like the ship that is bound for her "destined element,"

as the poets say. We got a good start, and left the spot as the
arrow leaves its bow.

Shall I own the truth, and confess I had a momentary pleasure
in the excitement produced by the rapidity of the motion, by
the race we were running with another sled, and by the skill and
ease with which Guert, almost without touching the ground, carried us unharmed through sundry narrow passages, and along
the line of wood-and-venison-loaded sleighs, barely clearing the
noses of their horses. I forgot that I was making this strange
exhibition of myself, in a strange place, and almost in strange
company. So rapid was our motion, however, that the danger
of being recognized was not very great; and there were so many
to divide attention, that the act of folly would have been overlooked, but for a most untimely and unexpected accident. We
had gone the entire length between the two churches with great
success — several steady, grave, and respectable-looking old
burghers calling out, on a high key, " Vell done, Guert! " — for
Guert appeared to be a general favorite, in the sense of fun and
frolic at least — when, turning an angle of the old Dutch temple,
in the ambitious wish of shooting past it, in order to run still
lower, and shoot off the wharf upon the river, we found ourselves
in imminent danger of running under the fore-legs of two foam-
ing horses, that were whirling a sleigh around the same corner
of the church. Nothing saved us but Guert's readiness and
physical power. By digging a heel into the snow, he caused
the sled to fly round at a right angle to its former course, and us
to fly off it, heels over head, without much regard to the proprieties, so far as posture or grace was concerned. The negro
who drove the sleigh pulled up, at the same instant, with so much
force as to throw his horses on their haunches. The result of
these combined movements was to cause Guert and myself to roll
over in such a way as to regain our feet directly alongside of the
sleigh. In rising to my feet, indeed, I laid a hand on the side of
the vehicle, in order to assist me in the effort.

What a sight met my eyes! In the front stood the negro,
grinning from ear to ear; for *he* deemed every disaster that occurred on runners a fit subject for merriment. Who ever did
any thing but laugh at seeing a sleigh upset? — and it was consequently quite in rule to do so on seeing two overgrown boys roll
over from a hand-sled. I could have knocked the rascal down,
with a good will, but it would not have done to resent mirth that
proceeded from so legitimate a cause. Had I been disposed to act

differently, however, the strength and courage necessary to effect such a purpose would have been annihilated in me, by finding myself standing within three feet, and directly in front of Anneke Mordaunt and Mary Wallace! The shame at being thus detected in the disastrous termination of so boyish a flight, at first nearly overcame me. How Guert felt I do not know, but, for a single instant, I wished him in the middle of the Hudson, and all Albany, its Dutch church, sleds, hill, and smoking burghers included, on top of him.

"Mr. Littlepage!" burst out of the rosy lips of Anneke, in a tone of voice that was not to be misunderstood.

"Mr. Guert Ten Eyck!" exclaimed Mary Wallace, in an accent and manner that bespoke chagrin.

"At your service, Miss Mary," answered Guert, who looked a little sheepish at the result of his exploit, though for a reason I did not at first comprehend, brushing some snow from his cap at the same time — "At your service, now and ever, Miss Mary. But, do not suppose it was awkwardness that produced this accident, I entreat of you. It was altogether the fault of the boy who is stationed to give warning of sleighs below the church, who must have left his post. Whenever either of you young ladies will do me the honor to take a seat with me, I will pledge my character, as an Albanian, to carry her to the foot of the highest and steepest hill in town without disturbing a ribbon."

Mary Wallace made no answer; and I fancied she looked a little sad. It is possible Anneke saw and understood this feeling, for she answered with a spirit that I had never seen her manifest before —

"No, no, Mr. Ten Eyck," she said; "when Miss Wallace or I wish to ride down hill, and become little girls again, we will trust ourselves with boys, whose constant practice will be likely to render them more expert than men can be, who have had time to forget the habits of their childhood. Pompey, we will return home."

The cold inclination of the head that succeeded, while it was sufficiently gracious to preserve appearances, proved too plainly that neither Guert nor myself had risen in the estimation of his mistress, by this boyish exhibition of his skill with the handsled. Had either of these young ladies been Albanians, it is probable they would have laughed at our mishap; but no high hill running directly into New York, the custom that prevailed at Albany did not prevail in the capital. Small boys alone used the hand-sled in that part of the colony, while the taste continued longer among the more stable and constant Dutch. Of course, we had nothing to do but to make profound bows, and suffer the negro to move on.

"There it is, Littlepage," exclaimed Guert, with a species of sigh; "I shall have nothing but iced looks for the next week, and all for riding down hill four or five years later than is the rule. Every body, hereabouts, uses the hand-sled until eighteen, or so; and I am only five-and-twenty. Pray, what may be your age, my dear fellow?"

"Twenty-one, only about a month since. I wish, with all my heart, it were ten!"

"Turned the corner! — well, that's unlucky; but we must make the best of it. My taste is for *fun*, and so I have admitted to Miss Wallace, twenty times; but she tells me that, after a certain period, men should look to graver things, and think of their country. She has lectured me already, once, on the subject of sliding; though she allows that skating is a manly exercise."

"When a lady takes the trouble to lecture, it is a sure sign she feels some interest in the subject."

"By St. Nicholas! I never thought of that, Littlepage!" cried Guert, who, notwithstanding the great advantages he possessed in the way of face and figure, turned out to have less personal vanity about him that almost any man I ever met with. "*Lectured* me she has, and that more than once, too!"

"The lady who lectures *me*, sir, will not get rid of me, at the end of the discourse."

"That's manly! I like it, Littlepage; and I like *you*. I foresee we shall be great friends; and we'll talk more of this matter another time. Now, Mary has spoken to me of the war, and hinted that a single man, like myself, with the world before him, might do something to make his name known in it. I did not like that; for a girl who loved a fellow would not wish to have him shot."

"A girl who took no interest in her suitor, Mr. Ten Eyck, would not care whether he did any thing or not. But I must now quit you, being under an engagement to meet Mr. Worden at the inn, at six."

Guert and I shook hands, for the tenth or twelfth time that day, parting with an understanding that he was to call for us, to accompany our party to the supper, at the previously appointed hour. As I walked toward the inn, I pondered on what had just occurred in a most mortified temper. That Anneke was displeased, was only too apparent; and I felt fearful that her displeasure was not entirely free from contempt. As for Guert's case, it did not strike me as being half so desperate as my own; for there was nothing unnatural, but something quite the reverse, in women of sense and stability, when they admire any youth of opposite temperament — and I remembered to have heard my grandfather say that such was apt to be the case — wishing to elevate their suitors in their pursuits and characters. Had Anneke taken the pains to remonstrate with me about the folly of what I had done, I should have been encouraged; but the cold indifference of her manner, not to call it contempt, cut me to the quick. It is true, Anneke seemed to feel most on her friend's account; but I could not mistake the look of surprise with which she saw me, Cornelius Littlepage, rise from under her sleigh, and stand brushing the snow from my clothes, like a great calf as I was! No man can bear to be rendered ridiculous in the presence of the woman he loves.

Near the inn I met Dirck, his whole face illuminated with a look of pleasure.

"I have just met Anneke and Mary Wallace!" he said, "and they stopped their sleigh to speak to me. Herman Mordaunt has been here half the winter, and he means to remain most of the summer. There will be no Lilacsbush this season, the girls told me, but Herman Mordaunt has got a house, where he lives with his own servants, and boils his own pot, as he calls it. We shall be at home there, of course, for you are such a favorite, Corny, ever since that affair of the lion! As for Anneke, I never saw her looking so beautiful!"

"Did Miss Mordaunt say she would be happy to see us on the old footing, Dirck?"

"Did she? — I suppose so. She said I shall be glad to see you, cousin Dirck, whenever you can come, and I hope you will bring with you sometimes the clergyman of whom you have spoken."

"But nothing of Jason Newcome or Corny Littlepage! Tell the truth at once, Dirck; my name was not mentioned?"

"Indeed, it was, t'ough; I mentioned it several times, and told them how long we had been on the roat, and how you trove, and how you had sold the sleigh and horses already, and a dozen other t'ings. Oh! we talked a great deal of you, Corny; that is, I dit, and the girls listened."

"Was my name mentioned by either of the young ladies, Dirck, in direct terms?"

"To be sure: Anneke had something to say about you, though it was so much out of the way, I can hardly tell you what it was now. Oh! I remember; she said 'I have seen Mr. Littlepage, and think he has grown since we last met; he promises to make a *man* one of these days.' What could t'at mean, Corny?"

"That I am a fool, a great overgrown boy, and wish I had never seen Albany; that's what it means. Come, let us go in; Mr. Worden will be expecting us. Ha! Who the devil's that, Dirck?"

A loud Dutch shout from Dirck broke out of him, regardless of the street, and his whole face lighted up into a broad sympathetic smile. I had caught a glimpse of a sled coming down the acclivity we were slowly ascending, which sled glided past us just as I got the words out of my mouth. It was occupied by Jason alone, who seemed just as much charmed with the sport as any other grown-up boy on the hill. There he went, the cocked-hat uppermost, the pea-green coat beneath, and the striped woollens and heavy plated buckles stuck out, one on each side, governing the movement of the sled with the readiness of a lad accustomed to the business.

"That must be capital fun, Corny!" my companion said, scarce able to contain himself for the pleasure he felt. "I have a great mind to borrow a sled and take a turn myself."

"Not if you intend to visit Miss Mordaunt, Dirck. Take my word for it, she does not like to see men following the pleasures of boys."

Dirck stared at me, but being taciturn by nature, he said nothing, and we entered the house. There we found Mr. Worden reading over an old sermon, in readiness for his next Sunday's business; and sitting down, we began to compare notes on the subject of the town and its advantages. The divine was in raptures. As for the Dutch he cared little for them, and had seen but little of them, overlooking them in a very natural, metropolitan sort of way; but he had found so many English officers, had heard so much from home, and had received so many invitations, that *his* campaign promised nothing but agreeables. We sat chatting over these matters until the tea was served, and for an hour or two afterward. My bargains were applauded, my promptitude — the promptitude of Guert would have been more just — was commended, and I was told that my parents should hear the whole truth in the matter. In a word, our Mentor being in good humor with himself, was disposed to be in good humor with every one else.

At the appointed hour, Guert came to escort us to the place of meeting. He was courteous, attentive, and as frank as the air he breathed, in manner. Mr. Worden took to him excessively, and it was soon apparent that he and young Ten Eyck were likely to become warm friends.

"You must know, gentlemen, that the party to which I have had the honor of inviting you, will be composed of some of the heartiest young men in Albany, if not in the colony. We meet once a month, in the house of an old bachelor, who belongs to us, and who will be delighted to converse with you, Mr. Worden, on the subject of religion. Mr. Van Brunt is very expert in religion, and we make him the umpire of all our disputes and bets on *that* subject."

This sounded a little ominous, I thought; but Mr. Worden was not a man to be frightened from a good hot supper, by half-a-dozen inadvertent words. He could tolerate even a religious discussion, with such an object in view. He walked on, side by side with Guert, and we were soon at the door of the house of Mr. Van Brunt, the Bachelor in Divinity, as I nicknamed him. Guert entered without knocking, and ushered us into the presence of our *quasi* host.

We found in the room a company of just twelve, Guert included; that being the entire number of the club. It struck me, at the first glance, that the whole set had a sort of slide-down-hill aspect, and that we were likely to make a night of it. My acquaintance with Dirck, and indeed my connection with the old race, had not left me ignorant of a certain peculiarity in the Dutch character. Sober, sedate, nay phlegmatic, as they usually appeared to be, their roystering was on a pretty high key, when it once fairly commenced. We thought one lad of the old race, down in Westchester, fully a match for two of the Anglo-Saxon breed, when it came to a hard set-to; no ordinary fun appeasing the longings of an excited Dutchman. Tradition had let me into a good many secrets connected with their excesses, and I had heard the young Albanians often mentioned as being at the head of their profession in these particulars.

Nothing could be more decorous, or considerate, however, than our introduction and reception. The young men seemed particularly gratified at having a clergyman of their party, and I make no doubt it was intended that the evening should be one of unusual sobriety and moderation. I heard the word "Dominie" whispered from mouth to mouth, and it was easy to see the effect it produced. Most eyes were fastened on Van Brunt, a red-faced, square-built, somewhat dissolute-looking man of forty-five, who seemed to find his apology for associating with persons so much his juniors, in his habits, and possibly in the necessity of the case; as men of his own years might not like his company.

"And, gentlemen, it is dry business standing here looking at each other," observed Mr. Van Brunt; "and we will take a little punch, to moisten our hearts, as well as our throats. Guert, yon is the pitcher."

Guert made good use of the pitcher, and each man had his glass of punch — a beverage then, as now, much used in the colony. I must acknowledge that the mixture was very knowingly put together, though I had no sooner swallowed my glass, than I discovered it was confounded strong. Not so with Guert. Not only did he swallow *one* glass, but he swallowed *two*, in quick succession, like a man who was thirsty; standing at the time in a fine, manly, erect attitude, as one who trifled with something that did not half tax his powers. The pitcher, though quite large, was emptied at that one assault, in proof of which it was turned bottom upward, by Guert himself.

Conversation followed, most of it being in English, out of compliment to the Dominie, who was not supposed to understand Dutch. This was an error, however, Mr. Worden making out tolerably well in that language, when he tried. I was felicitated on the bargains I had made with the contractor; and many kind and hospitable attempts were made to welcome me in a frank, hearty manner among strangers. I confess I was touched by these honest and sincere endeavors to put me at my ease, and when a second pitcher of punch was brought round, I took another glass with right good will, while Guert, as usual, took two; though the liquor *he* drank, I had many occasions to ascertain subsequently, produced no more visible effect on him, in the way of physical consequences, than if he had not swallowed it. Guert was no drunkard, far from it; he could only drink all near him under the table, and remain firm in his chair himself. Such men usually escape the imputation of being sots, though they are very apt to pay the penalty of their successes at the close of their career. These are the men who break down at sixty, if not

earlier, becoming subject to paralysis, indigestion, and other similar evils.

Such was the state of things, the company gradually getting
into a very pleasant humor, when Guert was called out of the
room by one of the blacks, who bore a most ominous physiog-
nomy while making his request. He was gone but a moment,
when he returned with a certain sort of consternation painted in
his own handsome face. Mr. Van Brunt was called into a corner,
where two or three more of the principal persons present soon
collected, in an earnest, half-whispered discourse. I was seated
so near this group, as occasionally to overhear a few expressions,
though to get no clear clue to its meaning. The words I overheard were " old Cuyler " — " capital supper " — " venison and
ducks " — " partridge and quails " — " knows us all " — " never
do " — " Dominie the man " — " strangers " — " how to do it? "
and several other similar expressions, which left a vague impression on my mind that our supper was in great peril from some
cause or other; but what that cause was I could not learn. Guert
was evidently the principal person in this consultation, every body
appearing to listen to his suggestions with respect and attention.
At length our friend came out of the circle, and in a courteous,
self-possessed manner communicated the difficulty in the following words:

" You must know, Rev. Mr. Worden, and Mr. Littlepage, and
Mr. Follock, and Mr. Newcome, that we have certain customs of
our own, among us youths of Albany, that perhaps are not familiar to you gentlemen nearer the capital. The trut' is, we are
not always as wise and sober as our parents, and grandparents
in particular, could wish us to be. It is t'ought a good thing
among us sometimes, to rummage the hen-roosts and poultry-
yards of the burghers, and to sup on the fruits of such a forage.
I do not know how it is with you, gentlemen; but I will own, that
to me, ducks and geese got in this innocent, game-like way, taste
sweeter than when they are bought in the market-hall; our own
supper for to-night was a *bought* supper, but it has become the
victim of a little enlargement of the practice I have mentioned."

" How! — how's that, friend Ten Eyck? " exclaimed Mr. Worden, in no affected consternation. " The *supper* a victim, do you
say? "

" Yes, sir; to be frank at once, it is gone; gone to a pullet, a
steak, and a potatoe. They have not left us a dish! "

" They! " echoed the parson — " and who can *they* be? "

"That is a point yet to be ascertained, for the operation has been carried on in so delicate and refined a way, that none of our blacks know any thing of the matter. It seems there was a cry of fire just now, and it took every one of the negroes into the street; during which all our game has been put up, and has flown."

"Bless me! bless me! what a calamity! what a rascally theft! Did you not mark it down?"

"No, sir, I am sorry to say we have not; nor do we apply such hard names to a frolic, even when we lose our supper by it. It is the act of some of our associates and friends, who hope to feast at our expense to-night; and who will, gentlemen, unless you consent to aid us in recovering our lost dishes."

"Aid you, my dear sir — I will do any thing you can wish — what will you have me attempt? Shall I go to the fort, and ask for succor from the army?"

"No, sir; our object can be effected short of t'at. I am quite certain we can find what we want, only two or three doors from this, if you will consent to lend us a little, a very little of your assistance."

"Name it — name it, at once, for Heaven's sake, Mr. Guert. The dishes must be getting cold, all this time," cried Mr. Worden, jumping up with alacrity, and looking about him for his hat and cloak.

"The service we ask of you, gentlemen, is just this," rejoined Guert, with a coolness that, when I came to reflect on the events of that night, has always struck me as singularly astonishing. "Our supper, and an excellent one it is, is close at hand, as I have said. Nothing will be easier than to get it on our own table, in the next room, could we only manage to get old Doortje off duty, and detain her for five minutes at the area gate of her house. She knows every one of *us*, and would smell a rat in a minute, did *we* show ourselves; but Mr. Worden and Mr. Littlepage, here, might amuse her for the necessary time, without any trouble. She is remarkably fond of Dominies, and would not be able to trace *you* back to this house, leaving us to eat our supper in peace. After *t'at*, no one cares for the rest."

"I'll do it! — I'll do it!" cried Mr. Worden, hurrying into the passage, in quest of his hat and cloak. "It is no more than just that you should have your own, and the supper will be either eaten, or overdone, should we go for constables."

"No fear of constables, Mr. Worden, we never employ them

in our poultry wars. All we, who will get the supper back again, can expect, will be a little hot water, or a skirmish with our friends."

The details of the movement were now intelligibly and clearly settled. Guert was to head a party provided with large clothes-baskets, who were to enter the kitchen during Doortje's absence, and abstract the dishes, which could not yet be served, as all in Albany, of a certain class, sat down to supper at nine precisely. As for Doortje, a negro who was in the house, in waiting on one of the guests, his master, would manage to get her out to the area gate, the house having a cellar kitchen, where it would depend on Mr. Worden to detain her, three or four minutes. To my surprise, the parson entered on the execution of the wild scheme with boyish eagerness, affirming that he could keep the woman half an hour, if it were necessary, by delivering her a lecture on the importance of observing the eighth command-ment. As soon as the preliminaries were thus arranged, the two parties proceeded on their respective duties, the hour ad-monishing us of the necessity of losing no time unnecessarily.

I did not like this affair from the first, the experiment of sliding down hill having somewhat weakened my confidence in Guert Ten Eyck's judgment. Nevertheless, it would not do for *me* to hold back, when Mr. Worden led, and, after all, there was no great harm in recovering a supper that had been ab-stracted from our own house. Guert did not proceed, like ourselves, by the street, but he went with his party, out of a back gate into an alley, and was to enter the house he assailed, by means of a similar gate in its rear. Once in that yard, the access to the kitchen, and the retreat, were very easy, provided the cook could be drawn away from her charge at so important a moment. Every thing, therefore, depended on the address of the young negro who was in the house, and ourselves.

On reaching the gate of the area, we stopped while our negro descended to invite Doortje forth. This gave us a moment to examine the building. The house was large, much larger than those round it, and what struck me as unusual, there was a lighted lamp over the door. This looked as if it might be a sort of tavern, or eating-house, and rendered the whole thing more intelligible to me. Our roystering plunderers doubtless intended to sup on their spoils at that tavern.

The negro was gone but a minute, when he came out with a young black of his own sex, a servant whom he was leading off his post, on some pretence of his own, and was immediately followed by the cook. Doortje made many courtesies as soon as she saw the cocked hat and black cloak of the Dominie, begging his pardon and asking his pleasure. Mr. Worden now began a grave and serious lecture on the sin of stealing, holding the confounded Doortje in discourse quite three minutes. In vain the cook protested she had taken nothing; that her master's property was sacred in her eyes, and ever had been; that she never gave away even cold meats without an order, and that she could not imagine why *she* was to be talked to in this way. To give him his due, Mr. Worden performed his part to admiration, though it is true he had only an ignorant wench, who was awed by his profession, to manage. At length we heard a shrill whistle from the alley, the signal of success, when Mr. Worden wished Doortje a solemn good-night, and walked away with all the dignity of a priest. In a minute or two we were in the house again, and were met by Guert with cordial shakes of the hand, thanks for our acceptable services, and a summons to supper. It appears that Doortje had actually dished up every thing, all the articles standing before a hot fire waiting only for the clock to strike nine to be served. In this state, then, the only change the supper had to undergo, was to bring it a short distance through the alley and to place it on our table, instead of that for which it was so lately intended.

Notwithstanding the rapidity with which the changes had been made, it would not have been very easy for a stranger to detect any striking irregularity in our feast. It is true, there were two sets of dishes on the table, or rather dishes of two different sets; but the ducks, game, etc., were not only properly cooked, but were warm and good. To work every body went, therefore, with an appetite, and for five minutes little was heard beyond the clatter of knives and forks. Then came the drinking of healths, and finally the toasts, and the songs, and the stories.

Guert sang capitally, in a fine, clear, sweet, manly voice, and he gave us several airs with words both in English and Dutch. He had just finished one of these songs, and the clapping of hands was still loud and warm, when the young man called on Mr. Worden for a lady, or a sentiment.

"Come, Dominie," he called out, for by this time the feast had produced its familiarity — "Come, Dominie, you have ac-

quitted yourself so well as a lecturer, that we are all dying to
hear you preach."

"A lady do you say, sir?" asked the parson, who was as
merry as any of us.

"A laty — a laty" — shouted six or seven at once. "The
Tominie's laty — the Tominie's laty."

"Well, gentlemen, since you will have it so, you shall have
one. You must not complain if she prove a little venerable —
but I give you 'Mother Church.'"

This produced a senseless laugh, as such things usually do,
and then followed my turn. Mr. Van Brunt very formally
called on me for a lady. After pausing a moment, I said, as I
flatter myself, with spirit:

"Gentlemen, I will give you another almost as heavenly —
Miss Anneke Mordaunt!"

"Miss Anneke Mordaunt!" was echoed round the table, and
I soon discovered that Anneke was a general favorite, and a
very common toast already at Albany.

"I shall now ask Mr. Guert Ten Eyck for his lady," I said,
as soon as silence was restored, there being very little pause
between the cups that night.

This appeal changed the whole character of the expression
of Guert's face. It became grave in an instant, as if the recollection of her whose name he was about to utter produced a
pause in his almost fierce mirth. He colored, then raised his
eyes and looked sternly round as if to challenge denial, and
gave:

"Miss Mary Wallace."

"Ay, Guert, we are used to that name, now," said Van Brunt,
a little dryly. "This is the tenth time I have heard it from
you within two months."

"You will be likely to hear it twenty more, sir; for I shall
give Mary Wallace, and nobody but Mary Wallace, while the
lady remains Mary Wallace. How, now, Mr. Constable! What
may be the reason we have the honor of a visit from you at this
time of night?"*

* In this whole affair of the supper, the reader will find incidents that bear a
striking resemblance to certain local characteristics portrayed by Mrs. Grant, of
Leggan, in her Memoirs of an American Lady; thus corroborating the fidelity of the
pictures of our ancient manners, as given by that respectable writer, by the unques-
tioned authority of Mr. Cornelius Littlepage. — EDITOR.

CHAPTER XIII

" Masters, it is proved already
That you are little better than false knaves;
And it will go near to be thought so, shortly."
DOGBERRY.

THE sudden appearance of the city constable, a functionary whose person was not unknown to most of the company, brought every man at table to his feet, the Rev. Mr. Worden, Dirck, and myself, included. For my own part, I saw no particular reason for alarm, though it at once struck me that this visit might have some connection with the demolished supper, since the law does not, in all cases, suffer a man to reclaim even his own, by trick or violence. As for the constable himself, a short, compact, snub-nosed, Dutch-built person, who spoke English as if it disagreed with his bile, he was the coolest of the whole party.

"Vell, Mr. Guert," he said, with a sort of good-natured growl of authority, "here I moost come ag'in! Mr. Mayor would be happy to see you, and ter Tominie, dat ist of your party; and ter gentleman dat acted as clerk, ven he lectured old Doortje, Mr. Mayor's cook."

Mr. Mayor's cook! here then, a secret was out, with a vengeance! Guert had not reclaimed his own lost supper, which, having passed into the hands of the Philistines, was hopelessly gone; but he had actually stolen and eaten the supper prepared for the mayor of Albany — Peter Cuyler, a man of note and standing in all respects; a functionary who had held his office from time immemorial; — the lamp was the symbol of authority, and not the sign of an inn, or an eating-house; — the supper, moreover, was never prepared for one man, or one family, but had certainly been got up for the honorable treatment of a goodly company — fifteen stout men had mainly appeased their appetites on it; and the fragments were that moment under discussion among half-a-dozen large-mouthed, shining negro faces, in the kitchen! Under circumstances like these, I looked inquiringly at the Rev. Mr. Worden — and the Rev. Mr. Worden looked inquiringly at me. There was no apparent remedy, however; but, after a brief consulation with Guert, we, the summoned parties, took our hats, and followed Dogberry to the residence of the mayor.

"You are not to be uneasy, gentlemen, at this little interruption of our amusements," said Guert, dropping in between Mr. Worden and myself, as we proceeded on our way, "these things happening very often among us. You are innocent, you know under all circumstances, since you supposed that the supper was our own — brought back by direct means, instead of having recourse to the shabby delays of the law."

"And whose supper may this have been, sir, that we have just eaten?" demanded Mr. Worden.

"Why, there can be no harm, now, in telling you the trut', Dominie; and I will own, therefore, it belonged in law to Mr. Mayor Cuyler. There is no great danger, however, as you will see, when I come to explain matters. You must know that the mayor's wife was a Schuyler, and my mother has some of that blood in her veins, and we count cousins as far as we can see, in Albany. It is just supping with one's relations, a little out of the common way, as you will perceive, gentlemen."

"Have you dealt fairly with Mr. Littlepage and myself, sir, in this affair?" Mr. Worden asked, a little sternly. "I might, with great propriety, lecture to a cook, on the eighth commandment, when that cook was a party to robbing you of your supper; but how shall I answer to his honor Mr. Mayor, on the charge which will now be brought against me? It is not for myself, Mr. Guert, that I feel so much concern, as for the credit and reputation of my sacred office, and that, too, among your disciples of the schools of Leyden."

"Leave it all to me, my dear Dominie — leave it all to me," answered Guert, well disposed to sacrifice himself, rather than permit a friend to suffer. "I am used to these little matters, and will take care of you."

"I will answer for t'at," put in the constable, looking over his shoulder. "No young fly-away in All*pon*ny hast more knowletge in t'ese matters t'an Mr. Guert, here. If any potty can draw his heat out of the yoke, Mr. Guert can. Yaas — yaas — he know all about t'ese little matters, sure enough."

This was encouraging, of a certainty! Our associate was so well known for his tricks and frolics, that even the constable who took him calculated largely on his address in getting out of scrapes! I did not apprehend that any of us were about to be tried and convicted of a downright robbery; for I knew how far the Dutch carried their jokes of this nature, and how tolerant the seniors were to their juniors; and especially how much all men are disposed to regard any exploit of the sort of that in which we had been engaged, when it has been managed adroitly, and in a way to excite a laugh. Still, it was no joke to rob a mayor of his supper; these functionaries usually passing to their offices through the probationary grade of alderman.* Guert was not free from uneasiness, as was apparent by a question he put to the officer, on the steps of Mr. Cuyler's house, and under the very light of the official lamp.

"How is the old gentleman, this evening, Hans?" the principal asked, with some little concern in his manner. "I hope he and his company have supped?"

"Vell, t'at is more t'an I can telt you, Mr. Guert. He look't more as like himself, when he hat the horse t'ieves from New Englant taken up, t'an he hast for many a tay. 'Twas most too pat, Mr. Guert, to run away wit' the mayor's *own* supper! I coult have tolt you who hast your own tucks and venison."

"I wish you had, Hans, with all my heart; but we were hard pushed, and had a strange Dominie to feed. You know a body must provide *well* for company."

"Yaas, yaas; I understants it, and knows how you moost have peen nonplush't to do sich a t'ing; put it was *mo-o-st* too pat. Vell, we are all young, afore we live to be olt—t'at effery potty knows."

By this time the door was open, and we entered. Mr. Mayor had issued orders we should all be shown into the parlor, where I rather think, from what subsequently passed, he intended to cut up Guert a little more than common, by exposing him before the eyes of a particular person. At all events, the reader can judge of my horror, at finding that the party whose supper I had just helped to demolish, consisted, in addition to three or four sons and daughters of the house, of Herman Mor-

---

* The American mayor is usually a different person from the English mayor. Until within the last five-and-twenty or thirty years, the mayor of New York was invariably a man of social and political importance, belonging strictly to the higher class of society. The same was true of the mayor of Albany. — At the present time, the rule has been so far enlarged, as to admit of a selection from all the more reputable classes, without any rigid adherence to the highest. The elective principle has produced the change. During the writer's boyhood, Philip Van Rensselaer, the brother of the late patroon, was so long mayor of Albany, as to be universally known by the *sobriquet* of "The Mayor." — Editor.

daunt, Mary Wallace, and Anneke! Of course, every body knew *what* had been done; but, until we entered the room, Mr. Mayor alone knew *who* had done it. Of Mr. Worden and myself even, he knew no more than he had learned from Doortje's account of the matter; and the cook, quite naturally, had represented us as rogues feigning our divinity.

Guert was a thoroughly manly fellow, and he did us the justice to enter the parlor first. Poor fellow! I can feel for him, even at this distance of time, when his eye first fell on Mary Wallace's pallid and distressed countenance. It could scarcely be less than I felt myself, when I first beheld Anneke's flushed features, and the look of offended propriety that I fancied to be sparkling in her estranged eye.

Mr. Mayor evidently regarded Mr. Worden with surprise, as indeed he did me; for, instead of strangers, he probably expected to meet two of those delinquents whose faces were familiar to him, by divers similar jocular depredations, committed within the limits of his jurisdiction. Then the circumstance that Mr. Worden was a real Dominie, could not be questioned by those who saw him standing, as he did, face to face, with all the usual signs of his sacred office in his dress and air.

" I believe there must be some mistake here, constable! " exclaimed Mr. Mayor. " Why have you brought these two strange gentlemen along with Guert Ten Eyck? "

" My orters, Mr. Mayor, wast to pring Doortje's ' rapscallion Tominie,' and his ' rapscallion frient; ' and t'at is one, and t'is ist t'ot'er."

" This gentleman has the appearance of being a *real* clergyman, and that too of the church of England."

" Yaas, Mr. Mayor, t'at is yoost so. He wilt preach fifteen minutes wit'out stopping, if you wilt give him a plack gownt; and pray an hour in a white shirt." *

" Will you do me the favor, Guert Ten Eyck, to let me have the names of the strangers I have the pleasure to receive," said the mayor, a little authoritatively.

" Certainly, Mr. Mayor; certainly, and with very great pleas-

---

* This opinion of the constable's must refer to the notion common amongst the non-Episcopal sects, that the value of spiritual provender was to be measured by the quantity. Preaching, however, *might* be overdone in the Dutch Reformed churches, for, quite within my recollection, a half-hour glass stood on the pulpit of the Dutch edifice named in the text, to regulate the dominie's wind. It was said it might be turned *once* with impunity; but woe betide him who should so far trespass on his people's patience as to presume to turn it *twice*. — EDITOR.

ure. I should have done this at once, had we been ushered into your house by any one but the city constable. Whenever I accompany that gentleman anywhere, I always wait to ascertain my welcome."

Guert laughed with some heart at this allusion to his own known delinquencies, while Mr. Cuyler only smiled. I could see, notwithstanding the severe measures to which he had resorted in this particular case, that the last was not unfriendly to the first, and that our friend Guert had not fallen literally among robbers, in being brought to the place where we were.

"This reverend dominie," continued Guert, as soon as he had had his laugh, and had ventured to cast a short, inquiring glance at Mary Wallace, "is a gentleman from England, Mr. Mayor, who is to preach in St. Peter's the day after to-morrow, by special invitation from the chaplain; when, I make no doubt, we shall all be much edified; Miss Mary Wallace among the rest, if she will do him the honor to attend service — good, and angelic, and *forgiving*, as I know she is by nature."

This speech caused all eyes to turn on the young lady, whose face crimsoned, though she made no reply. I now felt satisfied that Guert's manly, frank, avowed, and sincere admiration had touched the heart of Mary Wallace, while her reason condemned that which her natural tenderness encouraged; and the struggle in her mind was then, and long after, a subject of curious study with me. As for Anneke, I thought she resented this somewhat indiscreet, not to say indelicate though indirect avowal of his feelings toward his mistress; and that she looked on Guert with even more coldness than she had previously done. Neither of the ladies, however, said any thing. During this dumb-show, Mr. Cuyler had leisure to recover from the surprise of discovering that one of his prisoners was really a clergyman, and to inquire who the other might be.

"That gentleman then, is in fact a clergyman! " he answered. " You have forgotten to name the other, Guert."

"This is Mr. Corny Littlepage, Mr. Mayor — the only son of Mr. Littlepage, of Satansoe, Westchester."

The mayor looked a little puzzled, and I believe felt somewhat embarrassed as to the manner in which he ought to proceed. The incursion of Guert upon his premises much exceeded in boldness any thing of the kind that had ever before occurred in Albany. It was common enough for young men of his stamp to carry off poultry, pigs, etc., and feast on the spoils; and cases had occurred, as I afterward learned, in which rival parties of these depredators preyed on each other — the same materials for a supper having been known to change hands two or three times before they were consumed — but no one had ever presumed, previously to this evening, to make an inroad even on Mr. Mayor's hen-coop, much less to molest the domains of his cook. In the first impulse of his anger, Mr. Cuyler had sent for the constable; and Guert's club with its place of meeting being well known, that functionary having had many occasions to visit it, the latter proceeded thither forthwith. It is probable, however, a little reflection satisfied the mayor that a frolic could not well be treated as a larceny; and that Guert had some of his own wife's blood in his veins. When he came to find that two respectable strangers were implicated in the affair, one of whom was actually a clergyman, this charitable feeling was strengthened, and he changed his course of proceeding.

"You can return home, Hans," said Mr. Mayor, very sensibly mollified in his manner. "Should there be occasion for your further services, I will send for you. Now gentlemen," as soon as the door closed on the constable, "I will satisfy you that old Peter Cuyler can cover a table, and feed his friends, even though Guert Ten Eyck be so near a neighbor. Miss Wallace, will you allow me the honor to lead you to the table? Mr. Worden will see Mrs. Cuyler, in safety, to the same place."

On this hint, the missionary stepped forward with alacrity, and led Mrs. Mayoress after Mary Wallace, with the utmost courtesy. Guert did the same to one of the young ladies of the house; Anneke was led in by one of the young men; and I took the remaining young lady, who I presumed was also one of the family. It was very apparent we were respited; and all of us thought it wisest to appear as much at our ease as possible, in order not to balk the humor of the principal magistrate of the ancient town of Albany.

To do Mr. Mayor justice, the lost time had been so well improved by Doortje, that, on looking around the table, I thought the supper to which we were thus strangely invited, was, of the two, the best I had seen that evening. Luckily, game was plenty; and, by means of quails, partridges, oysters, venison patties, and other dishes of that sort, the cook had managed to send up quite as good a supper, at ten o'clock, as she had previously prepared for nine.

I will not pretend that I felt quite at my ease, as I took

my seat at the table, for the second time that night. All the younger members of the party looked exceedingly grave, as if they could very well dispense with our company; the old people alone appearing to enter into the scene with any spirit. Anneke did not even look at me, after the first astounded look given on my entrance; nor did Mary Wallace once cast her eyes toward Guert, when we reached the supper-room. Mr. Mayor, notwithstanding, had determined to laugh off the affair; and he and Mr. Worden soon became excellent friends, and began to converse freely and naturally.

"Come, cousin Guert," cried Mr. Mayor, after two or three glasses of Madeira had still further warmed his heart, "fill, and pledge me — unless you prefer to give a lady. If the last, every body will drink to her, with hearty good will. You eat nothing, and must drink the more."

"Ah! Mr. Mayor, I have toasted one lady, to-night, and cannot toast another."

"Not present company excepted, my boy?"

"No, sir, not even with that license. I pledge you, with all my heart, and thank you, with all my heart, for this generous treatment, after my own foolish frolic; but you know how it is, Mr. Mayor, with us Albany youths, when our pride is up, and a supper must be had — "

"Not I, Guert; I know nothing about it; but should very well like to learn. How came you in the first place to take such a fancy to my cook's supper? Did you imagine it better than Van Brunt's cook could give you?"

"The supper of Arent Van Brunt's cook has disappeared — gone on the hill, I fancy, among the red-coats; and to own the truth, Mr. Mayor, it was yours or nothing. I had invited these gentlemen to pass the evening with us. One of our blacks happened to mention what was going on here, and hospitality led us all astray. It was nothing more, I do assure you, Mr. Mayor."

"And so your hospitable feelings made your guests work for their supper, by sending them to preach to old Doortje, while you were dishing up my ducks and game?"

"Your pardon, Mr. Mayor; Doortje had dished up, before she went to lecture. Your cook is too well trained to neglect her duty, even to hear a sermon by the Rev. Mr. Worden! But, these gentlemen were quite as much deceived as the old woman; for they supposed we were after our own lost goods, and did not know that you dwelt here; and were as much my dupes as old Doortje herself. Truth obliges me to own this much in their justification."

There was a general clearing up of countenances at this frank avowal; and I saw that Anneke herself turned her looks inquiringly upon the speaker, and suffered a smile to relieve the extreme gravity of her sweet countenance. From that moment a very sensible change came over the feelings and deportment of the younger part of the company, and the conversation became easier and more natural. It was certainly much in our favor to have it known we had not boyishly and officiously joined in a gratuitous attempt to rob and insult this particular and unoffending family, but that Mr. Worden and I supposed we were simply aiding in getting back those things which properly belonged to our host, and getting them back, too, in a manner of which the party we supposed we were acting against, would certainly have no right to complain, inasmuch as they had set the example. Guert was encouraged to go on further with his explanations; which he did, in his own honest, candid manner, exculpating us, in effect, from every thing but being a little too much disposed to waggery, for a minister of the church and his pupil, who had just commenced his travels.

Anneke's face brightened up more and more, as the explanations proceeded; and soon after they were ended, she turned to me in a very gracious manner, and inquired after my mother. As I sat directly opposite her, and the table was narrow, we could converse without attracting much attention to ourselves; Mr. Mayor and his other guests keeping up a round of reasonably noisy jokes, on the events of the evening, nearer the foot of the table.

"You find some customs in Albany, Mr. Littlepage, that are not known to us in New York," Anneke observed, after a few preliminary remarks had opened the way to further communication.

"I scare know, Miss Anneke, whether you allude to what has occurred this evening or to what occurred this afternoon?"

"To both, I believe," answered Anneke, smiling, though she colored, as I thought, with a species of feminine vexation; "for certainly, one is no more a custom with us than the other."

"I have been most unfortunate, Miss Mordaunt, in the exhibitions I have made of myself in the course of the few hours I have passed in this, to me, strange place. I am afraid you regard me as little more than an overgrown boy who has been permitted by his parents to leave home sooner than he ought."

"This is your construction, and not mine, Mr. Littlepage. I suppose you know — but we will talk of this in the other room, or at some other time."

I took the hint, and said no more on the subject, while at table. Mr. Mayor, I suppose in consideration of our having gone through the exactions of one feast already that evening, permitted us to leave the supper-room much earlier than common, and the hour being late, the whole party broke up immediately afterward. Before we separated, however, Herman Mordaunt approached me in a friendly, free way, and invited me to come to his house at eight next morning to breakfast, requesting the pleasure of Dirck's company at the same time; the invitation to the latter going through me. It is scarcely necessary to say how gladly I accepted, and how much I was relieved by this termination of an adventure that at one moment menaced me with deep disgrace. Had Mr. Mayor seen fit to pursue the affair of the abstraction of his first supper in a serious vein, although the legal consequences could not probably have amounted to any thing very grave, they might prove very ridiculous; and I have no doubt they would have brought about a very abrupt termination of my visit to the north. As it was, my mind was vastly relieved, as I believe was the case also with that of the Rev. Mr. Worden.

"Corny," said that gentleman, after we had wished Guert good-night, and were well on our way to the inn again, "this second supper has helped surprisingly to digest the first. I doubt if our new acquaintance here will be likely to turn out very profitable to us."

"Yet, sir, you appeared to take to him exceedingly, and I had thought you excellent friends."

"I like the fellow well enough too; for he is hearty, and frank, and good-natured; but there was some little policy in keeping on good terms with him. I'm afraid, Corny, I did not altogether consult the dignity of my holy office, this morning, on the ice! It is exceedingly unbecoming in a clergyman, to be seen running in a public place like a schoolboy, or a youngster contending in a match. I thought, moreover, I overheard one of those young Dutchmen call me the 'Loping Dominie;' and so, taking altogether, it struck me it would be wisest to keep on good terms with this Guert Ten Eyck."

"I see your policy, sir, and it does not become me to deny it. As for myself, I confess I like Guert surprisingly, and shall not give him up easily; though he has already got me into two serious scrapes in the short time we have been acquainted. He is a hearty, good-natured, thoughtless young fellow, who Dutchman-like, when he does make an attempt to enjoy life, does it with all his heart."

I then related the affair of the hand-sled to Mr. Worden, who gave me some of that sort of consolation, of which a man receives a great deal, as he elbows his way through this busy, selfish world.

"Well, Corny," said my old master, "I am not certain you did not look more like a fool, as you rolled over from that sled, than I looked while 'loping' from our friends in the sleigh! "

We both laughed as we entered the tavern; I, to conceal the vexation I really felt, and Mr. Worden, as I presume, because he was flattered with the belief that I must have appeared quite as ridiculous as himself.

Next morning I proceeded to Herman Mordaunt's residence at the earliest hour the rules of society would allow. I found the family established in one of those Dutch edifices, of which Albany was mainly composed, and which stood a little removed from the street — having a tiny yard in front, with the *stoop* in the gable, and that gable toward the yard. The battlement-walls of this house diminished toward the high apex of a very steep roof by steps, as we are all so much accustomed to see, and the whole was surmounted by an iron weathercock, that was perched on a rod of some elevation. It was always a matter of importance with the Dutch to know which way the wind blew; nor did it comport with their habits of minute accuracy, to trust to the usual indications of the feeling on the skin, the bending of branches, the flying of clouds, or the driving of smoke; but they must and would have the certainty of a machine, that was constructed expressly to let them know the fact. Smoke might err, but a weathercock would not!

No one was in the little parlor into which I was shown by the servant who admitted me to the house, and in whom I recognized Herman Mordaunt's principal male attendant, of the household in New York. How pleasantly did that little room appear to me, in the minute or two that I was left in it alone. There lay the very shawl that Anneke had on the day I met her in the Pinkster Field; and a pair of gloves that it seemed to me no other hands but hers were small enough to wear, had been thrown on the shawl, carelessly, as one casts aside a thing of that sort, in a hurry. A dozen other articles were put here and there, that denoted the habits and presence of females of refinement. But the gloves most attracted my attention, and I must needs rise and examine them. It is true, these gloves might belong to Mary Wallace, for she, too, had a pretty little hand, but I fancied they belonged to Anneke. Under this impression, I raised them to my lips, and was actually pressing them there, with a good deal of romantic feeling, when a light footstep in the room told me I was not alone. Dropping the gloves, I turned and beheld Anneke herself. She was regarding me with an expression of countenance I did not then know how to interpret, and which I now hardly know how to describe. In the first place, her charming countenance was suffused with blushes, while her eyes were filled with an expression of softened interest, that caused my heart to beat so violently, that I did not know but it would escape by the channel of the throat. How near I was to declaring all I felt, at that moment; of throwing myself at the feet of the dear, dear creature, and of avowing how much and engrossingly she had filled both my waking and sleeping thoughts during the last year, and of beseeching her to bless the remainder of my days, by becoming my wife! Nothing prevented this sally, but the remark which Anneke made, the instant she had gracefully courtesied, in return to my confused and awkward bow, and which happened to be this:

"What do you find so much to admire in Miss Wallace's gloves?" asked the wilful girl, biting her lip, as I fancied, to suppress a smile, though her cheeks were still suffused, and her eyes continued to give forth that indescribable expression of bewitching softness. "It is a pair my father presented to her, and she wore them last evening in compliment to him."

"I beg pardon, Miss Mordaunt — Miss Anneke — that is — I beg pardon. Is there not a very delightful odor about those gloves — that is, I was thinking so, and was endeavoring to ascertain what it might be by the scent."

"It must be the lavender with which we young ladies are so coquettish as to sprinkle our gloves and handkerchiefs — or it may be musk. Mary is rather fond of musk, though I prefer lavender. But what an evening we had, Mr. Littlepage! and what an introduction you have had to Albany, and most of all, what a master of ceremonies!"

"Do you then dislike Guert Ten Eyck as an acquaintance, Miss Anneke?"

"Far from it. It is quite impossible to *dislike* Guert; he is so manly; so ready to admit his own weaknesses; so sincere in all he does and says; so good-natured; and, in short, so much that, were one his sister, she might wish him to be, and yet so much that a sister must regret."

"I thought last evening that all the ladies felt an interest in him, notwithstanding the numberless wild and ill-judged things he does. Is he not a favorite with Miss Wallace?"

The quick, sensitive glance that Anneke gave me, said plainly enough that my question was indiscreet, and it was no sooner put than it was regretted. A shadow passed athwart the sweet face of my companion, and a moment of deep, and, as I fancied, of painful thought succeeded. Then a light broke over all, a smile illumined her features, after which a light girlish laugh came to show how active were the agents within, and how strong was the native tendency to happiness and humor.

"After all, Corny Littlepage," said Anneke, turning her face toward me, with an indescribable character of fun and feeling so blended in it as fairly to puzzle me, "you must admit that your exploit in the hand-sled was sufficiently ridiculous to last a young man for some time!"

"I confess it all, Anneke, and shall have a care how I turn boy again in a strange place. I am rejoiced to find, however, that you look upon the foolish affair of the slide as more grave than that of the supper, which I was fearful might involve me in serious disgrace."

"Neither is very serious, Mr. Littlepage, though the last might have proved awkward, had not the mayor known the ways of the young men of the town. They say, however, that nothing so bold has ever before been attempted in that way, in Albany, great as are the liberties that are often taken with the neighbors' hen-coops."

And she laughed, and this time it was naturally, and without the least restraint.

"I hope you will not think it shabby in me, if I seem to wish to throw all the blame on this harum-scarum Guert Ten Eyck. He drew me into both affairs, and into the last, in a great measure, innocently and ignorantly."

"So it is understood, and so it would be understood, the moment Guert Ten Eyck was found to be connected with the affair at all."

"I may hope, then, to be forgiven, Anneke?" I said, holding out a hand to invite her to accept it as a pledge of pardon.

Anneke did not prudishly decline putting her own little hand in mine, though I got only the ends of two or three slender delicate fingers; and her color increased as she bestowed this grace.

"You must ask forgiveness, Corny," she answered — I believe she now used this familiar name simply to show how completely she had forgotten the little spleen she had certainly felt at my untoward exihibition in the street. "You must ask forgiveness of those who possess the right to pardon. If Corny Littlepage chooses to slide down hill, like a boy, what right has Anneke Mordaunt to say him nay?"

"Every right in the world — the right of friendship — the right of a superior mind, of superior manners — the right that my —— "

"Hush! — that is Mr. Bulstrode's footstep in the passage, and he will not understand this discussion on the subject of my manifold rights. It takes him some time, however, to throw aside his overcoats, and furs, and sword; and I will just tell you that Guert Ten Eyck is a dangerous master of ceremonies for Corny Littlepage."

"Yet, he has sense enough, feeling enough, *heart* enough to admire and love Mary Wallace."

"Has he told you this so soon! But I need not ask, as he tells his love to every one who will listen."

"And to Miss Wallace herself, I trust, among the number. The man who loves, and loves truly, should not long permit its object to remain in any doubt of his feelings and intentions. It has ever appeared to me, Miss Mordaunt, as a most base and dastardly feeling in a man to wish to be certain of a woman's returning his love, before he has the manliness to let his mistress understand his wishes. How is a sensitive female to know when she is safe in yielding her affections, without this frankness on the part of her suitor? I'll answer for it that Guert Ten Eyck has dealt thus honestly and frankly with Mary Wallace."

"That is a merit which cannot be denied him," answered Anneke, in a low, thoughtful tone of voice. "Mary has heard this from his own mouth, again and again. Even my presence has been no obstacle to his declarations, for three times have I heard him beg Mary to consider him as a suitor for her hand, and entreat her not to decide on his offer until he has had a longer opportunity to win her esteem."

" And this you will admit, Miss Mordaunt, is to his credit, is manly, and like himself? "

" It is certainly frank and honorable, Mr. Littlepage, since it enables Miss Wallace to understand the object of his attentions, and leaves nothing to doubt, or uncertainty."

" I am glad you approve of such fair and frank proceedings; — though but a moment remains to say what I wish, it will suffice to add, that the course Guert Ten Eyck has taken toward Mary Wallace, Cornelius Littlepage would wish to pursue toward Anneke Mordaunt."

Anneke started, turned pale; then showed cheeks that were suffused with blushes, and looked at me with timid surprise. She made no answer; though that earnest, yet timid gaze, long remained, and for that matter, still remains, vividly impressed upon my recollection. It seemed to express astonishment, startled sensibility, feminine bashfulness, and maiden coyness; but it did not appear to me that it expressed displeasure. There was no time, however, to ask for explanations, since the voices of Herman Mordaunt and Bulstrode were now heard at the very door, and at the next instant both entered the room.

CHAPTER XIV

" My beautiful! my beautiful! that standest meekly by,
With thy proudly arch'd and glossy neck, and dark and fiery eye — "

" Thus, thus I leap upon thy back, and scour the distant plains:
Away! who ovértakes me now, shall claim thee for his pains."

THE ARAB TO HIS STEED.

BULSTRODE seemed happy to meet me, complaining that I had quite forgotten the satisfaction with which all New York, agreeably to his account of the matter, had received me the past spring. Of course, I thanked him for his civility, and we soon became as good friends as formerly. In a minute or two Mary Wallace joined us, and we all repaired to the breakfast-table, where we were soon joined by Dirck, who had been detained by some affairs of his own.

Herman Mordaunt and Bulstrode had the conversation principally to themselves for the first few minutes. Mary Wallace was habitually silent; but Anneke, without being loquacious, was sufficiently disposed to converse. This morning, however, she said little beyond what the civilities of the table required from the mistress of the house, and that little in as few words as possible. Once or twice I could not help remarking that her hand remained on the handle of a richly-chased teapot, after that hand had performed its office; and that her sweet, deep blue eye was fixed on vacancy, or some object before her, with a vacant regard, in the manner of one that thought intensely. Each time as she recovered from these little *reveries*, a slight flush appeared on her face, and she seemed anxious to conceal the involuntary abstraction. This absence of mind continued until Bulstrode, who had been talking with our host on the subject of the movements of the army, suddenly directed his discourse to me.

" I hope we owe this visit to Albany," he said, " to an intention on your part, Mr. Littlepage, to make one among us in the next campaign. I hear of many gentlemen of the colonies who intend to accompany us in our march to Quebec."

"That is somewhat farther than I had thought of going,
Mr. Bulstrode," was my answer, "inasmuch as I have never supposed the king's forces contemplated quite so distant a march.
It is the intention of Mr. Follock and myself to get permission
to attach ourselves to some regiment, and to go forward as far
as Ticonderoga, at least; for we do not like the idea of the
French holding a post like that, so far within the limits of our
own province."

"Bravely said, sir; and I trust I shall be permitted to be
of some assistance when the time comes to settle details. Our
mess would always be happy to see you; and you know that I
am at its head, since the lieutenant-colonel has left us."

I returned my thanks, and the discourse took another direction.

"I met Harris, as I was walking hither this morning," Bulstrode
continued, "and he gave me, in his confused Irish — for I insist he is Irish, although he was born in London — but he gave
me a somewhat queer account of a supper he was at last night,
which he said had been borne off by a foraging party of young
Albanians, and brought into the barracks, as a treat to some
of our gentlemen. This was bad enough, though they tell me
a Dutchman always pardons such a frolic; but Harris makes
the matter much worse, by adding that the supperless party
indemnified itself by making an attack on the kitchen of Mr.
Mayor, and carrying off his ducks and partridges, in a way to
leave him without even a potato! "

I felt that my face was as red as scarlet, and I fancied every
body was looking at me, while Herman Mordaunt took on himself the office of making a reply.

"The story does not lose in travelling, as a matter of course,"
answered our host, "though it is true in the main. We all
supped with Mr. Cuyler last evening, and know that he had
much more than a potato on the table."

"All! — What, the ladies? "

"Even to the ladies — and Mr. Littlepage in the bargain,"
returned Herman Mordaunt, casting a glance at me, and smiling. "Each and all of us will testify he not only had a plenty
of supper, but that which was good."

"I see by the general smile," cried Bulstrode, "that there
is a *sous entendu* here, and shall insist on being admitted to the
secret."

Herman Mordaunt now told the whole story, not being particularly careful to conceal the more ludicrous parts, dwelling

with some emphasis on the lecture Mr. Worden had delivered to Doortje, and appealing to me to know whether I did not think it excellent. Bulstrode laughed, of course; though I fancied both the young ladies wished nothing had been said on the subject. Anneke even attempted, once or twice, to divert her father from certain comments that he made, in which he spoke rather lightly of such sort of amusements in general.

"That Guert Ten Eyck is a character!" exclaimed Bulstrode, "and one I am sometimes at a loss to comprehend. A more manly-looking, fine, bold, young fellow, I do not know; and he is often as manly and imposing in his opinions and judgments as he is to the eye; while at times he is almost childish in his tastes and propensities. How do you account for this, Miss Anneke?"

"Simply that nature intended Guert Ten Eyck for better things than accident and education, or the want of education, have enabled him to become. Had Guert Ten Eyck been educated at Oxford, he would have been a very different man from what he is. If a man has only the instruction of a boy, he will long remain a boy."

I was surprised at the boldness and decision of this opinion, for it was not Anneke's practice to be so open in delivering her sentiments of others; but it was not long ere I discovered that she did not spare Guert, in the presence of her friend, from a deep conviction he was not worthy of the hold he was sensibly gaining on the feelings of Mary Wallace. Herman Mordaunt, as I fancied, favored his daughter's views in this behalf; and there was soon occasion to observe that poor Guert had no other ally in that family, than the one his handsome, manly person, open disposition, and uncommon frankness had created in his mistress's own bosom. There was certainly a charm in Guert's habitual manner of underrating himself, that inclined all who heard him to his side; and, for myself, I will confess I early became his friend in all that matter, and so continued to the last.

Bulstrode and I left the house together, walking arm and arm to his quarters, leaving Dirck with the ladies.

"This is a charming family," said my companion, as we left the door: "and I feel proud of being able to claim some affinity to it, though it is not so near as I trust it may one day become."

I started, almost twitching my arm away from that of the major's, turning half round, at the same instant, to look him in

the face. Bulstrode smiled, but preserved his own self-possession in the stoical manner common to men of fashion and easy
manners, pursuing the discourse.

"I see that my frankness has occasioned you some little surprise," he added; "but the truth is the truth; and I hold it
to be unmanly for a gentleman, who has made up his mind
to become the suitor of a lady, to make any secret of his intentions; — is that not your own way of thinking, Mr. Littlepage?"

"Certainly, as respects the lady; and possibly, as respects her
family; but not as respects all the world."

"I take your distinction, which may be a good one, in ordinary cases; though, in the instance of Anneke Mordaunt, it
may be merciful to let wandering young men, like yourself,
Corny, comprehend the real state of the case. I very well
understand your own particular relation to the family of the
Mordaunts; but others may approach it with different and more
interested views."

"Am I to understand, Mr. Bulstrode, that Miss Mordaunt is
your betrothed?"

"Oh! by no means; for she has not yet made up her mind
to accept me. You are to understand, however, that I have
proposed to Herman Mordaunt, with my father's knowledge
and approbation, and that the affair is *in petto*. You can judge
for yourself of the probable termination, being a better judge,
as a looker-on, than I, as a party interested, of Anneke's manner of viewing my suit."

"You will remember I have not seen you together these ten
months, until this morning; and I presume you do not wish
me to suppose you have been waiting all that time for an answer."

"As I consider you an *ami de famille*, Corny, there is no
reason why there should not be a fair statement of things laid
before you, for that affair of the lion will ever render you half
a Mordaunt yourself. I had proposed to Anneke when you
first saw me, and got the usual lady-like answer that the dear
creature was too young to think of contracting herself, which
was certainly truer then than now; that I had friends at home
who ought to be consulted, that time must be given, or the
answer would necessarily be 'no,' and all the usual substance of
such replies, in the preliminary state of a negotiation."

"And there the matter has stood ever since?"

"By no means, my dear fellow; as far from that as possible. I heard Herman Mordaunt — for he did most of the talking on that side — with the patience of a saint, observed how proper it all was, and stated my intention to lay every thing before my father, and then advance to the assault anew, reinforced by his consent, and authority to offer settlements."

"All of which you got, by return of vessel, on writing home?" I added, unable to imagine how any man could hesitate about receiving Anneke Mordaunt for a daughter-in-law.

"Why, not exactly by return of vessel, though Sir Harry is much too well-bred to neglect answering a letter. I never knew him to do such a thing in his life; no, not when I have pushed him a little closely on the subject of my allowance having been out before the quarter was up, as will sometimes happen at college, you know, Corny. To tell you the truth, my dear boy, Sir Harry's consent did *not* come by return of vessel, though an answer did. It is a confounded distance across the Atlantic, and it takes time to argue a question when the parties are 'a thousand leagues asunder.'"

"Argue! — What argument could be required to convince Sir Harry Bulstrode of the propriety of your getting Anneke Mordaunt for a wife, *if you could?*"

"Quite plain and sincere, upon my honor! But, I love you for the simplicity of your character, Corny, and so shall view all favorably. If I *could!* Well, we shall know at the end of the approaching campaign, when you and I come back from our trip to Quebec."

"You have not answered my question, in the mean time, concerning Sir Harry Bulstrode."

"I beg Sir Harry's and your pardon. What argument could be required to convince my father? Why, you have never been at home, Littlepage, and cannot easily understand, therefore, what the feeling is precisely in relation to the colonies — much depends on that, you know."

"I trust the mother loves her children, as I am certain the children love their mother."

"Yes, you are all loyal; — I will say that for you, though Albany is not exactly Bath, or New York Westminster. I suppose you know, Littlepage, that the church upon the hill yonder, which is called St. Peter's, though a very good church and a very respectable church, with a very reputable congregation, is not exactly Westminster Abbey, or even St. James's?"

" I believe I understand you, sir; and so Sir Harry proved obstinate? "

" As the devil! — It took no less than three letters, the last of which was pretty bold, to get him round, which I did at last, and his consent, in due form, has been handed in to Herman Mordaunt. I contended with some advantages in the affair, or I never should have prevailed. But you will see how it was. Sir Harry is gouty and asthmatic both, and no great things of a life, at the best, and every acre he has on earth is entailed, just making the whole thing a question of time."

" All of which you communicated, of course, to Anneke and Herman Mordaunt? "

" If I did I'll be hanged! No, no; Master Corny, I am not so green as that would imply. You provincials are as thin-skinned as *raisons de Fontainebleau,* and are not to be touched so rudely. I do not believe Anneke would marry the Duke of Norfolk himself, if the family raised the least scruple about receiving her."

" And would not Anneke be right, in acting under so respectable a feeling? "

" Why, you know she would only marry the duke, and not his mother, and aunts, and uncles. I cannot see the necessity of a young woman's making herself uncomfortable on that account. But we have not come to that yet, for I would wish you to understand, Littlepage, that I am not accepted. No, no! justice to Anneke demands that I should say this much. She knows of Sir Harry's consent, however, and that is a good deal in my favor, you must allow. I suppose her great objection will be to quitting her father, who has no other child, and on him it *will* bear a little hard; and then it is likely she will say something about a change of country, for you Americans are all great sticklers for living in your own region."

" I do not see how you can justly accuse us of that, since it is universally admitted among us that every thing is better at home than it is in the colonies."

" I really think, Corny," rejoined Bulstrode, smiling good-naturedly, " were you to pay the old island a visit, now, you yourself would confess that some things *are."*

" I to visit! — I am at a loss to imagine why I am named as one disposed to deny it. Had it been Guert Ten Eyck, now, or even Dirck Follock, one might imagine such a thing; but I, who come from English blood, and who have an English-born grandfather, at this moment, alive and well at Satanstoe, am not to be included among the disaffected to England."

Bulstrode pressed my arm, and his conversation took a more confidential air, as it proceeded. " I believe you are right, Corny," he said; " the colony is loyal enough, heaven knows; yet I find these Dutch look on us red-coats more coldly than the people of English blood below. Should it be ascribed to the phlegm of their manners, or to some ancient grudge connected with the conquest of their colony? "

" Hardly the last, I should think, since the colony was traded away, under the final arrangement, in exchange for a possession the Dutch now hold in South America. There is nothing strange, however, in the descendants of the people of Holland preferring the Dutch to the English."

" I assure you, Littlepage, the coldness with which we are regarded by the Albanians has been spoken of among us; though most of the leading families treat us well, and aid us all they can. They should remember that we are here to fight their battles, and to prevent the French from overrunning them."

" To that they would probably answer that the French would not molest them, but for their quarrel with England. Here we must part, Mr. Bulstrode, as I have business to attend to. I will add one word, however, before we separate, and that is, that King George II, has not more loyal subjects in his dominions than those who dwell in his American provinces."

Bulstrode smiled, nodded in assent, waved his hand, and we parted.

I had plenty of occupation for the remainder of that day. Yaap arrived with his " brigade of sleighs " about noon, and I went in search of Guert, in whose company I repaired once more to the office of the contractor. Horses, harness, sleighs, provisions and all were taken at high prices, and I was paid for the whole in Spanish gold; joes and half-joes being quite as much in use among us in that day as the coin of the realm. Spanish silver has always formed our smaller currency, such a thing as an English shilling, or a sixpence, being quite a stranger among us. Pieces of eight, or dollars, are our commonest coin, it is true, but we make good use of the half-joe in all heavy transactions. I have seen two or three Bank of England notes in my day, but they are of rare occurrence in the colonies. There have been colony bills among us, but they are not favorites, most of our transactions being carried on by means of the Span-

ish gold and Spanish silver, that find their way up from the
islands and the Spanish main. The war of which I am now
writing, however, brought a great many guineas among us, most
of the troops being paid in that species of coin; but the contractors, in general, found it easier to command the half-joe
than the guinea. Of the former, when all our sales were made,
Dirck and myself had, between us, no less than one hundred and
eleven, or eight hundred and eighty-eight dollars in value.

I found Guert just as ready and just as friendly on this occasion, as he had been on the previous day. Not only were all
our effects disposed of, but all our negroes were hired to the
army for the campaign, Yaap excepted. The boys went off
with their teams toward the north that same afternoon, in high
spirits, as ready for a frolic as any white youths in the colony.
I permitted Yaap to go on with his sleigh, to be absent for a
few days, but he was to return and join us before we proceeded
in quest of the " patent," after the breaking up of the winter.

It was late in the afternoon before every thing was settled,
when Guert invited me to take a turn with him on the river in
his own sleigh. By this time I had ascertained that my new
friend was a young man of very handsome property, without
father or mother, and that he lived in as good style as was common for the simple habits of those around him. Our principal
families in New York were somewhat remarkable for the abundance of their plate, table-linen, and other household effects of
the latter character, while here and there one was to be found
that possessed some good pictures. The latter, I have reason
to think, however, were rare, though occasionally the work of
a master did find its way to America, particularly from Holland
and Flanders. Guert kept a bachelor's hall, in a respectable
house, that had its gable to the street, as usual, and which was
of no great size; but every thing about it proved that his old
black housekeeper had been trained under a *régime* of thorough
neatness; for that matter, every thing around Albany wore the
appearance of being periodically scoured. The streets themselves
could not undergo that process with snow on the ground; but
once beneath a roof, and every thing that had the character of
dirt was banished. In this particular Guert's bachelor residence
was as faultless as if it had a mistress at its head, and that mistress were Mary Wallace.

" If she ever consent to have me," said Guert, actually sighing as he spoke, and glancing his eyes round the very pretty little

parlor I had just been praising, on the occasion of the visit I first made to his residence that afternoon; " if she ever consent to have me, Corny, I shall have to build a new house. This is now a hundred years old, and though it was thought a great affair in its day, it is not half good enough for Mary Wallace. My dear fellow, how I envy you that invitation to breakfast this morning! what a favorite you must be with Herman Mordaunt! "

" We are very good friends, Guert " — for, with the freedom of our colony manners, we had already dropped into the familiarity of calling each other " Corny " and " Guert " — " we are very good friends, Guert," I answered, " and I have some reason to think Herman Mordaunt does not dislike me. It was in my power to be of a trifling service to Miss Anneke last spring, and the whole family are disposed to remember it."

" So I can see, at a glance; even Anneke remembers it. I have heard the whole story from Mary Wallace; it was about a lion. I would give half of what I am worth, to see Mary Wallace in the paws of a lion, or any other wild beast; just to let her see that Guert Ten Eyck has a heart, as well as Corny Littlepage. But, Corny my boy, there is one thing you must do; you are in such favor, that it will be easy for you to effect it; though I might try in vain, forever."

" I will do any thing that is proper, to oblige you, Guert, for you have a claim on me for services rendered by yourself."

" Pshaw! — Say nothing of such matters; I am never happier than when buying or selling a horse; and in helping you to get off your old cattle, why, I did the king no harm, and you some good. But it was about horses I was thinking. You must know, Littlepage, there is not a young man, or an old man, within twenty miles of Albany, that drives such a pair of beasts as myself."

" You surely do not wish to sell these horses to Mary Wallace, Guert! " I rejoined, laughing.

" Ay, my lad; and this house, and the old farm, and two or three stores along the river; and all I have, provided you can sell me with them. As the ladies have no present use for horses, however, Herman Mordaunt having brought up with him a very good pair, that came near running over you and me, Corny; so there is no need of any sale; but I *should* like to drive Mary and Anneke a turn of a few miles, with that team of mine, and in my own sleigh! "

" That cannot prove such a difficult affair; young ladies, ordinarily, consenting readily enough to be diverted with a sleigh-ride."

"The off-one carries himself more like a colonel at the head of his regiment, than like an ignorant horse!"

"I will propose the matter to Herman Mordaunt, or to Anneke, herself, if you desire it."

"And the near-one has the movement of a lady in a minuet, when you rein him in a little. I drove those cattle, Corny, across the pine-plains, to Schenectady, in one hour and twenty-six minutes! — sixteen miles as the crow flies, and nearer sixty if you follow all the turnings of the fifty roads."

"Well, what am I to do; tell this to the ladies, or beg them to name a day?"

"Name a day! — I wish it had come to that, Corny, with my whole soul. They are two beauties!"

"Yes, I think every body will admit *that*," I answered innocently; "yet, very different in their charms."

"Oh! not a bit more alike than is just necessary for a good match. I call one Jack, and the other Moses. I never knew an animal that was named 'Jack,' who would not do his work. I would give a great deal, Corny, that Mary Wallace could see that horse move!"

I promised Guert that I would use all my influence with the ladies, to induce them to trust themselves with his team; and, in order that I might speak with authority, the sleigh was ordered round to the door forthwith, with a view first to take a turn with me. The winter equipage of Guert Ten Eyck was really a tasteful and knowing thing. I had often seen handsomer sleighs, in the way of paint, varnish, tops and mouldings; for to these he appeared to pay very little attention. The point on which the owner most valued his sleigh, was the admirable manner in which it rested on its runners — pressing lightly both behind and before. Then the traces were nearer on a level with the horses than was common, though not so high as to affect the draft. The color without was a sky blue, a favorite Dutch tint; while within it was fiery red. The skins were very ample, all coming from the gray wolf. As these skins were lined with scarlet cloth, the effect of the whole was sufficiently cheering and warm. I ought not to forget the bells. In addition to the four sets buckled to the harness, the usual accompaniment of every sort of sleigh-harness, Guert had provided two enormous strings (always leathern straps), that passed from the saddles quite down under the bodies of Jack and Moses; and another string around each horse's neck, thus increasing the jingling music of his march at least fourfold beyond the usual quantity.*

In this style then, we dashed from the door of the old Ten Eyck house; all the blacks in the street gazing at us in delight, and shaking their sides with laughter — a negro always expresses his admiration of any thing, even to a sermon, in that mode. I remember to have heard a traveller who had been as far as Niagara, declare that his black did nothing but roar with laughter, the first half-hour he stood confronted with that mighty cataract.

Nor did the blacks alone stop to admire Guert Ten Eyck, his sleigh and his horses. All the young men in the place paid Guert this homage, for he was unanimously admitted to be the best whip, and the best judge of horse-flesh, in Albany; that is, the best judge for his years. Several young women who were out in sleighs, looked behind them, as we passed, proving that the admiration extended even to the other sex. All this Guert felt and saw, and its effect was very visible in his manner as he stood guiding his spirited pair, amid the wood-sleds that crowded the main street.

Our route lay toward the larger flats, that extend for miles along the west shore of the Hudson, to the north of Albany. This was the road usually taken by the young people of the place, in their evening sleigh-ride, not a few of the better class stopping to pay their respects to Madam Schuyler, a widow born of the same

* As it is possible this book may pass into the hands of others than Americans, it may be well to say that a sleigh-bell is a small hollow ball, made of bell-metal, having a hole in it that passes round half of its circumference, and containing a small *solid* ball, of a size not to escape. These bells are fastened to leathern straps, which commonly pass round the necks of the horses. In the time of Guert Ten Eyck, most of the bells were attached to small plates, that were buckled to various parts of the harness; but as this caused a motion annoying to the animals, Mr. Littlepage evidently wishes his readers to understand that his friend Ten Eyck was too knowing to have recourse to the practice. Even the straps are coming into disuse, the opinion beginning to obtain that sleigh-bells are a nuisance, instead of an advantage. Twenty years since, the laws of most large towns rendered them necessary, under the pretence of preventing accidents by apprising the footman of the approach of a sleigh; but more horses are now driven in the state of New York, without than with bells, in winter.

"Sleigh," as spelt, is purely an American word. It is derived from "slee," in Dutch, which is pronounced like "sleigh." Some persons contend that the Americans ought to use the old English words "sled," or "sledge." But these words do not precisely express the things we possess. There is as much reason for calling a pleasure conveyance by a name different from "sled," as there is for saying "coach" instead of "wagon." "Sleigh" *will* become English ere long as it is now American. Twenty millions of people not only can make a word, but they can make a language, if needed. — EDITOR.

family as that into which she had married, and who, from her
character, connections and fortune, filled a high place in the social
circle of the vicinity. Guert knew this lady, and proposed that I
should call and pay my respects to her — a tribute she was
accustomed to receive from most strangers of respectability.
Thither, then, we drove as fast as my companion's blacks could
carry us. The distance was only a few miles, and we were soon
dashing through the open gate, into what must have been a very
pretty, though an inartificial, lawn in the summer.

" By Jove, we are in luck! " cried Guert, the moment his eyes
got a view of the stables: " Yonder is Herman Mordaunt's sleigh,
and we shall find the ladies here! "

All this turned out as Guert had announced. Anneke and Mary
Wallace had dined with Madam Schuyler, and their coats and
shawls had just been brought to them, preparatory to returning
home, as we entered. I had heard so much of Madam Schuyler
as not to approach this respectable person without awe, and I
had no eyes at first for her companions. I was well received by
the mistress of the house, a woman of so large a size as to rise
from her chair with great difficulty, but whose countenance expressed equally intelligence, principles, refinement and benevolence.
She no sooner heard the name of Littlepage, than she threw a
meaning glance toward the young female friends, mine following
and perceiving Anneke coloring highly, and looking a little distressed. As for Mary Wallace she appeared to me then, as I
fancied was usually the case whenever Guert Ten Eyck approached
her, to be struggling with a species of melancholy pleasure.

" It is unnecessary for me to hear your mother's name, Mr.
Littlepage," said Madam Schuyler, extending a hand, " since I
knew her as a young woman. In *her* name you are welcome; as,
indeed, you would be in your own, after the all-important service
I hear you have rendered my sweet young friend, here."

I could only bow, and express my thanks; but it is unnecessary
to say how grateful to me was praise of this sort, coming, as I
knew it must, from Anneke in the first instance. Still I could
hardly refrain from laughing at Guert, who shrugged his shoulders,
and turned toward me with a look that repeated his ludicrous regrets he could not see Mary Wallace in a lion's paws! The conversation then took the usual turn, and I got an opportunity of
speaking to the young ladies.

After the character I had heard of Madam Schuyler, I was a
good deal surprised to find that Guert was somewhat of a favorite.

But even the most intellectual and refined women, I have since
had occasion to learn, feel a disposition to judge handsome, manly,
frank, flighty fellows like my new acquaintance, somewhat
leniently. With all his levity, and his disposition to run into the
excess of animal spirits, there was that about Guert which
rendered it difficult to despise him. The courage of a lion was
in his eye, and his front and bearing were precisely those that are
particularly attractive to women. To these advantages were
added a seeming unconsciousness of his superiority to most around
him, in the way of looks, and a humility of spirit that caused
him often to deplore his deficiencies in those accomplishments
which characterize the man of study and of intellectual activity.
It was only among the hardy, active, and reckless. that Guert
manifested the least ambition to be a leader.

"Do you still drive those spirited blacks, Guert," demanded
Madam Schuyler, in a gentle, affable way, that inclined her to
adapt her discourse to the tastes of those she might happen to be
with; "those, I mean, which you purchased in the autumn?"

"You may be certain of that, aunt" — every one who could
claim the most distant relationship to this amiable woman, and
whose years did not render the appellation disrespectful, called her
" aunt " — " you may be certain of that, aunt, for their equals are
not to be found in *this* colony. The gentlemen of the army pretend that no horse can be good that has not what they call *blood;*
but Jack and Moses are both of the Dutch breed, and the
Schuylers and the Ten Eycks will never own there is no ' blood '
in such a stock. I have given each of these animals my own name,
and call them Jack Ten Eyck and Moses Ten Eyck."

" I hope you will not exclude the Littlepages and the Mordaunts
from your list of dissenters, Mr. Ten Eyck," observed Anneke,
laughing, " since both have Dutch blood in their veins, too."

"Very true, Miss Anneke; Miss Wallace being the only true,
thorough Englishwoman here. But, as Aunt Schuyler has spoken
of my team, I wish I could persuade you and Miss Mary to let
me drive you back to Albany with it, this very evening. Your own
sleigh can follow; and your father's horses being English, we shall
have an opportunity of comparing the two breeds. The Anglo-
Saxons will have no load, while the Flemings will; still, I will
wager animal against animal, that the last do the work the most
nearly, and in the shortest time."

To this proposition, however, Anneke would not consent; her
instinctive delicacy, I make no doubt, at once presenting to her

mind the impropriety of quitting her own sleigh, to take an
evening's drive in that of a young man of Guert's established
reputation for recklessness and fun, and who was not always
fortunate enough to persuade young women of the first class to be
his companions. The turn the conversation had taken, nevertheless, had the effect to produce so many urgent appeals, that
were seconded by myself, to give the horses a trial, that Mary
Wallace promised to submit the matter to Herman Mordaunt,
and, should he approve, to accompany Guert, Anneke and myself, in an excursion the succeeding week.

This concession was received by poor Guert with profound
gratitude; and he assured me, as we drove back to town, that he
had not felt so happy for the last two months.

"It is in the power of such a young woman — young angel,
I might better say," added Guert, "to make any thing she may
please of me! I know I am an idler, and too fond of our Dutch
amusements, and that I have not paid the attention I ought to
have paid to books; but let that precious creature only take me
by the hand, and I should turn out an altered man in a month.
Young women can do any thing they please with us, Mr. Littlepage, when they set their minds about it in earnest. I wish I was
a horse, to have the pleasure of dragging Mary Wallace in this
excursion!"

CHAPTER XV

" When lo! the voice of loud alarm
His inmost soul appals:
What ho! Lord William, rise in haste!
The water saps thy walls!"

LORD WILLIAM.

THE visit to Madam Schuyler occurred of a Saturday evening; and the matter of our adventure in company with Jack and Moses, was to be decided on the following Monday. When I rose and looked out of my window on the Sunday morning, however, there appeared but very little prospect of its being effected that spring, inasmuch as it rained heavily, and there was a fresh south wind. We had reached the twenty-first of March, a period of the year when a decided thaw was not only ominous to the sleighing, but when it actually predicted a permanent breaking up of the winter. The season had been late, and it was thought the change could not be distant.

The rain and south wind continued all that day, and torrents of water came rushing down the short, steep streets, effectually washing away every thing like snow. Mr. Worden preached, notwithstanding, and to a very respectable congregation. Dirck and myself attended; but Jason preferred sitting out a double half-hour-glass sermon in the Dutch church, delivered in a language of which he understood very little, to lending his countenance to the rites of the English service. Both Anneke and Mary Wallace found their way up the hill, going in a carriage; though I observed that Herman Mordaunt was absent. Guert was in the gallery, in which we also sat; but I could not avoid remarking that neither of the young ladies raised her eyes once, during the whole service, as high as our pews. Guert whispered something about this, as he hastened down stairs to hand them to their carriage, when the congregation was dismissed, begging me at the same time, to be punctual to the appointment for the next day. What he meant by this last remembrancer I did not understand; for the hills were beginning to exhibit their bare breast, and it was somewhat surprising with what rapidity a rather

200

unusual amount of snow had disappeared. I had no opportunity to ask an explanation, as Guert was too busy in placing the ladies in the carriage, and the weather was not such as to admit of my remaining a moment longer in the street than was indispensably necessary.

A change occurred in the weather during the night, the rain having ceased, though the atmosphere continued mild, and the wind was still from the south. It was the commencement of the spring; and, as I walked round to Guert Ten Eyck's house, to meet him at breakfast, I observed that several vehicles with wheels were already in motion in the streets, and that divers persons appeared to be putting away their sleighs and sleds, as things of no further use, until the next winter. Our springs do not certainly come upon us as suddenly as some of which I have read, in the old world; but when the snow and winter endure as far into March as had been the case with that of the year 1758, the change is often nearly magical.

"Here, then, is the spring opening," I said to Dirck, as we walked along the well-washed streets; "and, in a few weeks, we must be off to the bush. Our business on the patent must be got along with before the troops are put in motion, or we may lose the opportunity of seeing a campaign."

With such expectations and feelings I entered Guert's bachelor abode; and the first words I uttered, were to sympathize in his supposed disappointment.

"It is a great pity you did not propose the drive to the ladies for Saturday," I begun; "for that was not only a mild day, but the sleighing was excellent. As it is, you will have to postpone your triumph until next winter."

"I do not understand you!" cried Guert; "Jack and Moses were never in better heart, or in better condition. I think they are equal to going to Kinderhook in two hours!"

"But who will furnish the roads with snow? By looking out of the window, you will see that the streets are nearly bare."

"Streets and roads! Who cares for either, while we have the river? We often use the river here, weeks at a time, when the snow has left us. The ice has been remarkably even the whole of this winter, and, now the snow is off it, there will be no danger from the air-holes."

I confess I did not much like the notion of travelling twenty miles on the ice, but was far too much of a man to offer any objections.

We breakfasted, and proceeded in a body to the residence of Herman Mordaunt. When the ladies first heard that we had come to claim the redemption of the half-promise given at Madam Schuyler's their surprise was not less than mine had been, half an hour before, while their uneasiness was probably greater.

"Surely, Jack and Moses cannot exhibit all their noble qualities without snow!" exclaimed Anneke, laughing, "Ten Eycks though they be?"

"We Albanians have the advantage of travelling on the ice, when the snow fails us," answered Guert. "Here is the river, near by, and never was the sleighing on it better than at this moment."

"But it has been many times safer, I should think. This looks very much like the breaking up of winter!"

"That is probably enough, and so much greater the reason why we should not delay, if you and Miss Mary ever intend to learn what the blacks can do. It is for the honor of Holland that I desire it, else would I not presume so far. I feel every condescension of this sort, that I receive from you two ladies, in a way I cannot express; for no one knows, better than myself, how unworthy I am of your smallest notice."

This brought the signs of yielding, at once, into the mild countenance of Mary Wallace. Guert's self-humiliation never failed to do this. There was so much obvious truth in his admission, so sincere a disposition to place himself, where nature and education, or a *want* of education had placed him, and most of all so profound a deference for the mental superiority of Mary herself, that the female heart found it impossible to resist. To my surprise, Guert's mistress, contrary to her habit in such things, was the first to join him, and to second his proposal. Herman Mordaunt entering the room at this instant, the whole thing was referred to him, as in reason it ought to have been.

"I remember to have travelled on the Hudson, a few years since," returned Herman Mordaunt, "the entire distance between Albany and Sing-Sing, and a very good time we had of it; much better than had we gone by land, for there was little or no snow."

"Just our case now, Miss Anneke!" cried Guert. "Good sleighing on the river, but none on the land."

"Was that near the end of March, dear Papa!" asked Anneke, a little inquiringly.

"No, certainly not, for it was early in February. But the

ice, at this moment, must be near eighteen inches thick, and strong enough to bear a load of hay."

"Yes, Masser Herman," observed Cato, a grey-headed black, who had never called his master by any other name, having known him from an infant; "yes, Masser Herman, a load do come over dis minute."

It appeared unreasonable to distrust the strength of the ice, after this proof to the contrary, and Anneke submitted. The party was arranged forthwith, and in the following manner: — the two ladies, Guert and myself, were to be drawn by the blacks, while Herman Mordaunt, Dirck, and any one else they could enlist, were to follow in the New York sleigh. It was hoped that an elderly female connection, Mrs. Bogart, who resided at Albany, would consent to be of the party, as the plan was to visit and dine with another, and a mutual connection of the Mordaunts, at Kinderhook. While the sleighs were getting ready, Herman Mordaunt walked round to the house of Mrs. Bogart, made his request, and was successful.

The clock in the tower of the English church struck ten as both sleighs drove from Herman Mordaunt's door. There was literally no snow in the middle of the streets; but enough of it, mingled with ice, was still to be found nearer the houses, to enable us to get down to the ferry, the point where sleighs usually went upon the river. Here Herman Mordaunt, who was in advance, checked his horses, and turned to speak to Guert on the propriety of proceeding. The ice near the shore had evidently been moved, the river having risen a foot or two, in consequence of the wind and thaw, and there was a sort of icy wave cast up near the land, over which it was indispensable to pass in order to get fairly on the river. As the top of this ridge or wave was broken, it exposed a fissure that enabled us to see the thickness of the ice, and this Guert pointed out in proof of its strength. There was nothing unusual in a small movement of the covering of the river, which the current often produces; but unless the vast fields below got in movement, it was impossible for those above materially to change their positions. Sleighs were passing too, still bringing to town hay from the flats on the eastern bank, and there was no longer any hesitation. Herman Mordaunt's sleigh passed slowly over the ridge, having a care to the legs of the horses, and ours followed in the same cautious manner, though the blacks jumped across the fissure in spite of their master's exertions.

Once on the river, however, Guert gave the blacks the whip and rein, and away we went like the wind. The smooth, icy surface of the Hudson was our road, the thaw having left very few traces of any track. The water had all passed beneath the ice, through cracks and fissures of one sort and another, leaving us an even, dry surface to trot on. The wind was still southerly, though scarcely warm, while a bright sun contributed to render our excursion as gay to the eye as it certainly was to our feelings. In a few minutes every trace of uneasiness had vanished. Away we went, the blacks doing full credit to their owner's boasts, seeming scarcely to touch the ice, from which their feet appeared to rebound with a sort of elastic force. Herman Mordaunt's bays followed on our heels, and the sleighs had passed over the well-known shoal of the Overslaugh, within the first twenty minutes after they touched the river.

Every northern American is familiar with the effect that the motion of a sleigh produces on the spirits, under favorable circumstances. Had our party been altogether composed of Albanians, there would probably have been no drawback on the enjoyment, for use would have prevented apprehension; but it required the few minutes I have mentioned to give Anneke and Mary Wallace full confidence in the ice. By the time we reached the Overslaugh, however, their fears had vanished; and Guert confirmed their sense of security, by telling them to listen to the sounds produced by his horses' hoofs, which certainly conveyed the impression of moving on a solid foundation.

Mary Wallace had never before been so gay in my presence, as she appeared to be that morning. Once, or twice, I fancied her eyes almost as bright as those of Anneke's, and certainly her laugh was as sweet and musical. Both the girls were full of spirits, and some little things occurred that gave me hopes Bulstrode had no reason to fancy himself as secure as he sometimes seemed to be. A casual remark of Guert's had the effect to bring out some of Anneke's private sentiments on the subject; or, at least, so they appeared to be to me.

"I am surprised that Mr. Mordaunt forgot to invite Mr. Bulstrode to be one of our party, to-day," cried Guert, when we were below the Overslaugh. "The major loves sleighing, and he would have filled the fourth seat in the other sleigh very agreeably. As for coming into this, that would be refused him, were he even a general! "

"Mr. Bulstrode is English," answered Anneke with spirit, " and fancies American amusements beneath the tastes of one who has been presented at the court of St. James."

"Well, Miss Anneke, I cannot say that I agree with you at all, in this opinion of Mr. Bulstrode," Guert returned, innocently. "It is true, he is English; that he fancies an advantage, as does Corny Littlepage, here; but we must make proper allowances for home-love and foreign dislike."

"'Corny Littlepage, here,' is only *half* English, and that half is colony-born and colony-bred," answered the laughing girl, "and he has loved a sleigh from the time when he first slid down hill —— "

"Ah! Miss Anneke — let me entreat —— "

"Oh! no allusion is intended to the Dutch church and its neighborhood; — but the sports of childhood are always dear to us, as are sometimes the discomforts. Habit and prejudice are sister handmaidens; and I never see one of these gentlemen from home taking extraordinary interest in any of our peculiarly colony usages, but I distrust an extra amount of complaisance, or a sort of enjoyment in which we do not strictly share."

"Is this altogether liberal to Bulstrode, Miss Anneke" I ventured to put in; "he seems to like us, and I am sure he has good reason so to do. That he likes *some* of us, is too apparent to be concealed or denied."

"Mr. Bulstrode is a skilful actor, as all who saw his Cato must be aware," retorted the charming girl, compressing her pouting lips in a way that seemed to me to be inexpressibly pleasing; "and those who saw his Scrub must be equally convinced of the versatility of his talents. No, no; Major Bulstrode is better where he is, or will be to-day, at four o'clock — at the head of the mess of the ——th, instead of dining in a snug Dutch parlor, with my cousin, worthy Mrs. Van der Heyden, at a dinner got up with colony hospitality, and colony good-will and colony plainness. The entertainment we shall receive to-day, sweetened, as it will be, by the welcome which will come from the heart, can have no competitor in countries where a messenger must be sent two days before the visit, to ask permission to come, in order to escape cold looks and artificial surprise. I would prefer surprising my friends from the heart, instead of from the head."

Guert expressed his astonishment that any one should not always be glad and willing to receive his friends; and insisted on it, that no such inhospitable customs *could* exist. I knew, however, that society could not exist on the same terms in old and in new countries — among a people that was pressed upon by numbers, and a people that had not yet felt the evils of a super-abundant population. Americans are like dwellers in the country, who are always glad to see their friends; and I ventured to say something of the causes of these differences in habits.

Nothing occurred worthy of being dwelt on, in our ride to Kinderhook. Mrs. Van der Heyden resided at a short distance from the river, and the blacks and the bays had some little difficulty in dragging us through the mud to her door. Once there, however, our welcome fully verified the theory of the colony habits, which had been talked over in our drive down. Anneke's worthy connection was not only glad to see her, as any body might have been, but she would have been glad to receive as many as her house would hold. Few excuses were necessary, for we were all welcome. The visit would retard her dinner an hour, as was frankly admitted — but that was nothing; and cakes and wine were set before us in the interval, did we feel hungry in consequence of a two hours' ride. Guert was desired to make free, and go to the stables to give his own orders. In a word, our reception was just that which every colonist has experienced, when he has gone unexpectedly to visit a friend, or a friend's friend. Our dinner was excellent, though not accompanied by much form. The wine was good; Mrs. Van der Heyden's deceased husband having been a judge of what was desirable in that respect. Every body was in good-humor; and our hostess insisted on giving us coffee before we took our departure.

"There will be a moon, cousin Herman," she said, "and the night will be both light and pleasant. Guert knows the road, which cannot well be missed, as it is the river; and if you quit me at eight, you will reach home in good season to go to rest. It is so seldom I see you, that I have a right to claim every minute you can spare. There remains much to be told concerning our old friends and mutual relatives."

When such words are accompanied by looks and acts that prove their sincerity, it is not easy to tear ourselves away from a pleasant house. We chatted on, laughed, listened to stories and colony anecdotes that carried us back to the last war, and heard a great many eulogiums on beaux and belles, that we young people had, all our lives, considered as respectable, elderly, common-place sort of persons.

At length the hour arrived when even Mrs. Bogart herself admitted we ought to part. Anneke and Mary were kissed, enveloped in their furs, and kissed again, and then we took our leave. As we left the house, I remarked that a clock in the passage struck eight. In a few minutes every one was placed, and the runners were striking fire from the flints of the bare ground. We had less difficulty in descending than in ascending the bank of the river, though there was no snow. It did not absolutely freeze, nor had it actually frozen since the commencement of the thaw, but the earth had stiffened since the disappearance of the sun. I was much rejoiced when the blacks sprang upon the ice, and whirled us away, on our return road at a rate even exceeding the speed with which they had come down it in the morning. I thought it high time we should be in motion on our return; and in motion we were, if flying at the rate of eleven miles in the hour could thus be termed.

The light of the moon was not clear and bright, for there was a haze in the atmosphere, as is apt to occur in the mild weather of March; but there was enough to enable Guert to dash ahead with as great a velocity as was at all desirable. We were all in high spirits; us two young men so much the more, because each of us fancied he had seen that day evidence of a tender interest existing in the heart of his mistress toward himself. Mary Wallace had managed, with a woman's tact, to make her suitor appear even respectable in female society, and had brought out in him many sentiments that denoted a generous disposition and a manly heart, if not a cultivated intellect; and Guert was getting confidence, and with it the means of giving his capacity fairer play. As for Anneke, she now knew my aim, and I had some right to construe several little symptoms of feeling, that escaped her in the course of the day, favorably. I fancied that, gentle as it always was, her voice grew softer, and her smile sweeter and more winning, as she addressed herself to, or smiled on me; and she did just enough of both not to appear distant, and just little enough to appear conscious; at least such were the conjectures of one who I do not think could be properly accused of too much confidence, and whose natural diffidence was much increased by the self-distrust of the purest love.

Away we went, Guert's complicated chimes of bells jingling their merry notes in a manner to be heard half a mile, the horses bearing hard on the bits, for they knew that their own stables lay at the end of their journey, and Herman Mordaunt's bays keeping so near us that, notwithstanding the noise we made with our own bells, the sounds of his were constantly in our ears. An hour went swiftly by, and we had already passed Coejeman's, and had a hamlet that stretched along the strand, and which lay quite beneath the high bank of the river, in dim distant view. This place has since been known by the name of Monkey Town, and is a little remarkable as being the first cluster of houses on the shores of the Hudson after quitting Albany. I dare say it has another name in law, but Guert gave it the appellation I have mentioned.

I have said that the night had a sombre, misty light, the moon wading across the heavens through a deep but thin ocean of vapor. We saw the shores plainly enough, and we saw the houses and trees, but it was difficult to distinguish smaller objects at any distance. In the course of the day twenty sleighs had been met or passed, but at that hour every body but ourselves appeared to have deserted the river. It was getting late for the simple habits of those who dwelt on its shores. When about half-way between the islands opposite Coejeman's and the hamlet just named, Guert, who stood erect to drive, told us that some one who was out late, like ourselves, was coming down. The horses of the strangers were in a very fast trot, and the sleigh was evidently inclining toward the west shore, as if those it held intended to land at no great distance. As it passed, quite swiftly, a man's voice called out something on a high key, but our bells made so much noise that it was not easy to understand him. He spoke in Dutch, too, and none of our ears, those of Guert excepted, were sufficiently expert in that language to be particularly quick in comprehending what he said. The call passed unheeded then, such things being quite frequent among the Dutch, who seldom passed each other on the highway without a greeting of some sort or other. I was thinking of this practice, and of the points that distinguished our own habits from those of the people of this part of the colony, when sleigh-bells sounded quite near me, and turning my head, I saw Herman Mordaunt's bays galloping close to us, as if wishing to get alongside. At the next moment the object was effected, and Guert pulled up.

"Did you understand the man who passed down, Guert?" demanded Herman Mordaunt, as soon as all noises ceased. "He called out to us, at the top of his voice, and would hardly do that without an object."

"These men seldom go home, after a visit to Albany, without filling their jugs," answered Guert, dryly; "what could he have to say, more than to wish us good-night!"

"I cannot tell, but Mrs. Bogart thought she understood something about 'Albany,' and 'the river.'"

"The ladies always fancy Albany is to sink into the river after a great thaw," answered Guert, good-humoredly; but I can show either of them that the ice is sixteen inches thick, here where we stand."

Guert then gave me the reins, stepped out of the sleigh, went a short distance to a large crack that he had seen while speaking, and returned with a thumb placed on the handle of the whip, as a measure to show that his statement was true. The ice at that spot was certainly nearer eighteen than sixteen inches thick. Herman Mordaunt showed the measure to Mrs. Bogart, whose alarm was pacified by this positive proof. Neither Anneke nor Mary exhibited any fear; but, on the contrary, as the sleighs separated again, each had something pleasant, but feminine, to say at the expense of poor Mrs. Bogart's imagination.

I believe I was the only person in our own sleigh who felt any alarm after the occurrence of this little incident. Why uneasiness beset *me*, I cannot precisely say. It must have been altogether on Anneke's account, and not in the least on my own. Such accidents as sleighs breaking through, on our New York lakes and rivers, happened almost every winter, and horses were often drowned; though it was seldom the consequences proved so serious to their owners. I recalled to mind the fragile nature of ice, the necessary effects of the great thaw and the heavy rains, remembering that frozen water might still retain most of its apparent thickness, after its consistency was greatly impaired. But I could do nothing! If we landed, the roads were impassable for runners, almost for wheels, and another hour might carry the ladies, by means of the river, to their comfortable homes. That day, however, which, down to the moment of meeting the unknown sleigh, had been the very happiest of my life, was entirely changed in its aspect, and I no longer regarded it with any satisfaction. Had Anneke been at home, I could gladly have entered into a contract to pass a week on the river myself, as the condition of her safety. I thought but little of the others, to my shame be it said, though I cannot do myself the injustice to imagine, had Anneke been away, that I would have deserted even a horse, while there was a hope of saving him.

Away we went! Guert drove rapidly, but he drove with judgment, and it seemed as if his blacks knew what was expected of them. It was not long before we were trotting past the hamlet

I have mentioned. It would seem that the bells of the two sleighs attracted the attention of the people on the shore, all of whom had not yet gone to bed; for the door of a house opened, and two men issued out of it, gazing at us as we trotted past at a pace that defied pursuit. These men also hallooed to us, in Dutch, and again Herman Mordaunt galloped up alongside, to speak to us.

"Did you understand these men?" he called out, for this time Guert did not see fit to stop the horses; "they, too, had something to tell us."

"These people always have something to tell an Albany sleigh, Mr. Mordaunt," answered Guert; "though it is not often that which it would do any good to hear."

"But Mrs. Bogart thinks they also had something to say about 'Albany,' and the 'river.'"

"I understand Dutch as well as excellent Mrs. Bogart," said Guert, a little dryly; "and I heard nothing; while I fancy I understand the river better. This ice would bear a dozen loads of hay, in a close line."

This again satisfied Herman Mordaunt and the ladies, but it did not satisfy me. Our own bells made four times the noise of those of Herman Mordaunt; and it was very possible that one, who understood Dutch perfectly, might comprehend a call in that language, while seated in his own sleigh, when the same call could not be comprehended by the same person, while seated in Guert's. There was no pause, however; on we trotted; and another mile was passed, before any new occurrence attracted attention.

The laugh was again heard among us, for Mary Wallace consented to sing an air, that was rendered somewhat ludicrous by the accompaniment of the bells. This song, or verse or two, for the singer got no further on account of the interruption, had drawn Guert's and my attention behind us, or away from the horses, when a whirling sound was heard, followed immediately by a loud shout. A sleigh passed within ten yards of us, going down, and the whirling sound was caused by its runners, while the shout came from a solitary man, who stood erect, waving his whip and calling to us in a loud voice, as long as he could be heard. This was but for a moment, however, as his horses were on the run; and the last we could see of the man, through the misty moonlight, he had turned his whip on his team, to urge it ahead still faster. In an instant, Herman Mordaunt was at our side, for the third time that night, and he called out to us somewhat authoritatively to stop.

"What can all this mean, Guert?" he asked. "Three times have we had warnings about 'Albany' and the 'river.' I heard this man myself utter those two words, and cannot be mistaken."

"I dare say, sir, that you may have heard something of the sort," answered the still incredulous Guert; "for these chaps have generally some impertinence to utter, when they pass a team that is better than their own. These blacks of mine, Herman Mordaunt, awaken a good deal of envy, whenever I go out with them; and a Dutchman will forgive you any other superiority, sooner than he will overlook your having the best team. That last man had a spur in his head, moreover, and is driving his cattle, at this moment, more like a spook than like a humane and rational being. I dare say he asked if we owned Albany and the river."

Guert's allusion to his horses occasioned a general laugh; and laughter is little favorable to cool reflection. We had looked out on the solemn and silent night, cast our eyes along the wide and long reach of the river, in which we happened to be, and saw nothing but the calm of nature, rendered imposing by solitude and the stillness of the hour. Guert smilingly renewed his assurances that all was right, and moved on. Away we went! Guert evidently pressed his horses, as if desirous of being placed beyond this anxiety as soon as possible. The blacks flew, rather than trotted; and we were all beginning to submit to the exhilaration of so rapid and easy a motion, when a sound which resembled that which one might suppose the simultaneous explosion of a thousand rifles would produce, was heard, and caused both drivers to pull up; the sleighs stopping quite near each other, and at the same instant! A slight exclamation escaped old Mrs. Bogart; but Anneke and Mary remained still as death.

"What means that sound, Guert?" inquired Herman Mordaunt; the concern he felt being betrayed by the very tone of his voice. "Something seems wrong!"

"Something *is* wrong," answered Guert, coolly, but very decidedly; "and it is something that must be seen to."

As this was said, Guert stepped out on the ice, which he struck a hard blow with the heel of his boot, as if to make certain of its solidity. A second report was heard, and it evidently came from *behind* us. Guert gazed intently down the river; then he laid his head close to the surface of the ice, and looked again.

At the same time, three or four more of these startling reports followed each other in quick succession. Guert instantly rose to his feet.

"I understand it, now," he said, "and find I have been rather too confident. The ice, however, is safe and strong, and we have nothing to fear from its weakness. Perhaps it would be better to quit the river notwithstanding, though I am far from certain the better course will not be to push on."

"Let us know the danger at once, Mr. Ten Eyck," said Herman Mordaunt, "that we may decide for the best."

"Why sir, I am afraid that the rains and the thaw together, have thrown so much water into the river, all at once, as it might be, as to have raised the ice and broken it loose, in spots, from the shores. When this happens *above*, before the ice has disappeared below, it sometimes causes dams to form, which heap up such a weight as to break the whole plain of ice far below it, and thus throw cakes over cakes until walls twenty or thirty feet high are formed. This has not happened *yet*, therefore there is no immediate danger; but by bending your heads low, you can see that such a *break* has just taken place about half a mile below us."

We did as Guert directed, and saw that a mound had arisen across the river nearer than the distance named by our companion, completely cutting off retreat by the way we had come. The bank on the west side of the Hudson was right at the point where we were, and looking intensely at it, I saw by the manner in which the trees disappeared, the more distant behind those that were nearer, that we were actually in motion! An involuntary exclamation caused the whole party to comprehend this startling fact at the same instant. We were certainly in motion, though very slowly, on the ice of that swollen river, in the quiet and solitude of a night in which the moon rather aided in making danger apparent than in assisting us to avoid it! What was to be done? It was necessary to decide, and that promptly and intelligently.

We waited for Herman Mordaunt to advise us, but he referred the matter at once to Guert's greater experience.

"We cannot land here," answered the young man, "so long as the ice is in motion, and I think it better to push on. Every foot will bring us so much nearer to Albany, and we shall get among the islands a mile or two higher, where the chances of landing will be greatly increased. Besides, I have often crossed the river on a cake, for they frequently stop, and I have known even loaded sleighs profit by them to get over the river. As yet there is nothing very alarming; — let us push on, and get nearer to the islands."

This, then, was done, though there was no longer heard the laugh or the song among us. I could see that Herman Mordaunt was uneasy about Anneke, though he could not bring her into his own sleigh, leaving Mary Wallace alone; neither could he abandon his respectable connection, Mrs. Bogart. Before we re-entered the sleighs, I took an occasion to assure him that Anneke should be my especial care.

" God bless you, Corny, my dear boy," Herman Mordaunt answered, squeezing my hand with fervor. " God bless you, and enable you to protect her. I was about to ask you to change seats with me; but, on the whole, I think my child will be safer with you than she could be with me. We will await God's pleasure as accident has placed us."

" I will desert her only with life, Mr. Mordaunt. Be at ease on that subject."

" I know you will not — I am *sure* you will not, Littlepage; that affair of the lion is a pledge that you will not. Had Bulstrode come, we should have been strong enough to — but Guert is impatient to be off. God bless you, boy — God bless you. Do not neglect my child."

Guert *was* impatient, and no sooner was I in the sleigh than we were once more in rapid motion. I said a few words to encourage the girls, and then no sound of a human voice mingled with the gloomy scene.

END OF VOLUME I

CHAPTER XVI

"He started up, each limb convulsed
  With agonizing fear,
He only heard the storm of night —
  'Twas music to his ear."

LORD WILLIAM.

AWAY we went! Guert's aim was the islands, which carried him nearer home, while it offered a place of retreat, in the event of the danger's becoming more serious. The fierce rapidity with which we now moved prevented all conversation, or even much reflection. The reports of the rending ice, however, became more and more frequent, first coming from above, and then from below. More than once it seemed as if the immense mass of weight that had evidently collected somewhere near the town of Albany, was about to pour down upon us in a flood — when the river would have been swept for miles, by a resistless torrent. Nevertheless, Guert held on his way; firstly, because he knew it would be impossible to get on either of the main shores, anywhere near the point where we happened to be; and secondly, because having often seen similar dammings of the waters, he fancied we were still safe. That the distant reader may understand the precise character of the danger we ran, it may be well to give him some notion of the localities.

The banks of the Hudson are generally high and precipitous, and in some places they are mountainous. No flats worthy of being mentioned, occur, until Albany is approached; nor are those which lie south of that town, of any great extent, compared with the size of the stream. In this particular the Mohawk is a very different river, having extensive flats that, I have been told, resemble those of the Rhine, in miniature. As for the Hudson, it is generally esteemed in the colony as a very pleasing river; and I remember to have heard intelligent people from home admit, that even the majestic Thames itself, is scarcely more worthy to be visited, or that it better rewards the trouble and curiosity of the enlightened traveller.*

---

* This remark of Mr. Cornelius Littlepage's may induce a smile in the reader. But few persons of fifty can be found, who cannot recall the time, when it was a rare

While there are flats on the shores of the Hudson, and of some extent, in the vicinity of Albany, the general formation of the adjacent country is preserved — being high, bold, and in some quarters, more particularly to the northward and eastward, mountainous. Among these hills the stream meanders for sixty or eighty miles north of the town, receiving tributaries as it comes rushing down toward the sea. The character of the river changes entirely, a short distance above Albany; the tides flowing to that point, rendering it navigable, and easy of ascent in summer, all the way from the sea. Of the tributaries, the principal is the Mohawk, which runs a long distance toward the west — they tell me, for I have never visited those remote parts of the colony — among fertile plains, that are bounded north and south by precipitous highlands. Now, in the spring, when the vast quantities of snow, that frequently lie four feet deep in the forests, and among the mountains and valleys of the interior, are suddenly melted by the south winds and rains, freshets necessarily succeed, which have been known to do great injury. The flats of the Mohawk, they tell me, are annually overflowed, and a moderate freshet is deemed a blessing; but occasionally a union of the causes I have mentioned, produces a species of deluge that has a very opposite character. Thus it is, that houses are swept away; and bridges from the smaller mountain streams, have been known to come floating past the wharves of Albany, holding their way toward the ocean. At such times the tides produce no counter-current; for it is a usual thing, in the early months of the spring, to have the stream pour downward for weeks, the whole length of the river, and to find the water fresh even as low as New York.

Such was the general nature of the calamity we had been so unexpectedly made to encounter. The winter had been severe, and the snows unusually deep; and, as we drove furiously onward, I remembered to have heard my grandfather predict ex-

---

thing to imagine *any thing* American as good as its English counterpart. The American who could write a book — a real, live book — forty years since, was a sort of prodigy. It was the same with him who could paint any picture beyond a common portrait. The very fruits and natural productions of the country were esteemed doubtingly; and he was a bold man who dared to extol even canvas-back ducks, in the year 1800! At the present day, the feeling is fast undergoing an organic change. It is now the fashion to *extol* every thing American, and from submitting to a degree that was almost abject, to the feeling of colonial dependency, the country is filled to-day with the most profound provincial self-admiration. It is to be hoped that the next change will bring us to something like the truth. — EDITOR.

traordinary freshets in the spring, from the character of the winter, as we had found it, even previously to my quitting home. The great thaw, and the heavy rains of the late storms, had produced the usual effect; and the waters thus let loose among the distant as well as the nearer hills, were now pouring down upon us in their collected might. In such cases, the first effect is, to loosen the ice from the shores; and local causes forcing it to give way at particular points, a breaking up of its surface occurs and dams are formed, that set the stream back in floods upon all the adjacent low land, such as the flats in the vicinity of Albany.

We did not then know it, but, at the very moment Guert was thus urging his blacks to supernatural efforts — actually running them as if on a race-course — there was a long reach of the Hudson, opposite to, for a short distance below, and for a considerable distance above the town, which was quite clear of stationary ice. Vast cakes continued to come down, it is true, passing on to increase the dam that had formed below, near and on the Overslaugh, where it was buttressed by the islands, and rested on the bottom; but the whole of that firm field, on which we had first driven forth that morning, had disappeared! This we did not know at the time, or it might have changed the direction of Guert's movements; but I learned it afterward, when placed in a situation to inquire into the causes of what had occurred.

Herman Mordaunt's bells, and the rumbling sound of his runners, were heard close behind us, as our own sleigh flew along the river at a rate that I firmly believe could not have been much less than that of twenty miles in the hour. As we were whirled northward, the reports made by the rending of the ice increased in frequency and force. They really became appalling! Still the girls continued silent, maintaining their self-command in a most admirable manner; though I doubt not that they felt, in the fullest extent, the true character of the awful circumstances in which we were placed. Such was the state of things, as Guert's blacks began sensibly to relax in their speed, for want of wind. They still galloped on, but it was no longer with the swiftness of the wind; and their master became sensible of the folly of hoping to reach the town ere the catastrophe should arrive. He reined in his panting horses, therefore, and was just falling into a trot, as a violent report was heard directly in our front. At the next instant the ice rose, positively beneath our horses' hoofs, to the height of several feet, taking the form of the roof of a house. It was too late to retreat, and Guert shouting out "Jack"—"Moses," applied the whip, and the spirited animals actually went over the mound, leaping a crack three feet in width, and reaching the level ice beyond. All this was done, as it might be, in the twinkling of an eye. While the sleigh flew over this ridge, it was with difficulty I held the girls in their seats; though Guert stood nobly erect, like the pine that is too firmly rooted to yield to the tempest. No sooner was the danger passed, however, than he pulled up, and came to a dead halt.

We heard the bells of Herman Mordaunt's sleigh on the other side of the barrier, but could see nothing. The broken cakes, pressed upon by millions of tons' weight above, had risen fully ten feet, into an inclination that was nearly perpendicular; rendering crossing it next to impossible, even to one afoot. Then came Herman Mordaunt's voice, filled with paternal agony and human grief, to increase the awe of that dreadful moment!

" Shore!—shore!—" he shouted, or rather yelled—" In the name of a righteous Providence, to the shore, Guert! "

The bells passed off toward the western bank, and the rumbling of the runners accompanied their sound. That was a breathless moment to us four. We heard the rending and grinding of the ice, on all sides of us; saw the broken barriers behind and in front; heard the jingling of Herman Mordaunt's bells, as it became more and more distant, and finally ceased; and felt as if we were cut off from the rest of our species. I do not think either of us felt any apprehension of breaking through; for use had so accustomed us to the field of the river, while the more appalling grounds of alarm were so evident, that no one thought of such a source of danger. Nor was there much, in truth, to apprehend from that cause. The thaw had not lasted long enough materially to diminish either the thickness or the tenacity of the common river ice; though it was found unequal to resisting the enormous pressure that bore upon it from above. It is probable that a cake of an acre's size would have upheld, not only ourselves, but our sleigh and horses, and carried us, like a raft, down the stream; had there been such a cake free from stationary impediments. Even the girls now comprehended the danger, which was in a manner suspended over us—as the impending wreath of snow menaces the fall of the *avalanche*. But it was no moment for indecision or inaction.

Cut off, as we were, by an impassable barrier of ice, from

the route taken by Herman Mordaunt, it was necessary to come to some resolution on our own course. We had the choice of endeavoring to pass to the western shore, on the upper side of the barrier, or of proceeding toward the nearest of several low islands which lay in the opposite direction. Guert determined on the last, walking his horses to the point of land, there being no apparent necessity for haste, while the animals greatly needed breath. As we went along, he explained to us that the fissure below cut us off from the only point where landing on the western shore could be practicable. At the same time, he put in practice a pious fraud, which had an excellent effect on the feelings and conduct of both the girls, throughout the remainder of the trying scenes of that fearful night; more especially on those of Anneke. He dwelt on the good fortune of Herman Mordaunt, in being on the right side of the barrier that separated the sleighs, in a way to induce those who did not penetrate his motive, to fancy the rest of the party were in a place of security, as the consequence of this accident. Thus did Anneke believe her father safe, and thus was she relieved from much agonizing doubt.

As soon as the sleigh came near the point of the island, Guert gave me the reins, and went ahead to examine whether it were possible to land. He was absent fifteen minutes; returning to us only after he had made a thorough search into the condition of the island, as well as of that of the ice in its eastern channel. These were fifteen fearful minutes; the rending of the masses above, and the grinding of cake on cake, sounding like the roar of the ocean in a tempest. Notwithstanding all the awful accessories of this dreadful night, I could not but admire Guert's coolness of manner, and his admirable conduct. He was more than resolute; for he was cool, collected, and retained the use of all his faculties in perfection. As plausible as it might seem, to one less observant and clear-headed, to attempt escaping to the western shore, Guert had decided right in moving toward the island. The grinding of the ice, in another quarter, had apprised him that the water was forcing its way through, near the mainland; and that escape would be nearly hopeless on that side of the river. When he rejoined us, he called me to the heads of the horses, for a conference; first solemnly assuring our precious companions that there were no grounds for immediate apprehension. Mary Wallace anxiously asked him to repeat this to *her*, on the faith due from man to woman; and he did it; when I was permitted to join him without further opposition.

"Corny," said Guert, in a low tone, "Providence has punished me for my wicked wish of seeing Mary Wallace in the claws of lions; for all the savage beasts of the old world, could hardly make our case more desperate than it now is. We must be cool, however, and preserve the girls, or die like men."

"Our fates are, and must be the same. Do you devote yourself to Mary, and leave Anneke to me. But why this language; surely our case is by no means so desperate?"

"It might not be so difficult for two active, vigorous young men to get ashore; but it would be different with females. The ice is in motion all around us; and the cakes are piling and grinding on each other in a most fearful manner. Were it light enough to see, we should do much better; but, as it is, I dare not trust Mary Wallace any distance from this island, at present. We may be compelled to pass the night here, and must make provision accordingly. You hear the ice grinding on the shore; a sign that every thing is going down stream. God send that the waters break through ere long; though they may sweep all before them, when they do come. I fear me, Corny, that Herman Mordaunt and his party are lost!"

"Merciful Providence! — can it be as bad as that! — I rather hope they have reached the land."

"*That* is impossible, on the course they took. Even a man would be bewildered and swept away, in the torrent that is driving down under the west shore. It is that vent to the water which saves us. But, no more words. You now understand the extent of the danger, and will know what you are about. We must get our precious charges on the island, if possible, without further delay. Half an hour — nay, half a minute may bring down the torrent."

Guert took the direction of every thing. Even while we had been talking, the ice had moved materially; and we found ourselves fifty feet further from the island than we had been. By causing the horses to advance, this distance was soon recovered; but it was found impossible to lead or drive them over the broken cakes with which the shore of the island now began to be lined. After one or two spirited and determined efforts, Guert gave the matter up, and asked me to help the ladies from the sleigh. Never did women behave better than did these delicate and lovely girls, on an occasion so awfully trying. Without remonstrances, tears, exclamations, or questions, both did as desired; and I cannot express the feeling of security I felt, when I had helped each over the broken and grinding border of white ice that separated us from the shore. The night was far from cold; but the ground was now frozen sufficiently to prevent any unpleasant consequences from walking on what would otherwise have been a slimy, muddy alluvion; for the island was so very low as often to be under water, when the river was particularly high. This, indeed, formed our danger, after we had reached it.

When I returned to Guert, I found him already drifted down some little distance; and this time we moved the sleigh so much above the point, as to be in less danger of getting out of sight of our precious wards. To my surprise, Guert was busy in stripping the harness from the horses, and Jack already stood only in his blinkers. Moses was soon reduced to the same state. I was wondering what was to be done next, when Guert drew each bridle from its animal, and gave a smart crack of his whip. The liberated horses started back with affright — snorted, reared, and, turning away, they went down the river, free as air, and almost as swift; the incessant and loud snapping of their master's whip, in no degree tending to diminish their speed. I asked the meaning of this.

"It would be cruel not to let the poor beasts make use of the strength and sagacity nature has given them to save their lives," answered Guert, straining his eyes after Moses, the horse that was behind, so long as his dark form could be distinguished, and leaning forward to listen to the blows of their hoofs, while the noises around us permitted them to be heard. "To us they would only be an encumbrance, since they could never be forced over the cracks and caked ice in harness; nor would it be at all safe to follow them, if they could. The sleigh is light, and we are strong enough to shove it to land, when there is an opportunity; or, it may be left on the island."

Nothing could have served more effectually to convince me of the manner in which Guert regarded our situation, than to see him turn loose beasts which I knew he so highly prized. I mentioned this; and he answered me with a melancholy seriousness, that made the impression so much the stronger —

"It is possible they may get ashore, for nature has given a horse a keen instinct. They can swim, too, where you and I would drown. At all events, they are not fettered with harness, but have every chance it is in my power to give them. Should they land, any farmer would put them in his stable, and

I should soon hear where they were to be found; if, indeed, I am living in the morning to make the inquiry."

" What is next to be done, Guert? " I asked, understanding at once both his feelings and his manner of reasoning.

" We must now run the sleigh on the island; after which it will be time to look about us, and to examine if it be possible to get the ladies on the mainland."

Accordingly, Guert and I applied ourselves to the task, and had no great difficulty in dragging the sleigh over the cakes, grinding and in motion as they were. We pulled it as far as the tree beneath which Anneke and Mary stood; when the ladies got into it and took their seats, enveloped in the skins. The night was not cold for the season, and our companions were thickly clad, having tippets and muffs; still, the wolves' skins of Guert contributed to render them more comfortable. All apprehension of immediate danger now ceased for a short time; nor do I think either of the females fancied they could run any more risk, beyond that of exposure to the night air, so long as they remained on *terra firma*. Such was not the case, however, as a very simple explanation will render apparent to the reader.

All the islands in this part of the Hudson are low, being rich alluvial meadows, bordered by trees and bushes; most of the first being willows, sycamores, or nuts. The fertility of the soil had given to these trees rapid growths, and they were generally of some stature; though not one among them had that great size which ought to mark the body and branches of a venerable tenant of the forest. This fact, of itself, proved that no one tree of them all was *very* old; a circumstance that was certainly owing to the ravages of the annual freshets. I say annual; for though the freshet which now encompassed us was far more serious than usual, each year brought something of the sort; and the islands were constantly increasing or diminishing under their action. To prevent the last, a thicket of trees was left at the head of each island, to form a sort of barricade against the inroads of the ice in the spring. So low was the face of the land, or meadow, however, that a rise of a very few feet in the river would be certain to bring it entirely under water. All this will be made more apparent by our own proceedings, after we had placed the ladies in the sleigh; and more especially by the passing remarks of Guert while employed in his subsequent efforts.

No sooner did Guert Ten Eyck believe the ladies to be temporarily safe, than he proposed to me that we should take a closer look at the state of the river, in order to ascertain the most feasible means of getting on the mainland. This was said aloud, and in a cheerful way, as if he no longer felt any apprehension, and evidently to me, to encourage our companions. Anneke desired us to go, declaring that now she knew herself to be on dry land all her own fears had vanished. We went accordingly, taking our first direction toward the head of the island.

A very few minutes sufficed to reach the limits of our narrow domain; and as we approached them Guert pointed out to me the mound of ice that was piling up behind it, as a most fearful symptom.

" *There* is our danger," he said, with emphasis, " and we must not trust to these trees. This freshet goes beyond any I ever saw on the river; and not a spring passes that we have not more or less of them. Do you not see, Corny, what saves us now? "

" We are on an island, and cannot be in much danger from the river while we stay here."

" Not so, my dear friend, not at all so. But come with me, and look for yourself."

I followed Guert, and did look for myself. We sprang upon the cakes of ice, which were piled quite thirty feet in height, on the head of the island, extending right and left, as far as our eyes could see, by that misty light. It was by no means difficult moving about on this massive pile, the movement in the cakes being slow, and frequently interrupted; but there was no concealing the true character of the danger. Had not the island, and the adjacent main interposed their obstacles, the ice would have continued to move bodily down the stream, cake shoving over cake, until the whole found vent in the wider space below, and floated off toward the ocean. Not only was our island there, however, but other islands lay near us, straitening the different channels or passages in such a way as to compel the formation of an icy dam; and, on the strength of this dam rested all our security. Were it to be ruptured anywhere near us, we should inevitably be swept off in a body. Guert thought, however, as has been said already, that the waters had found narrow issues under the mainland, both east and west of us; and should this prove to be true, there was a hope that the great calamity might be averted. In other words, if these floodgates sufficed, we *might* escape; otherwise the catastrophe was certain.

"I cannot excuse it to myself to remain here, without endeavoring to see what is the state of things nearer to the shore," said Guert, after we had viewed the fast accumulating mass of broken ice above us, as well as the light permitted, and we had talked over together the chances of safety, and the character of the danger. "Do you return to the ladies, Corny, and endeavor to keep up their spirits, while I cross this channel on our right, to the next island, and see what offers in that direction."

"I do not like the idea of your running all the risk alone; besides, something may occur to require the strength of two, instead of that of one, to overcome it."

"You can go with me as far as the next island, if you will, where we shall be able to ascertain at once whether it be ice or water that separates us from the eastern shore. If the first, you can return as fast as possible for the ladies, while I look for a place to cross. I do not like the appearance of this dam, to be honest with you; and have great fears for those who are now in the sleigh."

We were in the very act of moving away, when a loud cracking noise, that arose within a few yards, alarmed us both; and running to the spot whence it proceeded, we saw that a large willow had snapped in two, like a pipe-stem, and that the whole barrier of ice was marching, slowly, but grandly, over the stump, crushing the fallen trunk and branches beneath its weight, as the slow-moving wheel of the loaded cart crushes the twig. Guert grasped my arm, and his fingers nearly entered the flesh, under his iron pressure.

"We must quit this spot — " he said firmly, "and at once. Let us go back to the sleigh."

I did not know Guert's intentions, but I saw it was time to act with decision. We moved swiftly down to the spot where we had left the sleigh; and the reader will judge of our horror, when we found it gone! The whole of the low point of the island where we had left it, was already covered with cakes of ice that were in motion, and which had doubtless swept off the sleigh during the few minutes that we had been absent! Looking around us, however, we saw an object on the river, a little distance below, that I fancied was the sleigh, and was about to rush after it, when a voice, filled with alarm, took us in another direction. Mary Wallace came out from behind a tree, to which she had fled for safety, and seizing Guert's arm, implored him not to quit her again.

"Whither has Anneke gone?" I demanded, in an agony I cannot describe — "I see nothing of Anneke!"

"She would not quit the sleigh," answered Mary Wallace, almost panting for breath — "I implored — entreated her to follow me — said you *must* soon return; but she refused to quit the sleigh. Anneke is in the sleigh, if that can now be found."

I heard no more; but springing on the still moving cakes of ice, went leaping from cake to cake, until my sight showed me that, sure enough, the sleigh was on the bed of the river, over which it was in slow motion; forced downward before the new coating of ice that was fast covering the original surface. At first I could see no one in the sleigh; but, on reaching it, I found Anneke buried in the skins. She was on her knees; the precious creature was asking succor from God!

I had a wild but sweet consolation in thus finding myself, as it might be, cut off from all the rest of my kind, in the midst of that scene of gloom and desolation, alone with Anneke Mordaunt. The moment I could make her conscious of my presence, she inquired after Mary Wallace, and was much relieved on learning that she was with Guert, and would not be left by him, for a single instant, again that night. Indeed, I saw their figures dimly, as they moved swiftly across the channel that divided the two islands, and disappear in that direction, among the bushes that lined the place to which they had gone.

"Let us follow," I said, eagerly. "The crossing is yet easy, and we, too, may escape to the shore."

"Go you!" said Anneke, over whom a momentary physical torpor appeared to have passed. "Go you, Corny," she said; "a man may easily save himself; and you are an only child — the sole hope of your parents."

"Dearest, beloved Anneke! — why this indifference — this apathy on your own behalf? Are *you* not an only child, the sole hope of a widowed father? — do you forget *him?*"

"No, no, no!" exclaimed the dear girl, hurriedly. "Help me out of the sleigh, Corny; there, I will go with you anywhere — anyhow — to the end of the world, to save my father from such anguish!"

From that moment the temporary imbecility of Anneke vanished, and I found her, for the remainder of the time we remained in jeopardy, quick to apprehend, and ready to second all my efforts. It was this passing submission to an imaginary doom, on the one hand, and the headlong effect of sudden fright on the other, which had separated the two girls, and which had been the means of dividing the whole party as described.

I scarcely know how to describe what followed. So intense was my apprehension on behalf of Anneke, that I can safely say, I did not think of my own fate in the slightest degree as disconnected from hers. The self-devoted reliance with which the dear girl seemed to place all her dependence on me, would of itself have produced this effect, had she not possessed my whole heart, as I was now so fully aware. Moments like those make one alive to all the affections, and strip off every covering that habit, or the dissembling of our manners is so apt to throw over the feelings. I believe I both spoke and acted toward Anneke, as one would cling to, or address the being dearest to him in the world, for the next few minutes; but I can suppose the reader will naturally prefer learning what we did, under such circumstances, rather than what we said, or how we felt.

I repeat, it is not easy for me to describe what followed. I know we first rather ran than walked, across the channel on which I had last seen the dim forms of Guert and Mary, and even crossed the island to its eastern side, in the hope of being able to reach the shore in that quarter. The attempt was useless, for we found the water running down over the ice like a race-way. Nothing could be seen of our late companions; and my loud and repeated calls to them were unanswered.

"Our case is hopeless, Cornelius," said Anneke; speaking with a forced calmness, when she found retreat impossible in that direction. "Let us return to the sleigh, and submit to the will of God!"

"Beloved Anneke! — Think of your father, and summon your whole strength. The bed of the river is yet firm; we will cross it, and try the opposite shore."

Cross it we did, my delicate companion being as much sustained by my supporting arm as by her own resolution; but we found the same obstacle to retreat interposing there also. The island above had turned the waters aside, until they found an outlet under each bank — shooting along their willowy shores, with the velocity of arrows. By this time, owing to our hurried movement, I found Anneke so far exhausted, that it was absolutely necessary to pause a minute to take breath. This pause was also necessary, in order to look about us, and to decide understandingly as to the course it was necessary now to pursue. This pause, brief as it was, moreover contributed largely to the apparent horrors of our situation.

The grating or grinding of the ice above us, cake upon cake, now sounded like the rushing of heavy winds, or the incessant roaring of a surf upon the sea-shore. The piles were becoming visible, by their height and their proximity, as the ragged barriers set slowly but steadily down upon us; and the whole river seemed to me to be in motion downward. At this awful instant, when I began to think it was the will of Providence that Anneke and I were to perish together, a strange sound interrupted the fearful natural accessories of that frightful scene. I certainly heard the bells of a sleigh; at first they seemed distant and broken — then nearer and incessant, attended by the rumbling of runners on the ice. I took off my cap and pressed my head, for I feared my brain was unsettled. There it came, however, more and more distinctly, until the trampling of horses' hoofs mingled in the noise.

"Can there be others as unhappy as ourselves! " exclaimed Anneke, forgetting her own fears in generous sympathy. "See, Littlepage! — see, *dear* Cornelius — yonder surely comes another sleigh! "

Come it did, like the tempest, or the whirlwinds; passing within fifty feet of us. I knew it at a glance. It was the sleigh of Herman Mordaunt, empty; with the horses, maddened by terror, running wherever their fears impelled. As the sleigh passed, it was thrown on one side; then it was once more whirled up again; and it went out of sight, with the rumbling sound of the runners mingling with the jingling of bells and the tramp of hoofs.

At this instant a loud, distant cry from a human voice, was certainly heard. It seemed to me, as if some one called my name; and Anneke said, she so understood it, too. The call, if call it was, came from the south, and from under the western shore. At the next moment, awful reports proceeded from the barrier above; and, as passing an arm around the slender waist of my lovely companion, to support her, I began a rapid movement in the direction of that call. While attempting to reach the western shore, I had observed a high mound of broken ice, that was floating down; or rather, was pressed down on the smooth surface of the frozen river, in advance of the smaller cakes that came by in the current. It was increasing in size by accessions from these floating cakes, and threatened to form a new dam at some narrow pass below, as soon as of sufficient size. It occurred to me we should be temporarily safe could we reach that mound, for it rose so high as to be above danger from the water. Thither, then, I ran, almost carrying Anneke on my arm; our speed increased by the terrific sounds from the dam above us.

We reached the mound, and found the cakes so piled, as to be able to ascend them; though not without an effort. After getting up a layer or two, the broken mass became so irregular and ragged, as to render it necessary for me to mount first, and then to drag Anneke up after me. This I did, until exhausted; and we both seated ourselves on the edge of a cake, in order to recover our breath. While there, it struck me, that new sounds arose from the river; and, bending forward to examine, I saw that the water had forced its way through the dam above and was coming down upon us in a torrent.

CHAPTER XVII

"My heart leaps up when I behold
     A rainbow in the sky:
So was it when my life began;
So is it now I am a man;
So be it when I shall grow old,
          Or let me die!

"The child is father of the man;
     And I could wish my days to be
Bound each to each by natural piety."
WORDSWORTH.

FIVE minutes longer on the ice of the main channel, and we should have been swept away. Even as we still sat looking at the frightful force of the swift current, as well as the dim light of that clouded night would permit, I saw Guert Ten Eyck's sleigh whirl past us; and, only a minute later, Herman Mordaunt's followed; the poor exhausted beasts struggling in the harness for freedom, that they might swim for their lives. Anneke heard the snorting of those wretched horses; but her unpractised eyes did not detect them, immersed, as they were, in the current; nor had she recognized the sleigh that whirled past us, as her father's. A little later, a fearful shriek came from one of the fettered beasts; such a heart-piercing cry as it is known the horse often gives. I said nothing on the subject, knowing that love for her father was one of the great incentives which had aroused my companion to exertion; and being unwilling to excite fears that were now latent.

Two or three minutes of rest were all that circumstances permitted. I could see that every thing visible on the river was in motion downward; the piles of ice on which we were placed, as well as the cakes that glanced by us in their quicker descent. Our own motion was slow, on account of the mass which doubtless pressed on the shoals of the west side of the river; as well as on account of the friction against the lateral fields of ice, and occasionally against the shore. Still we were

in motion; and I felt the necessity, on every account, of getting
as soon as possible on the western verge of our floating island,
in order to profit by any favorable occurrence that might offer.

Dear Anneke! — How admirably did she behave that fearful
night! From the moment she regained her entire consciousness, after I found her praying in the bottom of the sleigh,
down to that instant, she had been as little of an encumbrance
to my own efforts, as was at all possible. Reasonable, resolute,
compliant, and totally without any ill-timed exhibition of womanly
apprehension, she had done all she was desired to do unhesitat-
ingly, and with intelligence. In ascending that pile of ice, by no
means an easy task under any circumstances, we had acted in
perfect concert, every effort of mine being aided by one of her
own, directed by my advice and greater experience.

" God has not deserted us, dearest Anneke," I said, now that
my companion's strength appeared to have returned, " and we
may yet hope to escape. I can anticipate the joy we shall
bring to your father's heart, when he again takes you to his
arms, safe and uninjured."

" Dear, *dear* father! — What agony he must now be suffering on my account. Come, Corny, let us go to him at once,
if it be possible."

As this was said, the precious girl arose, and adjusted her
tippet in a way that should cause her no encumbrance; like one
ready to set about the execution of a serious task with all her
energies. The muff had been dropped on the river; for neither
of us had any sensibility to cold. The night, however, was
quite mild, for the season; and we probably should not have
suffered, had our exertions been less violent. Anneke declared
herself ready to proceed, and I commenced the difficult and
delicate task of aiding her across an island composed of icy
fragments, in order to reach its western margin. We were
quite thirty feet in the air; and a fall into any of the numerous
caverns among which we had to proceed, might have been
fatal; certainly would have crippled the sufferer. Then the
surface of the ice was so smooth as to render walking on it an
exceedingly delicate operation; more especially as the cakes
lay at all manner of inclinations to the plane of the horizon.
Fortunately, I wore buckskin moccasins over my boots; and
their rough leather aided me greatly in maintaining my footing.
Anneke, too, had socks of cloth; without which I do not think
she could have possibly moved. By these aids, however, and by

proceeding with the utmost caution, we had actually succeeded in attaining our object, when the floating mass shot into an eddy, and turning slowly round under this new influence, placed us on the outer side of the island again! Not a murmur escaped Anneke, at this disappointment; but, with a sweetness of temper that spoke volumes in favor of her natural disposition, and a resignation that told her training, she professed a readiness to renew her efforts. To this I would not consent, however; for I saw that the eddy was still whirling us about; and I thought it best to escape from its influence altogether, before we threw away our strength fruitlessly. Instead of recrossing the pile, therefore, I told my fair companion that we would descend to a cake that lay level on the water, and which projected from the mass to such a distance as to be close to the shore, should we again get near it. This descent was made, after some trouble, though I was compelled to receive Anneke entirely into my arms, in order to effect it. Effect it I did; placing the sweet girl safely at my side, on the outermost and lowest of all the cakes in our confused pile.

In some respects this change was for the better, while it did not improve our situation in others. It placed both Anneke and myself behind a shelter, as respected the wind; which though neither very strong nor very cold, had enough of March about it to render the change acceptable. It took my companion, too, from a position where motion was difficult, and often dangerous; leaving her on a level, even spot, where she could walk with ease and security, and keep the blood in motion by exercise. Then it put us both in the best possible situation to profit by any contact with that shore, along and near which our island was now slowly moving.

There could no longer be any doubt of the state of the river in general. It had broken up; spring had come like a thief in the night; and the ice below having given way, while the mass above had acquired too much power to be resisted, every thing was set in motion; and like the death of the strong man, the disruption of fields in themselves so thick and adhesive, had produced an agony surpassing the usual struggle of the seasons. Nevertheless, the downward motion had begun in earnest, and the centre of the river was running like a sluice, carrying away in its current, those masses which had just before formed so menacing an obstacle above.

Luckily, our own pile was a little aside from the great downward rush. I have since thought, that it touched the bottom,

which caused it to turn, as well as retarded its movement. Be
this as it might, we still remained in a little bay slowly turning
in a circle; and glad was I to see our low cake coming round
again, in sight of the western shore. The moment now demanded decision; and I prepared Anneke to meet it. A
large, low, level cake had driven up on the shore, and extended
out so far as to promise that our own cake would touch it, in
its evolutions. I knew that the ice in general, had not broken
in consequence of any weakness of its own, but purely under
the weight of the enormous pressure from above, and the mighty
force of the current; and that we ran little, or no risk, in
trusting our persons on the uttermost limits of any considerable
fragment. A station was taken, accordingly, near a projection
of the cake we were on; when we waited for the expected contact. At such moments the slightest disappointment carries
with it the force of the greatest circumstances. Several times
did it appear to us that our island was on the point of touching the fastened cake, and as often did it incline aside; at no
time coming nearer than within six or eight feet. This distance
it would have been easy enough for *me* to leap across, but to
Anneke it was a barrier as impassable as the illimitable void.
The sweet girl saw this; and she acted like herself under the
circumstances. She took my hand, pressed it, and said earnestly,
and with patient sweetness —

"You see how it is, Corny; I am not permitted to escape;
but you can easily reach the shore. Go, then, and leave me in
the hands of Providence. Go; I never can forget what you
have already done; but it is useless to perish together!"

I have never doubted that Anneke was perfectly sincere in
her wish that I should, at least, save my own life. The feeling
with which she spoke; the despair that was coming over her;
and the movement of our island, which at that moment gave
signs of shooting away from the shore altogether, roused me to
a sudden, and certainly, to a very bold attempt. I tremble,
even at this distance of time, as I write the particulars. A small
cake of ice was floating in between us and that which lay firmly
fastened to the shore. Its size was such as to allow it to pass
between the two; though not without coming nearly, if not
absolutely, in contact with one, if not with both. I observed
all this; and saying one word of encouragement to Anneke, I
passed an arm around her waist — waited the proper moment —
and sprang forward. It was necessary to make a short leap,

with my precious burden on my arm, in order to gain this
floating bridge; but it was done, and successfully. Scarcely
permitting Anneke's foot to touch this frail support, which was
already sinking under our joint weight, I crossed it at two or
three steps, and threw all my power into a last and desperate
effort. I succeeded here, also; and fell upon the firmer cake
with a heart filled with gratitude to God. The touch told me
that we were safe; and in the next instant we reached the
solid ground. Under such circumstances, one usually looks back
to examine the danger he has just gone through. I did so;
and saw that the floating cake of ice had already passed down,
and was out of reach; while the mass that had been the means
of saving us, was slowly following, under some new impulse
received from the furious currents of the river. But we were
saved; and most devoutly did I thank my God, who had mercifully aided our escape from perils so imminent.

I was compelled to wait for Anneke, who fell upon her knees,
and remained there quite a minute, before I could aid her in
ascending the steep acclivity which formed the western bank of
the Hudson, at this particular point. We reached the top,
however, after a little delay, and pausing once or twice to take
breath: when we first became really sensible of the true character of the scene from which we had been delivered. Dim as
was the light, there was enough to enable us to overlook a considerable reach of the river, from that elevated stand. The
Hudson resembled chaos rushing headlong between the banks.
As for the cakes of ice — some darting past singly, and others
piled as high as houses — of course the stream was filled with
such; but, a large, dark object was seen coming through that
very channel over which Anneke and I had stood less than an
hour before, sailing down the current with fearful rapidity. It
was a house; of no great size, it is true, but large enough to
present a singular object on the river. A bridge, of some size,
followed; and a sloop, that had been borne away from the
wharves of Albany, soon appeared in the strange assemblage,
that was thus suddenly collected on this great artery of the
colony.

But the hour was late; Anneke was yet to care for; it was
necessary to seek a shelter. Still supporting my lovely companion, who now began to express her uneasiness on account of
her father and her other friends, I held the way inland; knowing that there was a high road parallel to the river, and at no

great distance from it. We reached the highway in the course
of ten minutes, and turned our faces northward, as the direction which led toward Albany. We had not advanced far
before I heard the voices of men, who were coming toward
us; and glad was I to recognize that of Dirck Follock among
the number. I called aloud, and was answered by a shout of
exultation, which, as I afterward discovered, spontaneously broke
out of his mouth, when he recognized the form of Anneke.
Dirck was powerfully agitated when we joined him; I had never,
previously, seen any thing like such a burst of feeling from him;
and it was some time before I could address him.

"Of course your whole party is safe?" I asked, a little doubtingly; for I had actually given up all who had been in Herman
Mordaunt's sleigh for lost.

"Yes, thank God! all but the sleigh and horses. But where
are Guert Ten Eyck and Miss Wallace?"

"Gone ashore on the other side of the river; we parted,
and they took that direction, while we came hither." I said
this to quiet Anneke's fears; but I had misgivings about their
having got off the river at all. "But let me know the manner
of your own escape."

Dirck then gave us a history of what had passed; the whole
party turning back to accompany us as soon as I told them
that their errand — a search for the horses — was useless. The
substance of what we heard was as follows: — in the first effort
to reach the western shore, Herman Mordaunt had been met
by the very obstacle which Guert had foreseen, and he turned
south, hoping to find some spot at which to land, by going
farther from the dam that had formed above. After repeated
efforts, and having nearly lost his sleigh and the whole party, a
point was reached at which Herman Mordaunt determined to
get his female companion on shore, at every hazard. This was
to be done only by crossing floating cakes of ice, in a current
that was already running at the rate of four or five miles in the
hour. Dirck was left in charge of the horses while the experiment was made; but seeing the adventurers in great danger, he
flew to their assistance — when the whole party were immersed,
though not in deep water. Left to themselves, and alarmed
with the floundering in the river and the grinding of the cakes,
Herman Mordaunt's bays went off in the confusion. Mrs.
Bogart was assisted to the land, and was helped to reach the
nearest dwelling — a comfortable farm-house, about a quarter

of a mile beyond the point where we had met the party. There
Mrs. Bogart had been placed in a warm bed, and the gentlemen
were supplied with such dry clothes, as the rustic wardrobe of
these simple people could furnish. The change made, Dirck
was on his way to ascertain what had become of the sleigh and
horses, as has been mentioned.

On inquiry, I found that the spot where Anneke and myself
had landed, was quite three miles below the island on which
Guert and I had drawn the sleigh. Nearly the whole of this
distance had we floated with the pile of broken ice, in the short
time we were on it; a proof of the furious rate at which the
current was setting downward. No one had heard any thing
of Guert and Mary; but I encouraged my companion to believe
that they were necessarily safe on the other shore. I certainly
deemed this to be very questionable, but there was no use in
anticipating evil.

On reaching the farm-house, Herman Mordaunt's delight and
gratitude may more easily be imagined than described. He
folded Anneke to his heart, and she wept like an infant on his
bosom. Nor was I forgotten in this touching scene, but came
in for a full share of notice.

"I want no details, noble young man — " I am professing to
write the truth, and must be excused for relating such things
as these, but — "I want no details, noble young man," said
Herman Mordaunt, squeezing my hand, "to feel certain that,
under God, I owe my child's life, for the second time, to you.
I wish to heaven! — but, no matter — it is now too late — some
other way may and *must* offer. I scarce know what I say,
Littlepage; but what I *mean* is, to express faintly, some small
portion of the gratitude I feel, and to let you know how sensibly and deeply your services are felt and appreciated."

The reader may think it odd, that this incoherent, but preg-
nant speech, made little impression on me at the time, beyond
the grateful conviction of having really rendered the greatest of
all services to Anneke and her father; though I had better
occasion to remember it afterward.

It is unnecessary to dwell more particularly on the occur-
rences at the farm-house. The worthy people did what they
could to make us comfortable, and we were all warm in bed in
the course of the next half-hour.

On the following morning a wagon was harnessed, and we
left these simple countrymen and women — who refused **every**

thing like compensation, as a matter of course — and proceeded homeward. I have heard it said that we Americans are mercenary; it may be so, but not a man, probably, exists in the colonies, who would accept money for such assistance. We were two hours in reaching Albany, on wheels; and entered the place about ten, in a very different style from that in which we had quitted it the day before. As we drove along, the highway frequently led us to points that commanded views of the river, and we had so many opportunities of noting the effects of the freshet. Of ice, very little remained. Here and there a cake or a pile was seen still adhering to the shore, and occasionally fragments floated downward; but, as a rule, the torrent had swept all before it. I particularly took notice of the island on which we had sought refuge. It was entirely under water, but its outlines were to be traced by the bushes which lined its low banks. Most of the trees on its upper end were cut down, and all that grew on it would unquestionably have gone, had not the dam given way as early as it did. A great number of trees had been broken down on all the islands; and large tops and heavy trunks were still floating in the current, that were lately tenants of the forest, and had been violently torn from their places.

We found all the lower part of Albany, too, under water. Boats were actually moving through the streets; a considerable portion of its inhabitants having no other means of communicating with their neighbors. A sloop of some size lay up on one of the lowest spots; and, as the water was already subsiding, it was said she would remain there until removed by the shipwrights. Nobody was drowned in the place; for it is not usual for the people of these colonies to remain in their beds, at such times, to await the appearance of the enemy in at their windows. We often read of such accidents destroying hundreds in the Old World; but in the New, human life is of too much account to be unnecessarily thrown away, and so we make some efforts to preserve it.

As we drove into the street in which Herman Mordaunt lived, we heard a shout, and turning our heads, we saw Guert Ten Eyck waving his cap to us, with joy delineated in every feature of his handsome face. At the next moment he was at our side.

"Mr. Herman Mordaunt," he cried, shaking that gentleman most cordially by the hand, "I look upon you as one raised from the dead; you and my excellent neighbor, Mrs. Bogart,

and Mr. Follock, here! How you got off the river is a mystery
to me, for I well know that the water commonly breaks through
first under the west shore. Corny and Miss Anneke — God bless
you both! Mary Wallace is in terror lest ill news come from
some of you; but I will run ahead and let her know the glad
tidings. It is but five minutes since I left her, starting at every
sound, lest it prove the foot of some ill-omened messenger."

Guert stopped to say no more. In a minute he was inside
of Herman Mordaunt's house — in another Anneke and Mary
Wallace were locked in each other's arms. After exchanging
salutes, Mrs. Bogart was conveyed to her own residence and
there was a termination to that memorable expedition.

Guert had less to communicate, in the way of dangers and
marvels, than I had anticipated. It seemed, that when he and
Miss Wallace reached the inner margin of the last island, a
large cake of ice had entered the strait, and got jammed; or
rather, that it went through, forced by the tremendous pressure
above; though not without losing large masses, as it came in
contact with the shores, and grinding much of its material into
powder, by the attrition. Guert's presence of mind and decision did him excellent service here. Without delaying an instant,
the moment it was in his power, he led Mary on that cake,
and crossed the narrow branch of the river, which alone separated him from the mainland, on it, dry-shod. The water was
beginning to find its way over this cake, as it usually did on all
those that lay low, and which even stopped in their progress;
but this did not offer any serious obstacles to persons who were
so prompt. Safe themselves, our friends remained to see if we
could not be induced to join them; and the call we heard, was
from Guert, who had actually recrossed to the island, in the
hope of meeting us, and directing us to a place of safety. Guert
never said any thing to me on the subject, himself; but I subsequently gathered from Mary Wallace's accounts, that the
young man did not rejoin her without a good deal of hazard
and difficulty, and after a long and fruitless search for his companions. Finding it useless to remain any longer on the river-
side, Guert and his companion held their way toward Albany.
About midnight they reached the ferry opposite to the town;
having walked quite six miles, filled with uneasiness on account
of those who had been left behind. Guert was a man of decision, and he wisely determined it would be better to proceed,
than to attempt waking up the inmates of any of the houses he

passed. The river was now substantially free from ice, though running with great velocity. But Guert was an expert oarsman; and finding a skiff, he persuaded Mary Wallace to enter it; actually succeeding, by means of the eddies, in landing her within ten feet of the very spot where the hand-sled had deposited him and myself, only a few days before. From this point, there was no difficulty in walking home; and Miss Wallace actually slept in her town bed, that eventful night, if indeed she *could* sleep.

Such was the termination of this adventure; one that I have rightly termed memorable. In the end, Jack and Moses came in safe and sound; having probably swum ashore. They were found in the public road, only a short distance from the town, and were brought in to their master the same day. Every one who took any interest in horses — and what Dutchman does not? — knew Jack and Moses, and there was no difficulty in ascertaining to whom they belonged. What is singular, however, both sleighs were recovered; though at long intervals of time, and under very different circumstances. That of Guert, wolves' skins and all, actually went down the whole length of the river on the ice; passing out to sea through the Narrows. It must have gone by New York in the night, or doubtless it would have been picked up; while the difficulty of reaching it, was its protector on the descent, *above* the town. Once outside of the Narrows, it was thrown by the tide and winds upon the shore of Staten Island; where it was hauled to land, housed, and being properly advertised in our New York paper, Guert actually got tidings of it in time to receive it, skins and all, by one of the first sloops that ascended the Hudson that year; which was within a fortnight after the river had opened. The year 1758 was one of great activity, on account of the movements of the army, and no time was then unnecessarily lost.

The history of Herman Mordaunt's sleigh was very different. The poor bays must have drowned soon after we saw them floating past us in the torrent. Of course, life had no sooner left them, than they sank to the bottom of the river, carrying with them the sleigh to which they were still attached. In a few days the animals rose to the surface — as is usual with all swollen bodies — bringing up the sleigh again. In this condition, the wreck was overtaken by a downward-bound sloop, the men of which saved the sleigh, harness, skins, foot-stoves, and such other articles as would not float away.

Our adventure made a good deal of noise in the circle of
Albany; and I have reason to think that my own conduct was
approved by those who heard it. Bulstrode paid me an especial
visit of thanks, the very day of my return, when the following
conversation took place between us:

"You seem fated, my dear Corny," the major observed,
after he had paid the usual compliments, "to be always serving
me in the most material way, and I scarcely know how to express all I feel on the occasion. First, the lion, and now this
affair of the river — but that Guert will drown or make away
with the whole family, before the summer is over, unless Mr.
Mordaunt puts a stop to *his* interference."

"This accident was one that might have overtaken the oldest
and most prudent man in Albany. The river seemed as solid
as the street when we went on it; and another hour, even as it
was, would have brought us all home in entire safety."

"Ay, but that hour came near bringing death and desolation
into the most charming family in the colony; and you have
been the means of averting the heaviest part of the blow. I
wish to heaven, Littlepage, that you would consent to come
into the army! Join us as a volunteer, the moment we move,
and I will write to Sir Harry to obtain a pair of colors for you.
As soon as he hears that we are indebted to your coolness and
courage for the life of Miss Mordaunt, he will move heaven
and earth to manifest his gratitude. The instant this good parent
made up his mind to accept Miss Mordaunt as a daughter, he
began to consider her as a child of his own."

"And Anneke — Miss Mordaunt herself, Mr. Bulstrode —
does she regard Sir Harry as a father?"

"Why, that must be coming by slow degrees, as a matter of
course, you know. Women are slower than us men to admit
such totally novel impressions; and I dare say Anneke fancies
one father enough for her, just at this moment; though she
sends very pleasant messages to Sir Harry, I can assure you,
when in the humor! But what makes you so grave, my good
Corny?"

"Mr. Bulstrode, I conceive it no more than fair, to be as
honest as yourself in this matter. You have told me that you
are a suitor for Miss Mordaunt's hand; I will now own to you
that I am your rival."

My companion heard this declaration with a quiet smile, and
the most perfect good-nature.

"So you actually wish to become the husband of Anneke Mordaunt, yourself, my dear Corny, do you?" he said, so coolly, that I was at a loss to know of what sort of materials the man could be made.

"I do, Major Bulstrode — it is the first and last wish of my heart."

"Since you seem disposed to reciprocate my confidence you will not take offence if I ask you a question or two!"

"Certainly not, sir; your own frankness shall be a rule for my government."

"Have you ever let Miss Mordaunt know that such are your wishes?"

"I have, sir; and that in the plainest terms — such as cannot well be misunderstood."

"What! last night? — On that infernal ice! — While she thought her life was in your hands!"

"Nothing was said on the subject, last night, for we had other thoughts to occupy our minds."

"It would have been a most ungenerous thing to take advantage of a lady's fears —"

"Major Bulstrode! — I cannot submit —"

"Hush, my dear Corny," interrupted the other, holding out a hand in a most quiet and friendly manner; "there must be no misunderstanding between you and me. Men are never greater simpletons than when they let the secret consciousness of their love of life push them into swaggering about their honor when their honor has, in fact, nothing to do with the matter in hand. I shall not quarrel with you; and must beg you, in advance, to receive my apologies for any little indecorum into which I may be betrayed by surprise; as for great pieces of indecorum, I shall endeavor to avoid *them*."

"Enough has been said, Mr. Bulstrode; I am no wrangler, to quarrel with a shadow; and, I trust, not in the least that most contemptible of all human beings, a social bully, to be on all occasions menacing the sword or the pistol. Such men usually *do* nothing when matters come to a crisis. Even when they fight they fight bunglingly and innocently."

"You are right, Littlepage, and I honor your sentiments. I have remarked that the most expert swordsman with his tongue, and the deadest shot at a shingle, are commonly as innocent as lambs of the shedding of blood on the ground. They can sometimes screw themselves up to *meet* an adversary, but it exceeds

their powers to use their weapons properly, when it comes to
serious work. The swaggerer is ever a coward at heart, however
well he may wear a mask for a time. But enough of this. We
understand each other, and are to remain friends under all circumstances. May I question further?"

"*Ask* what you please, Bulstrode—I shall answer, or not, at
my own discretion."

"Then permit me to inquire, if Major Littlepage has authorized you to offer proper settlements?"

"I am authorized to offer nothing. Nor is it usual for the
husband to make settlements on his wife, in these colonies,
further than what the law does for her, in favor of her own.
The father sometimes has a care for the third generation. I
should expect Herman Mordaunt to settle *his* estate on his
daughter, and her rightful heirs, let her marry whom she may."

"Ay, that is a very American notion; and one on which
Herman Mordaunt, who remembers his extraction, will be little
likely to act. Well, Corny, we are rivals, as it would seem;
but that is no reason we should not remain friends. We understand each other—though, perhaps, I ought to tell you all."

"I should be glad to know *all*, Mr. Bulstrode; and can
meet my fate, I hope, like a man. Whatever it may cost me,
if Anneke prefer another, her happiness will be dearer to me
than my own."

"Yes, my dear fellow, we all say and think so at one-and-
twenty; which is about your age, I believe. At *two*-and-twenty,
we begin to see that our own happiness has an equal claim on
us; and at *three*-and-twenty we even give it the preference.
However, I will be just if I am selfish. I have no reason to
believe Anne Mordaunt does prefer me; though my *perhaps*
is not altogether without a meaning either."

"In which case I may possibly be permitted to know to
what it refers?"

"It refers to the father; and I can tell you, my fine fellow,
that fathers are of some account, in the arrangement of marriages between parties of any standing. Had not Sir Harry
authorized my own proposals, where should I have been? Not
a farthing of settlement could I have offered, while he remained
Sir Harry; notwithstanding I had the prodigious advantage of
the entail. I can tell you what it is, Corny; the existing power
is always an important power, since we all think more of the
present time than of the future. That is the reason so few

of us get to heaven. As for Herman Mordaunt, I deem it no more than fair to tell you he is on my side, heart and hand. He likes my offers of settlement; he likes my family; he likes my rank, civil and military; and I am not altogether without the hope that he likes *me*."

I made no direct answer, and the conversation soon changed. Bulstrode's declaration, however, caused me to remember both the speech and manner of Herman Mordaunt, when he thanked me for saving his daughter's life. I now began to reflect on it; and reflected on it much during the next few months. In the end the reader will learn the effect it had on my happiness.

CHAPTER XVIII

"Good sir, why do you start; and seem to fear
Things that do sound so fair? I' the name of truth,
Are ye fantastical, or that indeed
Which outwardly ye show?"

BANQUO.

As I have said already, the adventure on the river made a good deal of noise in that simple community; and it had the effect to render Guert and myself a sort of heroes, in a small way; bringing me much more into notice than would otherwise have been the case. I thought that Guert, in particular, would be likely to reap its benefit; for various elderly persons, who were in the habit of frowning whenever his name was mentioned, I was given to understand could now smile; and two or three of the most severe among the Albany moralists, were heard to say that, "after all, there was some good about that Guert Ten Eyck." The reader will not require to be told, that a high-school moralist, in a place as retired and insulated as Albany, must necessarily be a being that became subject to a very severe code. Morality, as I understand the matter, has a good deal of convention about it. There is town morality and country morality, all over the world, as they tell me. But in America our morals were, and long have been, separated into three great and very distinct classes; viz. — New England or Puritan morals; middle colonies, or liberal morals; and southern colonies, or latitudinarian morals. I shall not pretend to point out all the shades of difference in these several schools; though that in which I had myself been taught, was necessarily the most in conformity with my own tastes. There were minor shades to be found in the same school; Guert and myself belonging to different classes. His morals were of the Dutch class; while mine more properly belonged to the English. The great characteristic of the Dutch school, was the tendency to excess that prevailed, when indulgences were sought. With them, it did not rain often; but when it did rain, it was pretty certain to pour. Old Colonel Follock was a case in point, on this score;

242

nor was his son Dirck, young and diffident as he was, altogether an exception to the rule. There was not a more respectable man in the colony, in the main, than Colonel Van Valkenburgh. He was well connected; had a handsome, unencumbered estate, and money at interest; was a principal prop in the church of his neighborhood; was esteemed as a good husband; a good father; a true friend; a kind neighbor; an excellent and loyal subject, and a thoroughly honest man. Nevertheless Colonel Van Valkenburgh had his weak times and seasons. He *would* have a frolic; and the Dominie was obliged to wink at this propensity. Mr. Worden often nicknamed him Colonel Frolic. His frolics might be divided into two clases; viz., the moderate and the immoderate. Of the first, he had two or three turns a year; and these were the occasions on which he commonly visited Satanstoe, or had my father with him at Rockrockarock, as his own place in Rockland was called. On these visits, whether to or from, there was a large consumption of tobacco, beer, cider, wine, rum, lemons, sugar, and the other ingredients of punch, toddy, and flip; but no outrageously durable excesses. There was much laughing, a great deal of good feeling, many stories, and regular repetitions of old adventures, in the way of traditional narrations; but nothing that could be called decided excesses. It is true, that my grandfather, and my father, and the Rev. Mr. Worden, and Colonel Follock, were much in the habit of retiring to their beds a little confused in their brains — the consequence of so much tobacco-smoke, as Mr. Worden always maintained; but every thing was decent, and in order. The parson, for instance, invariably pulled up on a Friday, and did not take his place in the circle until Monday evening again; which gave him fully twenty-four hours to cool off in, before he ascended the pulpit. I will say this for Mr. Worden, that he was very systematic and methodical in the performance of all his duties; and I have known him, when he happened to be late at dinner, on discovering that my father had omitted to say grace, insist on every body's laying down their knives and forks, while he asked a blessing; even though it were after the fish was actually eaten. No, no; Mr. Worden was a particular person about all such things; and it was generally admitted, that he had been the means of causing grace to be introduced into several families in Westchester, in which it had never been the practice to have it before his example and precepts were known to them.

I had not been acquainted with Guert Ten Eyck a fortnight, before I saw he had a tendency to the same sort of excesses as those to which Colonel Van Valkenburgh was addicted. There was an old French Huguenot living near Satanstoe — or rather, the son of one, who still spoke his father's language — and who used to call Colonel Follock's frolics his "*grands couchers*," and his "*petits couchers;*" * inasmuch as he usually got to bed at the last, without assistance; while at the first, it was indispensable that some aid should be proffered. It was these "grands couchers" at which my father never assisted. On these occasions, the colonel invariably held his orgies over in Rockland, in the society of men of purely Dutch extraction; there being something exclusive in the enjoyment. I have heard it said that these last frolics sometimes lasted a week, on really important occasions; during the whole of which time the colonel and all near him were as happy as lords. These "*grands couchers*," however, occurred but rarely — coming round, as it might be, like leap-years, just to regulate the calendar, and adjust the time.

As for my new friend, Guert, he made no manifestation toward a "*grand coucher*" during the time I remained at Albany — this his attachment to Mary Wallace forbade — but I discovered by means of hints and allusions, that he *had* been engaged in one or two such affairs, and that there was still a longing for them in his bones. It was owing to her consciousness of the existence of such weakness, and her own strong aversion to any thing of the sort, that I am persuaded Mary Wallace was alone induced to hesitate about accepting Guert's weekly offer of his hand. The tenderness she evidently felt for him, now shone too obviously in her eyes to leave any doubt in my mind of Guert's final success; for what woman ever re-

* In plain English, the "great go-to-bed," and the "little go-to-bed." There may be a portion of our readers who are not aware that the word "levee," meaning a morning reception by a great man, is derived from the French "lever," which means "to rise," or "to get up." The kings of France were in the habit of receiving homage at their morning toilets; a strange custom, that doubtless had its origin in the *empressement* of the courtier to inquire how his master had slept; which receptions were divided into two classes, the "*grand lever*," and the "*petit lever*"— the "great getting-up" or the "little getting-up." The first was an occasion of more state than the last. Even down to the time of Charles X., the court papers seldom went a week without announcing that the king had signed the contract of marriage — a customary compliment in France, among friends of this or that personage — at the "grand lever," or at the "petit lever;" the first, I believe, but am not certain, being the greater honor of the two. — EDITOR.

fused long to surrender, when the image of the besieger had taken its place in the citadel of her heart! Even Anneke received Guert with much favor, after his excellent behavior on the river; and I fancied that every thing was going on most flatteringly for my friend, while it seemed to me that I made no advances in my own suit. Such, at least, were my notions on the subject at the very moment when my new friend, as it appeared, was nearly driven to desperation.

It was near the end of April, or about a month after our perilous adventure on the ice, that Guert came to seek me, one fine spring morning, with something very like despair depicted in his fine manly face. During the whole of that month, it ought to be premised, I had not dared to speak of love to Anneke. My attentions and visits were incessant and pointed, but my tongue had been silent. The diffidence of real admiration had held me tongue-tied; and I foolishly fancied there would be something like presuming on the services I had so lately rendered, in urging my suit so soon after the occurrence of the events I have described. I had even the romance to think it might be taking an undue advantage of Bulstrode, to wish to press my claims at a moment when the common object of our suit might be supposed to feel the influence of a lively gratitude. These were the notions and sentiments of a very young man, it must be confessed; but I do not know that I ought to feel ashamed of them. At all events, they existed; and they had produced the effect I have mentioned, leaving me to fall each day, more desperately in love, while I made no sensible advances in preferring my suit. Guert was very much in the same situation, with this difference, however; he made it a point to offer himself, distinctly, each Monday morning, invariably receiving for an answer "no;" if the lady were to be pressed for a definite reply; but leaving some glimmering of hope, should time be given for her to make up her mind. The visit of Guert's, to which I have just alluded, was after one of the customary offers, and usual replies; the offer direct, and the "no," tempered by the doubting and thoughtful brow, the affectionate smile, and the tearful eye.

"Corny," said my friend, throwing down his hat with a most rueful aspect; for, winter having departed and spring come, we had all laid aside our fur caps — "Corny, I have just been refused again! That word, 'no,' has got to be so common with Mary Wallace, that I am afraid her tongue will never

know how to utter a 'yes!' Do you know, Corny, I have a
great mind to consult Mother Doortje!"

"Mother who?—You do not mean Mr. Mayor's cook, surely!"

"No; *Mother* Doortje. She is said to be the best fortune-
teller that has ever lived in Albany. But, perhaps, you do not
believe in fortune-tellers; some people I know do not?"

"I cannot say that I have much belief, or unbelief, on the
subject, never having seen any thing of that sort."

"Have they then no fortune-teller, no person who has the
dark art in New York?"

"I have heard of such people, but have never had an opportunity of seeing or hearing for myself. If you *do* go to see this
Mother Dorrichy, or whatever you call her, I should like amazingly to be of the party."*

Guert was delighted to hear this, and he caught eagerly at
the offer. If I would stand his friend he would go at once;
but he confessed he did not like to trust himself all alone in the
woman's company.

"I am, perhaps, the only man of my time of life, in Albany,
who has not, sooner or later, consulted Mother Doortje;"
he added. "I do not know how it is, but, *somehow*, I have never
liked to tempt fortune by going to question her! One never
can tell what such a being may say; and should it be evil, why
it might make a man very miserable. I am sure I want no
more trouble, as it is, than to find Mary Wallace so undeter-
mined about having me!"

"Then you do not mean to go after all! I am not only
ready, but anxious to accompany you."

"You mistake me, Corny. Go I will, now, though she tell
me that which will cause me to cut my throat—but we must
not go as we are; we must disguise ourselves, in order that she
may not know us. Every body goes disguised; and then they
have no opportunity of learning if she is in a good vein, or not,
by seeing if she can tell any thing about their business or
habits, in the first place. If she fail in that, I should not care
a straw for any of the rest. So, go to work, Corny, and dress
yourself for the occasion—borrow some clothes of the people in
the house here, and come round to me, as soon as you please;

---

* Doortje—pronounced Doort-yay—means Dorothea. Mr. Littlepage uses a sort
of corruption of the pronunciation. I well remember a fortune-teller of that name,
in Albany; though it could not have been the Doortje of 1758.—Editor.

I shall be ready, for I often go disguised to frolics — yes, unlucky devil that I am, and come back disguised too! "

Every thing was done as desired. By means of a servant in the tavern, I was soon equipped in a way that satisfied me was very successful; inasmuch as I passed Dirck, in quitting the house, and my old confidential friend did not recognize me. Guert was in as good luck, as I actually asked himself for himself, when he opened the door for my admission. The laugh, and the handsome face, however, soon let me into the secret, and we sallied forth in high spirits; almost forgetting our misgivings concerning the future, in the fun of passing our acquaintances in the street without being known.

Guert was much more artistically and knowingly disguised, than I was myself. We both had put on the clothes of laborers; Guert wearing a smock frock that he happened to own for his fishing occupations in summer — but I had my usual linen in view, and wore all the ordinary minor articles of my daily attire. My friend pointed out some of these defects, as we went along, and an attempt was made to remedy them. Mr. Worden coming in view, I determined to stop him, and speak to him in a disguised voice, in order to ascertain if it were possible to deceive him.

"Your sarvant, Tominie," I said, making an awkward bow, as soon as we got near enough to the parson to address him; " be you ter Tominie, that marries folk on a pinch? "

"Ay, or on a handful, liking the last best. Why, Corny, thou rogue, what does all this mean? "

It was necessary to let Mr. Worden into the secret; and he no sooner learned the business we were on, than he expressed a wish to be of the party. As there was no declining, we now went to the inn, and gave him time to assume a suitable disguise. As the divine was a rigid observer of the costume of his profession, and was most strictly a man of his *cloth*, it was a very easy matter for him to make such a change in his exterior, as completely to render him *incognito*. When all was ready, we went finally forth, on our errand.

"I go with you, Corny, on this foolish business," said the Rev. Mr. Worden, as soon as we were fairly on our way, "to comply with a promise made your excellent mother, not to let you stray into any questionable company, without keeping a fatherly eye over you. Now, I regard a fortune-teller's, as a doubtful sort of society; therefore, I feel it to be a duty, to make one of this party."

I do not know whether the Rev. Mr. Worden succeeded in deceiving himself; but I very well know, he did not succeed in deceiving me. The fact was, he loved a frolic; and nothing made him happier than to have an opportunity of joining in just such an adventure as that we were on. Judging from the position of the house, and the appearance of things in and around it, the business of Madame Doortje was not of the most lucrative sort. Dirt and poverty were two things not easily encountered in Albany; and I do not say that we found very positive evidence of either, here; but there was less neatness than was usual in that ultra-tidy community; and as for any great display of abundance, it was certainly not to be met with.

We were admitted by a young woman, who gave us to understand that Mother Doortje had a couple of customers already; but she invited us to sit down in an outer room, promising that our turn should be the next. We did so, accordingly, listening through a door that was a little ajar, with no small degree of curiosity, to what was passing within. I accidentally took a seat in a place that enabled me to see the legs of one of the fortune-teller's customers; and I thought immediately, that the striped stockings were familiar to me, when the nasal and very peculiar intonation of Jason, put the matter out of all doubt. He spoke in an earnest manner, which rendered him a little incautious; while the woman's tones were low and mumbled. Notwithstanding, we all overheard the following discourse: —

"Well, now, Mother Dorrichay," said Jason, in a very confiding sort of way, "I've paid you well for this here business, and I want to know if there is any chance for a poor man in this colony, who doesn't want for friends, or for that matter, merit?"

"That's *yourself*," mumbled the female voice, in the way one announces a discovery; "yes, I see by the cards, that your question applies to yourself. You are a *young* man, that wants not for friends; and you have *merit!* You have friends that you deserve; the cards tells me *that!*"

"Well, I'll not deny the truth of what you assert; and I must say, Dirck, it *is* a little strange, this woman, who never saw me before, should know me so well — my very natur', as it might be. But do you think I shall do well to follow up the affair I am now on, or that I had best give it up?"

"Give up nothing," answered the oracle, in a very oracular manner, shuffling the cards as she spoke; "no, give up nothing, but keep all you can. That is the way to thrive in this world."

"By the Hokey, Dirck, she gives good advice, and I think I shall follow it! But how about the land, and the mill-seat — or, rather, how about the particular things I'm thinking about?"

"You are thinking of purchasing — yes, the cards say purchasing; or is it 'disposing —'"

"Why, as I've got none to sell, it can't very well be disposing, mother."

"Yes, I'm right — this Jack of clubs settles the matter — you are thinking of buying some land — ah! there's water running down-hill; and here I see a pond — why, you are thinking of buying a mill-seat."

"By the Hokey! — Who would have thought this, Dirck!"

"Not a *mill; no,* there is *no* mill built; but a mill-*seat.* Six, king, three and an ace; yes, I see how it is — and you wish to get this mill-seat at much less than its real value. *Much* less; not less, but *much* less."

"Well, this is wonderful! I'll never gainsay fortin-tellin' ag'n!" exclaimed Jason. "Dirck, you are to say nothin' of this, or *think* nothin' of this — as it's all in confidence, you know. Now, jist put in a last word, about the end of life, mother, and I'll be satisfied. What you have told me about my fortin and earnin's must be true, I think, for my whole heart is in them; but I should like to know, after enjoying so much wealth and happiness as you've foretold, what sort of an end I am to make of it?"

"An excellent end — full of grace, and hope, and Christian faith. I see here, something that looks like a clergyman's gown — white sleeves — book under the arm —"

"That can't be *me,* mother, as I'm no lover of forms, but belong to the platform."

"Oh! I see how it is, now; you dislike Church of England people, and could throw dirt at them. Yes, yes — here *you* are — a Presbyterian deacon, and one that can lead in a private meeting, on an occasion."

"Come, Dirck, I'm satisfied — let us go; we have kept Mother Doorichaise long enough, and I heard some visitors come in just now. Thank you, mother — thank you, with all my heart; I think there *must* be some truth in this fortin-tellin' after all!"

Jason now arose, and walked out of the house, without even

deigning to look at us — and consequently without our being recognized. But Dirck lingered a minute, not yet satisfied with what had been already told him.

"Do you really think I shall never be married, mother?" he asked, in a tone that sufficiently betrayed the importance he attached to the answer. "I wish to know that particularly before I go away!"

"Young man," answered the fortune-teller in an oracular manner; "what has been said, has been said! I cannot *make* fortunes, but only reveal them. You have heard that Dutch blood is in your veins; but you live in an English colony. *Your* king is *her* king; while *she* is your *queen* — and you are not her master. If you can find a woman of English blood that has a Dutch heart, and has no English suitors, go forward, and you will succeed; but if you do not, remain as you are until time shall end. These are my words, and these are my thoughts; I can say no more."

I heard Dirck sigh — poor fellow! he was thinking of Anneke — and he passed through the outer room without once raising his eyes from the floor. He left Mother Doortje, as much depressed in spirits as Jason had left her elated; the one looking forward to the future with a selfish and niggardly hope, while the other regarded it with a feeling as forlorn as the destruction of all his youthful fancies could render any view of his after-life. The reader may feel disposed to smile at the idea of Dirck Van Valkenburgh's possessing youthful fancies — regarding the young man in the quiet, unassuming manner in which he has hitherto been enportrayed by me; but it would be doing great injustice to his heart and feelings, to figure him to the mind as a being without deep sensibilities. I have always supposed that this interview with Mother Doortje had a lasting influence on the fortunes of poor Dirck; nor am I at all certain its effects did not long linger in the temperament of some others that might be named.

As our turns had now come, we were summoned to the presence of this female soothsayer. It is unnecessary to describe the apartment in which we found Mother Doortje. It had nothing unusual in it, with the exception of a raven, that was hopping about the floor, and which appeared to be on the most familiar terms with his mistress. Doortje herself was a woman of quite sixty, wrinkled, lean, and hag-like; and I thought some care had been taken in her dress to increase the effect of this, certainly her natural appearance. Her cap was entirely of black muslin; though her dress itself was gray. The eye of this woman was of the color of her gown; and it was penetrating, restless, and deep-seated. Altogether, she looked the character well.

On our entrance, after saluting the fortune-teller, each of us laid a French crown on the table at which she was seated. This coin had become quite current among us, since the French troops had penetrated in our colony; and it was even said they purchased supplies with it from certain of our own people. As we had paid the highest price ever given for these glimpses into futurity, we thought ourselves entitled to have the pages of the sealed book freely opened to us.

" Do you wish to see me together; or shall I communicate with one at a time? " demanded Doortje, in her husky, sepulchral voice; which it struck me, obtained its peculiar tones partly from nature and partly from art.

It was settled that she should commence with Mr. Worden; but that all might remain in the room the whole time. While we were talking over this point, Doortje's eyes were by no means fixed; but I remarked that they wandered from person to person like those of one who was gathering information. Many persons do not believe at all in the art of the fortune-teller; but insist that there is nothing more in it than trick and management, pretending that this very woman kept the blacks of the town in pay to bring her information; and that she never told any thing of the past which was true, that had not been previously communicated to herself. I shall not pretend to affirm that the art goes as far as many imagine; but it strikes me that it is very presuming to deny that there is some truth in these matters. I do not wish to appear credulous; though at the same time I hold it to be wrong to deny our testimony to facts that we are convinced are true.*

Doortje commenced by shuffling an exceedingly dirty pack of cards; which had probably been used five hundred times on similar duty. She next caused Mr. Worden to cut these cards; when a close and musing examination succeeded. All this time

---

* It is quite evident that Mr. Cornelius Littlepage was, to a degree at least, a believer in the fortune-teller's art. Quite within my recollection, the Albanians had a celebrated dealer in the black art, who was regularly consulted on the subject of all lost spoons and the pilfering of servants, by the good housewives of the town, as recently as my school-boy days. The Dutch, like the Germans, appear to have been prone to this species of superstition; from which even the English of education were far from being free a century since. Mademoiselle Normand existed in the present century, even in the skeptical capital of France. But the somnambulist is taking the place of the ancient soothsayer in our times. — EDITOR.

not a syllable was said; though we were startled by a low whistle
from the woman which brought the raven upon her shoulder.

"Well, mother," cried Mr. Worden, with a little impatience
at what he fancied mummery, "I am dying to hear what *has*
happened, that I may put the more faith in what *is* to happen.
Tell me something of the crop of wheat I put into the ground
last autumn; how many bushels I sowed, and on how many
acres; whether on new land or on old?"

"Ay, ay you have sowed! — and you have sowed:" answered
the woman on a high key for her; "but your seed fell among
tares, and on the flinty ground; and you'll never reap a soul
among 'em all! Broadcast may you sow — but narrow will be
your harvest."

The Rev. Mr. Worden gave a loud hem — placed his arms
akimbo — and seemed determined to brazen it out; though I
could easily perceive that he felt excessively awkward.

"How is it, with my cattle? and shall I send much mutton
to market this season?"

"A wolf in sheep's clothing!" muttered Doortje. "No —
no — you like hot suppers, and ducks, and lectures to cooks more
than gathering in the harvest of the Lord!"

"Come, this is folly, woman!" exclaimed the parson, angrily.
"Give me some common sense for my good French crown.
What do you see in that knave of diamonds that you study its
face so closely?"

"A loping Dominie! — a loping Dominie!" screamed the hag
several times, rather than exclaiming aloud. "See! — he runs
for life; but Beelzebub will overtake him!"

There was a sudden and dead pause; for the Rev. Mr. Worden
had caught up his hat and darted from the room; quitting the
house as if already busily engaged in the race alluded to. Guert
shook his head, and looked serious; but perceiving that the woman
was already tranquil, and was actually shuffling the cards anew,
in his behalf, he advanced to learn his fate. I saw the eyes of
Doortje fastened keenly on him, as he took his stand near the
table, and the corners of her mouth curled in a significant smile.
What that meant exactly I have never been able to ascertain.

"I suppose you wish to know something of the past, like all
the rest of them," mumbled the woman, "so that you may have
faith in what you hear about the future?"

"Why, mother," answered Guert, passing his hand through
his own fine head of natural curls, and speaking a little hastily,

" I do not know that it is any great matter about the past. What is done is done, and there is an end of it. A young man may not wish to hear of such things at the moment, perhaps, when he is earnestly bent on doing better. We are all young once in our lives, and we can grow old only after having been so."

" Yes — yes — I see how it is! " muttered Doortje. " So — so — turkeys — turkeys; ducks — ducks — quaack — quaack — quaack — gobble, gobble, gobble." Here the old hag set up such an imitation of ducks, geese, turkeys, game-cocks, and other birds, that one who was in an outer room might well have imagined he heard the cries of a regular poultry-yard. I was startled myself, for the imitation was very admirable — but Guert was obliged to wipe the perspiration from his face.

" That will do — that will do, mother! " the young man exclaimed. " I see you know all about it; and there is no use in attempting disguises with you. Now, tell me, if I am ever to be a married man, or not. My errand here is to learn that fact; and I may as well own it at once."

" The world has many women in it — and fair faces are plenty in Albany," once more mumbled the woman, examining her cards with great attention. " A youth like you might marry twice even."

" No *that* is impossible; if I do not marry a particular lady, I shall never marry at all."

" Yes — yes — I see how it is! — You are in love, young man."

" D'ye hear that, Corny! Isn't it wonderful how these creatures can tell? I admit the truth of what you say; but describe to me the lady that I love."

Guert had forgotten altogether that the use of the word *lady*, completely betrayed the fact of his disguise; since no man truly of his dress and air, would think of applying such a word to his sweetheart.* I could not prevent these little betrayals of himself, however; for by this time my companion was too much excited to hear reason.

" The lady that you love," answered the fortune-teller, deliberately, and with the manner of one that proceeded with great confidence, " is *very* handsome, in the first place."

" True as the sun in the heavens, mother! "

* This might have been true in 1758, but is not true for 1845. — EDITOR.

"Then she is virtuous and amiable, and wise, and witty, and good."

"The gospel is not more certain! Corny, this surpasses belief!"

"Then, she is *young*. Yes, she is young and fair, and good; three things that make her much sought after."

"Why is she so long reflecting on my offers, mother; tell me that, I beg of you; or will she ever consent to have me?"

"I see — I see — it is all here on the cards. The lady cannot make up her mind."

"Listen to that now, Corny; and do not tell me there is nothing in this art. *Why* does she not make up her mind? For Heaven's sake let me know *that?* A man may tire of offering to marry an angel, and getting no answer. I wish to know the reason of her doubts."

"A woman's mind is not easily read. Some are in haste, while some are not. I am of opinion you wish to get an answer before the lady is ready to give it. Men must learn to wait."

"She really seems to know all about it, Corny! Much as I have heard of this woman, she exceeds it all! Good mother, can you tell me how I can gain the consent of the woman I love?"

"That is only to be had by asking. Ask once, ask twice, ask thrice."

"By St. Nicholas! I have asked already twenty times! If asking would do it, she would have been my wife a month since. What do you think, Corny — no, I'll not do it — it is not manly to get the secrets of a woman's heart by means like these — I'll not ask her!"

"The crown is paid and the truth must be said. The lady you love, loves you, and she does not love you; she will have you, and she won't have you; she thinks *yes*, and she says *no*."

Guert now trembled all over, like an aspen-leaf.

"I do not believe there is any harm, Corny, in asking whether I gained or lost by the affair of the river? I *will* ask her that much, of a certainty. Tell me, mother, am I better or worse, for a certain thing that happened about a month ago — about the time that the ice went, and that we had a great freshet?"

"Guert Ten Eyck, why do you try me thus?" demanded the fortune-teller, solemnly. "I knew your father, and I knew your mother; I knew your ancestors in Holland, and their children in America. Generations on generations have I known your people, and you are the first that I have seen so ill-clad. Do

you suppose, boy, that old Doortje's eyes are getting dim, and
that she cannot tell her own nation? I saw you on the river —
ha! ha! 'twas a pleasant sight — Jack and Moses, too; how they
snorted, and how they galloped! Crack — crack — that's the ice
— there comes the water! See, that bridge may hit you on the
head! Do *you* take care of this bird, and do *you* take care of
that — and all will come round with the seasons. Answer me
one thing, Guert Ten Eyck, and answer me truly. Know you
ever a young man who goes quickly into the bush?"

"I do, mother; this young man, my friend, intends to go in a
few days, or as soon as the weather is settled."

"Good! go you with him — absence makes a young woman
know her own mind, when asking will gain nothing. Go you
with him, I say; and if you hear muskets fired, go near them;
fear will sometimes make a young woman speak. You have your
answer, and I will tell no more. Come hither, young owner of
many half-joes, and touch that card."

I did as ordered; when the woman began to mumble to herself, and to run over the pack as rapidly as she could. Kings,
aces and knaves were examined, one after another, until she had
got the queen of hearts in her hand, which she held up to me in
triumph.

"That is *your* lady. She is a queen of too many hearts!
The Hudson did that for you that it has done for many a poor
man before you. Yes, yes; the river did you good; but water
will drown, as well as make tears. Do *you* beware of knights
barrownights!"*

Here Mother Doortje came to a dead stand in her communications, and not another syllable of any sort could either of us get
from her, though between us, as many as twenty questions were
asked. Signs were made for us to depart; and when the woman
found our reluctance, she laid a crown for each of us on the table
with a dignified air, and went into a corner, seated herself, and
began to rock her body, like one impatient of our presence.
After so unequivocal a sign that she considered her work as done,
we could not well do less than return, leaving the money behind
us as a matter of course.

* In the colony of New York, there lived but one titled man for a considerable
period. It was the celebrated Sir William Johnson, Bart., of Johnson Hall, Johns-
town, Albany, now Fulton county. The son of Sir William Johnson was knighted
during his father's lifetime, and was Sir John while Sir William was living. At the
death of his father he was Sir John Johnson, Kt. & Bart.; and it was usual for the
common class of people to style him a knight or barrow*night*. — EDITOR.

CHAPTER XIX

"Virtue, how frail it is!
Friendship, too rare!
Love, how it sells poor bliss
For proud despair!
But we, though soon they fall,
Survive their joy, and all
Which ours we call."
SHELLEY.

GUERT TEN EYCK was profoundly impressed with what he had heard, in his visit to the fortune-teller. It affected his spirits, and, as will be seen, it influenced all his subsequent conduct. As for myself, I will not say that I totally disregarded what has passed; though the effect was greatly less on me than it was on my friend. The Rev. Mr. Worden, however, treated the matter with great disdain. He declared that he had never before been so insulted in his life. The old hag, no doubt, had seen us all before, and recognized him. Profiting by a knowledge of this sort — that was very easily obtained in a place of the size of Albany — she had taken the occasion to make the most of the low gossip that had been circulated at his expense. "Loping Dominie indeed," he added; "as if any man would not run to save his life! You saw how it was with the river, Corny, when it once began to break up, and know that my escape was marvellous. I deserve as much credit for that retreat, boy, as Xenophon did for his retreat with ten thousand. It is true I had not thirty-four thousand six hundred and fifty stadia to retreat over; but acts are to be estimated more by quality than by quantity. The best things are always of an impromptu character; and generally they are on a small scale. Then, as for all you tell me about Guert; why, the hussy knew him — *must* have known him, in a town like Albany, where the fellow has a character that identifies him with all sorts of fun and roguery. Jack and Moses too! Do you think the inspiration of even an evil spirit, or of forty thousand devils would lead a fortune-teller to name any horse Moses? Jack might do, perhaps; but *Moses* would never enter the head of even an imp!

256

Remember, lad, Moses was the great lawgiver of the Jews; and
such a creature would be as apt to suppose a horse was named
Confucius, as to suppose he was named Moses! "

"I suppose the inspiration, as you call it, sir, would lead a
clever fortune-teller to give things as they are; and to call the
horses by their real names, let them be what they might."

"Ay, such inspiration as this miserable old, wrinkled, impu-
dent she-devil enjoys! Don't tell me, Corny; there is no such
thing as fortune-telling; at least, nothing that can be depended
on in all cases — and this is one of downright imposition.
'Loping Dominie,' forsooth! "

Such were the Rev. Mr. Worden's sentiments on the subject
of Mother Doortje's revelations. He exacted a pledge from us
all, to say nothing about the matter; nor were we much disposed to be communicative on the subject. As for Guert, Dirck,
Jason, and myself, we did not hesitate to converse on the circumstances of our visits among ourselves, however; and each
and all of us viewed the matter somewhat differently from our
Mentor. I ascertained that Jason had been highly gratified with
what had been predicted on his own behalf; for what was wealth
in his eyes had been foretold as his future lot: and a man rarely
quarrels with good fortune, whether in prospective or in possession. Dirck, though barely twenty, began to talk of living
a single life from this time; and no laughter of mine could induce
the poor lad to change his views, or to entertain livelier hopes.
Guert was deeply impressed, as has been said; and feeling no
restraint in the matter of his own case, he took occasion to speak
of his visit to the woman, one morning that Herman Mordaunt,
the two ladies, Bulstrode, and myself, were sitting together, chatting, in the freedom of what had now become a very constant
intercourse.

"Are such things as fortune-tellers known in England, Mr.
Bulstrode? " Guert abruptly commenced, fastening his eyes on
Mary Wallace, as he asked the question; for on her were his
thoughts running at the time.

"All sorts of silly things are to be found in Old England,
Mr. Ten Eyck, as well as some that are wise. I believe London
has one or two soothsayers; and I think I have heard elderly
people say that the fashion of consulting them has somewhat
increased since the court has been so German."

"Yes," Guert innocently replied; "I find it easy to believe
that; for it is a common saying among our people, that the

German and Low Dutch fortune-tellers are the best known. They have had, or pretend to have had, witches in New England; but no one hereabouts puts any faith in the pretence. It is like all the bragging of these boastful Yankees! "

I observed that Mary Wallace's color deepened; and that in biting off a thread, she profited by the occasion to avert her face in such a manner, that Bulstrode, in particular, could not see it.

" The meaning of all this," put in Major Bulstrode, " is, that our friend Guert has been to pay a visit to Mother Doortje; a woman of some note who lives on the hill, and who has a reputation in that way among these good Albanians! Several of our mess have been to see the old woman."

" It is, Mr. Bulstrode," Guert answered, in his manly way, and with a gravity which proved how much he was in earnest. " I have been to see Mother Doortje, for the first time in my life; and Corny Littlepage, here was my companion. Long as I have known the woman by reputation, I have never had any curiosity to pay her a visit until this spring. We have been, however; and I must say, I have been greatly surprised at the extent of the knowledge of this very extraordinary person."

" Did she tell you to look into the sweetmeat-pot for the lost spoon, Mr. Ten Eyck," Anneke inquired, with an archness of eye and voice that sent the blood to my own face in confusion. " They say that fortune tellers send all prudent yet careless housewives, to the sweetmeat-pots, to look for the lost spoons! Many have been found, I hear, by this wonderful prescience."

" Well, Miss Anneke, I see you have no faith," answered Guert, fidgeting; " and people who have no faith never believe. Notwithstanding, *I* put so much confidence in what Doortje has told me, that I intend to follow her advice, let matters turn out as they may."

Here Mary Wallace raised her thoughtful, full, blue eyes to the face of the young man; and they expressed an intense interest, rather than any light curiosity, that even her woman's instinct and woman's sensitiveness could not so far prevail, as to enable her to conceal. Still Mary Wallace did not speak, leaving the others present to maintain the discourse.

" Of course, you mean to tell us all about it, Ten Eyck," cried the major; " there is nothing more likely to succeed with an audience, than a good history of witchcraft, or something so very marvellous as to do violence to common sense, before we give it our faith."

"Excuse me, Mr. Bulstrode; these are things I cannot well mention; though Corny Littlepage will testify that they are very wonderful. At any rate, I shall go into the bush this spring; and Littlepage and Follock being excellent companions, I propose to join their company. It will be late before the army will be ready to move; and by that time, all three of us propose to join you before Ticonderoga; if indeed you succeed in getting so far."

"Say, rather, in front of Montreal; for I trust this new commander-in-chief will find something more for us to do than the last one did. Shall I have a sentinel placed at Doortje's door, in your absence, Guert?"

The smile this question produced was general; Guert himself joining in it; for his good-nature was of proof. When I say the smile was general, however, I ought to except Mary Wallace, who smiled little that morning.

"We shall be neighbors, then," Herman Mordaunt quietly observed; "that is to say, if you mean by accompanying Corny and Dirck to the bush, you intend to go with them to the patent lately obtained by Messrs. Littlepage and Van Valkenburgh. I have an estate in that quarter, which is now ten years old; and these ladies have consented to accompany me thither, as soon as the weather is a little more settled, and I can be assured that our army will be of sufficient force to protect us from the French and Indians."

It is unnecessary for me to say with what delight Guert and I heard this announcement! On Bulstrode, however, it produced an exactly contrary effect. He did not appear to me to be surprised at a declaration that was so new to us; but several expressions fell from him that showed he had no idea the two estates, that of Herman Mordaunt and that which belonged to us, lay so near together. It was by means of *his* questions, indeed, that I learned the real facts of the case. It appeared that Herman Mordaunt's business in Albany was to make some provisions in behalf of this property, on which he had caused mills to be erected, and some of the other improvements of a new settlement to be made, two or three years before; and which, by the progress and events of the war, was getting to be in closer proximity to the enemy than was desirable. Even where the French lay, at Ticonderoga, his mills in particular, might be

thought in some danger, though forty or more miles distant;
for parties of savages, led on by white men, frequently marched
that distance through the forests, in order to break up settlement and to commit depredations. But the enemy had crossed
Lake George the previous summer, and had actually taken
Fort William Henry, at its southern extremity, by siege. It is
true, this was the extent of their inroad; and it was now known
that they had abandoned this bold conquest, and had fallen back
upon Ty and Crown Point, two of the strongest military positions
in the British colonies. Still, Ravensnest, as Herman Mordaunt's
property was called, was far from being beyond the limits of
sorties; and the residence at Albany, was solely to watch the
progress of events in that quarter, and to be near the scene. If
he had any public employment, it remained a profound mystery.
A new source of embarrassment had arisen, however; and this it
was that decided the proprietor to visit the lands in person.
The fifteen or twenty families he had succeeded in establishing
on the estate, at much cost and trouble, had taken the alarm,
at the prospect of a campaign in their vicinity; and had announced an intention of abandoning their huts and clearings, as
a course most expedient for the times. Two or three had already
gone off toward the Hampshire grants, whence they had originally
come; profiting by the last of the snow; and it was feared that
others might imitate their caution.

Herman Mordaunt saw no necessity for this abandonment of
advantages over the wilderness, that had been obtained at so
much cost and trouble. The labor of a removal and a return,
was sufficient of itself to give a new direction to the movements of his settlers; and as their first entrance into the country had been effected through his agency, and aided by his
means, he naturally wished to keep the people he had got to
his estate with so much difficulty, and at so much cost, at their
several positions, as long, at least, as he considered prudent.
In these circumstances, therefore, he had determined to visit
Ravensnest in person, and to pass a part, if not most of the
summer among his people. This would give them confidence,
and would enable him to infuse new life into their operations. It would seem that Anneke and Mary Wallace had refused
to let Mr. Mordaunt go alone; and believing, himself, there was
no danger in the course he was about to take, the father and
guardian, for Mary Wallace was Herman Mordaunt's ward, had
yielded to the importunities of the two girls; and it had been

formally decided that they were all to proceed together, as soon as the season should get to be a little more advanced. Intelligence of this intention had been sent to the settlers; and its effect was to induce them to remain at their posts, by pacifying their fears.

I might as well add here what I learned subsequently, in the due course of events. Bulstrode had been made acquainted with Herman Mordaunt's plans, they being sworn friends, and the latter warmly in the interest of the former's suit; and he had known how to profit by the information. It was now time to put the troops in motion, and several parties had already marched toward the north, taking post at different points that it was thought desirable to occupy, previously to the commencement of the campaign. Among other corps under orders of this nature, was that commanded by Bulstrode; and he had sufficient interest at head-quarters, to get it sent to the point nearest Ravensnest, where it gave him the double advantage of having it in his power to visit the ladies on occasion, while at the same time he must appear to them somewhat in the character of a protector. The object of Dirck and myself in visiting the north was no secret; and it was generally understood that we were to go to Mooseridge; but we did not know ourselves that Herman Mordaunt had an estate so near us. This intelligence, as has been said, I now ascertained was as new to Bulstrode as it was to myself.

The knowledge of many little things I have just mentioned, was obtained by me only at intervals, and by means of observation and discourse. Nevertheless, the main points were determined on the morning on which Guert referred to his visit to the fortune-teller, and in the manner named. The conversation lasted an hour; nor did it cease until all present got a general idea of the course intended to be pursued by the different parties present, during the succeeding summer.

It happened that morning, that Bulstrode, Dirck, and Guert withdrew together, the two last to look at a horse the former had just purchased, leaving me alone with the young ladies. No sooner was the door closed on the retiring members of our party, than I saw a smile struggling about the handsome mouth of Anneke; Mary Wallace continuing the whole time thoughtful, if not sad.

"And *you* were of the party at the fortune-teller's, too, it seems, Mr. Littlepage," Anneke remarked, after appearing to be debating with herself on the propriety of proceeding any farther in the subject. "I knew there was such a person in Albany, and that thrifty housekeepers *did* sometimes consult her; but I was ignorant that men, and *educated* men paid her that honor."

"I believe there is no exception in the way of sex or learning, to her influence or her authority. They tell me that most of the younger officers of the army visit her, while they remain here."

"I would much like to know if Mr. Bulstrode has been of the number! He is young enough in years, though so high in rank. A major may have as much curiosity as an ensign; or, as it may appear, dear Mary, of a woman who has lost her grandmother's favorite dessert-spoon."

Mary Wallace gave a gentle sigh, and she even raised her eyes from her work; still she made no answer.

"You are severe on us, Anneke;" for since the affair on the river, the whole family treated me with the familiarity of a son or a brother; "I fancy we have done no more than Mr. Mordaunt has done in his day."

"This may be very true, Corny, and not make the consultation the wisest thing in nature. I hope, however, you do not keep your fortune a secret, but let your friends share in your knowledge!"

"To me the woman was far from being communicative, though she treated Guert Ten Eyck better. Certainly, she told him many extraordinary things of the past, even; unless, indeed, she knew who he was."

"Is it probable, Mr. Littlepage," said Mary Wallace, "that any person in Albany should not know Guert Ten Eyck, and a good deal of his past history? Poor Guert makes himself known wherever he is!"

"And often much to his advantage," I added — a remark that cost me nothing; but which caused Mary Wallace's face to brighten, and even brought a faint smile to her lips. "All that is true; yet there *was* something wild and unnatural in the woman's manner, as she told these things!"

"All of which you seem determined to keep to yourself?" observed Anneke, as one asks a question.

"It would hardly do to betray a friend's secrets. Let Guert answer for himself; he is as frank as broad day, and will not hesitate about letting you know all."

" I wish Corny Littlepage were only as frank as twilight! "

" I have nothing to conceal — and least of all from you, Anneke. The fortune-teller told me that the queen of my heart was the queen of *too many* hearts; that the river had done me no harm; and that I must particularly beware of what she called knights-barrow-*nights*."

I watched Anneke closely, as I repeated this warning of Mother Doortje; but could not read the expression of her sweet and thoughtful countenance. She neither smiled nor frowned; but she certainly blushed. Of course, she did not look at me — for that would have been to challenge observation. Mary Wallace, however, *did* smile, and she *did* look at me.

" You believe all the wizzard told you, Corny? " said Anneke, after a short pause.

" I believed that the queen of my heart was the queen of many hearts; that the river had done me no harm — though I could not say, or see, that it had done me much good; and that I had much to fear from knights-barrow*nights*. I believed all this, however, before I ever saw the fortune-teller."

The next remark that was made came from Anneke, and it referred to the weather. The season was opening finely, and fast; and it could not be long before the great movements of the year must commence. Several regiments had arrived in the colonies, and various officers of note and rank had accompanied them. Among others who had thus crossed the Atlantic for the first time, was my lord Howe, a young soldier of whom fame spoke favorably, and from whom much was expected in the course of the anticipated service of the year. While we were talking over these things, Herman Mordaunt re-entered the room after a short absence, and he took me with him to examine his preparations for transporting the ladies to Ravensnest. As we went along, the discourse was maintained, and I learned many things from my older and intelligent companion that were new to me.

" New lords, new laws, they say, Corny," continued Herman Mordaunt; " and this Mr. Pitt, the great commoner, as some persons call him, is bent on making the British empire feel the truth of the axiom. Every thing is alive in the colonies, and the sluggish period of Lord Loudon's command is passed. General Abercrombie, an officer from whom much is expected, is now at the head of the king's troops, and there is every prospect of an active and most important campaign. The disgraces of the few last years *must* be wiped out, and the English name be made once more to be dreaded on this continent. The Lord Howe of whom Anneke spoke, is said to be a young man of merit, and to possess the blood of our Hanoverian monarchs; his mother being a half-sister, in the natural way, of his present majesty."

Herman Mordaunt then spoke more fully of his own plans for the summer — expressed his happiness at knowing that Dirck and myself were to be what he called his neighbors — though, on a more exact computation, it was ascertained that the nearest boundaries of the two patents, that of Ravensnest, and that of Mooseridge, lay quite fourteen miles apart, with a dense and virgin forest between them. Nevertheless, this would be making us neighbors in a certain sense; as gentlemen always call men of their own class neighbors, when they live within visiting distance, or near enough to be seen once or twice in a year. And such men *are* neighbors in the sense that is most essential to the term — they know each other better; understand each other better; sympathize more freely; have more of the intercourse that makes us judges of motives, principles, and character, twenty-fold, than he who lives at the gate and merely sees the owner of the grounds pass in and out, on his daily avocations. There is, and can be no greater absurdity, than to imagine that the sheer neighborhood, or proximity of position, makes men acquainted. That was one of Jason Newcome's Connecticut notions. Having been educated in a state of society in which all associated on a certain footing of intimacy, and in which half the difficulties that occurred were "told to the church," he was forever fancying he knew all the gentry of Westchester, because he had lived a year or two in the county; when, in fact, he had never spoken to one in a dozen of them. I never could drive this notion out of his head, however; for *looking* often at a man, or occasionally exchanging a bow with him on the highway, he would insist was knowing him, or what he called, being "well acquainted;" a very favorite expression of the Danbury man's; though their sympathies, habits, opinions, and feelings, created so vast a void between the parties, they hardly understood each other's terms and ordinary language, when they did begin to converse, as sometimes happened. Notwithstanding all this, Jason insisted to the last that he *knew* every gentleman in the county, whom he had been accustomed to hear alluded to in discourse, and when he had seen them once or twice, though it were only at church. But Jason had a very flattering notion generally of his own acquisitions on all subjects.

Herman Mordaunt had made careful provision for the contemplated journey; having caused a covered vehicle to be constructed, that could transport not only himself and the ladies, but many articles of furniture that would be required during their residence in the forest. Another conveyance, strong, spacious, and covered, was also prepared for the blacks, and another portion of the effects. He pointed out all these arrangements to me with great satisfaction, dwelling on the affection and spirit of the girls with a pleasure he did not affect to conceal. For my own part, I have always been of opinion, that Anneke was solely influenced by pure, natural regard, in forming her indiscreet resolution; while her father was governed by the secret expectation that the movement would leave open the means of receiving visits and communications from Bulstrode, during most of the summer. I commended the arrangements, made one or two suggestions of my own in behalf of Anneke and Mary, and we returned to our several homes.

A day or two after this visit to the workshops, and the conversation related, the ——th took up its line of march for the north. The troops defiled through the narrow streets in the neighborhood of the barracks, half an hour after the appearance of the sun, preceded and followed by a long train of baggagewagons. They marched without tents, however, it being well understood that they were going into a region where the axe could at any time cover thousands of men, in about the time that a camp could be laid out, and the canvas spread. Hutting was the usual mode of placing an army under cover in the forest; and a dozen marches would take the battalion to the point where it was intended it should remain, as a support to two or three other corps still further in advance, and to keep open the communications.

Bulstrode, however, did not quit Albany in company with his regiment. I had been invited, with Guert and Dirck, to breakfast at Herman Mordaunt's that morning; and, as we approached the door, I saw the major's groom walking his own and his master's horse, in the street, near by. This was a sign we were to have the pleasure of Bulstrode's company at breakfast. Accordingly, on entering the room, we found him present, in the uniform of an officer of his rank, about to commence a march in the forests of America. I thought him melancholy, as if sad at parting; but my most jealous observation could detect no sign of similar feeling on the part of Anneke. She was not quite as gay as usual, but she was far from being sad.

"I leave you, ladies, with the deepest regret," said Bulstrode, while at table, "for you have made this country more than a home to me — you have rendered it *dear*."

This was said with feeling; more than I had ever seen Bulstrode manifest before, and more than I had given him credit for possessing. Anneke colored a little; but there was no tremor in the beautiful hand, that held a highly-wrought little tea-pot suspended over a cup, at that very moment.

"We shall soon meet again, Harry," Herman Mordaunt remarked, in a tone of strong affection; "for our party will not be a week behind you. Remember we are to be *good* neighbors, as well as neighbors; and if the mountain will not come to Mahomet, Mahomet must go to the mountain."

"Which means, Mr. Bulstrode," said Mary Wallace, with one of her sweet smiles, and one that was as open and natural as childhood itself, "that you are Mahomet, and we are the mountain. Ladies can neither travel, with comfort, in a wilderness, nor visit a camp, with propriety, if they would."

"They tell me, I shall not be in a camp at all," answered the soldier; "but in good, comfortable log-barracks that have been built for us by the battalion we relieve. I am not without hopes, they will be such as even ladies will not disdain to use, on an emergency. There ought to be no Mahomet, and no mountain, between such old and intimate friends."

The conversation then turned on the plans and expectations of the respective parties; and the usual promises were made of being sociable and good neighbors, as had just been suggested. Herman Mordaunt evidently wished to consider Bulstrode as one of his family; a feeling that might excuse itself to the world, on the score of consanguinity; but which, it was easy enough for me to see, had its origin in a very different cause. When Bulstrode rose to take his leave, I wished myself away on account of the exhibition of concern it produced; while the desire to watch the effect on Anneke, would have kept me rooted to the floor, even had it been proper that I should retire.

Bulstrode was more affected than I could have thought possible. He took one of Herman Mordaunt's hands into his own, and pressed it warmly for some little time before he could speak at all.

"God only knows what this summer is to see, and whether we are ever to meet again, or not," he then said; "but, come what may, the past, the *happy past*, is so much gained from the commonplace. If you never hear of me again, my dear kinsman, my letters to England will give you a better account of my gratitude than any thing I can say in words. They have been written as your kindnesses have been bestowed; and they faithfully portray the feelings to which your hospitality and friendship have given rise. In a possible event, I have requested that every one of them may be sent to America, for your special perusal — "

"Nay, my dear Harry, this is foreboding the very worst," interrupted Herman Mordaunt, dashing a tear from his eye, "and is making a very short separation a more serious matter than one ought — "

"Nay, sir, a soldier who is about to be posted within striking distance of his enemy, can never speak with confidence of separations that are to be short. This campaign will be decisive for me" — glancing toward Anneke — "I must return a conqueror, in one sense, or I do not wish to return at all. But God bless you, Herman Mordaunt, as your own countrymen call you; a thousand years could not efface from my heart the remembrance of all your kindness."

This was handsomely expressed; and the manner in which it was uttered, was as good as the language. Bulstrode hesitated a moment — looked at the two girls in doubt — and first approached Mary Wallace.

"Adieu, excellent Mary Wallace," he said, taking her offered hand and kissing it, with a freedom from emotion that denoted it was only friendship and respect which induced the act — "I believe you are a severe critic on Catos and Scrubs; but I forgive all your particular backbitings, on account of your general indulgence and probity. You may meet with a thousand mere acquaintances, before you find another who shall have the same profound respect for your many virtues as myself."

This was handsomely said, too; and it caused Mary Wallace to remove the handkerchief from her eyes, and to utter her adieus cordially, and with some emotion. Strangers say that our women want feeling — passion; or, if they have it, that it is veiled behind a mask of coldness, that takes away from its loveliness and warmth; that they are girlish and familiar, where they might better be reserved; and distant and unnatural, where feeling and nature ought to assert their sway. That they have less *manner*, in all respects, in that of self-control, and perhaps of self-respect, in their ordinary intercourse, and in that of *acting*, where it may seem necessary so to do, I believe to be true; but he who denies an American girl a heart, knows nothing about her. She is *all* heart; and the apparent coldness is oftener the consequence of not daring to trust her feelings, and her general dislike to every thing artificial, than to any want of affections. Two girls, educated, however, as had been Anneke and Mary Wallace, could not but acquit themselves better, in such a scene, than those who had been less accustomed to the usages of polite life, which are always, more or less, the usages of convention.

On the present occasion, Mary Wallace was strongly affected; it would not have been possible, for one of her gentle nature and warm affections, to be otherwise, when an agreeable companion, one she had now known intimately near two years, was about to take his leave of her, on an errand that he himself either thought, or affected so well to seem to think, might lead to the most melancholy issue. She shook hands with Bulstrode warmly; wished him good fortune, and various other pleasant things; thanked him for his good opinion, and expressed her hope, as well as her belief, that they should all meet again before the summer was over, and again be happy in each other's society.

Anneke's turn came next. Her handkerchief was at her eyes; and when it was removed, the face was pale, and the cheeks were covered with tears. The smile that followed, was sweetness itself; and I will own, it caused me a most severe pang. To my surprise, Bulstrode said nothing. He took Anneke's hand, pressed it to his heart, kissed it, left a note in it, bowed, and moved away. I felt ashamed to watch the countenance of Miss Mordaunt, under such circumstances, and turned aside, that observation might not increase the distress and embarrassment she evidently felt. I saw enough, notwithstanding, to render me more uncertain than ever, as to the success of my own suit. Anneke's color had come and gone, as Bulstrode stood near her, acting his dumb-show of leave-taking; and, to me, she seemed far more affected than Mary Wallace had been. Nevertheless, her feelings were always keener and more active than those of her friend; and that which my sensitiveness took for the emotion of tenderness, might be nothing more than ordinary womanly feeling and friendship. Besides, Bulstrode was actually her relative.

We men all attended Bulstrode to his horse. He shook us cordially by the hand; and after he had got into the saddle, he said: " This summer will be warmer than usual, even in your warmy-cold climate. My letters from home give me reason to think that there is, at last, a man of talent at the head of affairs;

and the British empire is likely to feel the impulse he will give
it, at its most remote extremities.   I shall expect you three young
men to join the ——th, as volunteers, as soon as you hear of our
moving in advance.   I wish I had a thousand like you; for that
affair of the river tells where a man will be found when the time
comes.   God bless you, Corny! " leaning forward in his saddle,
to give me another shake of the hand; " we *must* remain friends,
coute qui coute! "

There was no withstanding this frankness, and so much good
temper.   We shook hands most cordially; Bulstrode raised his
hat and bowed; after which he rode away, as I fancied at a slow,
thoughtful, reluctant pace.   Notwithstanding the kindness of this
parting, I had more cause than ever to regret Bulstrode had appeared among us; and the scenes of that morning only confirmed
me in a resolution previously adopted, not to urge Anneke to
any decision in my case in a moment when I felt there might be
so much danger it would be adverse.

CHAPTER XX

"Come, let a proper text be read,
    An' touch it aff wi' vigor,
How graceless Ham leugh at his dad,
    Which made Canaan a nigger."
                                BURNS.

TEN days after the departure of the ——th, Herman Mordaunt and his family, with our own party, left Albany, on the summer's business. In that interval, however, great changes had taken place in the military aspect of things. Several regiments of king's troops ascended the Hudson; most of the sloops on the river, of which there could not have been fewer than thirty or forty, having been employed in transporting them and their stores. Two or three corps came across the country, from the eastern colonies, while several provincial regiments appeared; every thing tending to a concentration at this point, the head of navigation on the Hudson. Among other men of mark, who accompanied the troops, was Lord Viscount Howe, the nobleman of whom Herman Mordaunt had spoken. He bore the local rank of brigadier,* and seemed to be the very soul of the army. It was not his personal consideration, alone, that placed him so high in the estimation of the public and the troops, but his professional reputation, and professional services. There were many young men of rank in the army present; and, as for younger sons of peers, there were enough to make honorables almost as plenty at Albany as they were at Boston. Most of the colonial families of mark had sons in the service, too; those of the middle and southern colonies bearing commissions in regular regiments; while the provincial troops from the eastern were led, as was very usual in that quarter of the country, by men of the class of yeomen, in a great degree; the habits of equality that prevailed in those

---

* The ordinary American reader may not know that the rank of brigadier in the British army, is not a step in the regular line of promotion, as with us. In England, the regular military gradations are from colonel to major-general, lieutenant-general, general, and field-marshal. The rank of brigadier is barely recognized, like that of commodore in the navy, to be used on emergencies; usually as brevet, *local* rank to enable the government to employ clever colonels at need.

provinces, making few distinctions on the score of birth or fortune.

Yet it was said, I remember, that obedience was as marked among the provincials from Massachusetts and Connecticut, as among those that came from farther south; the men deferring to authority, as the agent of the laws. They were fine troops, too; better than our own colony regiments, I must acknowledge; seeming to belong to a higher class of laborers; while it must be admitted that most of their officers were no very brilliant representatives of manners, acquirements, or habits, that would be likely to qualify them for command. It must have been that the officers and men suited each other; for it was said all round, that they stood well and fought very bravely, whenever they were particularly well led, as did not always happen to be the case. As a body of mere physical men, they were universally allowed to be the finest corps in the army, regulars and all included.

I saw Lord Howe two or three times, particularly at the residence of Madam Schuyler, the lady I have already had occasion to mention, and to whom I had given the letter of introduction procured by my mother, the Mordaunts visiting her with great assiduity, and frequently asking me with them. As for Lord Howe himself, he almost lived under the roof of excellent Madam Schuyler; where indeed all the good company assembled at Albany were at times to be seen.

Our party was a large one; and it might have passed for a small corps of the army itself, moving on in advance; as was the case with corps, or parts of corps, now almost daily. Herman Mordaunt had delayed our departure, indeed, expressly with a view to render the country safe, by letting it fill with detachments from the army; and our progress when we were once in motion, was literally from post to post; encampment to encampment. It may be well to enumerate our force, and to relate the order of our march, that the reader may better comprehend the sort of business we were on.

Herman Mordaunt took with him, in addition to the ladies, a black cook and a black serving-girl; a negro man to take care of his horses, and another as his house-servant. He had three white laborers in addition — men employed about the teams, and as axe-men, to clear the woods, bridge the streams, and to do other work of that nature, as it might be required. On our side there were us three gentlemen, Yaap, my own faithful negro, Mr. Traverse the surveyor, two chain-bearers, and two axe-men.

Guert Ten Eyck carried with him also a negro man, who was called Pete; it being contrary to *bonos mores* to style him Peter or Petrus; the latter being his true appellation. This made us ten men strong, of whom eight were white and two black. Herman Mordaunt mustered in all just the same number, of whom, however four were females. Thus by uniting our forces we made a party of twenty souls altogether. Of this number all the males, black and white, were well armed, each man owning a good rifle, and each of the gentlemen a brace of pistols in addition. We carried the latter belted to our bodies, with the weapons, which were small and fitted to the service, turned behind in such a way as to be concealed by our outer garments. The belts were also hid by the flaps of our nether garments. By this arrangement, we were well armed without seeming to be so; a precaution that is sometimes useful in the woods.

It is hardly necessary to say that we did not plunge into the forest in the attire in which we had been accustomed to appear in the streets of New York and Albany. Cocked hats were laid aside altogether; forest caps, resembling in form those we had worn in the winter, with the exception that the fur had been removed, being substituted. The ladies wore light beavers suited to their sex; there being little occasion for any shade for the face under the dense canopies of the forest. Veils of green, however, were added, as the customary American protection for the sex. Anneke and Mary travelled in habits made of light woman's cloth, and in a manner to fit their exquisite forms like gloves. The skirts were short, to enable them to walk with ease, in the event of being compelled to go afoot. A feather or two in each hat had not been forgotten — the offering of the natural propensity of their sex to please the eyes of men.

As for us men, buckskin formed the principal material of our garments. We all wore buckskin breeches, and gaiters, and moccasins. The latter, however, had the white man's soles; though Guert took a pair or two with him that were of the pure Indian manufacture. Each of us had a coatee, made of common cloth; but we all carried hunting-shirts, to be worn as soon as we entered the woods. These hunting-shirts, green in color, fringed and ornamented garments of the form of shirts to be worn over all, were exceedingly smart in appearance, and were admirably suited to the woods. It was thought that the fringes, form and color, blended them so completely with the foliage as to render them in a manner invisible to one at a distance, or at least undistinguished. They were much in favor with all the forest corps of America, and formed the usual uniform of the riflemen of the woods, whether acting against man or only against the wild beasts.

Neither Mr. Worden nor Jason moved with the main party; and it was precisely on account of these distinctions of dress. As for the divine, he was so good a stickler for appearances, he would have worn the gown and surplice even on a mission to the Indians; which, by the way, was ostensibly his present business; and at the several occasions on which I saw him at cock-fights, he kept on the clerical coat and shovel-hat. In a word, Mr. Worden never neglected externals so far as dress was concerned; and I much question, if he would have consented to read prayers without the surplice, or to preach without the gown, let the desire for spiritual provender be as great as it might. I very well remember to have heard my father say, that on one occasion the parson had refused to officiate of a Sunday, when travelling, rather than bring discredit on the church by appearing in the discharge of his holy office without the appliances that belonged to the clerical character.

"More harm than good is done to religion, Mr. Littlepage," said the Rev. Mr. Worden on that occasion, " by thus lessening its rites in vulgar eyes. The first thing is to teach men to respect holy things, my dear sir; and a clergyman in his gown and surplice, commands threefold the respect of one without them. I consider it, therefore, a sacred duty to uphold the dignity of my office on all occasions."

It was in consequence of these opinions, that the divine travelled in his clerical hat, clerical coat, black breeches and band, even when in pursuit of the souls of red men among the wilds of North America! I will not take it upon myself to say these observances had not their use; but I am very certain they put the reverend gentleman to a great deal of inconvenience.

As for Jason, he gave a Danbury reason for travelling in his best. Every body did so in his quarter of the country; and for his part, he thought it disrespectful to strangers to appear among them in old clothes! There was, however, another and truer reason, and that was economy; for the troops had so far raised the price of every thing, that Jason did not hesitate to pronounce Albany the dearest place he had ever been in. There was some truth in this allegation; and the distance from New York being no less than one hundred and sixty miles — so reported — the reader will at once see it was the business of quite a month, or even more, to refurnish the shelves of the shop that had been emptied. The Dutch not only moved slowly, but they were methodical; and the shopkeeper whose stores were exhausted in April, would not be apt to think of replenishing them until the regular time and season returned.

As a consequence of these views and motives, the Rev. Mr. Worden and Mr. Jason Newcome left Albany twenty-four hours in advance of the rest of our party, with the understanding they were to join us at a point where the road led into the woods, and where it was thought the cocked hat and the skin cap might travel in company harmoniously. There was, however, a reason for the separation I have not yet named, in the fact that all of my own set travelled on foot, three or four pack-horses carrying our necessaries. Now Mr. Worden had been offered a seat in a government conveyance, and Jason managed to worm himself into the party in some way that to me was ever inexplicable. It is, however, due to Mr. Newcome to confess that his faculty of obtaining favors of all sorts, was a most extraordinary character; and he certainly never lost any chance of preferment for want of asking. In this respect Jason was always a moral enigma to me; there being an absolute absence in his mind, of every thing like a perception of the fitness of things, so far as the claims and rights of persons were connected with rank, education, birth and experience. Rank, in the official sense, once possessed, he understood and respected; but of the claims to entitle one to its enjoyment, he seemed to have no sort of notion. For property he had a profound deference, so far as that deference extended to its importance and influence; but it would have cost him not the slightest qualm, either in the way of conscience or feeling, to find himself suddenly installed in the mansion of the patroons, for instance, and placed in possession of their estates, provided only he fancied he could maintain his position. The circumstance that he was dwelling under the roof that was erected by another man's ancestors, for instance, and that others were living who had a better moral right to it, would give him no sort of trouble, so long as any quirk of the law would sustain him in possession. In a word, all that was allied to sentiment, in matters of this nature, was totally lost on Jason Newcome, who lived and acted, from the hour he first came among us, as if the game of life were merely a game of puss in the corner, in which he who inadvertently left his own post unprotected, would be certain to find another filling

his place as speedily as possible. I have mentioned this propensity of Jason's at some little length, as I feel certain, should
this history be carried down by my own posterity as I hope and
design, it will be seen that this disposition to regard the whole
human family as so many tenants in common of the estate left by
Adam, will lead in the end, to something extraordinary. But
leaving the Rev. Mr. Worden and Mr. Jason Newcome to journey
in their public conveyance, I must proceed to our own party.

All of us men, with the exception of those who drove the two
wagons of Herman Mordaunt, marched afoot. Each of us carried a knapsack, in addition to his rifle and ammunition; and it
will be imagined that our day's work was not a very long one.
The first day we halted at Madam Schuyler's by invitation, where
we all dined; including the surveyor. Lord Howe was among
the guests, that day; and he appeared to admire the spirit of Anneke and Mary Wallace greatly, in attempting such an expedition
at such a time.

"You need have no fears, however, ladies, as we shall keep
up strong detachments between you and the French," he said,
more gravely, after some pleasant trifling on the subject. "Last
summer's work, and the disgraceful manner in which poor Munro
was abandoned to his fate, have rendered us all keenly alive to
the importance of compelling the enemy to remain at the north
end of Lake George; too many battles having already been fought
on this side it, for the credit of the British arms. We pledge
ourselves to your safety."

Anneke thanked him for this pledge, and the conversation
changed. There was a young man present who bore the name
of Schuyler, and who was nearly related to Madam, with whose
air, manner and appearance I was much struck. His aunt
called him "Philip;" and being about my own age, during
this visit I got into conversation with him. He told me he was
attached to the commissariat under General Bradstreet, and
that he should move on with the army as soon as the preparations for its marching were completed. He then entered into
a clear, simple explanation of the supposed plan of the approaching campaign.

"We shall see you and your friends among us then, I hope,"
he added, as we were walking on the lawn together, previously
to the summons to dinner; "for, to own to you the truth, Mr.
Littlepage, I do not half like the necessity of our having so
many eastern troops among us to clear this colony of its enemies.

It is true, a nation must fight its foes wherever they may happen to be found; but there is so little in common between us and the Yankees, that I could wish we were strong enough to beat back the French alone."

"We have the same sovereign and the same allegiance," I answered; "if you can call that something in common."

"That is true; yet, I think you must have enough Dutch blood about you to understand me. My duty calls me much among the different regiments; and I will own that I find more trouble with one New England regiment, than with a whole brigade of the other troops. They have generals and colonels, and majors enough for the army of the Duke of Marlborough!"

"It is certain there is no want of military rank among them — and they are particularly fond of referring to it."

"Quite true," answered young Schuyler, smiling. "You will hear the word 'general' or 'colonel' oftener used in one of their cantonments, in a day, than you shall hear it at headquarters in a month. They have capital points about them too; yet, somehow or other, we do not like each other."

Twenty years later in life, I had reason to remember this remark, as well as to reflect on the character of the man who had uttered it. I, or my successors, will probably have occasion to advert to matters connected with this feeling in the later passages of this record.

I had also a little conversation with Lord Howe, who complimented me on what had passed on the river. He had evidently received an account of that affair from some one who was much my friend, and saw fit to allude to the subject in a way that was very agreeable to myself. This short conversation was not worth repeating, but it opened the way to an acquaintance that subsequently was connected with some events of interest.

About an hour after dinner, our party took its leave of Madam Schuyler, and moved on. The day's march was intended to be short, though by this time the roads were settled, and tolerably good. Of roads, however, we were not long to enjoy the advantages, for they extended only some thirty miles to the north of Albany, in our direction. With the exception of the military route, which led direct to the head-waters of Lake Champlain, this was about the extent of all the avenues that penetrated the interior in that quarter of the country. Our direction was to the northward and eastward, both Ravensnest and Mooseridge lying slightly in the direction of the Hampshire grants.

As soon as we reached the point on the great northern road, or that which led toward Skeenesborough, Herman Mordaunt was obliged to quit his wagons, and to put all the females on horseback. The most necessary of the stores were placed on packhorse; and after a delay of half a day, time lost in making these arrangements, we proceeded. The wagons were to follow, but at a slow pace, the ladies being compelled to abandon them on account of the ruggedness of the ways, which would have rendered their motion not easy to be borne. Our cavalcade and train of footmen made a respectable display along the uneven road, which soon became very little more than a line cut through the forest, with an occasional wheel-track, but without the least attempt to level the surface of the ground by any artificial means. This was the place where we were to overtake Mr. Worden and Jason, and where we did find their effects; the owners themselves having gone on in advance, leaving word that we should fall in with them somewhere on the route.

Guert and I marched in front, our youth and vigor enabling us to do this with great ease to ourselves. Knowing that the ladies were well cared for on horseback, we pushed on in order to make provision for their reception at a house a few miles distant, where we were to pass the night. This building was of logs, of course, and stood quite alone in the wilderness, having however some twenty or thirty acres of cleared land around it; and it would not do to pass it at that time of the day. The distance from this solitary dwelling to the first habitation on Herman Mordaunt's property, was eighteen miles; and that was a length of road that would require the whole of a long May day to overcome under our circumstances.

Guert and myself might have been about a mile in advance of the rest of the party, when we saw a sort of semi-clearing before us, that we mistook at first for our resting-place. A few acres had been chopped over, letting in the light of the day upon the gloom of the forest, but the second growth was already shooting up, covering the area with high bushes. As we drew nearer we saw it was a small abandoned clearing. Entering it, voices were heard at no great distance, and we stopped; for the human voice is not heard in such a place without causing the traveller to pause, and stand to his arms. This we did; after which we listened with some curiosity and caution.

" High! " exclaimed some one very distinctly in English.

"Jack!" said another voice, in a sort of answering second that could not well be mistaken.

"There's three for low; — is that good?" put in the first speaker.

"It will do, sir; but here are a ten and an ace. Ten and three, and four and two make nineteen; — I'm game."

"High, low, jack, and game!" whispered Guert; "here are fellows playing at cards near us; let us go on and beat up their quarters."

We did so; and pushing aside some bushes, broke, quite unexpectedly to all parties, on the Rev. Mr. Worden and Jason Newcome playing the game of "all-fours on a stump;" or if not literally in the classic position of using "the stump," substituting the trunk of a fallen tree for their table. As we broke suddenly in upon the card-players, Jason gave unequivocal signs of a disposition to conceal his hand, by thrusting the cards he held into his bosom, while he rapidly put the remainder of the pack under his thigh, pressing it down in a way completely to conceal it. This sudden movement was merely the effect of a Puritanical education, which having taught him to consider that as a sin which was not necessarily a sin at all, exacted from him that hypocrisy which is the tribute that vice pays to virtue. Very different was the conduct of the Rev. Mr. Worden. Taught to discriminate better, and unaccustomed to set up arbitrary rules of his own as the law of God, this loose observer of his professional obligations in other matters, made a very proper distinction in this. Instead of giving the least manifestation of confusion or alarm, the log on which he was seated was not more unmoved than he remained at our sudden appearance at his side.

"I hope, Corny, my dear boy," Mr. Worden cried, "that you did not forget to purchase a few packs of cards; which I plainly see will be a great resource for us in this woody region. These cards of Jason's are so thumbed and handled, that they are not fit to be touched by a gentleman, as I will show you. Why, what has become of the pack, Master Newcome? It was on the log but a minute ago!"

Jason actually blushed! Yes, for a wonder, shame induced Jason Newcome to change color! The cards were reluctantly produced from beneath his leg, and there the schoolmaster sat, as it might be in the presence of his school, actually convicted of being engaged in the damning sin of handling certain spotted pieces of paper, invented for, and used in the combinations of a game played for amusement.

"Had it been 'push-pin,' now," Guert whispered, "it would give Mr. Newcome no trouble at all. But he does not admire the idea of being caught at 'all-fours, on a stump.' We must say a word to relieve the poor sinner's distress. I have cards, Mr. Worden, and they shall be much at your service, as soon as we can come at our effects. There is one pack in my knapsack, but it is a little soiled by use, though somewhat cleaner than that. If you wish it, I will hand it to you. I never travel without carrying one or two clean packs with me."

"Not just now, sir, I thank you. I love a game of whist, or piquet, but cannot say I am an admirer of all-fours. As Mr. Newcome knows no other, we were merely killing half an hour at that game; but I have enough of it to last me for the summer. I am glad that cards have not been forgotten, however; for I dare say we can make up a very respectable party at whist, when we all meet."

"That we can, sir, and a party that shall have its good players. Miss Mary Wallace plays as good a hand at whist as a woman should, Mr. Worden; and a very pretty accomplishment it is, for a lady to possess; useful, sir, as well as entertaining; for any thing is preferable to a dummy. I do not think a woman should play quite as well as a man, our sex having a natural claim to lead, in all such things; but it is very convenient sometimes, to find a lady who can hold her hand with coolness and skill."

"I would not marry a woman who did not understand piquet," exclaimed the Rev. Mr. Worden; "to say nothing of whist, and one or two other games. But let us be moving, since the hour is getting late."

Move on we did, and in due time we all reached the place at which we were to halt for the night. This looked like plunging into the wilderness indeed; for the house had but two rooms, one of which was appropriated to the use of the females, while most of us men took up our lodgings in the barn. Anneke and Mary Wallace, however, showed the most perfect good-humor; and our dinner, or supper might better be the name, was composed of deliciously fat and tender broiled pigeons. It was the pigeon season, the woods being full of the birds; and we were told we might expect to feast on the young to satiety.

About noon the next day, we reached the first clearing on the estate of Ravensnest. The country through which we were travelling was rolling rather than bold; but it possessed a feature of grandeur in its boundless forests. Our route that day, lay under lofty arches of young leaves, the buds just breaking into the first green of the foliage, tall, straight columns, sixty, eighty, and sometimes a hundred feet of the trunks of the trees, rising almost without a branch. The pines, in particular were really majestic, most of them being a hundred and fifty feet in height, and a few, as I should think, nearly if not quite two hundred. As every thing grows toward the upper light in the forest, this ought not to surprise those who are accustomed to see vegetation expand its powers in wide-spreading tops, and low, gnarled branches that almost touched the ground, as is the case in the open fields, and on the lawns of the older regions. As is usual in the American virgin forests, there was very little under-brush; and we could see frequently a considerable distance through these long vistas of trees; or, indeed, until the number of the stems intercepted the sight.

The clearings of Ravensnest were neither very large nor very inviting. In that day the settlement of new lands was a slow and painful operation, and was generally made at a great outlay to the proprietor. Various expedients were adopted to free the earth from its load of trees; * for at that time, the commerce of the colonies did not reward the toil of the settler in the same liberal manner as has since occurred. Herman Mordaunt, as we moved along, related to me the cost and trouble he had been at already, in getting the ten or fifteen families who were on his property, in the first place, to the spot itself; and in the second place, to induce them to remain there. Not only was he obliged

---

* The late venerable Hendrick Frey was a man well known to all who dwelt in the valley of the Mohawk. He had been a friend, contemporary, and it is believed an executor, of the celebrated Sir William Johnson, Bart. Thirty years since he related to the writer the following anecdote. Young Johnson first appeared in the valley as the agent of a property belonging to his kinsman, Admiral Sir Peter Warren, K.B.; who having married in the colony, had acquired several estates in it. Among other tracts was one called Warrensbush, on the Mohawk, on which young Johnson first resided. Finding it difficult to get rid of the trees around his dwelling, Johnson sent down to the admiral, at New York, to provide some purchases with which to haul the trees down to the earth, after grubbing and cutting the roots on one side. An acre was lowered in this manner, each tree necessarily lying at a larger angle to the earth than the next beneath it. An easterly wind came one night, and to Johnson's surprise he found half his trees erect again, on rising in the morning! The mode of clearing lands by " purchases " was then abandoned. — EDITOR.

to grant leases for three lives, or in some cases, for thirty or forty years, at rents that were merely nominal, but as a rule, the first six or eight years the tenants were to pay no rent at all. On the contrary, he was obliged to extend to them many favors in various ways, that cost no inconsiderable sum in the course of the year. Among other things, his agent kept a small shop, that contained the most ordinary supplies used by families of the class of the settler, and these he sold at little more than cost for their accommodation, receiving his pay in such articles as they could raise from their half-tilled fields, or their sugar-bushes, and turning those again into money, only after they were transported to Albany, at the end of a considerable period. In a word, the commencement of such a settlement was an arduous undertaking, and the experiment was not very likely to succeed, unless the landlord had both capital and patience.

The political economist can have no difficulty in discovering the causes of the circumstances just mentioned. They were to be found in the fact that people were scarce, while land was superabundant. In such a condition of society, the tenant had the choice of his farm, instead of the landlord's having a selection of his tenants, and the latter were to be bought only on such conditions as suited themselves.

"You see," continued Herman Mordaunt, as we walked together, conversing on this subject, "that my twenty thousand acres are not likely to be of much use to myself, even should they prove to be of any to my daughter. A century hence, indeed, my descendants may benefit from all this outlay of money and trouble; but it is not probable that either I or Anneke will ever see the principal and interest of the sums that will be expended in the way of roads, bridges, mills, and other things of that sort. Years must go by, before the light rents, which will only begin to be paid a year or two hence, and then only by a very few tenants, can amount to a sufficient sum to meet the expenses of keeping up the settlement, to say nothing of the quit-rents to be paid to the crown."

"This is not very encouraging to a new beginner in the occupation of a landlord," I answered; "and when I look into the facts, I confess I am surprised that so many gentlemen in the colony are willing to invest the sums they annually do in wild lands."

"Every man who is at his ease in his moneyed affairs, Corny, feels a disposition to make some provision for his posterity.

This estate, if kept together and in single hands, may make some descendant of mine a man of fortune. Half a century will produce a great change in this colony; and at the end of that period, a child of Anneke's may be thankful that his mother had a father who was willing to throw away a few thousands of his own, the surplus of a fortune that was sufficient for his wants without them, in order that his grandson may see them converted into tens, or possibly into hundreds of thousands."

"Posterity will, at least, owe us a debt of gratitude, Mr. Mordaunt; for I now see that Mooseridge is not likely to make either Dirck or myself very affluent patroons."

"On that you may rely. Satanstoe will produce you more than the large tracts you possess in this quarter."

"Do you no longer fear, sir, that the war, and apprehension of Indian ravages, may drive your people off?"

"Not much at present, though the danger was great at one time. The war *may* do me good as well as harm. The armies consume every thing they can get — soldiers resembling locusts in this respect. My tenants have had the commissaries among them; and I am told every blade of grass they can spare — all their surplus grain, potatoes, butter, cheese, and in a word, every thing that can be eaten, and with which they are willing to part, has been contracted for at the top of the market. The king pays in gold, and the sight of the precious metals will keep even a Yankee from moving."

About the time this was said, we came in sight of the spot Herman Mordaunt had christened Ravensnest; a name that had since been applied to the whole property. It was a log building that stood on the verge of a low cliff of rocks, at a point where a bird of that appellation had originally a nest on the uppermost branches of a dead hemlock. The building had been placed and erected with a view to defence, having served for some time as a sort of rallying point to the families of the tenantry, in the event of an Indian alarm. At the commencement of the present war, taking into view the exposed position of his possessions on that frontier — frontier as to settlement, if not as to territorial limits — Herman Mordaunt had caused some attention to be paid to his fortifications; which, though they might not have satisfied Mons. Vauban, were not altogether without merit, considered in reference to their use in case of a surprise.

The house formed three sides of a parallelogram, the open

portion of the court in the centre facing the cliff. A strong
picket served to make a defence against bullets on that side;
while the dead walls of solid logs were quite impregnable against
any assault known in forest warfare but that of fire. All the
windows opened on the court; while the single outer door was
picketed, and otherwise protected by coverings of plank. I was
glad to see by the extent of the rude structure, which was a
hundred feet long by fifty in depth, that Anneke and Mary
Wallace would not be likely to be straitened for room. Such
proved to be the fact; Herman Mordaunt's agent having prepared four or five apartments for the family, that rendered them
as comfortable as people could well expect to be in such a situation. Every thing was plain, and many things were rude; but
shelter, warmth and security had not been neglected.

CHAPTER XXI

"And long shall timorous fancy see,
  The painted chief and pointed spear;
And Reason's self shall bow the knee
  To shadows and delusions here."

FRENEAU.

IT is not necessary to dwell on the manner in which Herman Mordaunt and his companions became established at Ravensnest. Two or three days sufficed to render them as comfortable as circumstances would permit; then Dirck and I bethought us of proceeding in quest of the lands of Mooseridge. Mr. Worden and Jason both declined going any further; the mill-seat of which the last was in quest, being, as I now learned, on the estate of Herman Mordaunt, and having been for some time the subject of a negotiation between the pedagogue and its owner. As for the divine, he declared that he saw a suitable "field" for his missionary labor where he was; while it was easy to see that he questioned if there were fields of any sort, where we were going.

Our party on quitting Ravensnest, consisted of Dirck and myself, Guert, Mr. Traverse the surveyor, three chain-bearers, Jaap or Yaap, Guert's man Pete, and one woodsman or hunter. This would have given us ten vigorous and well armed men, for our whole force. It was thought best, however, to add two Indians to our number, in the double character of hunters and runners, or messengers. One of these Indians was called Jumper, in the language of the settlement where we found them, and the other Trackless; the latter *sobriquet* having been given him on account of a faculty he possessed of leaving little or no trail in his journeys and marches. This Indian was about six-and-twenty years of age, and was called a Mohawk, living with the people of that tribe; though I subsequently ascertained that he was in fact an Onondago* by birth. His true name

---

* Pronounced On-on-daw-ger, the latter syllable hard; or like ga, as it is sometimes spelled. This is the name of one of the midland counties of New York. The tribe from which it is derived, in these later times, has ever borne a better name for morals, than its neighbors, the Oneidas, the Mohawks, etc., etc. The Onondagoes belonged to the Six Nations. — EDITOR.

284

was Susquesus or Crooked Turns; an appellation that might or might not speak well of his character, as the "turns" were regarded in a moral or in a physical sense.

"Take that man, Mr. Littlepage, by all means," said Herman Mordaunt's agent, when the matter was under discussion. You will find him as useful in the woods as your pocket-compass, besides being a reasonably good hunter. He left here as a runner during the heaviest of the snows last winter, and a trial was made to find his trail within half an hour after he had quitted the clearing, but without success. He had not gone a mile in the woods before all traces of him were lost, as completely as if he had made the journey in the air."

As Susquesus had a reputation for sobriety, as was apt to be the case with the Onondagoes, the man was engaged, though one Indian would have been sufficient for our purpose. But Jumper had been previously hired; and it would have been dangerous under our circumstances, to offend a red man, by putting him aside for another, even after compensating him fully for the disappointment. By Mr. Traverse's advice therefore, we took both. The Indian, or Mohawk name of Jumper was Quissquiss, a term that I fancy signified nothing very honorable or illustrious.

The girls betrayed deep interest in us, on our taking leave; more, I thought, than either had before manifested. Guert had told me privately, of an intention on his part to make another offer to Mary Wallace; and I saw the traces of it in the tearful eyes and flushed cheeks of his mistress. But at such a moment, one does not stop to think much of such things; there being tears in Anneke's eyes, as well as in those of her friend. We had a thousand good wishes to exchange; and we promised to keep open the communication between the two parties, by means of our runners, semi-weekly. The distance, which would vary from fifteen to thirty miles, would readily admit of this, since either of the Indians would pass over it, with the greatest ease to himself, in a day at that season of the year.

After all, the separation was to be short, for we had promised to come over and dine with Herman Mordaunt on his fiftieth birth-day, which would occur within three weeks. This arrangement made the parting tolerable to us young men, and our constitutional gayety did the rest. Half an hour after the last breakfast at Ravensnest saw us all on our road, cheerful, if not absolutely happy. Herman Mordaunt accompanied us three miles; which led him to the end of his own settlements, and to the edge of the virgin forest. There he took his leave, and we pursued our way with the utmost diligence for hours, with the compass for our guide, until we reached the banks of a small river that was supposed to lie some three or four miles from the southern boundaries of the patent we sought. I say, "supposed to lie," for there existed then, and I believe there still exists, much uncertainty concerning the landmarks of different estates in the woods. On the banks of this stream, which was deep but not broad, the surveyor called a halt, and we made our dispositions for dinner. Men who had walked as far and as fast as we had done, made but little ceremony, and for twenty minutes every one was busy in appeasing his hunger. This was no sooner accomplished, however, than Mr. Traverse summoned the Indians to the side of the fallen tree on which we had taken our seats, when the first occasion occurred for putting the comparative intelligence of the two runners to the proof. At the same time the principal chain-bearer, a man whose life had been passed in his present occupation, was brought into the consultation, as follows.

"We are now on the banks of this stream, and about this bend in it," commenced the surveyor, pointing to the precise curvature of the river on a map he had spread before him, at which he supposed we were actually situated; "and the next thing is to find that ridge on which the moose was killed, and across which the line of the patent we seek is known to run. This abstract of the title tells us to look for a corner somewhere off here, about a mile or a mile and a half from this bend in the river — a black oak with its top broken off by the wind, and standing in the centre of a triangle made by three chestnuts. I think you told me, David, that you had never borne a chain on any of these ridges?"

"No, sir, never;" answered David, the old chain-bearer already mentioned; "my business never having brought me out so far east. A black oak with corner blazes on it, and its top broken down by the wind, and standing atween three chestnuts, howsomedever, can be nothing so very hard to find, for a person that's the least acquainted. These Injins will be the likeliest bodies to know that tree, if they've any nat'ral knowledge of the country."

Know a tree! There we were, and had been for many hours in the bosom of the forest, with trees in thousands ranged around us; trees had risen on our march, as horizon extends beyond horizon on the ocean, and this chain-bearer fancied it might be in the power of one who often passed through these dark and untenanted mazes, to recognize any single member of those countless oaks, and beeches, and pines! Nevertheless, Mr. Traverse did not seem to regard David's suggestion as so very extravagant, for he turned toward the Indians and addressed himself to them.

"How's this?" he asked; "Jumper, do you know any thing of the sort of tree I have described?"

"No," was the short, sentencious answer.

"Then, I fear there is little hope that Trackless is any wiser, as you are Mohawk born, and *he*, they tell me, is at bottom an Onondago. What say you, Trackless? can you help us to find the tree?"

My eyes were fastened on Susquesus, as soon as the Indians were mentioned. There he stood, straight as the trunk of a pine, light and agile in person, with nothing but his breech-cloth, moccasins, and a blue calico shirt belted to his loins with a scarlet band, through which was thrust the handle of his tomahawk, and to which were attached his shot-pouch and horn, while his rifle rested against his body, butt downward. Trackless was a singularly handsome Indian, the unpleasant peculiarities of his people being but faintly portrayed in his face and form; while their nobler and finer qualities came out in strong relief. His nose was almost aquiline; his eye, dark as night, was restless and piercing; his limbs Apollo-like; and his front and bearing had all the fearless dignity of a warrior, blended with the grace of nature. The only obvious defects were in his walk, which was Indian, or in-toed and bending at the knee; but to counterbalance these, his movements were light, springy and swift. I fancied him in figure, the very *beau-ideal* of a runner.

During the time the surveyor was speaking, the eye of Susquesus was seemingly fastened on vacancy, and I would have defied the nicest observer to detect any consciousness of what was in hand in the countenance of this forest stoic. It was not his business to speak while an older runner and an older warrior was present — for Jumper was both — and he waited for others, who might know more, to reveal their knowledge ere he produced his own. Thus directly addressed, however, all reserve vanished, and he advanced two or three steps, cast a curious glance at the map, even put a finger on the river, the devious course of which it followed across the map, much as a child would trace any similar object that attracted his attention. Susquesus knew but little of maps it was clear enough; but the result showed that he knew a great deal about the woods, his native field of action.

"Well, what do you make of my map, Trackless," repeated the surveyor. "Is it not drawn to suit your fancy?"

"Good"—returned the Onondago with emphasis. "Now show Susquesus *your* oak tree."

"Here it is, Trackless. You see it is a tree drawn in ink, with a broken top, and here are the three chestnuts in a sort of triangle around it."

The Indian examined the tree with some interest, and a slight smile illumined his handsome though dark countenance. He was evidently pleased at this proof of accuracy in the colony surveyors, and no doubt thought the better of them for the fidelity of their work.

"Good," he repeated in his low, guttural, almost feminine voice, so soft and mild in its tone. "*Very* good. The pale-faces know every thing! Now, let my brother find the tree."

"That is easier said than done, Susquesus," answered Traverse, laughing. "It is one thing to sketch a tree on a map, and another to go to its root, as it stands in the forest, surrounded by thousands of other trees."

"Pale-face must first see him, or how paint him? Where painter?"

"Ay, the surveyor saw the tree once, and marked it once, but that is not finding it again. Can you tell me where the oak stands? Mr. Littlepage will give the man who finds that corner a French crown. Put me anywhere on the line of the old survey, and I will ask favors of no one."

"Painted tree *there*," said Susquesus, pointing a little scornfully at the map, as it seemed to me. "Pale-face can't find him in wood. Live tree out yonder; Injun know."

Trackless pointed with great dignity toward the north-east, standing motionless as a statue the while, as if inviting the closest possible scrutiny into the correctness of his assertion.

"Can you lead us to the tree?" demanded Traverse eagerly. "Do it, and the money is yours."

Susquesus made a significant gesture of assent; then he set about collecting the scanty remains of his dinner, a precaution

in which we imitated him, as a supper would be equally agreeable as the meal just taken, a few hours later. When every
thing was put away, and the packs were on our shoulders — not
on those of the Indians, for *they* seldom condescended to carry
burdens, which was an occupation for women — Trackless led
the way in the direction he had already pointed out.

Well did the Onondago deserve his name, as it seemed to me,
while he threaded his way through that gloomy forest, without
path, mark, or sign of any sort that was intelligible to others.
His pace was between a walk and a gentle trot, and it required
all our muscles to keep near him. He looked to neither the
right nor the left, but appeared to pursue his course guided by
an instinct, or as the keen-scented hound follows the viewless
traces of his game. This lasted for ten minutes, when Traverse
called another halt, and we clustered together in council.

"How much further do you think it may be to the tree,
Onondago?" demanded the surveyor, as soon as the whole
party was collected in a circle. "I have a reason for asking."

"So many minutes," answered the Indian, holding up five
fingers, or the four fingers and thumb of his right hand. "Oak
with broken top, and pale-face marks, *there*."

The precision and confidence with which the Trackless pointed
not a little surprised me, for I could not imagine how any human
being could pretend to be minutely certain of such a fact under
the circumstances in which we were placed. So it was, however, and so it proved in the end. In the mean time, Traverse
proceeded to carry out his own plans.

"As we are so near to the tree," he said, for the surveyor
had no doubt of the red man's accuracy, "*we* must also be
near the line. The last runs north and south, on this part of
the patent, and we shall shortly cross it. Spread yourselves,
therefore, chain-bearers, and look for blazed trees; for, put me
anywhere on the boundaries, and I'll answer for finding any
oak, beech, or maple that is mentioned in the corners."

As soon as this order was received, all the surveyor's men
obeyed, opening the order of their march, and spreading themselves in a way to extend their means of observing materially.
When all was ready, a sign was made to the Indian to proceed.
Susquesus obeyed, and we were all soon in quick motion again.

Guert's activity enabled him to keep nearest to the Onondago, and a shout from his clear, full throat, first announced
the complete success of the search. In a moment the rest of

us pressed forward, and were soon at the end of our journey. There was Susquesus, quietly leaning against the trunk of the broken oak, without the smallest expression of triumph in either his manner or his countenance. That which he had done, he had done naturally, and without any apparent effort or hesitation. To him the forest had its signs and metes, and marks — as the inhabitant of the vast capital has his means of threading its mazes with the readiness of familiarity and habit. As for Traverse, he first examined the top of the tree, where he found the indicated fracture; then he looked round for the three chestnuts, each of which was in its place; after which he drew near to look into the more particular signs of his craft. There they were, three of the inner sides of the oak being blazed; the proof it was a corner; while that which had no scar on its surface looked outward or from the patent of Mooseridge. Just as all these agreeable facts were ascertained, shouts from the chain-bearers south of us, announced that they had discovered the line — men of their stamp being quite as quick-sighted in ascertaining their own peculiar traces, as the native of the forest is in finding his way to any object in it which he has once seen, and may desire to revisit. By following the line, these men soon joined us, when they gave us the additional information that they had also actually found the skeleton of the moose that had given its name to the estate.

Thus far all was well, our success much exceeding our hopes. The hunters were sent to look for a spring; and one being found at no great distance, we all repaired to the spot, and hutted for the night. Nothing could be more simple than our encampment; which consisted of coverings made of the branches of trees, with leaves and skins for our beds. Next day, however, Traverse finding the position favorable for his work, determined to select the spot as head-quarters; and we all set about the erection of a log-house, in which we might seek a shelter in the event of a storm, and where we might deposit our implements, spare ammunition, and such stores as we had brought with us on our backs. As every body worked with good-will at the erection of this rude building, and the laborers were very expert with the axe, we had it nearly complete by the setting of the next day's sun. Traverse chose the place because the water was abundant and good, and because a small knoll was near the spring, that was covered with young pines that were about fourteen or fifteen inches in diameter, while they grew to the height of near a hundred feet, with few branches, and straight as the Onondago. These trees were felled, cut into lengths of twenty and thirty feet, notched at the ends, and rolled alternately on each other, so as to enclose an area that was one-third longer than it was wide. The notches were deep, and brought the logs within two or three inches of each other; and the interstices were filled with pieces of riven chestnut, a wood that splits easily and in straight lines; which pieces were driven hard into their beds, so as to exclude the winds and the rains. As the weather was warm, and the building somewhat airy at the best, we cut no windows, though we had a narrow door in the centre of one of the longer sides. For a roof we used the bark of the hemlock, which, at that season, came off in large pieces, and which was laid on sticks raised to the desired elevation by means of a ridge-pole.

All this was making no more than one of the common log-houses of the new settlements, though in a more hurried and a less artificial manner than was usual. We had no chimney, for our cooking could be done in the open air; and less attention was paid to the general finish of the work than might have been the case had we expected to pass the winter there. The floor was somewhat rude, but it had the effect of raising us from the ground, and giving us perfectly dry lodgings, an advantage not always obtained in the woods. It was composed of logs roughly squared on three sides, and placed on sleepers. To my surprise Traverse directed a door to be made of riven logs, that were pinned together with cross-pieces, and which was hung on the usual wooden hinges. When I spoke of this as unnecessary labor, occupying two men an entire day to complete, he reminded me that we were much in advance from the settlements; that an active war was being waged around us, and that the agents of the French had been very busy among our own tribes, while those in Canada often pushed their war-parties far within our borders. He had always found a great satisfaction as well as security, in having a sort of citadel to retreat to, when on these exposed surveys; and he never neglected the necessary precaution, when he fancied himself in the least danger.

We were quite a week in completing our house; though after the first day neither the surveyor nor his chain-bearers troubled themselves with the labor, any further than to make an occasional suggestion. Traverse and his men went to work in their own pursuit, running lines to divide the patent into its great lots, each of which was made to contain a thousand acres. It should be mentioned that all the surveys in that day were made on the most liberal scale, our forty thousand acres turning out in the end to amount to quite three thousand more. So it was with the subdivisions of the patent, each of which was found to be of more than the nominal dimensions. Blazed trees, and records cut into the bark, served to indicate the lines, while a map went on *pari passu* with the labor, the field-book containing a description of each lot, in order that the proprietor of the estate might have some notions of the nature of its soil and surface, as well as of the quality and sizes of the trees it bore.

The original surveyors, those on whose labors the patent of the king was granted, had a comparatively trifling duty to perform. So long as they gave a reasonably accurate outline of an area that would contain forty thousand acres of land, more or less, and did not trespass on any prior grant, no material harm could be done, there being no scarcity of surface in the colony; but Mr. Traverse had to descend to a little more particularity. It is true he ran out his hundreds of acres daily, duly marking his corners and blazing his line-trees, but something very like a summer's work lay before him. This he understood, and his proceedings were as methodical and deliberate as the nature of his situation required.

In a very few days, things had gotten fairly in train, and everybody was employed in some manner that was found to be useful. The surveying party were making a very satisfactory progress, running out their great lots between sun and sun, while Dirck and myself made the notes concerning their quality under the dictation of Mr. Traverse. Guert did little besides shoot and fish, keeping our larder well supplied with trout, pigeons, squirrels, and such other game as the season would allow, occasionally knocking over something in the shape of poor venison. The hunters brought us their share of eatables also; and we did well enough in this particular, more especially as trout proved to be very abundant. Yaap, or Jaap, as I shall call him in future, and Pete performed domestic duty, acting as scullions and cooks, though the first was much better fitted to perform the service of a forester. The two Indians did little else for the first fortnight but come and go between Ravensnest and Mooseridge, carrying missives and acting as guides to the hunters, who went through once or twice within that period to bring us out supplies of flour, groceries, and other similar necessaries; no inducement being able to prevail on the Indians to carry any thing that approached a burden, either in weight or appearance.

The surveying party did not always return to the hut at night, but it "camped out," as they called it, whenever the work led them to a distance on the other side of the tract. Mr. Traverse had chosen his position for head-quarters more in reference to its proximity to the settlement at Ravensnest, than in reference to its position on the patent. It was sufficiently central to the latter as regarded a north and south line, but was altogether on the western side of the property. As his surveys extended east, therefore, he was often carried too far from the building to return to it each night, though his absences never extended beyond the evening of the third day. In consequence of this arrangement, his people were enabled to carry the food they required, without inconvenience, for the periods they were away, coming back for fresh supplies as the lines brought them west again. Sundays were strictly observed by us all as days of rest, a respect to the day that is not always observed in the forest; he who is in the solitude of the woods, like him who roams athwart the wastes of the ocean, often forgetting that the spirit of the Creator is abroad equally on the ocean and on the land, ready to receive that homage of his creatures which is a tribute due to beneficence without bounds, a holiness that is spotless, and a truth that is inherent.

As Jumper or the Trackless returned from his constantly recurring visits to our neighbors, we young men waited with impatience for the letter that the messenger was certain to bear. This letter was sometimes written by Herman Mordaunt himself, but oftener by Anneke or Mary Wallace. It was addressed to no one by name, but uniformly bore the superscription of " To the Hermits of Mooseridge; " nor was there any thing in the language to betray any particular attention to either of the party. We might have liked it better, perhaps, could we have received epistles that were a little more pointed in this particular; but those we actually got were much too precious to leave any serious grounds of complaint. One from Herman Mordaunt reached us on the evening of the second Saturday, when our whole party were at home and assembled at supper. It was brought in by the Trackless, and among other matters contained this paragraph:

"We learn that things hourly assume a more serious aspect with the armies. Our troops are pushing north in large bodies, and the French are said to be reinforcing. Living, as we do, out of the direct line of march, and fully thirty miles in the rear of the old battle-grounds, I should feel no apprehension, were it not for a report I hear that the woods are full of Indians. I very well know that such a report invariably accompanies the near approach of hostilities in the frontier settlements, and is to be received with many grains of allowance; but it seems so probable the French should push their savages on this flank of our army, to annoy it on the advance, that I confess the rumor has some influence on my feelings. We have been fortifying still more, and I would advise you not to neglect such a precaution altogether. The Canadian Indians are said to be more subtle than our own; nor is government altogether without the apprehension that our own have been tampered with. It was said in Albany that much French silver had been seen in the hands of the people of the Six Nations; and that even French blankets, knives and tomahawks were more plentiful among them than might be accounted for by the ordinary plunder of their warfare. One of your runners, the man who is called the Trackless, is said to live out of his own tribe, and such Indians are always to be suspected. Their absence is sometimes owing to reasons that are creditable, but far oftener to those that are not. It may be well to have an eye on the conduct of this man. After all, we are in the hands of a beneficent and gracious God, and we know how often his mercy has saved us, on occasions more trying than this! "

This letter was read several times among ourselves, including Mr. Traverse. As the *oi polloi* of our party were eating out of ear-shot, and the Indians had left us, it naturally induced a conversation that turned on the risks we ran, and on the probability of Susquesus being false.

"As for the rumor that the woods are full of Indians," the surveyor quietly observed, "it is very much as Herman Mordaunt says — there is never a blanket seen, but fame magnifies it into a whole bale. There is danger to be apprehended from savages, I will allow, but not one-half that the settlers ordinarily imagine. As for the French, they are likely to need all their savages at Ty; for they tell me General Abercrombie will go against them with three men to their one."

"With that superiority, at least," I answered; "but after

all, would not a sagacious officer be likely to annoy his flank in the manner here mentioned? "

" We are every mile of forty to the eastward of the line of march; and why should parties keep so distant from their enemies? "

" Even such a supposition would place our foes between us and our friends; no very comfortable consideration of itself. But what think you of this hint concerning the Onondago? "

" There may be truth in *that* — more than in the report that the woods are full of savages. It is usually a bad sign when an Indian quits his tribe; and this runner of ours is certainly an Onondago; *that* I know, for the fellow has twice refused rum. Bread he will take as often as offered; but rum has not wet his lips, since I have seen him, offered in fair weather or foul."

" T'at *is* a bad sign " — put in Guert, a little dogmatically for him. " T'e man t'at refuses his glass, in good company, has commonly something wrong in his morals. I always keep clear of such chaps."

Poor Guert! — How true that was, and what an influence the opinion had on his character and habits. As for the Indian, I could not judge him so harshly. There was something in his countenance that disposed me to put confidence in him, at the very moment his cold, abstracted manners — cold and abstracted even for a red-skin in pale-face company — created doubts and distrust.

" Certainly, nothing is easier than for a man in his situation to sell us," I answered, after a short pause, " if he be so disposed. But what could the French gain by cutting off a party as peaceably employed as this? It can be of no moment to them, whether Mooseridge be surveyed into lots this year, or the next."

" Quite true; and I am of opinion that Monsieur Montcalm is very indifferent whether it be ever surveyed at all," returned Traverse, who was an intelligent and tolerably educated man. " You forget, however, Mr. Littlepage, that both parties offer such things as premiums on scalps. A Huron may not care about our lines, corners, and marked trees; but he *does* care a great deal whether he is to go home with an empty string, or with half-a-dozen human scalps at his girdle."

I observed that Dirck thrust his finger through his bushy hair, and that his usually placid countenance assumed an indignant and semi-ferocious appearance. A little amused at this,

I walked toward the log on which Susquesus was seated, having ended his meal in silent thought.

"What news do you bring us from the red-coats, Trackless?" I asked, with as much of an air of indifference as I could assume. "Are they out in sufficient numbers to eat the French?"

"Look at leaves; count 'em; " answered the Indian.

"Yes, I know they are in force; but what are the red-skins about? Is the hatchet buried among the Six Nations, that you are satisfied with being a runner when scalps may be had near Ticonderoga?"

"Susquesus *Onondago*" — the red man replied, laying a strong emphasis on the name of his tribe. "No Mohawk blood run in him. *His* people no dig up hatchet this summer."

"Why not, Trackless? You are allies of the Yengeese, and ought to give us your aid, when it is wanted."

"Count leaves — count Yengeese. Too much for one army. No want Onondago."

"That may be true, possibly, for we are certainly very strong. But, how is it with the woods — are they altogether clear of red-skins, in times as troublesome as these?"

Susquesus looked grave, but he made no answer. Still, he did not endeavor to avoid the keen look I fastened on his face, but sat composed, rigid, and gazing before him. Knowing the uselessness of attempting to get any thing out of an Indian when he was indisposed to be communicative, I thought it wisest to change the discourse. This I did by making a few general inquiries as to the state of the streams, all of which were answered, when I walked away.

CHAPTER XXII

I CANNOT say I was quite satisfied with the manner of Susquesus; nor on the other hand was I absolutely uneasy. All might be well; and if it were not, the power of man to injure us could not be very great. A new occurrence, however, raised very unpleasant doubts of his honesty. Jumper being out on a hunt, the Onondago was sent across to Ravensnest the next trip, out of his turn; but instead of returning, as had been the practice of both, the next day, we saw no more of him for near a fortnight. As we talked over this sudden and unexpected disappearance, we came to the conclusion that, perceiving he was distrusted, the fellow had deserted and would be seen no more. During his absence we paid a visit to Ravensnest ourselves, spending two or three happy days with the girls, whom we found delighted with the wildness of their abode, and as happy as innocence, health, and ceaseless interest in the forest and its habits could make them. Herman Mordaunt having fortified his house sufficiently, as he fancied, to remove all danger of an assault, returned with us to Mooseridge, and passed two or three days in walking over and examining the quality of the land, together with the advantages offered by the watercourses. As for Mr. Worden and Jason, the former had gone to join the army, craving the flesh-pots of a regimental mess, in preference to the simple fare of the woods; while Jason had driven a hard bargain with Herman Mordaunt for the possession of the millseat, which had been the subject of frequent discussion between the parties, and about which the pedagogue had deemed it prudent to draw on the wisdom of Mother Doortje. As the reader may have some curiosity to know how such things were conducted in the colony in the year 1758, I will recapitulate the terms of the bargain that was finally agreed on, signed and sealed.

Herman Mordaunt expected no emolument to himself, from Ravensnest, but looked forward solely to a provision for posterity.

In consequence of these views he refused to sell, but gave leases on such conditions as would induce tenants to come into his terms, in a country in which land was far plentier than men. For some reason that never was very clear to me, he was particularly anxious to secure Jason Newcome, and no tolerable terms seemed extravagant to effect his purpose. It is not surprising therefore that our miller in perspective got much the best of the bargain, as its conditions will show.

The lease was for three lives, and twenty-one years afterward. This would have been thought equal to a lease for forty-two years in that day in Europe; but experience is showing that it is in truth for a much longer period, in America.* The first ten years, no rent at all was to be paid. For the next ten, the land, five hundred acres, was to pay sixpence currency an acre, the tenant having the right to cut timber at pleasure. This was a great concession, as the mill-lot contained much pine. For the remainder of the lease, be it longer or shorter, a shilling an acre, or about sixpence sterling, was to be paid for the land, and forty pounds currency, or one hundred dollars a year, for the mill-seat. The mills to be taken by the landlord, at an appraisal "made by men," at the expiration of the lease; the tenant to pay the taxes. The tenant had the privilege of using all the materials for his dams, buildings, etc., he could find on the land.

The policy of the owners of Mooseridge was different. We intended to sell at low prices at first, reserving for leases hereafter such farms as could not be immediately disposed of, or for which the purchaser failed to pay. In this manner it was thought we should sooner get returns for our outlay, and sooner "build up a settlement," as the phrase goes. In America, the reader should know every thing is "built." The priest "builds up" a flock; the speculator a fortune; the lawyer a reputation; and the landlord a settlement; sometimes with sufficient accuracy in language, he even builds a town.

Jason was a very happy man the moment he got his lease signed and sealed in his own possession. It made him a sort of a landholder on the spot, and one who had nothing to pay for ten years to come. God forgive me, if I do the man injustice; but, from the first I had a suspicion that Jason trusted to fortune to prevent any pay-day from ever coming at all. As for Herman Mordaunt, he seemed satisfied, for he fancied that

* It has been found that a three-lives' lease, in the state of New York, is equal to a term of more than thirty years. — EDITOR.

he had got a man of some education on his property, who might answer a good purpose in civilizing, and in otherwise advancing the interests of his estate.

Just as the rays of the rising sun streamed through the crevices of our log tenement, and ere one of us three idlers had risen from his pallet, I heard a moccasined foot moving near me, in the nearly noiseless tread of an Indian. Springing to my feet, I found myself face to face with the missing Onondago!

"You here, Susquesus!" I exclaimed; "we supposed you had abandoned us. What has brought you back?"

"Time to go, now," answered the Indian, quietly. "Yengeese and Canada warrior soon fight."

"Is this true! — And do you, *can* you know it to be true! Where have you been this fortnight past?"

"Been see — have see — know him just so. Come — call young men; go on war-path."

Here, then, was an explanation of the mystery of the Onondago's absence! He had heard us speak of an intention of moving with the troops, at the last moment, and he had gone to reconnoitre, in order that we might have seasonable notice when it would be necessary to quit the "Ridge," as we familiarly termed the patent. I saw nothing treasonable in this, but rather deemed it a sign of friendly interest in our concerns; though it was certainly "running" much farther than the Indian had been directed to proceed, and "running" a little off the track. One might overlook such an irregularity in a savage, however, more especially as I began to weary of the monotony of our present manner of living, and was not sorry to discover a plausible apology for a change.

The reader may be certain, it was not long before I had communicated the intelligence brought by the Trackless, to my companions; who received it as young men would be apt to listen to tidings so stirring. The Onondago was summoned to our council, and he renewed his protestation that it was time for us to be moving.

"No stop" — he answered, when questioned again on the subject; "time go. Canoe ready — gun loaded — warrior counted — chief woke up — council-fire gone out. Time, go."

"Well then, Corny," said Guert, rising and stretching his fine frame like a lion roused from his lair, "here's off. We can go to Ravensnest to sleep, to-day; and to-morrow we will work our way out into the highway, and fall into the line of march of the army. I shall have another opportunity of seeing Mary Wallace, and of telling her how much I love her. That will be so much gained, at all events."

"No see squaw — no go to Nest!" said the Indian, with energy. "War-path *this* way," pointing in a direction that might have varied a quarter of a circle from that to Herman Mordaunt's settlement. "Bad for warrior to see squaw when he dig up hatchet — only make woman of him. No; go this way — path there — no here — scalp there — squaw here."

As the gestures of the Onondago were quite as significant as his language, we had no difficulty in understanding him. Guert continued his questions, however, while dressing, and we all soon became convinced by the words of the Indian, broken and abrupt as they were, that Abercrombie was on the point of embarking with his army on Lake George, and that we must needs be active, if we intended to be present at the contemplated operations in front of Ticonderoga.

Our decision was soon reached, and our preparations made. By packing and shouldering his knapsack, and arming himself, each man would be ready; though a short delay grew out of the absence of Traverse and his chain-bearers. We wrote a letter, however, explaining the reason of our intended absence, promising to return as soon as the operations in front of Ty should be terminated. This letter we left with Pete, who was to remain, as cook, though Jaap bestirred himself, loaded his broad shoulders with certain indispensables for our march, took his rifle, pack and horn, and was ready to move as soon as any of us. All this the fellow did, moreover, without orders; deeming it a part of his duty to follow his young master, even if he followed him to evil. No dog, indeed, could be truer in this particular, than Jaap or Jacob Satanstoe, for he had adopted the name of the Neck as his patronymic; much as the nobles of other regions style themselves after *their* lands.

When all was ready and we were on the point of quitting the hut, the question arose seriously, whether we were to go by Ravensnest, or by the new route that the Onondago had mentioned. Path there was not, in either direction; but we had landmarks, springs, and other known signs on the former; while of the latter we literally knew nothing. Then Anneke and Mary Wallace, with their bright, blooming, sunny faces — bright and happy whenever we appeared, most certainly, of late — were in the former direction, and even Dirck cried out "for Ravens-

nest." But on that route, the Onondago refused to stir one foot.
He stood, resembling a finger-post, pointing north-westerly, with
an immovable obstinacy that threatened to bring the order of
our march into some confusion.

"We know nothing of that route, Trackless," Guert observed,
or rather replied, for the Indian's manner was so expressive as to
amount to a remark, "and we would rather travel a road with
which we are a little acquainted. Besides, we wish to pay our
parting compliments to the ladies."

"Squaw no good, now — war-path no go to squaw. Huron —
French warrior, here."

"Ay, and they are there, too. We shall be on their heels soon
enough, by going to Ravensnest."

"No soon 'nough — can't do him. Path long, time short.
Pale-face warrior in great hurry."

"Pale-face warriors' friends are in a hurry, too — so you will
do well to follow us, as we do not intend to follow you. Come,
gentlemen, we will lead the Indian, as the Indian does not seem
disposed to lead us. After a mile or two he will think it more
honorable to go in advance; and for that distance, I believe I can
show you the way."

"That road good for young men who don't want see enemy!"
said Susquesus, with ironical point.

"By St. Nicholas! Indian, what do you mean?" cried Guert,
turning short on his heels and moving swiftly toward the
Onondago, who did not wait for the menacing blow, but wheeled in
his tracks and led off at a quick pace, directly toward the north-
west.

I do believe that Guert pursued, for the first minute, with no
other intention than that of laying his powerful arm on the
offender's shoulder; but I dropped in on his footsteps so soon,
Dirck following me and Jaap Dirck, that we were all moving off
Indian file, or in the fashion of the woods, at the rate of four miles
in the hour, almost before we knew it. An impulse of that angry
nature is not over in a minute, and before either of us had sufficiently cooled to be entirely reasonable, the whole party were
fairly out of sight of the hut. After that no one appeared to think
of the necessity or of the expediency of reverting to the original
intention. It was certainly indiscreet, thus to confide absolutely
in the good faith of a savage, or a semi-savage, at least, whom we
scarcely knew, and whom we had actually distrusted; but we did
it, and precisely in the manner and under the feelings I have

described. I know that we all thought of the indiscretion of which we had been guilty, after the first mile; but each was too proud to make the other acquainted with his misgivings. I say all, but Jaap ought to be excepted, for nothing in the shape of danger ever gave that negro any concern, unless it was "spooks." He *was* afraid of spooks, but he did not fear man.

Susquesus manifested the same confidence in his knowledge of the woods, while now leading the way league after league through the dark forest, as he had done when he took us to the oak with the broken top. On this occasion, he guided us more by the sun and the course generally, than by any acquaintance with objects that we passed; though three times that day did he point out to us particular things that he had before seen while traversing the woods in directions that crossed, at angles more or less oblique, the line of our present route. As for us, it was like a sailor's pointing to a path on the trackless ocean. We had our pocket-compasses, it is true, and understood well enough that a north-west course would bring us out somewhere near the foot of Lake George; but I much doubt if we could have made by any means as direct a line, by their aid, as we did by that of the Indian.

On this subject we had a discussion among ourselves, I well remember, when we halted to eat and rest, a little after the turn of the day. For five hours had we walked with great rapidity, much as the bird flies, so far as course was concerned, never turning aside unless it might be to avoid some impassable obstacle; and our calculation was that we had made quite twenty of the forty miles we had to go over, according to the Onondago's account of the probable length of our journey. We had strung our sinews and hardened our muscles in such a way as to place us above the influence of common fatigue; yet it must be confessed the Indian was much the freshest of the five when we reached the spring where we dined.

"An Indian does seem to have a nose much like that of a hound," said Guert, as our appetites began to be appeased; " *that* must be admitted. Yet I think, Corny, a compass would carry a man through the woods with more certainty than any signs on the bark of trees, or looks at the sun."

"A compass cannot err, of course; but it would be a troublesome thing to be stopping every minute or two to look at your compass, which must have time to become steady, you will remember, or it would become a guide that is worse than none."

"Every minute or two! Say once in an hour, or once in half

an hour, at most. I would engage to travel as straight as the
best Indian of them all, by looking at my compass once in half an
hour."

Susquesus was seated near enough to us three to overhear our
conversation, and he understood English perfectly, though he spoke
it in the usual clipped manner of an Indian. I thought I could
detect a covert gleam of contempt in his dark countenance, at this
boast of Guert's; but he made no remark. We finished our meal,
rested our legs, and when our watches told us it was one o'clock, we
rose in a body to resume our march. We were renewing the
priming of our rifles, a precaution each man took twice every day
to prevent the effects of the damps of the woods, when the
Onondago quietly fell in behind Guert, patiently waiting the leisure
of the latter.

"We are all ready, Trackless," cried the Albanian; "give us
the lead and the step as before."

"No," answered the Indian. "Compass lead now; Susquesus
no see any longer — blind as young dog."

"Oh! that is your game, is it? Well, let it be so. Now, Corny,
you shall learn the virtue there is in a compass."

Hereupon Guert drew his compass from a pocket in his hunting-
shirt, placed it on a log in order to get a perfectly accurate start,
and waited until the quivering needle had become perfectly
stationary. Then he made his observation, and took a large hemlock, which stood at the distance of some twenty rods, a great
distance for a sight in the forest, as his landmark, gave a shout,
caught up his compass and led off. We followed of course, and
soon reached the tree. As Guert now fancied he was well entered
on the right course, he disdained to turn to renew his observation,
but called out for us to "come on," as he had a new tree for his
guide, and that in the true direction. We may have proceeded in
this manner for half a mile, and I began to think that Guert was
about to triumph — for to me it did really seem that our course
was as straight as it had been at any time that day. Guert now
began to brag of his success, talking *to* me and *at* the Indian,
who was between us, over his shoulder.

"You see, Corny," he said, "I am used to the bush, after all,
and have often been up among the Mohawks, and on their hunts.
The great point is to begin right; after which you can have no
great trouble. Make certain of the first ten rods, and you can
be at ease about the ten thousand that are to follow. So it is
with life, Corny, boy; begin right, and a young man is pretty

certain of coming out right. I made a mistake at the start, and you see the trouble it has given me. But I was left an orphan, Littlepage, at ten years of age; and the boy that has neither father nor money, must be an uncommon boy not to kick himself out of the traces before he is twenty. Well, Onondago, what do you say to following the compass, now?"

"Best look at him — he tell," answered Susquesus, our whole line halting to let Guert comply.

"This d——d compass will never come round!" exclaimed Guert, shaking the little instrument in order to help the needle round to the point at which he wished to see it stand. "These little devils are very apt to get out of order, Corny, after all."

"Try more — got three," said the Indian, holding up the number of fingers he mentioned, as was his wont when mentioning numbers of any sort.

On this hint, Dirck and I drew out our compasses, and the three were placed on a log, at the side of which we had come to our halt. The result showed that the three "little devils" agreed most accurately, and that we were marching exactly south-east, instead of north-west! Guert looked on that occasion, very much as he did when he rose from the snow after the hand-sled had upset with us. There was no resisting the truth; we had got turned completely round, without knowing it. The fact that the sun was so near the zenith probably contributed to our mistake; but any one who has tried the experiment, will soon ascertain how easy it is for him to lose his direction beneath the obscurity and amid the inequalities of a virgin forest. Guert gave it up like a man as he was, and the Indian again passed in front without the slightest manifestation of triumph or discontent. It required nothing less than a thunderbolt to disturb the composure of that Onondago!

From that moment our progress was as swift as it had been previously to the halt, while our course was seemingly as unerring as the flight of the pigeon. Susquesus did not steer exactly north-west, as before, however, but he inclined more northerly. At length, it was just as the sun approached the summits of the western mountains, an opening appeared in our front beneath the arches of the wood, and we knew that a lake was near us, and that we were on the summit of high land, though at what precise elevation could not yet be told. Our route had lain across hills and through valleys, and along small streams; though as I after- ward ascertained, the Hudson did not run far enough north to intercept our march, or rather, by a sudden turn to the west, it left our course clear. Had we inclined westwardly ourselves, we might have almost done that which Colonel Follock had once laughingly recommended to my mother in order to avoid the dangers of the Powles Hook Ferry — gone round the river.

A clearing now showed itself a little on our right; and thither the Indian held his way. This clearing was not the result of the labors of man, but was the fruit of one of those forest accidents that sometimes let in the light of the sun upon the mysteries of the woods. This clearing was on the bald cap of a rocky mountain, where Indians had doubtless often encamped; the vestiges of their fires proving that the winds had been assisted by the sister element in clearing away the few stunted trees that had once grown in the fissures of the rocks. As it was, there might have been an open space of some two or three acres, that was now as naked as if it had never known any vegetation more ambitious than the bush of the whortleberry or the honeysuckle. Delicious water was spouting from a higher ridge of the rocks, that led away northerly, forming the summit of an extensive range in that direction. At this spring Susquesus stooped to drink; then he announced that our day's work was done.

Until this announcement, I do not believe that one of us all had taken the time to look about him, so earnest and rapid had been our march. Now, however, each man threw aside his pack, laid down his rifle, and thus disencumbered, we turned to gaze on one of the most surprisingly beautiful scenes eye of mine had ever beheld.

From what I have read and heard, I am now fully aware that the grandest of our American scenery falls far behind that which is to be found among the lakes and precipices of the Alps, and along the almost miraculous coast of the Mediterranean; and I shall not pretend that the view I now beheld, approached in magnificence many that are to be met with in those magic regions. Nevertheless, it was both grand and soft; and it had one element of vastness in the green mantle of its interminable woods, that is not often to be met with in countries that have long submitted to the sway of man. Such as it was, I shall endeavor to describe it.

Beneath us, at the distance of near a thousand feet, lay a lake of the most limpid and placid water, that was beautifully diversified in shape, by means of bluffs, bays and curvatures of the shores, and which had an extent of near forty miles. We were on its eastern margin, and about one-third of the distance from its southern to its northern end. Countless islands lay almost under our feet, rendering the mixture of land and water at that particular point, as various and fanciful as the human imagination could desire. To the north, the placid sheet extended a great distance, bounded by rocky precipices, passing by a narrow gorge into a wider and larger estuary beyond. To the south, the water lay expanded to its oval termination, with here and there an island to relieve the surface. In that direction only were any of the results of human industry to be traced. Everywhere else the gorges, the receding valleys, the long ranges of hills, and the bald caps of granite, presented nothing to the eye but the unwearying charms of nature. Far as the eye could reach, mountain behind mountain, the earth was covered with its green mantle of luxuriant leaves, such as vegetation bestows on a virgin soil beneath a beneficent sun. The rolling and variegated carpet of the earth resembled a firmament reversed, with clouds composed of foliage.

At the southern termination of the lake, however, there was an opening in the forest of considerable extent; and one that had been so thoroughly made as to leave few or no trees. From this point we were distant several miles, and that distance necessarily rendered objects indistinct; though we had little difficulty in perceiving the ruins of extensive fortifications. A thousand white specks we now ascertained to be tents, for the works were all that remained of Fort William Henry, and there lay encamped the army of Abercrombie; much the largest force that had then ever collected in America, under the colors of England. History has since informed us that this army contained the formidable number of sixteen thousand men. Hundreds of boats, large batteaux, that were capable of carrying forty or fifty men, were moving about in front of the encampment, and, remote as we were, it was not impossible to discover the signs of preparation, and of an early movement. The Indian had not deceived us thus far, at least, but had shown himself an intelligent judge of what was going on as well as a faithful guide.

We were to pass the night on the mountain. Our beds were none of the best, as the reader may suppose, and our cover slight; yet I do not remember to have opened my eyes from the moment they were closed, until I awoke in the morning. The fatigue of a forced march did that for us which down cannot obtain for the voluptuary, and we all slept as profoundly as children. Consciousness returned to me, by means of a gentle shake of the shoulder, which proceeded from Susquesus. On arising, I found the Indian still near me, his countenance, for the first time since I had known him, expressing something like an animated pleasure. He had awoke none of the others, and he signed for me to follow him, without arousing either of my companions.   Why I had been thus particularly selected for the scene that succeeded, I cannot say, unless the Onondago's native sagacity had taught him to distinguish between the educations and feelings of us three young men.   So it was, however, and I left the rude shelter we had prepared for the night, alone.

A glorious sight awaited me!   The sun had just tipped the mountain-tops with gold, while the lake and the valleys, the hill-sides even, and the entire world beneath, still reposed in shadow. It appeared to me like the awakening of created things from the sleep of nature.   For a moment or more, I could only gaze on the wonderful picture presented by the strong contrast between the golden hill-tops and their shadowed sides — the promises of day and the vestiges of night.   But the Onondago was too much engrossed with his own feelings, to suffer me long to disregard what he conceived to be the principal point of interest.   Directed by his finger and eye, for he spoke not, I turned my look toward the distant shore of William Henry, and at once perceived the cause of his unusual excitement.   As soon as the Indian was certain that I saw the objects that attracted himself so strongly, he exclaimed with a strong, guttural, emphatic cadence —

" Good! "

Abercrombie's army was actually in motion!   Sixteen thousand men had embarked in boats, and were moving toward the northern end of the lake, with imposing force, and a most beautiful accuracy. The unruffled surface of the lake was dotted with the flotilla, boats in hundreds stretching across it in long, dark lines, moving on toward their point of destination with the method and concert of an army with its wings displayed.   The last brigade of boats had just left the shore when I first saw this striking spectacle, and the whole picture lay spread before me at a single glance.   America had never before witnessed such a sight; and it may be long before she will again witness such another.   For several minutes I stood entranced; nor did I speak until the rays of the sun had penetrated the dusky light that lay on the inferior world, as low as the bases of the western mountains.

" What are we to do, Susquesus? " I then asked, feeling how much right the Indian now might justly claim to govern our movements.

" Eat breakfast first " — the Onondago quietly replied: " then go down mountain."

" Neither of which will place us in the midst of that gallant army, as it is our wish to be."

" See, bye'm by. Injin know — no hurry now. Hurry come when Frenchman shoot."

I did not like this speech, nor the manner in which it was uttered; but there were too many things to think of just then, to be long occupied by vague conjecture, touching the Onondago's evasive allusions. Guert and Dirck were called, and made to share in the pleasure that such a sight could not fail to communicate. Then I got the first notion of what I should call the truly martial character of Ten Eyck. His fine, manly figure appeared to me to enlarge, his countenance actually became illuminated, and the expression of his eye, usually so full of good-nature and fun, seemed to change its nature entirely, to one of sternness and severity.

" This is a noble sight, Mr. Littlepage," Guert remarked, after gazing at the measured but quick movement of the flotilla for some time in silence — " a truly noble sight, and it is a reproach to us three for having lost so much time in the woods, when we ought to have been *there*, ready to aid in driving the French from the province."

" We are not too late, my good friend, as the first blow yet remains to be struck."

" You say true, and I shall join that army, if I have to swim to reach the boats. It will be no difficult thing for us to swim from one of those islands to another, and the troops must pass through the midst of them in order to get into the lower lake. Any reasonable man would stop to pick us up."

" No need," said the Onondago, in his quiet way. " Eat breakfast; then go. Got canoe — that 'nough."

" A canoe! By St. Nicholas! Mr. Susquesus, I'll tell you what it is — you shall never want a friend as long as Guert Ten Eyck is living, and able to assist you. That idea of the canoe is a most thoughtful one, and shows that a reasoning man has had the care of us. We can now join the troops with the rifles in our hand, as becomes gentlemen and volunteers."

By this time Jaap was up, and looking at the scene with all his eyes. It is scarcely necessary to describe the effect on a negro. He laughed in fits, shook his head like the Chinese figure of a mandarin, rolled over on the. rocks, arose, shook himself like a dog that quits the water, laughed again, and finally shouted. As we were all accustomed to these displays of negro sensibility, they only excited a smile among us, and not even that from Dirck. As for the Indian, he took no more notice of these natural, but undignified signs of pleasure in Jaap, than if the latter had been a dog, or any other unintellectual animal. Perhaps no weakness would be so likely to excite his contempt, as to be a witness of so complete an absence of self-command, as the untutored negro manifested on this occasion.

As soon as our first curiosity and interest were a little abated, we applied ourselves to the necessary duty of breaking our fasts. The meal was soon dispatched; and, to say the truth, it was not of a quality to detain one long from any thing of interest. The moment we had finished, the whole party left the cap of the mountain, following our guide as usual.

The Onondago had purposely brought us to that look-out, a spot known to him, in order that we might get the view of its panorama. It was impossible to descend to the lake-shore at that spot, however, and we were obliged to make a detour of three or four miles, in order to reach a ravine, by means of which, and not without difficulty either, that important object was obtained. Here we found a bark canoe, of a size sufficient to hold all five of us, and we embarked without a moment's delay.

The wind had sprung up from the south, as the day advanced, and the flotilla of boats was coming on, at a greatly increased rate, as to speed. By the time we had threaded our way through the islands, and reached the main channel, if indeed any one passage could be so termed, among such a variety, the leading boat of the army was within hail. The Indian paddled, and waving his hand in sign of amity, he soon brought us alongside of the batteau. As we approached it, however, I observed the fine, large form of the Viscount Howe, standing erect in its bows, dressed in his light infantry forest uniform, as if eager to be literally the foremost man of a movement, in the success of which the honor of the British empire itself was felt to be concerned.

CHAPTER XXIII

"My sons? It may
Unman my heart, and the poor boys will weep;
And what can I reply, to comfort them,
Save with some hollow hopes, and ill-worn smiles?"

SARDANAPALUS

MY LORD HOWE did not at first recognize us, in our hunting-shirts. With Guert Ten Eyck, however, he had formed such an acquaintance, while at Albany, as caused him to remember his voice, and our welcome was both frank and cordial. We inquired for the ——th, declaring our intention to join that corps, from the commander of which all three of us had reiterated and pressing invitations to join his mess. The intention of seeking our friend immediately, nevertheless was changed by a remark of our present host, if one may use such a term as applied to the commander of a brigade of boats.

"Bulstrode's regiment is in the centre, and will be early in the field," he said; "but not as early as the advanced guard. If you desire good living, gentlemen, I am far from wishing to dissuade you from seeking the flesh-pots of the ——th; there being a certain Mr. Billings in that corps, who has an extraordinary faculty, they tell me, in getting up a good dinner out of nothing; but if you want service, we shall certainly be the first brigade in action; and, to such fare as I can command, you will be most acceptable guests. As for any thing else, time must show."

After this, no more was said about looking for Bulstrode; though we let our noble commander understand, that we should tax his hospitality no longer than to see him fairly in the field, after driving away the party that it was expected the enemy would send to oppose our landing.

Susquesus no sooner learned our decision, than he took his departure, quietly paddling away toward the eastern shore; no one attempting to intercept a canoe that was seen to quit the batteau that was known to carry the commander of the advanced brigade.

The wind freshened, as the day advanced, and most of the boats

310

having something or other in the shape of a sail, our progress now became quite rapid. By nine o'clock we were fairly in the lower lake, and there was every prospect of our reaching our point of destination by mid-day. I confess, the business we were on, the novelty of my situation, and the certainty that we should meet in Montcalm an experienced as well as a most gallant foe, conspired to render me thoughtful, though I trust not timid during the few hours we were in the batteau. Perfectly inactive, it is not surprising that so young a soldier should feel sobered by the solemn reflections that are apt to get possession of the mind, at the probable approach of death — if not to myself, at least to many of those who were around me. Nor was there any thing boastful or inflated in the manner or conversation of our distinguished leader, who had seen much warm service in Germany, in the wars of his reputed grandfather and uncle, young as he was. On the contrary, my lord Howe that day was grave and thoughtful, as became a man who held the lives of others in his keeping, though he was neither depressed nor doubting. There were moments, indeed, when he spoke cheerfully to those who were near him; though, as a whole, his deportment was, as I have just said, grave and thoughtful. Once I caught his eye fastened on me, with a saddened expression; and, I suppose that a question he soon after put to me, was connected with the subject of his thoughts.

"How would our excellent and respectable friend Madam Schuyler feel, did she know our precise position at this moment, Mr. Littlepage? I do believe that excellent woman feels more concern for those in whom she takes an interest, than they often feel for themselves."

"I think, my lord, that in such a case we shall certainly receive the benefit of her prayers."

"You are an only child, I think she told me, Littlepage?"

"I am, my lord; and thankful am I that my mother cannot foresee this scene."

"I too have those that love me, though they are accustomed to think of me as a soldier, and liable to a soldier's risks. Happy is the military man who can possess his mind in the moment of trial, free from the embarrassing, though pleasing, and otherwise so grateful ties of affection. But we are nearing the shore and must attend to duty."

This is the last conversation I held with that brave soldier; and these were the last words of a private nature I ever heard him utter. From that moment his whole soul seemed occupied with the discharge of his duty, the success of our arms, and the defeat of the enemy.

I am not soldier enough to describe what followed, in a very military or intelligible manner. As the brigade drew near the foot of the lake, where there was a wide extent of low land principally in forest, however, some batteaux were brought to the front, on which were mounted a number of pieces of heavy artillery. The French had a party of considerable force to oppose our landing; but as it appeared, they had not made a sufficient provision of guns on their part, to contend with success; and our grape scouring the woods, we met with but little real resistance. Nor did we assail them precisely at the point where we were expected, but proceeded rather to the right of their position. At the signal, the advanced brigade pushed for the shore, led by our gallant commander, and we were all soon on *terra firma*, without sustaining any loss worth naming. We four, that is, Guert, Dirck, myself and Jaap, kept as near as was proper to the noble brigadier, who instantly ordered an advance to press the retreating foe. The skirmishing was not sharp, however, and we gained ground fast, the enemy retiring in the direction of Ticonderoga, and we pressing on their rear quite as fast as prudence and our preparations would allow. I could see that a cloud of Indians were in our front, and will own that I felt afraid of an ambush; for the artful warfare practised by those beings of the wood, could not but be familiar, by tradition at least, to one born and educated in the colonies. We had landed in a cove, not literally at the foot of the lake, but rather on its western side; and room was no sooner obtained, than General Abercrombie got most of his force on shore, and formed it as speedily as possible, in columns. Of these columns we had four, the two in the centre being composed entirely of king's troops, six regiments in all, numbering more than as many thousand men; while five thousand provincials were on the flanks, leaving quite four thousand of the latter with the boats, of which this vast flotilla actually contained the large number of one thousand and twenty-five! All our boats, however, had not reached the point of debarkation; those with the stores, artillery, etc., etc., being still some distance in the rear.

Our party was now placed with the right centre column, at the head of which marched our noble acquaintance. The enemy had posted a single battalion in a log encampment, near the ordinary landing; but finding the character of the force with which he was about to be assailed, its commandant set fire to the huts and retreated. The skirmishing was now even of less moment than it had been on landing, and we moved forward in high spirits, though the want of guides, the density of the woods, and the difficulties of the ground, soon produced a certain degree of confusion in our march. The columns got entangled with each other, and no one seemed to possess the means of promptly extricating them from this awkward embarrassment. Want of guides was the great evil under which we labored; but it was an evil that it was now too late to remedy.

Our column, notwithstanding, or its head rather, continued to advance, with its gallant leader keeping even pace with its foremost platoon. We four volunteers acted as look-outs, a little on its flank; and I trust there will be no boasting, if I say, we kept rather in advance of the leading files, than otherwise. In this state of things, French uniforms were seen in front, and a pretty strong party of the enemy were encountered, wandering, like ourselves, a little uncertain of the route they ought to take in order to reach their intrenchments in the shortest time. As a matter of course, this party could not pass the head of our column without bringing on a collision, though it were one that was only momentary. Which party gave the first fire, I cannot say, though I thought it was the French. The discharge was not heavy, however, and was almost immediately mutual. I know that all four of us let off our rifles, and that we halted, under a cover, to reload. I had just driven the ball down, when my eye caught the signs of some confusion in the head of the column, and I saw the body of an officer borne to the rear. It was that of Lord Howe! He had fallen at the first serious discharge made by the enemy in that campaign! The fall of its leader, so immediately in its presence, seemed to rouse the column into a sense of the necessity of doing something effective, and it assaulted the party in its front with the rage of so many tigers, dispersing the enemy like chaff; making a considerable number of prisoners, besides killing and wounding not a few.

I never saw a man more thoroughly aroused than was Guert Ten Eyck, in this little affair. He had been much noticed by Lord Howe, during the residence of that unfortunate nobleman at Albany; and the loss of the last appeared to awaken all that there was of the ferocious in the nature of my usually kind-hearted Albany friend. He acted as our immediate commander; and he led us forward on the heels of the retreating French, until we actually came in sight of their intrenchments. Then, indeed, we all saw it was necessary to retreat in our turn; and Guert consented to fall back, though it was done surlily, and like a lion at bay. A party of Indians pressed us hard, in this retreat, and we ran an imminent risk of our scalps; all of which I have ever believed would have been lost, were it not for the resolution and Herculean strength of Jaap. It happened, as we were dodging from tree to tree, that all four of our rifles were discharged at the same time; a circumstance of which our assailants availed themselves to make a rush at us. Luckily the weight of the onset fell on Jaap, who clubbed his rifle, and literally knocked down in succession the three Indians that first reached him. This intrepidity and success gave us time to reload; and Dirck, ever a cool and capital shot, laid the fourth Huron on his face, with a ball through his heart. Guert then held his fire, and called on Jaap to retreat. He was obeyed; and under cover of our two rifles, the whole party got off; the red-skins being too thoroughly rebuked to press us very closely, after the specimen they had just received of the stuff of which we were made.

We owed our escape, however, as much to another circumstance, as to this resolution of Jaap, and the expedient of Guert. Among the provincials was a partisan of great repute, of the name of Rogers. This officer led a party of riflemen on our left flank, and he drove in the enemy's skirmishers, along his own front, with rapidity, causing them to suffer a considerable loss. By this means, the Indians before us were held in check; as there was the danger that Major Rogers's party might fall in upon their rear, should they attempt to pursue us, and thus cut them off from their allies. It was well it was so; inasmuch as we had to fall back more than a mile, ere we reached the spot where Abercrombie brought his columns to a halt, and encamped for the night. This position was distant about two miles from the works before Ticonderoga; and consequently at no great distance from the outlet of Lake George. Here the army was brought into good order, and took up its station for some little time.

It was necessary to await the arrival of the stores, ammunition and artillery. As the bringing up these materials, through a country that was little else than a virgin forest, was no easy task, it occupied us quite two days. Melancholy days they were too; the death of Lord Howe acting on the whole army much as if it had been a defeat. He was the idol of the king's troops, and he had rendered himself as popular with us Americans as with his own countrymen. A sort of ominous sadness prevailed among us, each common man appearing to feel his loss as he might have felt that of a brother.

We looked up the ——th, and joined Bulstrode, as soon as we reached the ground chosen for the new encampment. Our reception was friendly, and even kind; and it became warmer still, as soon as it was understood that we composed the little party that had skirmished so freely on the flank of the right centre column, and which was known to have gone farther in advance than any one else, in that part of the field. Thus we joined our corps with some *éclat*, at the very outset, every body welcoming us cordially, and with seeming sincerity.

Nevertheless, the general sadness existed in the ——th, as well as in all the other corps. Lord Howe was as much beloved in that regiment, as in any other; and our meeting and subsequent intercourse could not be called joyful. Bulstrode had an extensive and important command for his rank and years, and he certainly was proud of his position; but I could see that even his elastic and usually gay temperament was much affected by what had occurred. That night we walked together, apart from our companions, when he spoke on the subject of our loss.

"It may appear strange to you, Corny," he said, "to find so much depression in camp, after a debarkation that has certainly been successful, and a little affair that has given us, as they assure me, a couple of hundred prisoners. I tell you, however, my friend, it were better for this army to have seen its best corps annihilated, than to have lost the man it has. Howe was literally the soul of this entire force. He was a soldier by nature, and made all around him soldiers. As for the commander-in-chief, he does not understand you Americans, and will not use you as he ought; then he does not understand the nature of the warfare of this continent, and will be very likely to make a blunder. I'll tell you how it is, Corny; Howe had as much influence with Abercombie, as he had with every one else; and an attempt will be made to introduce his mode of fighting; but such a man as Lord Howe requires another Lord Howe to carry out his own conceptions. That is the point on which I fear we shall fail."

All this sounded very sensible to me, though it sounded discouragingly; I found, however, that Bulstrode did not entertain these feelings alone, but that most around me were of the same way of thinking. In the mean time, the preparations proceeded; and it was understood that the 8th was to be the day that was to decide the fate of Ticonderoga. The fort proper, at this celebrated station, stands on a peninsula, and can only be assailed on one side. The outworks were very extensive on that side, and the garrison was known to be formidable. As these outworks, however, consisted principally of a log breastwork, and it could be approached through open woods, which of itself afforded some cover, it was determined to carry it by storm, and, if possible, enter the main work with the retreating enemy. Had we waited for our artillery, and established batteries, our success would have been certain; but the engineer reported favorably of the other project; and perhaps it better suited the temper and impatience of the whole army, to push on, rather than proceed by the slow movements of a regular siege.

On the morning of the 8th, therefore, the troops were paraded for the assault, our party falling in on the flank of the ——th, as volunteers. The ground did not admit of the use of many horses, and Bulstrode marched with us on foot. I can relate but little of the general movements of that memorable day, the woods concealing so much of what was done on both sides. I know this, however; that the flower of our army were brought into the line, and were foremost in the assault; including both regulars and provincials. The 42d, a Highland corps that had awakened much interest in America, both by the appearance and character of its men, was placed at a point where it was thought the heaviest service was to be performed. The 55th, another corps on which much reliance was placed, was also put at the head of another column. A swamp extending for some distance along the only exposed front of the peninsula, these two corps were designated to carry the log breastwork that commenced at the point where the swamp ceases — much the most arduous portion of the expected service, since this was the only accessible approach to the fortress itself. To render their position more secure, the French had placed several pieces of artillery in battery, along the line of this breastwork; while we had not yet a gun in front to cover our advance.

It was said, that Abercombie did not take counsel of any of the American officers with him, before he decided on the attack of the 8th of July. He had directed his principal engineer to reconnoitre; and that gentleman having reported that the defences offered no serious scientific obstacles, the assault was decided on. This report was accurate, doubtless, agreeably to the principles and facts of European warfare; but it was not suited to those of the conflicts of this continent. It was to be regretted, however, that the experience of 1755, and the fate of Braddock, had not inculcated a more extensive lesson of discretion among the royal commanders, than was manifested by the incidents of this day.

The ——th was placed in column directly in the rear of the Highlanders, who were led on this occasion by Colonel Gordon Graham; a veteran officer of great experience, and of an undaunted courage.* Of course, I saw this officer and this regiment, being, as they were, directly in my front, but I saw little else; more especially after the smoke of the first discharge was added to the other obstacles to vision.

A considerable time was consumed in making the preparations; but when every thing was supposed to be ready, the columns were set in motion. It was generally understood that the troops were to receive the enemy's fire, then rush forward to the breastwork, cross the latter at the bayonet's point, if it should be necessary, and deliver their own fire at close quarters; or on their retreating foes. Permission was given to us volunteers, and to divers light parties of irregulars, to open on any of the French of whom we might get glimpses, as little was expected from us in the charge.

Nearly an hour was consumed in approaching the point of attack, owing to the difficulties of the ground, and the necessity of making frequent halts, in order to dress. At length the important moment had arrived when the head of the column was ready to unmask itself, and consequently to come under fire. A short halt sufficed for the arrangements here, when the bagpipes commenced their exciting music, and we broke out of cover, shouting and cheering each other on. We must have been within two hundred yards of the breastwork at the time, and the first gun discharged was Jaap's, who, by working his way into the cover of the swamp, had got some distance ahead of us, and who actually shot down a French officer who had got upon the logs of his defences, in order to reconnoitre. That assault, however, was fearfully avenged! The Highlanders were moving on like a whirlwind, grave, silent and steady, cheered

* Holmes's Annals says, that Lord John Murray commanded the 42d, on this occasion. I presume, as Mr. Littlepage was there, and was posted so near the corps in question, he cannot well be mistaken. Mrs. Grant, of Laggan, who was at Albany at the time, and whose father was in the battle, agrees with Mr. Littlepage, in saying that Gordon Graham led the 42d. — EDITOR.

only by their music, when a sheet of flame glanced along the
enemy's line, and the iron and leaden messengers of death came
whistling in among us like a hurricane. The Scotsmen were
staggered by that shock; but they recovered instantly and
pressed forward. The ——th did not escape harmless, by any
means; while the din told us that the conflict extended along
the whole of the breastwork, toward the lake-shore. How
many were shot down in our column, by that first discharge, I
never knew; but the slaughter was dreadful, and among those
who fell was the veteran Graham himself. I can safely say,
however, that the plan of attack was completely deranged from
this first onset; the columns displaying and commencing their
fire as soon as possible. No men could have behaved better
than all that I could see; the whole of us pushing on for the
breastwork, until we encountered fallen trees; which were made
to serve the purpose of chevaux-de-frise. These trees had been
felled along the front of the breastwork, while their branches
were cut, and pointed like stakes. It was impossible to pass in
any order, and the troops halted when they reached them, and
continued to fire by platoons, with as much regularity as on
parade. A few minutes of this work, however, compelled different corps to fall back, and the vain conflict was continued for
four hours, on our part almost entirely by a smart but ineffec-
tive fire of musketry; while the French sent their grape into
our ranks almost with as much impuity as if they had been on
parade. It had been far better for our men had they been less
disciplined, and less under the control of their officers; for the
sole effect of steadiness under such circumstances, is to leave
the gallant and devoted troops who refuse to fall back, while
they are unable to advance, only so much the longer in jeopardy.

Guert had shouted with the rest, and I soon found that by
following him for a leader, we should quickly be in the midst
of the fray. He actually led us up to the fallen trees, and finding something like a cover there, we three established ourselves
among them as riflemen, doing fully our share of service. When
the troops fell back, however, we were left in a manner alone,
and it was rather dangerous work to retire; and finding ourselves out of the line of fire from our own men, no immaterial
point in such a fray, we maintained our post to the last. Admonished, after a long time, of the necessity of retreating, by
the manner in which the fire of our own line lessened, we got

off with sound skins, though Guert retired the whole distance
with his face to the enemy, firing as he withdrew. We all did
the last, indeed, using the trees for covers. Toward the close
we attracted especial attention; and there were two or three
minutes during which the flight of bullets around us might
truly, without much exaggeration, be likened to a storm of
hail!

Jaap was not with us in this sally, and I went into the swamp
to look for him. The search was not long, for I found my fellow retreating also, and bringing in with him a stout Canadian
Indian as a prisoner. He was making his captive carry three
discharged rifles, and blankets, one of which had been his own
property once, and the others that of two of his tribe, whom
the negro had left lying in the swamp as bloody trophies of
his exploits. I cannot explain the philosophy of the thing,
but that negro ever appeared to me to fight as if he enjoyed
the occupation as an amusement.

These facts were scarcely ascertained, when we learned the
important intelligence that a general retreat was ordered. Our
proud and powerful army was beaten, and that too by a force
two-thirds less than its own! It is not easy to describe the
miserable scene that followed. The transporting of the wounded
to the rear had been going on the whole time; and, as usually
happens when it is permitted, it had contributed largely to
thin the ranks. These unfortunate men were put into the batteaux in hundreds, while most of the dead were left where they
lay. So completely were our hopes frustrated, and our spirits
lowered, that most of the boats pulled off that night, and all
the remainder quitted the foot of the lake early next day.

Thus terminated the dire expedition of 1758 against Ticonderoga, and with it our expectations of seeing Montreal or
Quebec that season. I dare say we had fully ten thousand
bayonets in the field that bloody day, and quite five thousand men
closely engaged. The mistake was in attempting to carry a
post that was so nearly impregnable by assault, and this, too,
without the cover of artillery. The enemy was said to have
four or five thousand men present; and this may be true as
applied to all within the defences, though I question if more
than half that number pulled triggers on us in the miserable
affair. There is always much of exaggeration in both the boasting and the apologies of war.

Our own loss on this sad occasion was reported at 548 slain,

and 1,356 wounded. This was probably within the truth; though
the missing were said to be surprisingly few, some thirty or
forty in all, the men having no place to repair to but the boats.
Of the Highlanders, it was said that nearly half the common
men, and twenty-five or nearly *all* the officers were either killed
or wounded. One account, indeed, said that *every* officer of that
corps who was on the ground suffered. The 55th also was
dreadfully cut up. Ten of its officers were slain outright and
many were wounded. As for the ——th, it fared a little better,
not heading a column; but its loss was fearful. Bulstrode was
seriously wounded early in the attack, though his hurt was
never supposed to be dangerous. Billings was left dead on the
field, and Harris got a scratch that served him to talk of in after-
life.

The confusion was tremendous after such a conflict and such
a defeat. The troops re-embarked without much regard to
corps or regularity of movement; and the boats moved away
as fast as they received their melancholy cargoes. An immense
amount of property was lost, though I believe all the customary
military trophies were preserved. As the provincials had been
the least engaged, and had suffered much the least in proportion to numbers, a large body of them was kept as a rear-guard,
while the regular corps removed their wounded and *matériel*.

As for us three or four, including Jaap, who stuck by his
prisoner, we scarcely knew what to do with ourselves. Every
body who felt any interest in us was either killed or wounded.
Bulstrode we could not see, nor could we even find the regiment. Should we succeed in the attempt at the last, very few
now remained in it who would have taken much, or indeed any
concern in us. Under the circumstances, therefore, we held a
consultation on the lake-shore, uncertain whether to ask admission into one of the departing boats, or to remain until morning
that our retreat might have a more manly aspect.

"I'll tell you what it is, Corny," said Guert Ten Eyck, in a
somewhat positive manner, "the less *we* say about this campaign, and of our share in it, the petter. We are not soldiers
in a regular way, and if we keep quiet, nobody will know what
a t'rashing we t'ree, in particular, haf received. My advice is,
t'at we get out of this army as we got into it — t'at is, py a one-
sided movement, and forever after holt our tongues about our
having had anyt'ing to do with it. I never knew a worsted
man any the more respected for his mishap; and I will own

that I set down flogging as a very material part of a fight."

"I am quite sure, Guert, I am as little disposed to brag of my share in this affair, as you or any one can possibly be; but it is much easier to talk about getting away from this confused crowd than really to do the thing. I doubt if any of these boats will take us in; for an Englishman, flogged, is not apt to be very good-natured; and all our friends seem to be killed or wounded."

"You want go?" asked a low Indian voice at my elbow. "Got 'nough, eh?"

Turning, I saw Susquesus standing within two feet of me. Our consultation was necessarily in the midst of a moving throng; and the Onondago must have approached us, unnoticed, at the commencement of our conference. There he was, however, though whence he came or how he got there, I could not imagine at the time, and have never been able to learn since.

"Can you help us to get away, Susquesus?" was my answer. "Do you know of any means of crossing the lake?"

"Got canoe. That good. Canoe go, though Yengeese run."

"That in which we came off to the army, do you mean?"

The Indian nodded his head, and made a sign for us to follow. Little persuasion was necessary, and we proceeded at his heels, in a body, in the direction he led. I will confess, that when I saw our guide proceeding eastward, along the lake-shore, I had some misgivings on the subject of his good faith. That was the direction which took us toward, instead of *from* the enemy; and there was something so mysterious in the conduct of this man, that it gave me uneasiness. Here he was, in the midst of the English army in the height of its confusion, though he had declined joining it previously to the battle. Nothing was easier than to enter the throng, in its present confused state, and move about undetected for hours, if one had the nerve necessary for the service; and, in that property, I felt certain the Onondago was not deficient. There was a coolness in the manner of the man, a quiet observation, both blended with the seeming apathy of a red-skin, that gave every assurance of his fitness for the duty.

Nevertheless, there was no remedy but to follow, or to break with our guide on the spot. We did not like to do the last, although we conferred together on the subject, but followed, keeping our hands on the locks of our rifles, in readiness for a brush, should we be led into danger. Susquesus had no such

treacherous intention, however, while he had disposed of his
canoe in a place that denoted his judgment. We had to walk
quite a mile ere we reached this little bush-fringed creek in
which he had concealed it. I have always thought we ran a
grave risk, in advancing so far in that direction, since the enemy's
Indians would certainly be hanging around the skirts of our
army, in quest of scalps; but I afterward learned the secret of
the Onondago's confidence, who first spoke on the subject after
we had left the shore, and then only in an answer to a remark
of Guert's.

"No danger," he said; " red man gettin' Yengeese scalps
on the war-path. Too much kill, now, to want more."

As both governments pursued the culpable policy of paying
for human scalps, this suggestion probably contained the whole
truth.

Previously to quitting the creek, however, there was a difficulty
to dispose of. Jaap had brought his Huron prisoner with him;
and the Onondago declared that the canoe could not carry
six. This we knew from experience, indeed, though five went
in it very comfortably.

"No room," said Susquesus, "for red man. Five good —
six bad."

"What shall we do with the fellow, Corny?" asked Guert,
with a little interest. " Jaap says he is a proper devil, by daylight, and that he had a world of trouble in taking him, and in
bringing him in. For five minutes, it was heads or tails which
was to give in; and the nigger only got the best of it, by his
own account of the battle, because the red-skin had the un-
accountable folly to try to beat in Jaap's brains. He might as
well have battered the rock of Gibraltar, you know, as to attempt to break a nigger's skull, and so your fellow got the best
of it. What shall we do with the rascal? "

"Take scalp," said the Onondago, sententiously; "got good
scalp — war lock ready — paint, war paint — capital scalp."

"Ay, that may do better for you, Master Succetush " — so
Guert always called our guide, " than it will do for us Christians.
I'm afraid we shall have to let the ravenous devil go, after dis-
arming him."

"Disarmed he is already; but he cannot be long without a
musket, on this battle-ground. I am of your opinion, Guert;
so, Jaap, release your prisoner at once, that we may return to
Ravensnest as fast as possible."

"Dat berry hard, Master Corny, sah!" exclaimed Jaap, who did not half like the orders he received.

"No words about it, sir, but cut his fastening" — Jaap had tied the Indian's arms behind him with a rope, as an easy mode of leading him along. "Do you know the man's name?"

"Yes, sah — he say he name be Muss" — probably Jaap's defective manner of repeating some Indian sound; "and a proper muss he get in, Masser Corny, when he try to cotch Jaap by the wool!"

Here I was obliged to clap my hand suddenly on the black's mouth, for the fellow was so delighted with the recollection of the manner in which he had got the better of his red adversary, that he broke out into one of the uncontrollable fits of noisy laughter that are so common to his race. I repeated the order, somewhat sternly, for Jaap to cut the cords, and then to follow us to the canoe, in which the Onondago and my two friends had already taken their places. My own foot was raised to enter the canoe, when I heard heavy stripes inflicted on the back of some one. Rushing back to the spot where I had left Jaap and his captive, Muss, I found the former inflicting a severe punishment on the naked back of the other, with the end of the cord that still bound his arms. Muss, as Jaap called him, neither flinched nor cried. The pine stands not more erect or unyielding, in a summer's noontide, than he bore up under the pain. Indignantly I thrust the negro away, cut the fellow's bonds with my own hands, and drove my slave before me to the canoe.

CHAPTER XXIV

"Pale set the sun — the shades of evening fell,
The mournful night-wind sung their funeral knell;
And the same day beheld their warriors dead,
Their sovereign captive and their glory fled!"

MRS. HEMANS.

I SHALL never forget the journey of that fearful night. Susquesus paddled the canoe, unaided by us, who were too much fatigued with the toil of the day to labor much, as soon as we found ourselves in a place of safety. Even Jaap lay down and slept for several hours, the sleep of the weary. I do not think any of us, however, actually slept for the first hour or two, the scenes through which we had just passed, and that, indeed, through which we were then passing, acting as preventives to such an indulgence.

It must have been about nine in the evening, when our canoe quitted the ill-fated shore at the south end of Lake George, moving steadily and silently along the eastern margin of the sheet. By that time, fully five hundred boats had departed for the head of the lake, the retreat having commenced long before sunset. No order was observed in this melancholy procession, each batteau moving off as her load was completed. All the wounded were on the placid bosom of the "holy lake," as some writers have termed this sheet of limpid water, by the time we ourselves got in motion; and the sounds of parting boats told us that the unhurt were following as fast as circumstances would allow.

What a night it was! There was no moon, and a veil of dark vapor was drawn across the vault of the heavens, concealing most of the mild summer stars, that ought to have been seen twinkling in their Creator's praise. Down between the boundaries of hills, there was not a breath of air, though we occasionally heard the sighings of light currents among the tree-tops above us. The eastern shore having fewer sinuosities than the western, most of the boats followed its dark, frowning mass, as the nearest route, and we soon found ourselves near the line of the retir-

ing batteaux. I call it the line, for though there was no order
observed, each party making the best of its way to the common
point of destination, there were so many boats in motion at the
same time, that, far as the eye could penetrate by that gloomy
light, an unbroken succession of them was visible. Our motion
was faster than that of these heavily-laden and feebly-rowed batteaux, the soldiers being too much fatigued to toil at the oars,
after the day they had just gone through. We consequently
passed nearly every thing, and soon got on a parallel course
with that of the boats, moving along at a few rods in-shore of
them. Dirck remarked, however, that two or three small craft
even passed us. They went so near the mountain, quite within
its shadows, in fact, as to render it difficult to say what they
were; though it was supposed they might be whale-boats, of
which there were more than a hundred in the flotilla, carrying
officers of rank.

No one spoke. It appeared to me that not a human voice
was raised among those humiliated and defeated thousands. The
plash of oars, so long as we were at a distance from the line,
alone broke the silence of night; but that was incessant. As
our canoe drew ahead, however, an hour or two after we had
left the shore, and we overtook the boats that had first started,
the moaning and groans of the wounded became blended with
the monotonous sounds of the oars. In two respects, these unfortunate men had reason to felicitate themselves, notwithstanding their sufferings. No army could have transported its wounded
with less pain to the hurt; and the feverish thirst that loss of
blood always induces, might be assuaged by the limpid element
on which we all floated.

After paddling for hours, Susquesus was relieved by Jaap —
Dirck, Guert and myself occasionally lending our aid. Each
had a paddle, and each used it as he saw fit, while the Onondago slept. Occasionally I caught a nap myself, as did my
companions; and we all felt refreshed by the rest and sleep.
At length we reached the narrow pass that separated the upper
from the lower lake, and we entered the former. This is near
the place where the islands are so numerous, and we were unavoidably made to pass quite close to some of the batteaux.
I say to some, for the line became broken at this point, each
boat going through the openings it found the most convenient.

"Come nearer with that bark canoe," called out an officer
from a batteau; "I wish to learn who is in it."

"We are volunteers, that joined the ——th the day the army moved up, and were guests of Major Bulstrode. Pray, sir, can you tell us where that officer can be found?"

"Poor Bulstrode! He got a very awkward hit early in the day, and was taken past me to the rear. He will be able neither to walk nor to ride for some months, if they save his leg. I heard the commander-in-chief order him to be sent across the lake in the first boat with the wounded; and some one told me Bulstrode himself expressed an intention to be carried some distance to a friend's house, to escape from the abominations of an army hospital. The fellow has horses enough to transport him on a horse-litter to Cape Horn, if he wishes it. I'll warrant you Bulstrode works his way into good quarters, if they are to be had in America. I suppose this arm of mine will have to come off, as soon as we reach Fort William Henry; and that job done, I confess I should like amazingly to keep him company. Proceed, gentlemen; I hope I have not detained you; but observing a bark canoe, I thought it my duty to ascertain we were not followed by spies."

"This then was another victim of war! He spoke of the loss of his arm, notwithstanding, with as much coolness as if it were the loss of a tooth; yet I question not, that in secret he mourned over the calamity in bitterness of heart. Men never wear the mask more completely than when excited and stimulated by the rivalry of arms. Bulstrode, too, at Ravensnest! He could be carried nowhere else so easily; and should his wound be of a nature that did not require constant medical treatment, where could he be so happily bestowed as under the roof of Herman Mordaunt? Shall I confess that the idea gave me great pain, and that I was fool enough to wish that I too could return to Anneke, and appeal to her sympathies, by dragging with me a wounded limb!"

Our canoe now passed quite near another batteau, the officer in command of which was standing erect, seemingly watching our movements. He appeared to be unhurt, but was probably intrusted with some special duty. As we paddled by, the following curious conversation occurred.

"You move rapidly to the rear, my friends," observed the stranger; "pray, moderate your zeal; others are in advance of you with the evil tidings!"

"You must think ill of our patriotism and loyalty, sir, to **imagine** we are hastening on with the intelligence of a check to

the British arms," I answered as dryly, and almost as equivo-
cally in manner, as the other had spoken.

"The check! — I beg a thousand pardons — I see you *are*
patriots, and of the purest water! Check is just the word;
though check-*mate* would be more descriptive and significant!
A charming time we've had of it, gentlemen! What say you?
— it is your move now."

"There has been much firmness and gallantry manifested by
the troops," I answered, "as we who have been merely volunteers, will always be ready to testify."

"I beg your pardon, again and again," returned the officer,
raising his hat and bowing profoundly — "I did not know I had
the honor to address volunteers. You are entitled to superlative
respect, gentlemen, having come voluntarily into such a field.
For my part, I find the honor oppressive, having no such supere-
rogatory virtue to boast of. Volunteers! On my word, gentlemen, you will have many wonders to relate, when you get back
into the family circle."

"We shall have to speak of the gallantry of the Highlanders,
for we saw all they did and all they suffered."

"Ah! Were you, then, near that brave corps?" exclaimed
the other, with something like honest, natural feeling, for the
first time exhibited in his voice and meaning; "I honor men who
were only *spectators* of so much courage, especially if they took
a tolerably near *view* of it. May I venture to ask your names,
gentlemen?"

I answered, giving him our names, and mentioning the fact
that we had been the guests of Bulstrode, and how much we
were disappointed in having missed not only our friend, but his
corps.

"Gentlemen, I honor courage, let it come whence it may,"
said the stranger, with strong feeling and no acting, "and most
admire it when I see it exhibited by natives of these colonies,
in a quarrel of their own. I have heard of you as being with
poor Howe when he fell, and hope to know more of you. As
for Bulstrode, he has passed southward now some hours, and
intends to make his cure among some connections that he has
in this province. Do not let this be the last of our intercourse,
I beg of you; but look up Captain Charles Lee, of the ——th,
who will be glad to take each and all of you by the hand, when
we once more get into camp."

We expressed our thanks, but Susquesus causing the canoe

to make a sudden inclination toward the shore, the conversation
was suddenly interrupted.

By this time the Indian was awake, and exercising his authority in the canoe again. Gliding among the islands, he shortly
landed us at the precise point where we had embarked only five
days before. Securing his little bark, the Onondago led the way
up the ravine, and brought us out on the naked cap of the mountain where we had before slept, after an hour of extreme effort.

If the night had been so memorable, the picture presented
at the dawn of day was not less so! We reached that lofty
look-out about the same time in the morning as the Indian had
awakened me on the previous occasion, and had the same natural outlines to the view. In one sense also, the artificial accessories were the same, though exhibited under a very different aspect. I presume the truth will not be much, if any
exceeded, when I say that a thousand boats were in sight, on
this as on a former occasion. A few, a dozen or so at most,
appeared to have reached the head of the lake; but all the rest
of that vast flotilla were scattered along the placid surface of the
lovely sheet, forming a long, straggling line of dark spots that
extended to the beach under Fort William Henry in one direction, and as far as eye could reach in the other. How different
did that melancholy, broken procession of boats appear, from
the gallant array, the martial bands, the cheerful troops, and
the multitude of ardent young men who had pressed forward in
brigades less than a week before, filled with hope, and exulting
in their strength! As I gazed on the picture, I could not but
fancy to myself the vast amount of physical pain, the keen
mental suffering, and the deep mortification that might have
been found, amid that horde of returning adventurers. We
had just come up from the level of this scene of human agony,
and our imaginations could portray details that were beyond the
reach of the senses, at the elevation on which we stood.

A week before, and the name of Abercrombie filled every
mouth in America; expectation had almost placed his renown
on that giddy height where performance itself is so often inse-
cure. In the brief interval, he was destroyed. Those who had
been ready to bless him, would now heap curses on his devoted
head, and none would be so bold as to urge aught in his favor.
Men in masses, when goaded by disappointment, are never just.
It is, indeed, a hard lesson for the individual to acquire; but
released from his close, personal responsibility, the single man

follows the crowd, and soothes his own mortification and wounded pride by joining in the cry that is to immolate a victim. Yet Abercrombie was not the foolhardy and besotted bully that Braddock had proved himself to be. His misfortune was, to be ignorant of the warfare of the region in which he was required to serve, and possibly to overestimate the imaginary invincible character of the veterans he led. In a very short time he was recalled, and America heard no more of him. As some relief to the disgrace that had anew alighted on the British arms, Bradstreet, a soldier who knew the country, and who placed much reliance on the young man of her name and family whom I had met at Madam Schuyler's, marched against Frontenac, in Canada, at the head of a strong body of provincials; an enterprise that, as it was conducted with skill, resulted in a triumph.

But with all this my narrative has no proper connection. No sooner did we reach the bald mountain top, than the Onondago directed Jaap to light a fire, while he produced from a deposit left on the advance, certain of the materials that were necessary to a meal. As neither of us had tasted food since the morning of the previous day, this repast was welcome, and we all partook of it like so many famished men. The negro got his share, of course, and then we called a council as to future proceedings.

"The question is, whether we ought to make a straight path to Ravensnest," observed Guert, "or proceed first to the surveyor's, and see how things are going on in that direction."

"As there can be no great danger of a pursuit on the part of the French, since all their boats are in the other lake," I remarked, "the state of the country is very much what it was before the army moved."

"Ask that question of the Indian," put in Dirck, a little significantly.

We looked at Susquesus inquiringly, for a look always sufficed to let him comprehend us, when a tolerably plain allusion had been previously made.

"Black man do foolish t'ing," observed the Onondago.

"What I do, you red-skin devil?" demanded Jaap, who felt a sort of natural antipathy to all Indians, good or bad, excellent or indifferent; a feeling that the Indians repaid to his race by contempt indifferently concealed. "What I do, red-devil, ha? dat you dares tell Masser Corny *dat!*"

Susquesus manifested no resentment at this strong and somewhat rude appeal, but sat as motionless as if he had not heard it. This vexed Jaap so much the more; and my fellow being exceedingly pugnacious on all occasions that touched his pride, there might have been immediate war between the two, had I not raised a finger, at once effectually stilling the outbreak of Jacob Satanstoe's wrath.

"You should not bring such a charge against my slave, Onondago," I said, "unless able to prove it."

"He beat red warrior like dog."

"What of dat!" growled Jaap, who was only half-quieted by my sign. "Who ebber hear it hurt red-skin to rope-end him?"

"Warrior back like squaw's. Blow hurt him. He never forget."

"Well, let him remember, den," grinned the negro, showing his ivory teeth from ear to ear. "Muss was *my* prisoner, and what *good* he do me, if he let go widout punishment. I wish you tell Masser Corny *dat*, instead of tellin' him nonsense. When he flog me, who ebber hear me grumble?"

"You have not had half enough of it, Jaap, or your manners would be better," I thought it necessary to put in, for the fellow had never before manifested so quarrelsome a disposition in my presence; most probably because I had never before seen him at variance with an Indian. "Let me hear no more of this, or I shall be obliged to pay off the arrears on the spot."

"A little hiding does a nigger good, sometimes," observed Guert significantly.

I observed that Dirck, who loved my very slave principally because he was mine, looked at the offender reprovingly; and by these combined demonstrations, we succeeded in curbing the fellow's tongue.

"Well, Susquesus," I added, "we all listen to hear what you mean."

"Musquerusque chief — Huron chief — got very tender back; never forget rope."

"You mean us to understand that my black's prisoner will be apt to make some attempt to revenge himself for the flogging he got from his captor?"

"Just so. Indian good memory — no forget friend — no forget enemy."

"But your Huron will be puzzled to find us, Onondago. He

will suppose us with the army, and should he even venture to look for us there, you see he will be disappointed."

"Never know. Wood full of paths — Injin full of cunning. Why talk of Ravensnest?"

"Was the name of Ravensnest mentioned in the presence of that Huron?" I asked, more uneasy than such a trifle would probably have justified me in confessing.

"Ay, something was said about it, but not in a way the fellow could understand," answered Guert, carelessly. "Let him come on, if he has not had enough of us yet."

This was not my manner of viewing the matter, however; for the mentioning of Ravensnest brought Anneke to my mind, surrounded by the horrors of an Indian's revenge.

"I will send you back to the Huron, Susquesus," I added, "if you can name me the price that will purchase his forgiveness."

The Onondago looked at me meaningly a moment; then bending forward, he passed the fore-finger of his hand around the head of Jaap, along the line that is commonly made by the knife of the warrior, as he cuts away the trophy of success from his victim. Jaap comprehended the meaning of this very significant gesture as well as any of us, and the manner in which he clutched the wool, as if to keep the scalp in its place, set us all laughing. The negro did not partake of our mirth; but I saw that he regarded the Indian, much as the bull-dog shows his teeth before he makes his spring. Another motion of my finger, however, quelled the rising. It was necessary to put an end to this, and Jaap was ordered to prepare our packs, in readiness for the expected march. Relieved from his presence, Susquesus was asked to be more explicit.

"You know Injin," the Onondago answered. "Now he t'ink red-coats driv' away and skeared, he go look for scalp. Love all sort scalp — old scalp, young scalp — man scalp, woman scalp — boy scalp, gal scalp — all get pay, all get honor. No difference to him."

"Ay!" exclaimed Guert, with a strong respiration, such as escapes a man who feels strongly; "he is a devil incarnate, when he once gets fairly on the scent of blood! So you expect these French Injins will make an excursion in among the settlers, out here to the south-east of us?"

"Go to nearest — don't care where he be. Nearest your friend; won't like that, s'pose?"

"You are right enough, Onondago, in saying that. I shall

not like it, nor will my companions here like it; and the first thing you will have to do, will be to guide us, straight as the bird flies, to the Ravensnest; the picketed house, you know, where we have left our sweethearts."

Susquesus understood all that was said without any difficulty; in proof of which he smiled at this allusion to the precious character of the inmates of the house Guert told him to seek.

"Squaw pretty 'nough," he answered, complacently. "No wonder young man like him. But can't go there now. First find friends measure land. All Injin land, once!"

This last remark was made in a way I did not like; for the idea seemed to cross the Onondago's brain so suddenly, as to draw from him this brief assertion in pure bitterness of spirit.

"I should be very sorry if it had not been, Susquesus," I observed, "myself, since the title is all the better for its having been so, as our Indian deed will show. You know, of course, that my father and his friend Colonel Follock, bought this land of the Mohawks, and paid them their own price for it."

"Red man nebber measure land so. He p'int with finger, break bush down, and say, ' there, take from that water to that water.' "

"All very true, my friend; but as that sort of measurement will not answer to keep farms separate, we are obliged to survey the whole off into lots of smaller size. The Mohawks first gave my father and his friend as much land as they could walk around in two suns, allowing them the night to rest in."

"*That* good deed!" exclaimed the Indian, with strong emphasis. "Leg can't cheat — pen great rogue."

"Well, we have the benefit of both grants; for the proprietors actually walked round the estate, a party of Indians accompanying them, to see that all was fair. After that, the chiefs signed a deed in writing, that there might be no mistake, and then we got the king's grant."

"Who give king land at all? All land here red man's land; who give him to the king?"

"Who made the Delawares women? The warriors of the Six Nations, was it not, Susquesus?"

"Yes, my people help. Six Nation great warrior, and put petticoat on Delawares, so they can't go on war-path any more. What that to do with king's land?"

"Why, the king's warriors, you know, my friend, have taken

possession of this country, just as the Six Nations took possession of the Delawares, before they made them women."

"What become of king's warrior, now?" demanded the Indian, quick as lightning. "Where he run away to? Where
land Ticonderoga, now! Whose land t'oder end lake, now?"

"Why, the king's troops have certainly met with a disaster;
and for the present, their rights are weakened, it must be admitted. But another day may see all this changed, and the
king may get his land again. You will remember he has not
sold Ticonderoga to the French, as the Mohawks sold Mooseridge to us; and that you must admit, makes a great difference.
A bargain is a bargain, Onondago."

"Yes, bargain bargain — that good. Good for red man good
for pale-face — no difference — what Mohawk sell, he no take
back, but let pale-face keep — but how come Mohawk and king
sell, too? Bot' own land, eh?"

This was rather a puzzling question to answer to an Indian.
We white people can very well understand that a humane government, which professes, on the principles recognized by civilized nations to have jurisdiction over certain extensive territories
that lie in the virgin forest, and which are used only, and that
occasionally, by certain savage tribes as hunting-grounds, should
deem it right to satisfy those tribes by purchase, before they
parcelled out their lands for the purposes of civilized life; but
it would not be so easy to make an unsophisticated mind understand that there could be two owners to the same property.
The transaction is simple enough to us, and it tells in favor of
our habits, for we have the power to grant these lands without
"extinguishing the Indian title," as it is termed; but it presents difficulties to the understandings of those who are not
accustomed to see society surrounded by the multifarious interests of civilization. In point of fact, the Indian purchases give
no other title, under our laws, than the right to sue out, in
council, a claim to acquire by the grant of the crown; paying
to the latter such a consideration as in its wisdom it shall see
fit to demand. Still, it was necessary to make some answer to
the Onondago's question, lest he might carry away the mistaken
notion that we did not justly own our possessions.

"Suppose you find a rifle to your fancy, Susquesus," I said,
after reflecting a moment on the subject, "and you find two
Indians who both claim to own it; now, if you pay each warrior

his price, is your right to the title any the worse for having done so? Is it not rather better?"

The Indian was struck with this reply, which suited the character of his mind. Thrusting out his hand, he received mine, and shook it cordially, as much as to say he was satisfied. Having disposed of this episode thus satisfactorily, we turned to the more interesting subject of our immediate movements.

"It would seem that the Onondago expects the French Indians will now strike at the settlements," I remarked to my companions, "and that our friends at Ravensnest may need our aid; but, at the same time, he thinks we should first return to Mooseridge, and join the surveyors. Which mode of proceeding strikes you as the best, my friends?"

"Let us first hear the Injin's reasons for going after the surveyors," answered Guert. "If he has a sufficient reason for his plan, I am ready to follow it."

"Surveyor got scalp, as well as squaw," said Susquesus, in his brief, meaning manner.

"That must settle the point!" exclaimed Guert. "I understand it all, now. The Onondago thinks the Mooseridge party may be cut off, as being alone and unsupported, and that we ought to apprise them of this danger."

"All perfectly just," I replied, "and it is what they, being our own people, have a right to expect from us. Still, Guert, I should think those surveyors might be safe where they are, in the bosom of the forest, for a year to come. Their business there cannot be known, and who then is to betray them?"

"See," said Susquesus, earnestly. "Kill deer, and leave him in the wood. Won't raven find carcass?"

"That may be true enough; but a raven has an instinct, given him by nature, to furnish him with food. He flies high in the air, moreover, and can see further than an Indian."

"Nuttin' see farther than Injin! Red man fly high, too. See from salt lake to sweet water. Know ebbery t'ing in wood. Tell him nuttin' he don't know."

"You do not suppose, Susquesus, that the Huron warriors could find our surveyors at Mooseridge?"

"Why not find him? Find moose; why no find ridge, too? Find Mooseridge, sartain; find land measurer."

"On the whole, Corny," Guert remarked after musing a little, "we may do well to follow the Injin's advice. I have heard of so many misfortunes that have befallen people in the

bush, from having despised Indian counsels, that I own to a
little superstition on the subject. Just look at what happened
yesterday! Had red-skin opinions been taken, Abercrombie
might now have been a conqueror, instead of a miserable beaten
man."

Susquesus raised a finger, and his dark countenance became
illumined by an expression that was more eloquent even than
his tongue.

"Why no open ear to red man?" he asked with dignity.
"Some bird sing a song that good — some sing bad song — but
all bird know his own song. Mohawk warrior use to wood, and
follow a crooked war-path, when he meet much enemy. Great
Yengeese chief think his warrior have two life, that he put him
before cannon and rifle to stand up and be shot. No Injin do
so foolish — no — never!"

As this was too true to be controverted, the matter was not
discussed; but having determined among ourselves to let the
Onondago take us back on the path by which we had come, we
announced our readiness to start as soon as it might suit his
convenience. Being sufficiently rested, Susquesus, who did every
thing on system, manifesting neither impatience nor laziness,
arose and quietly led the way. Our course was just the reverse
of that on which we had travelled when we left Mooseridge;
and I did not fail to observe that so accurate was the knowledge
of our guide, we passed many of the same objects as we had
previously gone near. There was nothing like a track, with the
exception of occasional footprints left by ourselves; but it was
evident the Onondago paid not the least attention to these, possessing other and more accessible clues to his course.

Guert marched next to the Indian, and I was third in the line.
How often that busy day did I gaze at my file-leader, in admiration of his figure and mien! Nature appeared to have
intended him for a soldier. Although so powerful, his frame
was agile — a particular in which he differed from Dirck, who,
although so young, already gave symptoms of heaviness at no
distant day. Then Guert's carriage was as fine as his form.
The head was held erect; the eye was intrepid in its glance;
and the tread elastic, though so firm. To the last hour, on that
long and weary march, Guert leaped logs, sprang across hollows in the ground, and otherwise manifested that his iron
sinews and hardened muscles still retained all their powers. As
he moved in my front I saw for the first time, that some of the

fringe of his hunting-shirt had been cut away in the fight, and that a musket-ball had passed directly through his cap. I afterward ascertained that Guert was aware of these escapes, but his nature was so manly he did not think of mentioning them.

We made a single halt as before, to dine; but little was said at this meal, and no change in our plan was proposed. This was the point where we ought to have diverged from the former course, did we intend to proceed first to Ravensnest; but though all knew it, nothing was said on the subject.

"We shall carry unwelcome tidings to Mr. Traverse and his men," Guert observed, a minute or two before our halt was up; "for I take it for granted, the news cannot have gone ahead of *us*."

"We first," answered the Onondago. "Too soon for Huron yet. T'ink so — nobody know."

"I wish, Corny," pursued the Albanian, "we had thought of saying a word to Doortje about this accursed expedition. There is no use in a man's being above his business; and he who puts himself in the way of fortune, might profit by now and then consulting a fortune-teller."

"Had we done so, and had all that has happened been foretold, do you suppose it would have made any change in the result?"

"Perhaps not, since we should have been the persons to relate what we had heard. But Abercrombie himself need have had no scruples about visiting that remarkable old woman. She's a wonderful creature, Corny, as we must allow, and a prudent general would not fail to respect what she told him. It is a thousand pities that either the commander-in-chief or the adjutant-general had not paid Doortje a visit before they left Albany. My lord Howe's valuable life might then have been saved."

"In what way, Guert? I am at a loss to see in what manner any good could come of it."

"In what manner? Why, in the plainest possible. Now suppose Doortje had foretold this defeat; it is clear Abercrombie, if he put any faith in the old woman, would not have made the attack."

"And thus defeat the defeat. Do you not see, Guert, that the soothsayer can at the best but foretell what *is* to happen, and that which *must* come *will*. It would be an easy matter for any of us to get great reputations for fortune-telling, if all we had to do was to predict misfortunes, in order that our friends might avoid them. As nothing would ever happen, in consequence of the precautions taken to avert the evils, a name would be easily and cheaply maintained."

"By St. Nicholas! Corny, I never thought of that! But you have been college-taught; and a thousand things are picked up at colleges that one never dreams of at an academy. I see reason every day to lament my idleness when a boy; and fortunate shall I be, if I do not lament it all my life."

Poor Guert! He was always so humble when the subject of education arose, however accidentally or unintentionally on my part, that it was never commented on, that it did not give me pain, exciting a wish to avoid it. As the time for the halt was now up, it was easy to terminate the present discussion, by declaring as much, and proceeding on our way.

We had a hard afternoon's walk of it, though neither of the five manifested the least disposition to give in. As for Susequesus, to me he never seemed to know either fatigue or hunger. He was doubtless acquainted with both; but his habits of self-command were so severe, as to enable him completely to conceal his sufferings in this, as well as in most other respects.

The sun was near setting when we entered within the limits of the Mooseridge estate. We ascertained this fact by passing the line-trees, some of which had figures cut into their bark, to denote the numbers of the great subdivisions of the property. Guert pointed out these marks; being far more accustomed to the woods than either Dirck or myself. Aided by such guides, we had no difficulty in making a sufficiently straight course to the hut.

Susquesus thought a little caution necessary as we drew near to the end of our journey. Causing us to remain behind, he advanced in front himself to reconnoitre. A signal, however, soon took us to the place where he stood, when we discovered the hut just as we had left it, but no one near it. This might be the result of mere accident, the surveying party frequently "camping out," in preference to making a long march after a fatiguing day's work; and Pete would be very likely to prefer going to join these men to remaining alone in the hut. We advanced to the building therefore with confidence. On reaching it, we found the place empty, as had been anticipated, though with every sign about it of its tenants having left it but a short time previously; that morning, at the furthest.

Jaap set about preparing a supper out of the regular supplies of the party; all of which were found in their places, and in abundance. On inquiry of the fellow, I ascertained it was his opinion Mr. Travers had gone off that very day, most probably to some distant portion of the patent, taking Pete with him, as every thing was covered up and put away with that sort of care that denotes an absence of some little time. The Indian heard the negro's remark to this effect, and tossing his head significantly, he said —

" No need guess — go see — light enough — plenty time. Injin soon tell."

He quitted the hut on the spot, and immediately set about this self-assigned duty.

CHAPTER XXV

"Thou tremblest; and the whiteness in thy cheek,
Is apter than thy tongue to tell thy errand."
                                        SHAKSPEARE.

CURIOSITY induced me to follow the Indian, in order to watch his movements. Susquesus proceeded a short distance from the hut, quitting the knoll entirely, until he reached lower land, where a footprint would be most likely to be visible, when he commenced a slow circuit of the place, with eyes fastened on the earth, as the nose of the hound follows the scent. I was so much interested in the Onondago's manner as to join him, falling in in his rear, in order not to interfere with his object.

Of footmarks there were plenty, more particularly on the low, moist ground, where we were; but they all appeared to me to have no interest with the Indian. Most of our party wore moccasins; and it was not easy to see how, under such circumstances, and amid such a maze of impressions, it could be possible for any one to distinguish a hostile from a friendly trail. That Susquesus thought the thing might be done, however, was very evident by his perseverance, and his earnestness.

At first, my companion met with no success, or with nothing that he fancied success; but after making half the circuit of the hut, keeping always a hundred yards distant from it, he suddenly stooped quite to the earth; then arose, and, sticking a broken knot into the ground as a mark, signed to me to keep a little on one side, while he turned at right angles to his former course, and moved inward toward our dwelling. I followed slowly, watching his movements, step by step.

In this manner we reached the hut, deviating from a direct line, in order to do so. At the hut itself Susquesus made a long and minute examination; but even I could see, that the marks here were so numerous as to baffle even him. After finishing his search at this point, the Indian turned, and went back to the place where he had stuck the knot in the ground. In doing this, however, he followed his own trail, returning by precisely the same deviating course as that by which he had come. This alone would have satisfied me that he saw more than I did; for, to own the truth, I could not have done the same thing.

When we reached the knot, Susquesus followed that (to me invisible) trail outside of the circle, leading off into the forest in a direct line from the hut and spring. I continued near him, although neither had spoken during the whole of this examination, which had now lasted quite half an hour. As it was getting dark, however, and Jaap showed the signal that our supper was ready, I thought it might be well, at length, to break the silence.

" What do you make of all this, Trackless? " I inquired. " Do you find any signs of a trail? "

" Good trail " — Susequesus answered; " new trail, too; look like Huron! "

This was startling intelligence, certainly; yet, much as I was disposed to defer to my companion's intelligence in such matters, in general, I thought he must be mistaken in his fact. In the first place, though I had seen many footprints near the hut, and along the low land on which the Indian made his circuit, I could see none where we then were. I mentioned this to the Indian, and desired him to show me, particularly, one of the signs which had led him to his conclusion.

" See," said Susquesus, stooping so low as to place a finger on the dead leaves that ever make a sort of carpet to the forest, "here been moccasin — that heel; this toe."

Aided, in this manner, I could discover a faint footprint, which might, by aid of the imagination, be thus read; though the very slight impression that was to be traced, might almost as well be supposed any thing else, as it seemed to me.

" I see what you mean, Susquesus; and I allow, it *may* be a footprint," I answered; " but then it may also have been left by any thing else which has touched the ground just at that spot. It may have been made by a falling branch of a tree."

" Where branch? " asked the Indian, quick as lightning.

" Sure enough; that is more than I can tell you. But I cannot suppose *that* a Huron footprint, without more evidence than you now give."

" What you call that? — this — that — t'other? " added the Indian, stepping quickly back, and pointing to four other similar, but very faint impressions on the leaves; " no see him, eh? — Just leg apart, too! "

This was true enough; and now my attention was thus directed, and my senses were thus aided, I confess I did discover certain proofs of footsteps, that would, otherwise, have baffled my most serious search.

"I can see what you mean, Susquesus," I said, "and will allow that this line of impressions, or marks, does make them look more like footsteps. At any rate, most of our party wear moccasins as well as the red men, and how do you know that some of the surveyors have not passed this way?"

"Surveyor no make such mark. Toe turn in."

This was true, too. But it did not follow that a footprint was a Huron's merely because it was Indian. Then where were the enemy's warriors to come from, in so short a time as had intervened between the late battle and the present moment? There was little question all the forces of the French — pale-face and red man, had been collected at Ticonderoga to meet the English; and the distance was so great as almost to render it impossible for a party to reach this spot so soon, coming from the vicinity of the fortress after the occurrence of the late events. Did not the lake interpose an obstacle, I might have inferred that parties of skirmishers would be thrown on the flanks of the advancing army, thus bringing foes within a lessened distance of us; but there was the lake, affording a safe approach for more than thirty miles, and rendering the employment of any such skirmishers useless. All this occurred to me at the moment, and I mentioned it to my companion as an argument against his own supposition.

"No true," answered Susquesus, shaking his head. "That trail — he Huron trail too. Don't know red man to say so."

"But red men are human as well as pale-faces. It must be seventy miles from this spot to the foot of Lake George, and your conjecture would make it necessary that a party should have travelled that distance in less than twenty-four hours, and be here some time before us."

"We no travel him, eh?"

"I grant you that, Trackless; but we came a long bit of the road in a canoe, each and all of us sleeping and resting ourselves in turns. These Hurons must have come the whole distance by land."

"No so. Huron paddle canoe as well as Onondago. Lake there — canoe plenty. Why not come?"

"Do you suppose, Trackless, that any of the French Indians

would venture on the lake while it was covered with our boats, as was the case last night?"

"What 'our boat' good for, eh? Carry wounded warrior — carry runaway warrior — what he care? T'ink Huron 'fraid of boat? Boat got eye, eh? Boat see; boat hear; boat shoot, eh?"

"Perhaps not; but those who were in the boats can do all this, and would be apt at least to speak to a strange canoe."

"Boat speak my canoe, eh? Onondago canoe strange canoe too."

All this was clear enough, when I began to reflect on it. It was certainly possible for a canoe with two or three paddles, to go the whole length of the lake in much less time than we had employed in going two-thirds of the distance; and a party landing in the vicinity of William Henry, could certainly have reached the spot where we then were, several hours sooner than we had reached it ourselves. Still there existed all the other improbabilities on my side of the question. It was improbable that a party should have proceeded in precisely this manner; it was still more improbable that such a party, coming on a war-path from a distant part of the country, should know exactly where to find our hut. After a moment's pause, and while we both slowly proceeded to join our companions, I suggested these objections to the Onondago.

"Don't know Injin," answered the other, betraying more earnestness of manner than was usual with him when he condescended to discuss any of the usages of the tribes with a pale-face. "He fight first, then he want scalp. Ever see dead horse in wood — well, no crow there, eh? Plenty crow, isn't he? Just so Injin. Wounded soldier carry off, and Injin watch in wood, behind army, to get scalp. Scalp good after battle. Want him very much. Wood full of Huron, along path to Albany. Yengeese down in heart; Huron up. Scalp so good, t'ink of nuttin' else."

By this time we had reached the hut, where I found Guert and Dirck already at their supper. I will own that my appetite was not as good as it might have been but for the Onondago's conjectures and discoveries, though I took a seat and began to eat with my friends. While at the meal, I communicated to my companions all that had passed, particularly asking of Guert, who had a respectable knowledge of the bush, what he thought of the probabilities of the case.

"If hostile red skins have really been here lately," the Albanian answered, "they have been thoroughly cunning devils; for not an article in or about the hut has been disturbed. I had an eye to that myself, the moment we arrived; for I have thought it far from unlikely that the Hurons would be out on the road between William Henry and the settlements, trying to get scalps from the parties that would be likely to be sent to the rear with wounded officers."

"In which case our friend Bulstrode might be in danger?"

"He must take his chance, like all of us. But he will probably be carried to Ravensnest, as the nearest nest for him to nestle in. I don't half like this trail, however, Corny; it is seldom a red skin of the Onondago's character, makes a mistake in such a matter!"

"It is too late, now, to do any thing to-night," Dirck observed. "Besides, I don't think any great calamity is likely to befall any of us, or Doortje would have dropped some hint about it. These fortune-tellers seldom let any thing serious pass without a notice of some sort or other. You see, Corny, we went through all this business at Ty, without a scratch, which is so much in favor of the old woman's being right."

Poor Dirck! that prediction had made a deep impression on his character, and on his future life. A man's faith must be strong, to fancy that a negative of this nature could carry with it any of the force of a positive, affirmative prediction. Nevertheless Dirck had spoken the truth, in one respect. It was too late to do any thing that night, and it only remained to prepare to take our rest as securely as possible.

We consulted on the subject, calling on the Indian to aid us. After talking the matter over, it was determined to remain where we were, securing the door, and bringing every body within the building; for the negroes and the Indians had been much in the habit of sleeping about, under brush covers that they had erected for themselves. It was thought that, having once visited the hut, and finding it empty, the enemy, if enemy there were, would not be very likely to return to it immediately, and that we might consider ourselves as comparatively safe, from that circumstance alone. Then, there were all the chances that the trail might have been left by friendly instead of hostile Indians, although Susquesus shook his head in the negative, whenever this was mentioned. At all events, we had but a choice of three expedients — to abandon the patent, and seek safety in flight; to "camp out;" or to shut ourselves up in our fortress. Of the first, no one thought for a moment; and of the two others, we decided on the last, as far the most comfortable, and on the whole, as the safest.

An hour after we had come to this determination, I question if either of the five knew any thing about it. I never slept more profoundly in my life, and my companions subsequently gave the same account of their several conditions. Fatigue, and youth, and health, gave us all refreshing sleep; and as we lay down at nine, two o'clock came after so much time totally lost in the way of consciousness. I say two o'clock; for my watch told me that was just the hour, when the Indian awoke me by shaking my shoulder. One gets the habits of watchfulness in the woods, and I was on my feet in an instant.

Dark as it was, for it was deep night, I could distinguish that Susquesus was alone stirring, and that he had unbarred the door of our cabin. Indeed, he passed through that open space, into the air of the forest, the moment he perceived I was conscious of what I was about. Without pausing to reflect, I followed, and soon stood at his side some fifteen or twenty feet from the hut.

"This good place to hear," said the Indian, in a low, suppressed tone. "Now, open ear."

What a scene was that, which now presented itself to my senses! I can see it, at this distance of time, after years of peaceful happiness, and years of toil and adventure. The morning, or it might be better to say the night, was not very dark in itself; but the gloom of the woods being added to the obscurity of the hour, it lent an intensity of blackness to the trunks of the trees, that gave to each a funereal and solemn aspect. It was impossible to see for any distance, and the objects that were visible were only those that were nearest at hand. Notwithstanding, one might imagine the canopied space beneath the tops of the trees, and fancy it, in the majesty of its gloomy vastness. Of sounds there were literally none, when the Indian first bade me listen. The stillness was so profound, that I thought I heard the sighing of the night air among the upper branches of the loftier trees. This might have been mere imagination; nevertheless, all above the summits of the giant oaks, maples and pines, formed a sort of upper world as regarded us; a world with which we had little communication, during our sojourn in the woods below. The raven, and the eagle, and the hawk, sailed in that region, above the clouds of leaves beneath them, and occasionally stooped, perhaps, to strike their quarry; but to all else it was inaccessible, and to a degree invisible.

But my present concern is with the world I was in; and what a world it was! Solemn, silent, dark, vast and mysterious. I listened in vain to catch the footstep of some busy squirrel, for the forest was alive with the smaller animals, by night quite as much as by day; but every thing at that moment seemed stilled to the silence of death.

"I can hear nothing, Trackless," I whispered — "why are you out here?"

"You hear soon — wake me up, and I hear twice. Soon come ag'in."

It did soon come again. It was a human cry, escaping from human lips in their agony! I heard it once only; but should I live to be a hundred it would not be forgotten. I often hear it in my sleep, and twenty times have I awoke since, fancying that agonizing call was in my ears. It was long, loud, piercing, and the word "help" was as distinct as tongue could make it.

"Great God!" I exclaimed — "some one is set upon, and calls for aid in his extremity. Let us arouse our friends, and go to his assistance. I cannot remain here, Susquesus, with such a cry in my ears."

"Best go, t'ink too," answered the Onondago. "No need call, though; two better than four. Stop minute."

I did remain stationary that brief space, listening with agonized uncertainty, while the Indian entered the hut, and returned, bringing out his rifle and my own. Arming ourselves, and shutting the door of the cabin, to exclude the night-air at least, Susquesus led off with his noiseless step, in a south-west direction, or that in which we had heard the sound.

Our march was too swift and earnest to admit of discourse. The Onondago had admonished me to make as little noise as possible; and between the anxiety I felt, and the care taken to comply, there was, indeed, but little opportunity for conversing. My feelings were wrought up to a high pitch; but my confidence in my companion being great, I followed in his footsteps as diligently as my skill would allow. Susquesus rather trod on air than walked; yet I kept close at his heels, until we had gone, as I should think, full half a mile in the direction from

which that awful cry had come. Here Susquesus halted, saying to me, in a low voice —

"No far from here — best stop."

I submitted in all things to the directions of my Indian guide.
The latter had selected the dark shadows of two or three young
pines for our cover, where, by getting within their low branches,
we were completely concealed from any eye that was distant from
us eight or ten feet. No sooner were we thus posted, than the
Onondago pointed to the trunk of a fallen tree, and we took our
seats silently on it. I observed that my companion kept his
thumb on the cock of his rifle, while his forefinger was passed
around the trigger. It is scarcely necessary to say that I observed the same precaution.

"This good," said Susquesus, in a voice so low and soft that
it could not attract more attention than a whisper; "this very
good — hear him ag'n, soon; then know."

A stifled groan *was* heard, and that almost as soon as my
companion ceased to speak. I felt my blood curdle at these
frightful evidences of human suffering; and an impulse of humanity caused me to move, as if about to rise. The hand of
Trackless checked the imprudence.

"No good," he said, sternly. "Sit still. Warrior know how
to sit still."

"But, Heavenly Providence! There is some one in agony,
quite near us, man. Did you not hear a groan, Trackless?"

"To be sure hear him. What of that? Pain make groan
come alway, from pale-face."

"You think, then, it is a white man who suffers? if so, it
must be one of our party, as there is no one else near us. If I
hear it again, I must go to his relief, Onondago."

"Why you behave like squaw? What of little groan? Sartain, he pale-face; Injin never groan on war-path. Why he
groan, you t'ink? Cause Huron meet him. That reason he
groan. You groan too, no sit still. Injin know time to shoot
— know time not to shoot."

I had every disposition to call aloud to inquire who needed
succor; yet the admonitions of my companion, aided as they
were by the gloomy mysteries of that vast forest in the hour of
deepest night, enabled me to command the impulse. Three
times, notwithstanding, was that groan repeated, and as it appeared to me, each time more and more faintly. I thought,
too, when all was still in the forest — when we sat ourselves in

breathless expectation of what might next reach our ears —
attentive to each sighing of the night-air, and distrustful even
of the rustling leaf — that the last groan of all, though certainly
the faintest of any we had heard, was much the nearest. Once,
indeed, I heard, or fancied I heard, the word "water," mur-
mured in a low, smothered tone, almost in my ear. I thought,
too, I knew the voice — that it was familiar to me; though I
could not decide, in the state of my feelings, exactly to whom
it belonged.

In this manner we passed what to me were two of the most
painful hours of my life, waiting the slow return of light. My
own impatience was nearly ungovernable; though the Indian
sat the whole of that time, seemingly as insensible as the log
which formed his seat, and almost as motionless. At length
this intensely anxious, and even physically painful watch drew
near its end. Signs of day gleamed through the canopy of leaves,
and the rays of dull light appeared to struggle downward,
rendering objects dimly discernible.

It was not long ere we could ascertain that we had so completely covered ourselves, as to be in a position where the
branches of the pines completely shut out the view of objects
beyond. This was favorable to reconnoitring, however, previously to quitting our concealment, and enabled us to have some
care of ourselves while attending to the duties of humanity.

Susquesus used the greatest caution in looking around before
he left the cover. I was close at his side peeping through such
openings as offered, for my curiosity was so intense, that I
almost forgot the causes for apprehension. It was not long
before I heard the familiar Indian interjection "hugh!" from
my companion, a proof that something had caught his eye of
a more than ordinarily exciting character. He pointed in the
way I was to look, and there, indeed, I beheld one of those
frightful instances of barbarous cruelty, that the usages of savage
warfare have sanctioned as far back as our histories extend,
among the forest warriors of this continent. The tops of two
saplings had been brought down near each other by main force,
the victim's hands attached firmly to upper branches of each,
and the trees permitted to fly back to their natural positions, or
as near them as the revolting means of junction would allow.
I could scarce believe my senses when my first sight revealed
the truth. But there hung the victim suspended by his arms,
at an elevation of at least ten or fifteen feet from the earth. I

confess I sincerely hoped he was dead, and the motionless attitude of the body gave me reason to think it might be so. Still, the cries for "help," uttered wildly, hopelessly, in the midst of a vast and vacant forest, the groans extorted by suffering, must have been his. He had probably been thus suspended and abandoned while alive!

Even the Onondago could not restrain me, after I fully saw and understood the nature of the cruelty which had been exercised on the miserable victim who was thus suspended directly before my eyes, and I broke out of the cover, ready, I am willing to confess, to pull trigger on the first hostile red man I saw. Fortunately for myself, most probably, the place had long been deserted. As the back of the sufferer was toward me, I could not tell who he was; but his dress was coarse, and of the description that belongs to the lowest class. Blood had flowed freely from his head, and I made no doubt he had been scalped; though the height at which he hung, and the manner in which his head had fallen forward upon his breast, prevented me from ascertaining the fact at once, by the aid of sight. Thus much did I perceive, however, ere the Indian joined me.

"See!" said Susquesus, whose quick eye never let any thing escape it long, "told you so; Huron been here."

As this was said, the Indian pointed significantly at the naked skin, which was visible between the heavy, coarse shoes of the victim, and the trowsers he wore, when I discovered it was black. Moving quickly in front, so as to get a view of the face, I recognized the distorted features of Petrus, or Pete, Guert Ten Eyck's negro. This man had been left with the surveyors, it will be remembered, and he had either fallen into the hands of his captors while at the hut, engaged in his ordinary duties, or he had been met in the forest while going to or coming from those he served, and had thus been treated. We never ascertained the facts, which remain in doubt to this hour

"Give me your tomahawk, Trackless," I cried, as soon as horror would permit me to speak, "that I may cut down this sapling, and liberate the unfortunate creature!"

"No good — better so," answered the Indian. "Bear — wolf can't get him now. Let black-skin hang — good as bury — no safe stay here long. Look round and count Huron, then go."

"Look round and count the Hurons," I thought to myself; "and in what manner is this to be done?" By this time, however, it was sufficiently light to see footprints, if any there were,

and the Onondago set about examining such traces of what had
passed at that terrible spot, as might be intelligible to one of his
experience.

At the foot of a huge oak, that grew a few yards from the
fatal saplings, we found the two wooden covered pails in which
we knew Pete had been accustomed to carry food to Mr. Traverse
and the chain-bearers. They were empty, but whether the
provisions they unquestionably had contained fell to the share of
those for whom they were intended, or to that of the captors,
we never learned. No traces of bones, potato-skins, or other
fragments, were discovered; and if the Hurons had seized the
provisions, they doubtless transferred them to their own reposi-
tories, without stopping to eat. Susquesus detected proof that
the victim had been seated at the foot of the oak, and that he
had been seized at that spot. There were the marks of many
feet there, and some proofs of a slight scuffle. Blood, too, was
to be traced on the leaves, from the foot of the oak to the place
where poor Pete was suspended; a proof that he had been hurt
previously to being abandoned to his cruel fate.

But the point of most interest with Trackless was to ascertain
the number of our foes. This might be done in some measure,
according to his view of the matter, by means of the footprints.
There was no want of such signs, the leaves being much disturbed in places, though after a short but anxious search, my
companion thought it wisest to repair to the hut, lest those it
contained might be surprised in their sleep. He gave me to
understand that the enemy did not appear to be numerous at
that spot, three or four at most, though it was quite possible,
nay highly probable, that they had separated, and that their
whole force was not present at this miserable scene.

It was broad daylight when we came in sight of the hut
again, and I perceived Jaap was up and busy with his pots and
kettles near the spring. No one else was visible, and we inferred that Guert and Dirck were still on their pallets. We
took a long and distrustful survey of the forest around the cabin,
from the height where we stood, ere we ventured to approach
it any nearer. Discovering no signs of danger, and the forest
being quite clear of the underbrush or cover of any sort, large
trees excepted, for some distance from the hut, we then advanced
without apprehension. This open character of the woods near
our dwelling was felt to be a very favorable circumstance, rendering it impossible for an enemy to get very near us by daylight,

without being seen. It was owing to the fact that we had used so much of the smaller timber in our own operations, while the negroes had burned most of the underbrush for fuel.

Sure enough, I found my two friends fast asleep, and certainly much exposed. When aroused and told all that had occurred to me and the Indian, their surprise was great, nor was their horror less. Jaap, who, missing us on rising, supposed we had gone in pursuit of game, had followed us into the hut, and heard my communications. His indignation was great at the idea of one of his own color being thus treated, and I heard him vowing vengeance between his set teeth, in terms that were by no means measured.

" By St. Nicholas! " exclaimed Guert, who had now finished dressing, and who accompanied me out into the open air, " my poor fellow shall be revenged, if the rifle will do it! Scalped, too, do you say, Corny? "

" As far as we could ascertain, suspended as he was from the tree. But scalped he must be, as an Indian never permits a dead captive to escape this mutilation."

" And you have been out in the forest three hours, you tell me, Corny? you and Trackless? "

" About that time, I should judge. The heart must have been of stone that could resist those cries! "

" I do not blame you, Littlepage, though it would have been kinder and wiser had you taken your friends with you. We must stick together, in future, let what may happen. Poor Petrus! I wonder Doortje should have hinted nothing of that nigger's fate! "

We then held a long consultation on the subject of our mode of proceeding next. It is unnecessary to dwell on this conference, as its conclusions will be seen in the events of the narrative; but it was brought to a close by a very sudden interruption, and that was the sound of an axe in the forest. The blows came in the direction of the scene of Pete's murder, and we had collected our rifles and were preparing to move toward the suspected point, when we saw Jaap staggering along, coming to the hut, beneath the load of his friend's body. The fellow had stolen away unseen on this pious duty, and had executed it with success. In a minute or two he had reached the spring, and began to wash away the revolting remains of the massacre from the head of the Huron's victim.

We now ascertained that poor Pete had been badly cut by

knives, as well as scalped, and suspended in the manner related.
Both arms appeared to be dislocated, and the only relief to our
feelings was in the hope that an attempt to inflict so much
suffering must have soon defeated itself. Guert, in particular,
expressed his hope that such was the case, though the awful
sounds of the past night were still too fresh in my ears to
enable me to believe all I could wish on that subject. A grave
was dug, and we buried the body at once, rolling a large log or
two on the spot, in order to prevent wild beasts from disinterring
it. Jaap worked hard in the performance of these rites, and
Guert Ten Eyck actually repeated the Lord's Prayer and the
Creed over the grave, when the body was placed in it, with a
fervor and earnestness that a little surprised me.

"He was but a nigger, Corny, it is true," said the Albanian,
a little apologetically perhaps, after all was over, "but he was
a very goot nigger in the first place; then he had a soul as well
as a white man — Pete had his merits as well as a Tominie, and
I trust they will not be forgotten in the last great account. He
was an excellent cook, as you must have seen, and I never knew
a nigger that had more of the dog-like fidelity to his master. The
fellow never got into a frolic without coming honestly to ask
leave; though to be sure, I was not a hard master in these particulars on reasonable occasions."

We next ate our breakfast with as much appetite as we could.
Shouldering our packs, and placing all around and in the hut
as much as possible in the condition in which we had found the
place, we then commenced our march, Susquesus leading as
usual.

We went in quest of the surveyors, who were supposed to be
in the south-east corner of the patent, employed as usual, and
ignorant of all that had passed. At first, we had thoughts of
discharging our rifles as signals to bring them in; but these
signals might apprise our enemies, as well as our friends, of our
presence, and the distance was too great moreover, to render
it probable the reports could be heard by those for whom alone
they would be intended.

The route we took was determined by our general knowledge
of the quarter of the patent in which the surveyors ought now
to be, as well as by the direction in which the body of Pete
had been found. The poor fellow was certainly either going to
or coming from the party, and being in constant communication
with them, he doubtless knew where they were at work. Then

the different trails of the surveyors were easily enough found by Trackless, and he told us that the most recent led off in the direction I have named. Toward the south-east, therefore, we held our way, marching, as before, in Indian file; the Onondago leading, and the negro bringing up the rear.

CHAPTER XXVI

" 'Tis too horrible!
The weariest and most loathed worldly life
That age, ache, penury, and imprisonment
Can lay on nature, is a paradise,
To what we fear of death."

MEASURE FOR MEASURE.

WE were not long in reaching the point of the patent in which
the surveyors had been at work, after which we could have but
little difficulty in finding their present actual position. The
marked trees were guides that told the whole story of their
labors. For an hour and a half, however, we moved rapidly
forward, Susquesus on the lead, silent, earnest, watchful, and
I fear I must add, revengeful. Not a syllable had been uttered
during the whole of that time, though our senses were keenly
on the alert; and we avoided every thing like a cover that
might conceal an ambush. Suddenly the Indian halted; at the
next instant he was behind a tree. Each of us imitated him,
quick as thought, for this was our previous training in the event
of encountering an enemy; and we all well knew the importance
of a cover in forest warfare. Still, no foe could be seen. After
examining around us in every direction, for a minute or two,
and finding the woods vacant and silent as ever, Guert and I
quitted our own trees, and joined the Trackless, at the foot of
his own huge pine.

" Why this, Susquesus? " demanded the Albanian, sharply;
for he began to suspect a little acting, got up to magnify the
Indian's usefulness; " here is neither pale-face nor red-skin.
Have done with this folly, and let us go forward."

" No good — warrior been here; p'rhaps gone, p'rhaps no;
soon see. Open eye, and look."

As a gesture accompanied this speech, we did look again,
and this time in the right direction. At the distance of a hundred yards from us was a chestnut, that might be seen from
its roots to its branches. On the ground, partly concealed by
the tree, and partly exposed, was the leg of a man placed as the

limb would be apt to lie, on the supposition that its owner lay
on his back asleep. It showed a moccasin, and the usual legging
of an Indian; but the thigh and all the rest of the frame was
concealed. The quick eye of the Onondago had caught this small
object, even at that distance, comprehended it at a glance, when
he instantly sought a cover, as described. Guert and I had some
difficulty at first, even after it was pointed out to us, in recognizing this object; but it soon became distinct and intelligible.

"Is that a red-skin's leg?" asked Guert, dropping the muzzle
of his rifle, as if about to try his skill on it.

"Don't know," answered the Indian; "got leggin, got moccasin; can't see color. Look most pale-face; leg big."

What there was to enable one, at that distance, to distinguish
between the leg of a white man and the leg of an Indian, at
first greatly exceeded our means of conjecturing; but the Onondago explained it, when asked, in his own usual sententious manner, by saying:

"Toe turn out — Injin turn in — no like, at all. Pale-face
big; Injin no very big."

The first was true enough in walking, and it did seem probable that the difference might exist in sleep. Guert now declared there was no use in hesitating any longer; if asleep he
would approach the chestnut cautiously, and capture the stranger,
if an Indian, before he could rise; and if a white man, it must be
some one belonging to our own set, who was taking a nap,
probably, after a fatiguing march. Susquesus must have satisfied
himself, by this time, that there was no immediate danger; for
merely saying, "all go together," he quitted the cover, and led
down toward the chestnut with a rapid but noiseless step. As
we moved in a body all five of us reached the tree at the same
instant, where we found Sam, one of our own hunters, and whom
we supposed to be with Mr. Traverse, stretched on his back, dead;
with a wound in his breast that had been inflicted by a knife.
He, too, had been scalped!

The looks we exchanged, said all that could be said on the
subject of the gravity of this new discovery. Susquesus alone
was undisturbed; I rather think he expected what he found.
After examining the body, he seemed satisfied, simply saying,
"kill, last night."

That poor Sam had been dead several hours was pretty certain, and the circumstance removed all apprehension of any
immediate danger from his destroyers. The ruthless warriors

of the woods seldom remained long near the spot they had desolated, but passed on, like the tornado or the tempest. Guert, who was ever prompt when any thing was to be done, pointed to a natural hollow in the earth — one of those cavities that are so common in the forest, and which are so usually attributed to upturning of trees, in remote ages — and suggested that we should use it as a grave. The body was accordingly laid in the hole, and we covered it in the best manner we could; succeeding in placing over it something like a foot deep of light loam, together with several flat stones, rolling logs on all, as we had done at the grave of Pete. By this time Guert's feelings were so thoroughly aroused, that in addition to the prayer and the Creed, which he again repeated in a very decorous and devout manner, he concluded the whole ceremony by a brief address. Nor was Guert any thing but serious in what he did or said on either of these solemn occasions; his words, like his acts, being purely the impulses of a simple mind, which possesses longings after devotion and scriptural truths, without knowing exactly how to express them; and this, moreover, in spite of the mere animal propensities, and gay habits of his physical conformation and constitutional tendencies.

"Deat', my friends," said Guert, most seriously, becoming Dutch as usual, as he became interested; "Deat' is a sutten visitor. He comes like a t'ief in the night, as you must all have often he'rt the Tominie say; and happy is he whose loins are girtet and whose lamp is trimmed. Such I trust is the case with each of you, for it is not to be concealet that we are likely to have serious work before us. Here have been Injins, beyont a question; and they are Injins, too, that are out on the war-path in search of English scalps, or what is of equal importance to Mr. Follock and myself, Dutch scalps in the pargain; which makes it so much the more necessary for every man to be on his guart, and to stant up to his work when it may come, as the pull-dog stants up to the ox. Got forpit t'at I should preach revenge over t'e grave of a frient; but the soltier fights none the worse for knowing t'at he has been injuret in his feelin's, as has certainly peen the case with ourselves. Perhaps I ought to say a wort in behalf of the teat, as this is the last and only time that a fellow-creature will ever have occasion to speak of him. Sam was an excellent hunter, as his worst enemy must allow; and now he is gone, few petter remain pehint. He had one weakness, which, stanting over his grave, an honest man ought not to conceal; he dit love liquor; but in this he was not alone. Nevertheless he was honest; and his wort might pass where many a man's bond would be wort'less; and I leave him in the merciful hants of his Creator. My frients, I haf but little more to say, and that is this — that life is uncertain, and deat' is sure. Samuel has gone before us only a little while; and may we all be equally preparet to meet our great account. Amen."

Did any one smile at this address? Far from it! Singular, disconnected, and unsophisticated as it may seem to certain persons, it had one great merit that is not always discernable in the speeches of those who officiate at the most elaborate funeral rites. Guert was sincere, though he might not be either logical or very clear. This was apparent in his countenance, his voice, his whole manner. For myself, I will allow I saw nothing particularly out of place in this address at the time, nor do I now regard it as either irreverent or unseasonable.

We left the grave of the hunter, in the depths of that interminable forest, as the ship passes away from the spot on the ocean where she has dropped her dead. At some future day, perhaps, the plough share may turn up the bones, and the husbandman ruminate on the probable fate of the lonely man, whose remains will then again be brought to the light of day. As we left the spot, the Indian detained us a moment, to put us on our guard.

"Huron do that," he said meaningly. "No see difference, eh? Saw no hang up like Pete?"

"That is true enough, Susquesus," Guert answered; for Guert, by his age, his greater familiarity with the woods, his high courage and his personal prowess, had now assumed, unresistingly on our part, a sort of chieftainship over us. "Can you tell us the reason, however?"

"Muss, you call him, back sore — that all. Know him well; don't love flog. No Injin love flog."

"And you think, then, Jaap's prisoner has had a hand in this, and that the war-path is open to revenge as well as public service — that we are hunted less for our scalps than to put a plaster on the Huron's back?"

"Sartain. T'ree canoe go by on lake — t'at Muss, you call him — know him well. He no want sleep till back get well. See how he use nigger! Hang him on tree — only kill paleface and take away scalp."

"Do you suppose that he made this difference in the treatment of his two captives, on account of the color? That he was so cruel to Petrus because Jaap, another nigger, had flogged him?"

"Sartain — just so. Back feel better after t'at. Good for back to hang nigger. Jaap see, some time."

I will do my fellow the justice to say, that in the way of courage, few men were his equals. As I have said before, he only feared spooks, or Dutch ghosts; for the awe he had of me was so blended with love, as not to deserve the name of fear. In general, unless the weather happened to be cold, his face was of a deep, glistening black; coffin-color, as the boys sometimes called it; but I observed, notwithstanding his nerve and his keen desire to be revenged for the cruel treatment bestowed on his companion and brother, that his skin now assumed a grayish hue, such as is seen only in hard frosts, as a rule, in the people of his race. It was evident that the Trackless's manner of speaking had produced an effect; and I have always thought the impression then made on Jaap was of infinite service to us, by setting in motion, and keeping in lively activity, every faculty of his mind and body. I had a specimen of this, as we moved off, Jaap walking for some distance close at my heels, in order to make me the repository of his griefs and solicitude.

"I hopes, Masser Corny, sah," commenced the negro, "you doesn't t'ink anyt'ing of what dis here Injin say?"

"I think, Jaap, it will be necessary for you to keep your eyes open, and by no means to fall into the hands of your friend Muss, as you call him, or he may serve you even worse than he served poor Pete. I hope, too, this will be a warning to you of the necessity of treating your prisoners kindly, should you ever make another."

"I don't tink, Masser Corny, you consider pretty much, sah. What good it do a nigger to captivate an Injin, if he let him go ag'in, and don't lick him little? Only little, Masser Corny. Ebery t'ing so handy too, sah — rope all ready, back bare, and feelin' up, like, after such a time in takin' 'e varmint, sah!"

"Well, Jaap, what is done, is done, and there is no use in regretting it, in words. Of one thing, however, you may be certain; no mercy will be shown *you*, should this fellow, Muss, be actually out here, on our heels, and should you be so unfortunate as to fall into his hands."

The negro growled out his discontent, and I could see that

his mind was made up to give stout battle, ere *his* wool should be disturbed by the knife of a savage. A moment later, he stepped aside, and respectfully permitted Dirck to take his proper place next to me in the line.

We may have proceeded two miles from the spot where we had buried Sam, the hunter, when on rising a little hillock, the Indian tossed his arm, the sign that a new discovery was made. This time, however, the gesture was rather made in exultation than in horror. As he came to a dead halt at the same instant, we all closed eagerly up, and got an early view of the cause of this exhibition of feeling.

The ground fell away, in a sort of swell, for some distance in our front; and the trees being all of the largest size, and totally without underbrush, the place had somewhat of the appearance of a vast forest edifice, to which the canopy of leaves above formed the roof, and the stems of oaks, lindens, beeches and maples, might be supposed to be the columns that upheld it. Within this wide, gloomy, yet not unpleasant hall, a sombre light prevailed, like that which is cast through the casements of an edifice of the ancient style of architecture, rendering every thing mellow and grave. A spring of sweet water gushed from a rock, and near it were seated, in a circle, Mr. Traverse and his two chain-bearers, seemingly taking their morning's meal; or, rather, reclining after it, with the pail, platters and fragments before them; like men reposing after appeasing their hunger, and passing a few minutes in idle talk. Tom, the second hunter and axe-man, lay asleep, a little apart.

"Here has been even no alarm, thank Got," said Guert, cheerfully, "and we are in time to let them know their danger. I will give the call; it will sound sweetly to their ears."

"No call," said Trackless, quickly; "holla no good, now. Soon get there, and tell him in low voice."

As this was clearly prudent, we pushed forward in a body, taking no pains, however, to conceal our approach, but making somewhat of a measured tread with our footsteps. A strange sensation came over me as we advanced, and I found that neither of the surveyors stirred! A suspicion of the dread truth forced itself on my mind; but I can hardly say that the shock was any the less, when on getting near, we saw by the pallid countenances, fixed, glassy eyes and fallen jaws, that all our friends were dead. The savage ingenuity of Indians had propped the bodies in reclining positions, and thrown them into attitudes that had a

horrible resemblance to the species of indulgence that I have just
described.

"Holy heaven!" exclaimed Guert, dropping the butt of his
rifle on the ground; "we are too late!"

No one else spoke. On removing the caps, it was found that
each man had been scalped, and that all of those whom we had
left a few days before, proud of their strength and instinct with
life, had departed in spirit, soon to be seen no more. Jumper,
the other Indian, alone remained to be accounted for. Rifle-
balls had been at work here, each of the four having been shot;
Mr. Traverse in no less than three places.

I will confess that a suspicion of the Oneida crossed my
mind now, for the first time; and I did not scruple to mention
it to my companions, as soon as either of us had power to speak
or listen.

"No true," said Trackless, positively. "Jumper poor Injin
— that so — love rum — no rascal, to kill friend. Musohoeenah
warrior to do so. Just like him. No; Jumper fool — love rum
— no bad Injin."

Where, then, was Jumper? He alone, of all whom we had
left behind us, remained to be found. We made a long search
for his body, but without success. Susquesus examined the
trails, and the bodies, and gave it as his opinion that the surveyor and chain-bearers might have been killed about three or
four hours; and that the murderers, for such, in our eyes, they
who had done the foul deed were to be accounted, had not
been away from the place more than twenty minutes when we
arrived. This might well have happened, and we not hear the
rifles, as the distance from the hut was several miles; and two
hours before, we must not have been far from the place where
we had passed the night. That the attack occurred after daylight was reasonably certain; and as Pete was surely seized
while alive, some intelligence might have been obtained from
him, that directed the savages to the point where the outlying
party would probably be expecting him. Nevertheless, this was
pretty much conjecture, and we never knew which victim fell
first, or whether the negro was taken at all near the spot where
he was gibbeted. The infernal cruelty of his conquerors may have
kept him as a prisoner, for some time before the final catastrophe, and caused them to carry him about with them as a captive,
in order to subject the wretch to as much misery as possible, for
as Susquesus said, Muss' "back very sore."

We buried poor Traverse and his chain-bearers near the spring, using one of the same natural hollows in the earth, as that in which we had interred the hunter. On a search, it was ascertained that their arms and ammunition had been carried off, and that the pockets of the dead men had been rifled. The American Indian is seldom a thief, in the ordinary sense of the term; but he treats the property of those whom he slays as his own. In this particular he does not differ materially from the civilized soldier, I believe, plunder being usually considered as a legitimate benefit of war. The Hurons had laid their hands on the compass and chains, for we could discover neither; but they had left the field-book and notes of Traverse, as things that, to them, were useless. In other respects, the visit of the savages to this fatal spot left the appearance of having been hurried.

On this occasion Guert made no attempt at morals or eloquence. The shock had disqualified us all for any thing of the sort, and we discharged our duties with the earnest diligence, and grave thoughtfulness of men who did not know but the next moment might bring themselves into the midst of a scene of deadly strife. We worked hard and a little hastily, and were soon ready to start. It was determined, on a hurried consultation, to follow the trail of the Hurons, as the most certain method of surprising them on the one hand, and of preventing them from surprising us on the other. The Indian would have no difficulty in pursuing the very obvious trail that was left, and which bore all the proofs of having been left by a dozen men.

The reader who is unacquainted with the usages of the American savage, is not to suppose that this party had moved through the forest in a disorderly group, regardless of the nature of the vestiges of their passage left behind them. The native warrior never does that; usually he marches in a line of single files, which has obtained the name of Indian file with us; and whenever there are strong reasons for concealing his numbers, it is his practice for each succeeding man to follow, as nearly as possible, in the footsteps of the warrior who precedes him; thereby rendering a computation difficult, if not impossible. In this manner our foes had evidently marched; but Susquesus, who had been busy examining the marks around the spring, the whole time we were occupied in burying the dead, gave it as his opinion that our enemies could not number less than a dozen warriors. This was not very pleasing intelligence, since it would render success in a conflict next to hopeless. So, at least, I viewed the matter, though Guert saw things differently. This highly intrepid man could not find it in his heart to abandon the idea of driving foes so ruthless out of the country; and I do believe he would have faced a hundred savages at once when we quitted the spring.

The Onondago had no difficulty in following the trail, which led us, at first, for some distance in a line toward Ravensnest, then made a sudden inclination in the direction of the hut. It was probably owing to this circuit, and want of settled purpose in the Hurons, that we did not encounter them on our advance toward the "bloody spring," as the spot where Traverse was slain has been subsequently called.

It was not long ere we found ourselves quite near our own trail, though, perhaps fortunately for us, we did not actually strike it. Had our movement been discovered, doubtless the enemy would have got into our rear, a position in which Indians are always most formidable. As it was, however, we possessed that great advantage ourselves, and pursued our way with so much the greater confidence, knowing full well that danger was only to be apprehended in our front, the quarter on which all our eyes were fixed.

Although our return march was swift, it was silent as that of a train of mourners. Mourners we were, indeed, for it was not possible for human hearts to be so obdurate as to feel insensible to the amount of misery that our late companions must have suffered, and to the suddenness of their fates. No one spoke, and Susquesus had never found us so close on his heels as we kept ourselves all that morning. The foot of the file-leader was scarcely out of its place, ere that of his successor covered the same spot!

The trail led us quite close to the hut, which we reached as near as might be to noon. On approaching the cabin, we used the utmost caution lest our enemies might then be in it, in ambush. The trail did not extend quite to the building, however, but diverged in a westerly direction, from a point that may have been a hundred yards distant from our habitation, though in full view of it. Here we found the signs of a gathering of the party into a cluster, and we inferred that a counsel had been held on the subject of once more going to the hut or of turning aside to pursue some other object. Susquesus made a close examination at this spot, and gave it as his opinion again, that the hostiles must, at least, number the dozen he had already mentioned. Leaving us to watch the signs about our dwelling from covers we took for that purpose, he followed the trail for half a mile, in order to make certain it did not approach the log-house on its opposite side. So far from this proving to be the case, however, he ascertained that it led off in a straight line toward Ravensnest. This was, if any thing, more unpleasant news to Guert and myself, than if the Onondago had brought back a confirmation of his first suspicion that the Hurons might be waiting for us in our own temporary house. Complaints were useless, however, and we smothered our apprehensions as well as we could.

Susquesus was not a warrior to confide entirely in the signs of an open march. Experienced woodsmen frequently left their trails visible expressly to deceive; and the Onondago, who personally knew Muss, as Jaap called his prisoner, was fully aware that he had to deal with a profoundly artful foe. Not satisfied with even what he had seen, he cautioned us about quitting the cover, except under his guidance, and then commenced a mode of approach that was purely Indian, and which, in its way, had much of the merit of the approaches of more civilized besiegers, by means of their intrenchments and zigzags. Our advance was regulated in this way. Each man was told to select the nearest tree that led him toward the hut, and to pass from the old to the new cover, in as rapid and sudden a manner as his agility would allow. By observing this precaution, and by using great activity, we had got within twenty yards of the door of the cabin, in the course of ten minutes. Guert could not submit to this slow, and as he called it, unmanly procedure any longer; but quitting his cover, he now walked straight and steadily to the door of the cabin, threw it open, and announced to us that the place was empty. Susquesus made another close examination around the building, and told us he felt quite certain that the spot had not been visited since we had left it that morning. That was grateful intelligence to us all, since it was the only probable clue by which our enemies could have learned our return to the patent at all.

The question now arose as to future proceedings. Nothing was to be gained by remaining on the property, while prudence and the danger of our friends, united to call us away. We felt it would be a most hazardous thing to attempt reaching Ravensnest; though we felt it was a hazard we were bound to incur. While the matter was talked over, those among us who had any appetite, profited by the halt, to dine. An Indian on a war-path is equally ready to eat or to fast; his powers of endurance both ways, more especially when the food is game, amounting to something wonderful.

While Susquesus and Jaap, in particular, were performing their parts in a very serious manner in this way, and the rest of us were picking up a few morsels, more like men whose moral feelings checked their physical propensities, I caught a distant glimpse of a man's form, as it glided among the trees, at some distance from us. Surprise and awe were so strong in me, that I did not speak, but pointed with a finger eagerly in the necessary direction, in order to let the Onondago see the same object too. Susquesus was not slow in detecting the stranger, however; for I think he must have seen him, even before he was descried by myself. Instead of manifesting any emotion, however, the Onondago did not even cease to eat; but merely nodded his head, and muttered, " Good — now hear news — Jumper come."

Sure enough, it was Jumper; and his appearance in the flesh, not only alive, but unharmed, produced a general shout among us as he came in, on such a long, loping gait, as usually marked a runner's movement. In a moment he was among us, calm, collected, and without motion. He gave no salutation, but seated himself quietly on a log, waiting to be questioned before he spoke; impatience being a womanly weakness.

" Jumper, my honest fellow," cried Guert, not without emotion, for joy was struggling powerfully with his organs of speech, " you are heartily welcome! These devils incarnate, the Hurons, have not injured *you*, at least! "

Liquor had rendered Jumper's faculties somewhat obtuse, in general, though he was now perfectly sober. He gave a sort of dull look of recognition at the speaker, and muttered his answer in a low, sluggish tone:

" Plenty Huron," he said; " clearin' full. Pale-face in fort send Jumper with message."

We should have overwhelmed the fellow with questions, had he not unfolded a corner of his calico shirt, and exhibited several letters, each of which was soon in the hand of the individual to whom it was addressed. Guert, Dirck, and myself, severally got his communication; while there was a fourth, in the hand-writing of Herman Mordaunt that bore the superscription of poor Traverse's name. Subsequent events have placed it in my power to give copies of all the letters thus received. My own was in the following words:

"My dearest father is so much occupied, as to desire *me* to write you this note. Mr. Bulstrode sent an express yesterday, who was bearer of the sad tidings from Ticonderoga. He also announced his own approach; and we expect him, in a horse-litter, this evening. Reports are flying about the settlement, that savages have been seen in our own woods. I endeavor to hope that this is only one of those idle rumors of which we have had so many lately. My father, however, is taking all necessary precautions, and he desires *me* to urge on *you* the necessity of collecting all your party, should you be again at Mooseridge, and of joining us *without delay*. We have heard of your safety, and gallant conduct, through the man sent forward by Mr. Bulstrode; his master having heard of you all, safe in a canoe on the lake, the night after the battle, through a Mr. Lee; a gentleman of great eccentricity of character, though, it is said of much talent, with whom papa happens to be acquainted. I trust this note will find you at your hut, and that we shall see you all, with the least possible delay.

"ANNEKE."

This certainly was not a note to appease the longings of a lover; though I had infinite gratification in seeing the pretty characters that had been traced by Anne Mordaunt's hand, and of kissing the page over which that hand must have passed. But there was a postscript, the part of a letter in which a woman is said always to give the clearest insight into her true thoughts. It was in these words, viz:

"I see that I have underscored the 'me,' when I speak of papa's desire that *I* should write to you, in preference to another. We have gone through one dreadful scene in company, and I confess, Corny, I should feel far happier, if another is to occur, that *you* and *yours* should be with us here, behind the defences of this house, than exposed as you otherwise might be, in the forest. Come to us, then, I repeat, with the least possible de-lay."

This postscript afforded me far more satisfaction than the body of the note; and I was quite as ready to comply with Anneke's request, as the dear girl could be to urge it. Guert's letter was as follows:

"Mr. Mordaunt has commanded Anneke and myself to write to those of your party with whom he fancies each has the most influence, to urge you to come to Ravensnest as speedily as possible. We have received most melancholy news; and a panic prevails among the poor people of this settlement. We learn that Mr. Bulstrode, accompanied by Mr. Worden, is within a few hours' journey of us, and the families of the vicinity are coming to us, frightened and weeping. I do not know that I feel much alarmed myself; my great dependence is on a merciful Providence; but the dread Being on whom I rely, works through human agents; and I know of none in whom I can place more confidence than in Guert Ten Eyck.

" MARY WALLACE."

"By St. Nicholas! Corny, these are such summonses as a man never hesitates about obeying," cried Guert, rising and beginning to replace his knapsack. "By using great diligence we may reach the Nest yet, before the family go to bed, and make not only them but ourselves so much the more comfortable and secure."

Guert had a willing auditor in me; nor was Dirck at all backward about complying. The letters certainly much quickened our impulses, though in fact there remained nothing else to do; unless indeed, we intended to lie out, exposed to all the risks of a vindictive and savage warfare. Dirck's letter was from Herman Mordaunt; and it told the truth in plainer language than it had been related by either of the ladies. Here it is:

"DEAR DIRCK — The savages are certainly approaching us, my young kinsman, and it is for the good of us all to unite our forces. Come in, for God's sake, with your whole party, as speedily as possible. I have had scouts out, and they have all come in with reports that signs of trails in the forest abound. I expect at least a hundred warriors will be upon us by to-morrow, and am making my preparations accordingly. In approaching the Nest, I would advise you to enter the ravine north of the house, and to keep within its cover until you get to its southern termination. This will bring you within a hundred yards of the gate, and greatly increase your chances of entering, should we happen to be invested when you get here. God bless you, dear Dirck, and guide you all safely to your friends.

"HERMAN MORDAUNT.

"Ravensnest, July 11th, 1758."

Guert and I read this letter hastily, before we commenced our march. Then, abandoning the hut and all it contained to the mercy of any who might pass that way, we set off for our point of destination on a quick step, carrying little beside our arms, ammunition, and the food that was necessary to assure our strength.

As before, Trackless led, keeping the Jumper a little on his flank, the danger of encountering foes being now considered to be greatly increased. It was true, we were still in the rear of the party that had committed the deeds at Mooseridge; but the Onondago no longer followed its trail, pursuing a different course, or one that led directly to its object.

CHAPTER XXVII

" My father had a daughter lov'd a man,
   As it might be perhaps, were I a woman,
   I should your lordship."

VIOLA.

As the reader must by this time have a pretty accurate idea
of our manner of marching in the wilderness, I shall not dwell
on this part of our proceeding any longer. On we went, and
at a rapid rate, the guide having abandoned the common route,
which had got to be a pretty visible trail, and taking another
on which, as it appeared to me, he had no other clue than an
instinct. Guert had told Susquesus of the ravine, and how desirable it was to reach it, getting for an answer a quiet nod of
the head, and a low ejaculation. It was understood, however,
that we were to approach Herman Mordaunt's fortress by that
avenue.

It was past the turn of the day when we quitted Mooseridge,
and none of us hoped to reach Ravensnest before dark. It fell
out as we expected, night drawing its veil over the scene about
half an hour before the Trackless plunged into the northern or
forest end of the ravine. Thus far, we had got no evidence
whatever of the proximity of foes. Our march had been silent,
rapid and watchful, but it proved to be perfectly undisturbed.
We knew, however, that the critical portion of it was still before
us; and just as the sun set we had made a halt, in order to look
to our arms. It may now be well to say a word or two on the
subject of the position of Herman Mordaunt's " garrison," as
well of the adjacent settlement. I call Ravensnest the " garrison," for that is the word which New York custom has long
applied to the fortress itself, as well as those who defend it.
Some critics pretend there is authority to justify the practice,
and I see by the dictionaries that they are not entirely in the
wrong.

The Nest stood quite half a mile from the nearest point of
the forest, a belt of trees that fringed the margin and which
filled the cavity of the ravine, excepted. Near it, and in plain

367

sight, was the heart of the settlement itself, which extended in
an east and west direction, fully four miles. This area, however, was cleared only in a settlement fashion, having patches
of virgin forest scattered profusely over its surface. The mill-
lot, as Jason's purchase was termed, lay at the most distant extremity of the view, but as yet the axe had not been applied to
it. I had remarked in my last visit to the place, that standing
before Herman Mordaunt's door, something like a dozen log-
cabins were to be seen at a time in different parts of the settlement, and that this number might have been increased to twenty
by varying the observer's position.

Of course, the whole of the open space was more or less dis-
figured by stumps, dead and girdled trees, charred stubs, log-
heaps, brush, and all the other unseemly accompaniments of
the first eight or ten years of the existence of a new settlement.
This period in the history of a country, may be likened to the
hobbledehoy condition in ourselves, when we have lost the graces
of childhood, without having attained the finished forms of men.

Herman Mordaunt's settlement would have been thought a
strong country in one sense, for a field fight, had there been
men enough to contend with a hostile party of any force. But
I had heard him say that he had but about seventeen rifles and
muskets that could be in the least relied on, inasmuch as some
of his people were Europeans and had no knowledge of fire-
arms, while experience had shown that others on the occurrence
of an alarm, invariably fled to the woods with their families,
instead of rallying round the settlement colors. Such delinquencies usually take place I believe, on all emergencies; love of
life being even a stronger instinct than love of property. Here
and there a sturdy fellow, however, would bar himself in, with a
determination to go for the whole, under his own bark roof;
and occasionally defences were made that would do credit to a
hero.

It should be apparent to those who have any accurate notion of
savage warfare, that the ravine, being, as it was, the only wooded
spot near Herman Mordaunt's fortress, would be the place of
all others most likely to contain an enemy who made his approaches against a garrison by means of natural facilities alone.
We were aware of this; and Guert, who took an active command among us, as we drew near to danger, issued his commands for every man to be on the alert, in order that there
might be no confusion. We were instructed as to the manner

of proceeding the moment an alarm was given; and Guert, who
was a capital mimic, had previously taught us several calls and
rallying signals, all of which were good imitations of the cries
of different tenants of the woods, principally birds. These signals had their origin with the red man, who often resorted to
them, and were said to be more successfully practised by our
own hunters and riflemen than even by those with whom they
originated.

On entering the ravine the order of our march was changed.
While Susquesus and Jumper were still kept in advance, Guert,
Dirck, Jaap and myself moved abreast, and quite close together.
The density of the foliage, and the deep obscurity that prevailed
in the bottom of this dell-like hollow, rendered this precaution
necessary. It soon became so dark, indeed, that our only guide
was the brook that gurgled along the bottom of the ravine, and
which we knew issued into the open ground at its termination,
to join a small river that meandered through some natural meadows to the westward of the Nest, but which in the language
of the country was called a " creek." This abuse of good old
English words, I am sorry to say is getting to be only too common among us; yet I have heard Americans boast that we speak
the language better than the mother country! That we have
no class among us that uses an unintelligible dialect, like that of
Lancashire or Yorkshire, is true enough; and that we have fewer
persons who use decided vulgarisms in the way of false gram-
mar than is the case in England, may be also accurate; but it
might be well for us to correct a great many faults into which
we have certainly fallen, before we declaim with so much confidence about the purity of our English.* To return to the ravine.

We had gone so far in the hollow, dark dell, as to have reached
a point where the faint light of the open ground and the stars

* It is *northern* American to call a small " lake " a " pond," a small " river " a
" creek," even though it should be an " outlet," instead of an " inlet," etc., etc. It
is a more difficult thing than is commonly supposed to make two great nations, each
of which is disposed to innovate, speak the same language with precise uniformity.
The Manhattanese, who have probably fewer of the peculiarities of the inhabitants
of a capital than the population of any other town in the world of four hundred
thousand souls, the consequences of a rapid growth, and of a people who have come
principally from the country, are much addicted to introducing new significations
for words, which arise from their own provincial habits. In Manhattanese parlance,
for instance, a " square " is a " park," or even a " garden " is a " park." A
promenade on the water is a " battery " ! It is a pity that in this humor for
change they have not thought of altering the complex and imitative name of their
town. — EDITOR.

in the firmament became visible to us, when we suddenly found ourselves alongside of the Trackless and Jumper. These Indians had halted; for their quick, jealous, eagle-like glances had detected the signs of enemies. Nor was this discovery very difficult to make, though some pains had actually been taken to conceal what was going on in our front. A party of some forty savages, every one of whom was in his war-paint, had lighted a fire beneath a shelving rock, and were gathered around it at supper. The fire had already done its duty, and was now merely smouldering, throwing a faint, flickering light on the dark, fierce features of the group that was clustered round. We might have approached the spot in any other direction, without seeing the danger in time to avoid it; but a kind Providence had carried the two Indians directly to a point where the dying embers immediately caught their attention, and where they halted as has been said. I do not think we were more than forty yards from this fearful band of savages, when they first met my eye; and hardened as I had certainly somewhat become by the service and scenes I had so lately gone through, I will confess that my blood was a little chilled at the sight.

Our conference was in whispers; there we stood, huddled together beneath a huge oak, the shade of which rendered the darkness that formed our only safeguard, so much the more intense. So close were we in fact, that even Jaap's body was in absolute contact with my own. Susquesus proposed making a *détour* by crossing the brook, which fortunately tumbled down some rocks at this point, making a very favorable noise, and thus pass our enemies, who would not probably end their meal until we had time to reach the " garrison." To this Guert applied his veto. He was of opinion, and I have always thought it was the decision of a man born to be a soldier, that we were exactly in the position we might desire to occupy in order to be of great service to the family, and to strike the enemy with a panic. By attacking, we should certainly surprise the party in our front, and might make such an impression as would induce them to abandon the settlement. Both Dirck and myself coincided in this opinion, which even received the support of Jaap's voice.

" Yes, sah! — yes, Masser Corny, now 'e time to wengeance poor Pete! " he muttered, and that rather louder than was thought quite prudent.

As soon as the Trackless found how things were going, he and Jumper prepared for the conflict as coolly as any of us. Our

arrangements were very simple, and were soon made. We were
to deliver a single fire from the spot where we stood, shout, and
charge with the knife and tomahawk. No time was to be wasted,
however; and instead of remaining near the light, small as it
was, we were to push for the mouth of the ravine, and thence
make the best of our way, singly or in company, as the chance
should offer, to the gate of Ravensnest. In a moment we were
in open files, and had our orders.

"Remember Traverse!" said Guert, sternly, — "remember
poor Sam, and all our murteret frients!"

The reader knows that Guert was apt to be very Dutch, when
much excited. We *did* remember the dead; and I have often
thought, but never knew precisely, that each of us sacrificed a
victim to the manes of our lost companions on that stern occasion.
Our rifles rang, or cracked would be the better word, almost simul-
taneously; a yell arose from the savages around the fire; our own
shouts mingled with that yell, and forward we went, endeavoring to make our numbers appear as if we were a hundred.

One retains but very indistinct notions of a charge like that,
made as it was in the dark, beyond its general characteristics.
We swept directly among the slain and wounded, and I heard
Jaap deal one or two awful blows on the bodies; but no one
opposed us. A moment after we had passed the smouldering
fire, three or four shot were discharged at us, but there was no
sign of their telling on any of our party. The distance from
the fire to the mouth of the ravine might have been a hundred
yards; and the external light, or lesser darkness may be a better expression, served us for a guide. Thither we pushed, fast
as we could, though by no means in compact order.

For this part of the affair, I can only speak for myself. I saw
men moving swiftly among the trees, and supposed them to be
my companions; but we had become separated, it being understood that each man was now to shift for himself. As our
rifles were discharged, and there was no time to reload them,
there was little use, indeed, in any halt. Perceiving this, I did
not issue from the ravine at the brook, but clinging more to its
side, left it at a little height above the level of the adjacent
plain. Here I paused to load, the cover being good, and the
position every way favorable. While thus employed, I had time
to look around me, and to ascertain the situation of things in the
settlement, so far as the hour and the obscurity would permit.

The plain was glimmering with the remains of a dozen large

fires, the ruins of so many log-houses and barns. Their light amounted to no more than to render the darkness of the night distinctly visible, and to afford some small clews to the extent of the ravages that had been already committed. The house of Ravensnest, however, was untouched. There it stood, looking dark and gloomy; for having no external windows, no other light was to be seen than a single candle, that was probably placed in a loophole as a signal. Profound stillness reigned in and around the building, producing a species of mystery that was in itself, under such circumstances, an element of force. There was not light enough to distinguish objects at any distance, and having reloaded my rifle, I thought it wisest to make the best of my way to the gate. At that moment the stillness in my rear seemed to possess something affirmative fearful about it.

It was certainly a somewhat hazardous thing to break cover at such a moment, and under such circumstances; but it was absolutely necessary to incur its risks. My first leap carried me half-way down the declivity, and I was soon on the level land. In my front were two men, one of whom seemed to me to be in the grasp of the other. As they were moving, though slowly, in the direction of the house, I ventured to ask, "Who goes there?"

"Oh, Corny, my lad, is that you?" answered Guert. "Got be praised! you seem unhurt, and are just in time to help me along with this Huron, on whom I blundered in the dark, and have disarmed and captured. Give him a kick or a push, if you please, for the fellow holds back like a hog."

I had too much knowledge of Indian vindictiveness, however, to adopt the means recommended; but seizing the captive by one arm while Guert held the other, we ran him up to the *abbattis* that covered the gate of the " garrison " with very little difficulty. Here we found Herman Mordaunt and a dozen of his people all armed, ready to receive us. They were in expectation of our appearance, both on account of the hour, and on account of the clamor in the ravine, which had been distinctly heard at the house. In less than a minute every body was in, safe and unharmed. The fact was, that our attack had been so sudden as to sweep every thing before it, and the enemy had not time to recover from his panic before we were all snugly housed. Once within the gates of Ravensnest, we ran no risks beyond those which were common to all such log fortresses in the warfare of the wilderness.

It would not be easy for a pen as unskilful as mine, to portray the change from the gloom of the ravine, the short, but
bloody assault, the shouts, the rush, and the retreat of the outer
world, to the scene of domestic security we found within the
Nest, embellished, as was the last, by woman's loveliness and
graces, and in many respects, by woman's elegance. Anneke
and her friend received us in a bright, cheerful, comfortable
apartment, that was rendered so much the more attractive by
their tears and their smiles, neither of which were spared. I
could see that both had been dreadfully agitated; but joy restored their color, and brought back the smiles to their sweet
faces. The situation of the place was such, perhaps, as to render
cheerfulness neither very lasting nor very lively; but the tender-
est female can find her heart suddenly so lightened from its
burden of apprehensions, as to be able to seem momentarily
happy even when environed by the horrors of war. Such, in a
measure, was the character of the reception we now received,
together with a thousand thanks for having so promptly answered their letters in person. The dear creatures had the ingenuity not to seem to ascribe that prompt obedience to their own
request which we had manifested, to any care for ourselves, but
solely to a wish to oblige and protect them. The reader will
understand that all explanations still remained to be made, on
both sides. These soon came, however, facts pressing themselves
on the attention, at such times, with a weight that is irresistible.
The ice was broken by Herman Mordaunt's entering the room,
and speaking to us like one who felt that a great omission had
been made.

"We had closed the gate and set the look-out at the loops
again," he said, "before I ascertained that all your party is not
here. I see nothing of Traverse and his chain-bearers, nor of
Sam or Tom, your hunters. Surely, they are not left behind in
the forest?"

Neither of us three spoke. Our looks must have told the sad
story, for Herman Mordaunt seemed to understand us on the
instant.

"No!" he exclaimed — "Can it be possible? Not *all*, surely!"

"*All*, Mr. Mordaunt, even to my poor slave, Petrus," answered
Guert, solemnly. "They were set upon, while dispersed, I suppose, and have been murdered, while we were still absent on our
expedition."

The dear girls clasped their hands, and I thought Anneke's

pallid lips moved, as if in prayer. Her father shook his head, and for some time he paced the room in silence. Then rousing himself, like one conscious of the necessity of calmness and exertion, he resumed the discourse.

"Thank God, Mr. Bulstrode reached us safely last evening, just after we dispatched the runner; and *he* is beyond the reach of these demons for the present! "

After this we were enabled to converse more connectedly, exchanging such statements as enabled each party to understand the precise condition of the other. We were then carried to Bulstrode's room, for he had expressed a desire to see us as soon as we could be spared. Our fellow-campaigner received us in good spirits, for one in his situation, speaking of the events in front of Ticonderoga sensibly, and without any attempt to conceal the mortification that he felt in common with the whole British empire. His hurt was by no means a bad one; likely to cripple him for a few weeks, but the leg was in no danger.

"I have had the resolution and address, Corny, to work my way into good quarters, this unexpected siege excepted," he observed to me, when the others had withdrawn, leaving us alone. "This rivalry of ours is a generous one, and may now have fair play. If we quit this nest of Herman Mordaunt's without ascertaining the true state of Anneke's feelings, we shall deserve to be condemned to celibacy for the remainder of our lives. There never were two such opportunities of wooing to advantage! "

"I confess our situation does not strike me as being quite as favorable, Mr. Bulstrode," I answered. "Anneke must have too many apprehensions on her own account, and on account of others, to be as sensible to the tender sentiments of love, as might be the case in the peace and security of Lilacsbush."

"Ah! It is very evident you know nothing of the female sex, Corny, by that remark. I will grant you that, unwooed previously, and without any foundation laid, if I may express myself so irreverently, your theory might turn out to be true; but not so under actual circumstances. Here is a young lady in her nineteenth year, who knows she is not only sought, but has long been sought, ay, warmly, ardently sought by two reasonably unobjectionable young men placed in the very situation to have all her sensibilities excited by one or the other, and depend on it, the matter will be determined within this blessed week. If I should prove to be the fortunate man, I hope to be able to manifest a generous sympathy; and *vice versa,* I shall expect the same. Though this sad, sad business before Ty has been a good preparative for humiliation."

I could not avoid smiling at Bulstrode's singular views of our suit; but as Anneke was ever with me an engrossing theme, spite of our situation, which certainly was not particularly appropriate to love, I did not feel equal to quitting it abruptly. The matter was consequently pursued. As I asked Bulstrode to explain himself, I got from him the following account of his theory.

"Why, I reason in this wise, Corny. Anneke loves *one* of us two, beyond all question. That she *loves,* I will swear; her blushes, her beaming eyes, even her beauty is replete with the loveliness of the sentiment. Now, it is not possible that she should love any other person than one of us two, for the simple reason that she has no other suitor. I shall be frank with you, and confess that I think I am the favored fellow, while I dare say, you are just as sanguine and think it is yourself."

"I give you my honor, Major Bulstrode, so presuming, so improper a thought has never —— "

"Yes, yes — I understand all that. You are not worthy of Anne Mordaunt's love, and therefore have never presumed to imagine that she could bestow it on such a poor, miserable, worthless, good-for-nothing fellow as yourself. I have a great deal of the same very proper feeling; but at the same time, each of us is quite confident of his own success, or he would have given up the pursuit long since."

"I do assure you, Bulstrode, any thing but confidence mingles with *my* feelings on this subject. *You* may have reasons for your own security, but I can boast of none."

"I have no other than self-love, of which every man has a just portion for his own comfort and peace of mind. I say that hope is indispensable to love, and hope is allied to confidence. My reasoning on these points is very simple. And now for the peculiar advantages we enjoy for bringing matters to a crisis. In the first place I am hurt, you will understand; suffering under an honorable wound received in open battle, fighting for king and country. Then I have been brought fresh from the field on my litter, into the presence of my mistress, bearing on my person the evidence of my risk, and I hope of my good conduct. There is not one woman in a thousand, if she hesitated between us, that would not decide in my favor on these grounds alone. You have no notion, Corny, how the hearts of these sweet, gentle, devoted, generous little American girls melt to sympathy, at the sufferings of a poor wretch that they know adores them! Make a nurse out of a female, and she is yours, nine times out of ten. This has been a master-stroke of mine, but I hope you will pardon it. Stratagems are excusable in love, as in war."

"I have no difficulty in understanding your policy, Bulstrode; though I confess to some in understanding your frankness. Such as it is, however, I trust you feel certain it will not be abused. Now as to my situation, what peculiar countervailing advantages do I enjoy?"

"Those of a defender. Oh, *that* is a battering-ram of itself! This confounded assault on the settlement, which they tell me is rather serious, and may keep alive apprehensions for some days yet, is a most unlucky thing for me, while it is of great advantage to you. A wounded man cannot excite one-half the interest he otherwise might, when there is a chance that others may be slain every minute. Then the character of a defender is a great deal; and being a generous rival, as I have always told you, Corny, my advice is, to make the most of it. I conceal nothing, and intend to do all I can with my wound."

It was scarcely possible not to laugh at this strangely frank, yet I fully believe strangely sincere communication; for Bulstrode was a humorist, with all his conventionalism and London notions, and was more addicted to saying precisely what he thought, than is common with men of his class. After sitting and chatting with him half an hour longer on the subject of the late military operations, of which he spoke with both feeling and good sense, I took my leave for the night.

"God bless you, Corny," he said, squeezing my hand, as I left him; "improve the opportunity in your own way, for I assure you I shall do it in mine. It is present valor against past valor. If it were not my own case that was concerned, there is not a man living to whom I should more freely wish success."

And I believe Bulstrode did not exceed the truth in his declarations. That I should succeed with Anneke, he did not think, as was apparent to me by his general manner, and the consciousness he must have possessed of his own advantages in the way of rank and fortune, as well as in having Herman Mordaunt's good wishes. Oddly enough, in quitting my rival and, under circumstances so very peculiar, I was accidentally thrown into the presence of my mistress, and that too alone! Anneke was the sole occupant of the little room in which the girls habitually staid, when I returned to it; Guert having induced Mary Wallace to walk with him in the court, the only place the ladies now possessed for exercise; while Herman Mordaunt, Mr. Worden, and Dirck were together in the public room making some arrangement with the confused body of settlers who had crowded into the Nest, for the night-watch. I shall not stop to express the delight I felt at finding Anneke there; nor was it in any degree diminished as I met the soft expression of her sweet eyes, and saw the blushes that suffused her cheek. The conversation I had just held doubtless had its effect; for I determined at once that so favorable an occasion for pressing my suit should not be lost. I was goaded on, if the truth must be told, by apprehension of Bulstrode's wound.

What I said precisely, at the commencement of that interview, is more than I could record, did I think it would redound to my advantage, as I fear it would not; but I made myself understood, which is more, I fancy, than happens to all lovers in such scenes. At first I was confused and a little incoherent, I suspect; but feeling so far got the better of these defects as to enable me to utter what I wished to express. Toward the end, if I spoke in the least as warmly and distinctly as I felt, there must have been some slight touch of eloquence about my manner and language. This being the first occasion, too, on which I had ever had an opportunity of urging my suit very directly, there was so much to be said, so many things to be explained, and so many seemingly slighted occasions to account for, that Anneke had little else to do, for the first ten minutes, but to listen. I have always ascribed the self-possession which my companion was enabled to command during the remainder of this interview, to the time that was thus accorded her to rally her thoughts.

Dear, precious Anneke! How admirably did she behave that memorable night! It was certainly an extraordinary situation in which to speak of love; yet I much question if the feelings be not more likely to be true and natural at such times, than when circumstances admit of more of the expedients of everyday life. I could see that my sweet listener was touched from the moment I commenced, and that her countenance betrayed a tender interest in what I said. Presuming on this, or encouraged by her blushes and her downcast eyes, I ventured to take a hand, and perceived I was not repulsed. Then it was that I found words that actually brought tears to my companion's eyes, and Anneke was enabled to answer me.

"This is so unusual — so extraordinary a time to speak of such things, Corny," she said, "that I hardly know what ought to be my reply. Of one thing, however, I feel certain; persons surrounded as we are, by dangers that may at any instant involve our destruction, have an unusual demand on them for sincerity. Affectation, I hope, I am never much addicted to, and prudery I know *you* would condemn. I have a feeling uppermost at this instant, that I wish to express, yet scarce know how — "

"Do not suppress it, beloved Anneke; be as generous as I am certain you are sincere."

"Corny, it is this. I know we are in danger — very great danger of being overcome, captured, perhaps slain by the ruthless beings who are prowling around our dwelling, and that no one in this house can count on a single day of existence, even with the ordinary vain security of man. Now should any thing befall *you* after this, and I survive you, I should survive for the remainder of my days to mourn your loss, and to feel the keenest regrets that I had hesitated to own how much interest I have long felt in you, and how happy I have been with the consciousness of the preference that you so frankly and honestly avowed in my favor months ago."

As the tears as well as blushes of Anneke accompanied these admissions, it was not possible for me to doubt what I heard. From that moment a world of confidence, and a flow of pure sweet, strong, natural feeling bound us more and more closely together. Guert was in a happy mood to detain Mary Wallace, and business greatly befriended me, as respected the others. More than an hour had I Anne Mordaunt all to myself; and when the heart is open, how much can be uttered and understood on such a subject as love, in an hour of unreserved confidence and of strong feeling! Anneke admitted to me before we separated, that she had often thought of the chivalrous boy who had volunteered to do battle in her behalf, when she was little more than a child herself, and thought of him as a generous-minded girl would be apt to think of a lad under the circumstances. This very early preference had been much quickened and increased by the affair of the lion, and our subsequent intercourse. Bulstrode, that formidable, encouraged rival, encouraged by her father if not by herself, had never interested her in the least, beyond the feeling natural to the affinity of blood; and I might have spared myself many hours of anxious concern on his account could I only have seen what was now so unreservedly told to me. Poor Bulstrode! a feeling of commiseration came over me, as I listened to my companion's assurances that he had never in the least touched her heart, while at the same time, blushing very red, she confessed my own power over it. An expression to this effect even escaped her aloud.

"Have no concern on Mr. Bulstrode's account, Corny," Anneke answered, smiling archly, like one who had well weighed the pros and cons of the whole subject in her own mind; "he may be a little mortified, but his fancy will soon be forgotten in rejoicing that he had not yielded to a passing inclination, and connected himself with a young, inexperienced American girl, who is hardly suited to move in the circles in which his wife must live. I do believe Mr. Bulstrode prefers me, just now, to any other female he may happen to know; but his attachment, if it deserve the name, has not the heart in it, dear Corny, that I know is to be found in yours. We women are said to be quick in discovering when we are really loved, and I confess that my own little experience inclines me to believe that the remark does us no more than justice."

I then spoke of Guert, and expressed a hope that his sincere, obvious, manly devotion, might finally touch her heart, and that my new friend, toward whom, however, I began already to feel as toward an old friend, might finally meet with a return for a passion that I was persuaded was as deep and as sincere as my own; a comparison that I felt was as strong as any I could make in Guert's behalf.

"On this subject, you are not to expect me to say much, Corny," answered Anneke, smiling. "Every woman is the mistress of her own secrets on such a subject; and did I know fully Mary Wallace's mind or wishes in reference to Mr. Ten Eyck, as I do not profess to know either, I should not feel at liberty to betray her, even to you. I have no longer any secret of my own, as respects Corny Littlepage, but must not be expected to be as weak in betraying my whole sex, as I have been in betraying myself!"

I was obliged to be satisfied with this sweet admission and with the knowledge that I had been long loved. When Anneke left me, which at the expiration of more than an hour, she insisted on doing, under the consciousness of all that had passed between us, I had a good deal of difficulty in believing that I was not dreaming. This *ecclaircissement* was so sudden, so totally unexpected I fancy to us both, that well might it so seem to either; yet I fancy we did not part without a deep conviction that both were happier than when we met. I solemnly declare, notwithstanding, that I felt sorrow, almost regret, on behalf of Bulstrode. The poor fellow had been so evidently confident of success only an hour or two before, that I could not have acquainted him with my own success, had he been up, and able to prefer his own suit; in his actual situation, such a procedure would have appeared brutal.

As for Guert Ten Eyck, he rejoined me sadder and more despairing than ever.

" It struck me, Corny, that if Mary Wallace had the smallest inclination in my behalf, she would manifest it at a moment when we may all be said to be hanging between life and deat'. I have often heard it said that the woman who would trifle with a young fellow at a ball, or on a sleigh-ride, and use him like a dog, while every one was laughing and making merry, would come round like one of the weathercocks on our Dutch barns, at a shift of the wind, the instant that distress or unhappiness alighted on her suitor. In other worts, that the very girl who would be capricious and uncertain, in happiness and prosperity, would suddenly become tender and truthful, as soon as sorrow touched the man who wished to have her. On the strength of this, then, I thought I would urge Mary, to the best of my abilities, and you know they are no great matter, Corny, to give me only a glimmering of hope; but without success. Not a syllable more could I get out of her than that the time was unseasonable to talk of such things; and I do think I should be ready to go and meet these Huron devils, hand to hand, were it not for the fact that the very girl who thus remonstrated, staid with me quite two hours, listening to what I had to say, though I spoke of nothing else. There was a crumb of comfort in that, lad, or I do not understand human nature."

There was truly. Still I could not but compare Anne Mordaunt's generous confessions, under the influence of the same facts, and fancy that the prospects of the simple-minded, warm-hearted, manly young Albanian, were far less flattering than my own.

CHAPTER XXVIII

" Between two worlds life hovers like a star,
    'Twixt night and morn, upon the horizon's verge:
How little do we know that which we are!
    How less what we may be! The eternal surge,
Of time and tide rolls on, and bears afar
    Our bubbles: as the old burst, new emerge,
Lashed from the foam of ages; while the graves
    Of empires heave but like some passing wave."

                                          BYRON.

IT was now announced by Herman Mordaunt in person, that the watch was set for the night, and that each man might seek his rest. The crowded state of the Nest was such as to render it no easy matter to find a place in which to sleep, straw being our only beds. At length we found our pallets, such as they were; and spite of all that had passed that evening, truth compels me to admit that I was soon in a profound sleep. There was no exception to this rule among the Mooseridge party, I believe, fatigue proving to be more powerful than either successful love, unsuccessful love, or personal apprehension.

It was about three o'clock when I felt a significant pressure of the arm, such as one gives when he especially wishes to attract attention. It was Jason Newcome, employed in awakening the men of the house, without giving such an alarm as might reach the ears without. In a few minutes every body was up and armed.

As the morning, just before the appearance of light, when sleep is heaviest, is the hour when savages usually attack, no one was surprised at these preparations, which were understood to be ordered by Herman Mordaunt, who was afoot, and on the look-out himself, at a place favorable to observation. In the mean time, we men, three or four-and-twenty in all, assembled in the court, in waiting for a summons to the gate, or the loop. Jason had executed his trust so dexterously, that neither female nor child knew any thing of our movement; all sleeping,

381

or seeming to sleep, in the security of a peaceful home. I took an occasion to compliment the ex-pedagogue and new miller, on the skill he had shown; and we fell into a low discourse, in consequence.

"I have been thinking that this warfare may put a new face on these settlements, Corny," continued Jason, after we had conversed some little time, "more especially as to the titles."

"I cannot see how they are to be affected, Mr. Newcome, unless the French should happen to conquer the colony, a thing not very likely to happen."

"That's just it; exactly what I mean, as to principle. Have not these Hurons conquered this particular settlement? I say they have. They are in possession of the whull of it, this house excepted; and it appears to me that if we ever get repossession, it will be by another conquest. Now, what I want to know is this — does not conquest give the conquerors a right to the conquered territory? I have no books here, yet; but I'm dreadful forgetful, or I *have* read that such is the law."

I may say that this was the first direct demonstration that Jason ever made on the property of Herman Mordaunt. Since that time he has made many more, some of which I, or he who may be called on to continue this narrative, will probably relate; but I wish to record, here, this as the first in a long series of attempts which Jason Newcome has practised, in order to transfer the fee-simple of the mill-lot at Ravensnest, from the ownership of those in whom it is vested by law, to that of his own humble but meritorious person.

I had little time to answer this very singular sort of reasoning; for just then Herman Mordaunt appeared among us, and gave us serious duty to perform. The explanations with which his orders were preceded, were these. As had been anticipated, the Indians had adopted the only means that could prove effective against such a fortress as the Nest without the aid of artillery. They were making their preparations to set the building on fire, and had been busy all night in collecting a large amount of pine-knots, roots, etc., which they had succeeded in piling against the outer logs, at the point where one wing touched the cliff, and where the formation of the ground enabled them to approach the building without incurring much risk. Their mode of proceeding is worthy of being related. One of the boldest and most skilful of their number had crept to the spot, and posted himself so close to the logs as to be safe from observation,

as well as reasonably safe from shot. His associates had then
extended to him one end of a long pole, they standing below, some
on a shelf of the cliff, and the rest on the ground; all being
safe from harm so long as they kept close to their respective
covers. Thus disposed, these children of the forest passed
hours in patient toil, in forwarding by means of a basket, the
knots, and other combustibles up to the warrior, who kept
his position close under the building, and who piled them in
the way most favorable to his object.

Susquesus had the merit of discovering the projected attempt,
the arrangements for which had completely escaped the vigilance
of the sentinels. It would seem that the Onondago, aware of the
artifices of the red man, and acquainted in particular with the
personal character of Jaap's friend, Muss, did not believe the
night would go by without some serious attempt upon the house.
The side of the cliff was much the weakest point of the fortress,
having no other protection than the natural obstacle of the rocks
— which were not inaccessible, though somewhat difficult of
ascent — and the low picketing already mentioned. Under such
circumstances, the Indian felt certain the assault would be made
on that side. Placing himself on watch, therefore, he discovered
the first attempts of the Hurons, but did not let them be known
to Herman Mordaunt until they were nearly completed; his
reason for the delay being the impatience of the pale-faces,
which would not have suffered the enemy to accomplish his
object, so far as preparations were concerned — the thing of all
others he himself thought to be the most desirable. By allowing the Hurons to waste their time and strength in making
arrangements for an assault that was foreseen, and which might
be met and defeated, a great advantage was obtained; whereas,
by driving them prematurely from an artifice they were known to
be engaged in, they would have recourse to another, and the
difficulty of discovery would be added to our other disadvantages.
So Susquesus reasoned, as we said at the time; and it is certain that so he acted.

But the time had come to meet these covert preparations.
Herman Mordaunt now held a consultation on the subject of
our proceedings. The question submitted was, whether we
ought to let the Hurons go any further; whether we should
shoot the adventurous savage who was known still to be posted
under the logs of the house, and scatter his pile of knots by a
sortie; or whether it were wiser to let the enemy proceed to

the extremity of actually lighting his fire, before we unmasked. Something was to be said in favor of each plan. By shooting the savage who had made a lodgment under our walls, and scattering his pile, we should unquestionably defeat the present attempt; but in all probability another would be made on the succeeding night; whereas by waiting to the last moment, such an effectual repulse might be given to our foes, as would at once terminate their expedition.

On consultation, and weighing all the points as they offered, it was decided to adopt the latter policy. But one spot commanded a view of the pile at all, and that was a loop that had been cut only the day before, and which looked directly down on the place, from a projection that existed in the second story, and which ran around the whole building. These projections were common enough in the architecture of the provinces at that day, being often adopted in exposed positions purposely to afford the means of protecting the inferior and external portions of the dwellings. The Nest possessed this advantage, though the loops necessary to complete the arrangement, had only quite recently been cut. At this loop, then, I stationed myself for a short time, watching what was going on below. The night was dark, but there was no difficulty in distinguishing the pile of knots, which to me seemed several feet high, besides being of some length, or in noting the movements of the Indian who had built it. At the moment I took my stand at the loop, this man was actually engaged in setting fire to his combustibles.

For several minutes Guert and I watched our enemy while he was thus employed, for the Huron was obliged to proceed with the utmost caution, lest a light prematurely shed around should betray him. He cautiously lighted his knots quite within the pile, having left a place for that purpose; and his combustibles were well in flames before the latter began to throw their rays to any distance. We had a quantity of water provided in the room from which we beheld all those movements, and might at any time have extinguished the fire by pouring a stream through our loop, provided we did not wait too long. But Guert objected to "spoiling the sport," as he called it, insisting that the logs of the house would be slow to ignite, and that we might at any moment scatter the knots, by a rapid sortie. His wish was, to let the enemy proceed in his designs as far as would be at all safe, in order to render his defeat more overwhelming.

Owing to our position, directly over his head, we had no

chance to see the face of the incendiary while he was thus engaged. At length he cast a glance upward as if to note the effect of the flames, which were beginning to throw their forked tongues above the pile, when we both recognized Jaap's prisoner, Muss. The sight proved too much for Guert's philosophy, and thrusting the muzzle of his rifle through the loop, he blazed away at him without much regard to aim. This report was a sort of signal for action, the whole house, and all the outer world appearing to be in a clamor in an instant. I had no means of seeing Muss, but some of our look-outs, who had him in view most of the time, told me, after all was over, that the fellow seemed much astonished at the suddenness of this assault; that he gazed up at the loop an instant, uttered a loud exclamation, then yelled the war-whoop at the top of his voice, and went bounding off into the darkness, like a buck put up unexpectedly from his lair. The fields all around the Nest seemed to be alive with whooping demons. Herman Mordaunt had done little toward embellishing the place; and stumps were standing in hundreds all about it, many having been left within twenty yards of the buildings. It now seemed as if every one of these stumps had an Indian warrior lodged behind it; while bands of them appeared to be leaping about in the gloom under the rocks. At one time I fancied we must be surrounded by hundreds of these ruthless foes, though I now suppose that their numbers were magnified by their activity and their infernal yells. They manifested no intention to attack, nevertheless, but kept screaming around us in all directions, occasionally discharging a rifle, but as a whole, waiting the moment when the flames should have done their work.

Considering the fearful circumstances in which he was placed, Herman Mordaunt was wonderfully collected. For myself, I felt as if I had fifty lives to lose, Anneke being uppermost in my thoughts. The females, however, behaved uncommonly well; making no noise, and using all the self-command they could assume, in order not to distract the exertions of their husbands and friends. Some of the wives of the sturdy settlers indeed actually exhibited a species of stern courage that would have done credit to soldiers; appearing in the court armed, and otherwise rendering themselves useful. It often happened that women of this class, by practising on deer, and wolves, and bears, got to be reasonably expert with fire-arms, and did good service in attacks on their dwellings. I remarked in all the commoner class of females that night, a sort of fierce hostility to their savage foes, in whom they doubtless saw only the murderers of children, and wretches who made no distinction of sex or age, in pursuing their heartless warfare. Many of them appeared like the dams of the inferior animals when their young were in danger.

An interval of ten or fifteen minutes must have occurred between the moment when Guert discharged his rifle and that in which the battle really began. All this time the fire was gathering head, our tardy attempts to extinguish it proving a complete failure. But little apprehension was felt on this account, however, the flames proving an advantage, by casting their light far into the fields, and even below the rocks, while they did not reach the court at all; thus placing a portion of the enemy, should they venture to attack, under a bright light, while it left us in darkness. The only point, however, at which we could fear a serious assault, was on the side of the rocks, where the court had no other protection than the low, but close and tolerably strong picket. Fortunately, the formation of the ground on that side prevented one who stood on the meadows below from firing into the court from any point within the ordinary range of the rifle. It was this circumstance that had determined the site of the garrison.

Such was the state of things when Anneke's own girl came to ask me to go to her mistress, if it were possible for me to quit my station, were it only for a minute. Having no particular duty to perform, there was no impropriety in complying with a request which, in itself, was every way so grateful to my feelings. Guert was near me at the time, and heard what the young negress said; this induced him to inquire if there was no message for himself; but even at that serious moment, Mary Wallace did not relent. She had been kinder than common in manner, the previous night, as the Albanian had admitted; but at the same time, she had appeared to distrust her own resolution so much as even to give less direct encouragement than had actually escaped her on previous occasions.

I found Anneke expecting me in that little parlor where I had recently listened to her confessions of tenderness the evening before. She was alone, the instinct of her sex teaching her the expediency of having no witness to the feelings and language that might escape two hearts that were united as were ours, under circumstances so trying. The dear girl was pale as death when I entered; she had doubtless been thinking of the approaching conflict and of what might be its frightful consequences; but my presence instantly caused her face to be suffused with blushes, it being impossible for her sensitive mind not to revert to what had so lately occurred. This truth to the instinctive principle of her nature could hardly be extinguished in woman, even at the stake itself. Notwithstanding the liveliness and varying character of her feelings, Anneke was the first to speak.

"I have sent for you, Corny," she said, laying a hand on her heart, as if to quiet its throbbings, " to say one word in the way of caution — I hope it is not wrong."

"You *can* do nothing wrong, beloved Anneke," I answered; " or nothing that would seem so in my eyes. Be not thus agitated. Your fears have increased the danger, which we consider as trifling. The risks Guert, Dirck and myself have already run, are tenfold those which now beset us."

The dear girl submitted to have an arm of mine passed around her waist, when her head dropped on my breast, and she burst into tears. Enabled by this relief to command her feelings a little, it was not long ere Anneke raised herself from the endearing embrace I felt impelled to give her, though still permitting me to hold both her hands; and she looked up into my face with the full confidence of affection, renewing the discourse.

"I could not suffer you to engage in this terrible scene, Corny," she said, "without one word, one look, one sign of the interest I feel in you. My dear, dear father has heard all; and though disappointed, he does not disapprove. You know how warmly he has wished Mr. Bulstrode for a son, and can excuse that preference; but he desired me not ten minutes since, as he left me, after giving me his kiss and his blessing, to send for you and say that he shall hereafter look upon you, as my and his choice. Heaven alone knows whether we are to be permitted to meet again, dear Corny; but should that never be granted us, I feel that it will relieve your mind to know that we shall meet as the members of one family."

"We are the only children of our parents, Anneke, and our union will gladden their hearts almost as much as it can gladden our own."

"I have thought of this already. I shall have a mother, now; a blessing I hardly ever knew."

"And one that will dearly, dearly love you, as I know by

her own opinions, again and again expressed in my presence."

"Thank you, Corny — and thanks to that respected parent, too. Now go, Corny; I am fearful this selfish gratification only adds to the danger of the house — go; I will pray for your safety."

"One word, dearest; — poor Guert! — you cannot know how disappointed he is, that I alone should be summoned here at such a moment."

Anneke seemed thoughtful, and it struck me she was a little distressed.

"What can I do after this?" she said, after a short pause. "A woman's judgment and her feelings may not impel her the same way; then Mary Wallace is a girl who appreciates propriety so highly!"

"I understand you, Anneke. But Guert is of so noble a disposition, and acknowledges all his defects so meekly, and with so much candor. Man cannot love woman better than he loves Mary Wallace. Her extreme prudence is a virtue in his eyes, even while he suffers by it."

"I cannot change Mary Wallace's nature, Corny," said Anneke, smiling sadly, and, as I fancied, in a way that said "Were it I, the virtues of Guert should soon outweigh his defects;" "but Mary will be Mary, and we must submit. Perhaps to-morrow may bring her wavering mind to something like decision; for these late events have proved greatly Mr. Ten Eyck's friends. But Mary is an orphan, and prudence has been taught her as her great protection. Now go, Corny, lest you be missed."

The dear girl parted from me hurriedly, but not without strong manifestation of feeling. I folded her to my heart; that being no moment for affectations or conventional distance; and I know *I* was, while I trusted Anneke might be, none the less happy for remembering we had exchanged these proofs of mutual attachment.

Just as I reached the court, I heard a yell without, which my experience before Ty had taught me was the whoop the Hurons give when they attack. A rattling fire succeeded, and we were instantly engaged in a hot conflict. Our people fought under one advantage, which more than counterbalanced the disadvantage of their inferiority in numbers. While two sides of the buildings, including that of the meadows, or the one on which an assault could alone be successful, were in bright light, the court still remained sufficiently dark to answer all the purposes of defence. We could see each other, but could not be distinguished at any distance. Our persons, when seen from without, must have been confounded too, with the waving shadows of the pickets.

As I approached the pickets, through the openings of which our people were already keeping up a dropping fire on the dark-looking demons who were leaping about on the meadows below, I learned from Herman Mordaunt himself, who received me by an affectionate squeeze of the hand, that a large body of the enemy was collected directly under the rocks; and that Guert had assumed the duty of dislodging them. He had taken with him, on his service, Dirck, Jaap, and three or four more of the best men, including both of our Indians. The manner in which he proposed to effect this object was bold, and like the character of the leader of the party. As so much depended on it, and on its success, I will explain a few of its more essential details.

The front of the house ranged north and south, facing westward. The two wings consequently extended east and west. The fire had been built at the verge of the cliff, and at the northeast angle of the building. This placed the north and east sides of the square in light, while it left the west and south in deep darkness. The gate opening to the west, it was not a very hopeless thing to believe it practicable to lead a small party round the south-west angle of the house, to the verge of the cliff, where the formation of the ground would allow of a volley's being given upon those savages who were believed to be making a lodgment directly beneath our pickets, with a view of seizing a favorable moment to scale them. On this errand, then, Herman Mordaunt now gave me to understand my friends had gone.

"Who guards the gate, the while?" I asked, almost instinctively.

"Mr. Worden, and your old acquaintance and my new tenant, Newcome. They are both armed, for a parson will not only fight the battles of the spirit, but he will fight those of the field, when concerned. Mr. Worden has shown himself a man in all this business."

Without replying, I left Herman Mordaunt, and proceeded to the gate myself, since there was little to be done in the court. *There* we were strong enough; stronger perhaps than was

necessary; but I greatly distrusted Guert's scheme, the guard
at the gate, and most of all the fire.

I was soon at Mr. Worden's side. There the reverend gentleman was, sure enough, with Jason Newcome at his elbow.
Their duty was, to keep the gate in that precise condition in
which it could be barred, or unbarred, at the shortest notice,
as friends or foes might seek admission. The parties appeared
to be fully aware of the importance of the trust they filled, and
I asked permission to pass out. My first object was the fire,
for it struck me Herman Mordaunt felt too much confidence in
his means of extinguishing it, and that our security had been
neglected in that quarter. I was no sooner outside the buildings, therefore, than I turned to steal along the wall to the
north-west corner, where alone I could get a view of the dangerous pile.

The brightness of the glare that was gleaming over the fields
and stumps that came within the compass of the light from the
fire, added to my security by the contrast, though it did not
tell well for that particular source of danger. The dark stumps,
many of which were charred by the fires of the clearing, and
were absolutely black, seemed to be dancing about in the fields,
under the waving light, and twice I paused to meet imaginary
savages ere I had gained the corner of the house. Each alarm,
however, was idle, and I succeeded in obtaining the desired
view. Not only were the knots burning fiercely, but a large
sheet of flame was clinging to the logs of the house, menacing
us with a speedy conflagration. The danger would have been
greater, but a thunder-shower had passed over the settlement
only an hour before we were alarmed, and coming from the
north, all that side of the house had been well drenched with
rain. This occurred after "Muss" had commenced his pile, or
he might have chosen another side of the building. The deep
obscurity of that gust, however, was probably one of the means
of his success. He must have been at work during the whole
continuance of the storm.

I was not absent from the gate two minutes. That brief
space was sufficient for my first purpose. I now desired Jason
to enter the court and to tell Herman Mordaunt not to delay a
moment in applying the means for extinguishing the flames.
There was greater danger from them than there possibly could
be from any other attack upon the pickets, made in the darkness of the morning. Jason was cool by temperament, and he

was a good agent to be employed on such a duty. Promising to be quick, he left us, and I turned my face toward Guert and his party. As yet, nothing had been heard of the last. This very silence was a source of alarm, though it was difficult to imagine the adventurer had met with an enemy, since such a collision must have been somewhat noisy. A few scattering shots, all of which came from the west side of the buildings, and the flickering light of the fire, were the only interruptions to the otherwise deathlike calm of the hour.

The same success attended me in reaching the south-west as in reaching the north-west angle of the house. To me it seemed as if the savages had entirely abandoned the fields in my vicinity. When I took my stand at this corner of the building, I found all its southern side in obscurity, though sufficient light was gleaming over the meadows to render the ragged edges of the cliff visible in that direction. I looked along the log walls to this streak of light, but could see no signs of my friends. I was certain they were not under the house, and began to apprehend some serious indiscretion on the part of the bold Albanian. While engaged in endeavoring to get a clew to Guert's movements, by devouring every dark object I could perceive with my eyes, I felt an elbow touched lightly, and saw a savage in his half-naked, fighting attire at my side. I could see enough to ascertain this, but could not distinguish faces. I was feeling for my hunting-knife, when the Trackless's voice stayed my hand.

" He wrong," said the Onondago, with emphasis. " Head too young — hand good — heart good — head very bad. Too much fire — dark here — much better."

This characteristic criticism on poor Guert's conduct served to tell the whole story. Guert had put himself in a position in which the Onondago had refused to remain; in other words he had gone to the verge of the cliff, where he was exposed to the light of the fire, and where he was necessarily in danger of being seen. Still, no signs of him were visible, and I was on the point of moving along the south side of the building to the margin of the rocks, when the Trackless again touched my arm, and said " There! "

There our party was, sure enough! It had managed to reach the verge of the rocks at a salient point, which placed them in an admirable position for raking the enemy, who were supposed to be climbing to the pickets with a view to a sudden spring, but at a dangerous distance from the buildings. The darkness had been the means of their reaching that point, which was about a hundred yards from the spot where I had expected to find them, and admirably placed for the intended object. The whole procedure was so much like Guert's character, that I could not but admire its boldness, while I condemned its imprudence. There was, however, no time to join the party, or to warn its leader of the risks he ran. We, who stood so far in the rear, could see and fully appreciate all the danger, while he probably did not. There the whole party of them stood, plainly though darkly drawn in high relief against the light beyond, each poising his rifle and making his disposition for the volley. Guert was nearest to the verge of the rocks, actually bending over them; Dirck was close at his side; Jaap just behind Dirck; Jumper close at Jaap's elbow; and four of the settlers, bold and hardy men, behind the Oneida.

I could scarcely breathe for painful expectation, when I saw Guert and his companions thus rising from the earth, bringing their entire figures in front of the background of light. I could have called out to warn them of the danger they ran; but it would have done no good, nor was there time for remonstrances. Guert must have felt he occupied a dangerous position, and what he did was done very promptly. Ten seconds after I saw the dark forms, all their rifles were discharged as it might be at a single crack. One instant passed in deathlike stillness, through all the fields, and in the court; then came a volley from among the stumps, at a little distance from our side of the building, and the adventurers on the rocks, or those that could, rushed toward the gate. Two of the settlers, however, and the Oneida, I saw fall myself. The last actually leaped upward into the air, and went down the cliff. But Guert, Dirck, Jaap, and the other two settlers had moved away. It was at that moment that my ears were filled with such yells as I had not supposed the human throat could raise, and all the fields on our side of the house seemed alive with savages. To render the scene more appalling, that was the precise instant when the water, previously provided by Herman Mordaunt, fell upon the flames, and the light vanished almost as one extinguishes a candle. But for this providential coincidence, there was scarce a chance for the escape of one of the adventurers. As it was, rifle followed rifle from among the stumps, though it was no longer with any certain aim.

The battle had now become a *mêlée*. The savages went
leaping and whooping forward in the darkness, and heavy blows
were given and taken. Guert's clear, manly voice was heard
rising above the clamor, encouraging his companions to press
through the throng of their assailants, in tones full of confidence.
Both the Trackless and myself discharged our rifles at the foremost of the Hurons, and each certainly brought down his man,
but it was not easy to see what we could do next. To stand aloof
and see my friends borne down by numbers was impossible,
however, and Susquesus and myself fell upon the enemy's rear.
This charge of ours had the appearance of a sortie, and it produced a decided effect on the result, opening a passage by which
Dirck and the two settlers issued from the throng and joined us.
This was no sooner done than we all had to stand at bay, retreating little by little as we could. The result would still have
been doubtful, even after we had succeeded in reaching the
south-western angle of the building, had it not been for a forward movement on the part of Herman Mordaunt, at the head
of half a dozen of his settlers. This reinforcement came into
the affair with loaded rifles, and a single discharge, given as
soon as we were in a line with our friends, caused our assailants
to vanish as suddenly as they had appeared. On reflecting on
the circumstances of that awful night, in after-life, I have thought
that the force in the rear of the Hurons began to melt away,
even before Herman Mordaunt's support was received, leaving
their front weak and unsustained. At any rate, the enemy fled
to their covers, as has just been related, and we entered the gate
in a body, closing and barring it as soon as possible.

I can scarcely describe the change that had come over the
appearance of things in that eventful night. The fire was extinguished, even to the embers, and deep darkness had succeeded
to the glimmering, waving red light of the flames. The yells,
and whoops, and screams, and shouts — for our men had frequently thrown back the defiance of their foes in cheers — were
done; a stillness as profound as that of the grave reigning over
the whole place. The wounded seemed ashamed even to groan;
but our hurt, of whom there were four, went into the house to
be cared for, stern and silent. No enemy was any longer to
be apprehended beneath the pickets, for the streak of morning
was just appearing above the forest, in the east, and Indians
rarely attack under the light of day. In a word, *that* night at
least was passed, and we were yet protected by Providence.

Herman Mordaunt now bethought him of ascertaining his precise situation, the extent of his own loss, and as far as possible of that which we had inflicted on the enemy. Guert was called for to aid in this inquiry, but no Guert was to be found! Jaap, too, was absent. A muster was had, and then it was found that Guert Ten Eyck, Jaap Satanstoe, Gilbert Davis and Moses Mudge were all wanting. The Jumper, too, did not appear; but I accounted for him, and for the two settlers named, having actually seen them fall. Day returned to us slowly, while agitated by the effect of these discoveries; but it brought no relief. We soon ventured to reopen the gates, knowing no Indian would remain very near the building while it was light; and having examined all the dangerous covers, we passed outside of the court with confidence, in quest of the bodies of our friends. Not an Indian was seen, Jumper excepted. The Oneida lay at the foot of the rocks, dead, and scalped; as did Davis and Mudge on the summit. Every thing else human had disappeared. Dirck was confident that six or seven of the Hurons fell by the volley from the cliff, but the bodies had been carried off. As to Guert and Jaap, no traces of them remained, dead or alive.

CHAPTER XXIX

" She looked on many a face with vacant eye,
On many a token without knowing what;
She saw them watch her without asking why,
And reck'd not who around her pillow sat;
Not speechless, though she spoke not; not a sigh
Relieved her thoughts: dull silence and quick chat
Were tried in vain by those who served; she gave
No sign, save breath, of having left the grave."

BYRON.

IT was a most painful moment to me, when Herman Mordaunt, an hour after all these facts were established, came to summon me to the presence of Anneke and Mary Wallace. One gleam of joy, one ray of the sunshine of the heart, shone on Anneke's sweet countenance as she saw me unharmed enter the room, but it quickly disappeared in the strong sympathy she felt for the sufferings of her friend. As for Mary Wallace, death itself could hardly have left her more colorless, or with features more firmly impressed with the expression of mental suffering. Anneke was the first to speak.

"God be praised that this dreadful night is passed and you and my dearest father are spared!" the precious girl said, with fervor pressing the hand that had taken one of hers, in both her own. "For this much, at least, we can be grateful; would I could add for the safety of us all!"

"Tell me the worst at once, Mr. Littlepage," added Mary Wallace; "I can bear any thing better than uncertainty. Mr. Mordaunt says that you know the facts better than any one else, and that you must relate them. Speak, then, though it break my heart to hear it! — is he killed?"

"I hope, through Heaven's mercy, not. Indeed I think not; though I fear he must be a prisoner."

"Thank you for that, dear, dear Mr. Littlepage! Oh! thank you for that, from the bottom of my heart. But may they not torture him? Do not these Hurons torture their prisoners? Conceal nothing from me, Corny; you cannot imagine how

395

much self-command I have, and how well I can behave. Oh! conceal nothing."

Poor girl! At the very moment she was boasting of her fortitude and ability to endure, her whole frame was trembling from head to foot, her face was of the hue of death, and the smile with which she spoke was frightfully haggard. That pent-up passion, which had so long struggled with her prudence, could no longer be suppressed. That she really loved Guert, and that her love would prove stronger than her discretion, I had not doubted, now, for some months; but never having before witnessed the strength of any feeling that had been so long and so painfully suppressed, I confess that this exhibition of a suffering so intense, in a being so delicate, so excellent, and so lovely, almost unmanned me. I took Mary Wallace's hand and led her to a chair, scarce knowing what to say to relieve her mind. All this time, her eye never turned from mine, as if she hoped to learn the truth by the aid of the sense of sight alone. How anxious, jealous, distrustful, and yet beseeching was that gaze!

"Will he be tortured?" She rather whispered huskily, than asked aloud.

"I trust, by God's mercy, not. They have taken my slave, Jaap, also; and it is far more probable that *he* would be the victim in such a case, than Mr. Ten Eyck——"

"Why do you call him Mr. Ten Eyck? You have always called him Guert, of late — you are his friend — you think well of him — you cannot be less his friend, now that he is miserable, than when he was happy, and the pride of all human eyes, in his strength and manly beauty!"

"Dear Miss Wallace, compose yourself, I do entreat of you — no one will cling to Guert longer than I."

"Yes; I have always thought this — always *felt* this. Guert cannot be low, or mean in his sentiments, while an educated gentleman like Corny Littlepage is his friend. I have written to my aunt, and we must not be too hasty in our judgments. The spirit and follies of youth will soon be over, and then we shall see a shining character in Guert Ten Eyck. Is not this true, Anneke?"

Anneke knelt at the side of her friend, folded her in her arms, drew the quivering head down upon her own sympathizing bosom, and held it there a moment, in the very attitude of protecting, solacing love. After a brief pause, Mary Wallace burst into tears, and I have ever thought that relief, under God's mercy, saved her reason. In a few minutes, the sufferer became more calm, when she retired into herself, as was her wont, leaving Anneke and me to discuss the subject.

After turning all the chances and probabilities in our minds, I promised my companions not to lose a moment, but to use immediate means of ascertaining all that could be ascertained, in Guert's behalf, and of doing every thing that could be done to save him.

"You will not deceive me, Corny," whispered Mary Wallace, pressing my hand at leave-taking, in both her own. "I know I can depend on *you*, for he *boasts* of being your friend."

Anneke's painful smile added force to this request, and I tore myself away, unwilling to quit such a sufferer, yet unable to remain. Herman Mordaunt was seen conversing with Susquesus in the court, and I joined him at once, determined to lose no time.

"I was speaking to the Trackless on this very subject," answered Herman Mordaunt, as soon as I had explained my purpose, "and am now waiting for his answer. Do you think it, then, safe to send a messenger out to the Hurons, in order to inquire after our friends, and to treat with them?"

"No send? — Why not?" returned the Indian. "Red man glad to see messenger. Go when he want; come back when he want. How can make bargain, if scalp messenger?"

I had heard that the most savage tribes respected a messenger; and, indeed, the necessity of so doing was, of itself, a sort of security that such must be the case. It was true, that the bearer of a flag might be in more danger, on such an errand, than would be the case in a camp of civilized men; but these Canada Indians had been long serving with the French, and their chiefs, beyond a question, had obtained some of the notions of pale-face warfare. Without much reflection, therefore, and under an impulse in behalf of my friend, and my slave — for Jaap's fate was of lively interest with me — I volunteered to bear a flag myself. Herman Mordaunt shook his head, and seemed reluctant to comply.

"Anneke would hardly pardon me for consenting to that," he answered. "You must remember now, Corny, that a very tender and sensitive heart is bound up in you, and you must no longer act like a thoughtless single man. It would be far better to send this Onondago, if he will agree to go. He under-

stands the red men, and will be able to interpret the omens
with more certainty than any of us. What say you, Susquesus;
will you be a messenger to the Hurons?"

"Sartain; — why no go, if he want? Good to be messenger,
sometime. Where wampum — what tell him?"

Thus encouraged, we deliberated together, and soon had Susquesus in readiness to depart. As for the Indian, he laid
aside all his arms, washed the war-paint from his face, put a
calico shirt over his shoulders, and assumed the guise of peace.
We gave him a small white flag to carry, feeling certain that
the Huron chiefs must understand its meaning; and thinking it might be better, in bearing a message from pale-faces,
that he who carried it should have a pale-face symbol of his
errand. Susquesus found some wampum, too; having as much
faith in that, probably, as in any thing else. He then set
forth, being charged to offer liberal ransom to the Hurons,
for the living, uninjured bodies of Guert Ten Eyck and Jaap
Satanstoe.

We entertained no doubt that the enemy would be found in
the ravine, for that was the point in every respect most favorable to the operations of the siege; being near the house, having
perfect cover, possessing water, wood, and other conveniences.
From that point the Nest could be watched, and any favorable
chance improved. Thither, then, Susquesus was told to proceed;
though it was not thought advisable to fetter one so shrewd
with too many instructions. Several of us accompanied the
Onondago to the gate, and saw him moving across the fields
toward the wood, in his usual loping trot. A bird could scarcely
have flown more directly to its object.

The half-hour that succeeded the disappearance of Susquesus
in the mouth of the ravine, was one of intensely painful sus-
pense. We all remained without the gate waiting the result,
including Dirck, Mr. Worden, Jason, and half-a-dozen of the
settlers. At length the Onondago reappeared; and to our great
joy, a group followed him, in which were both the prisoners.
The last were bound, but able to walk. This party might have
contained a dozen of the enemy, all of whom were armed. It
moved slowly out of the ravine, and ascended to the fields
that were on a level with the house, halting when about four
hundred yards from us. Seeing this movement, we counted out
exactly the same number of men, and went forward, halting at
a distance of two hundred yards from the Indians. Here we

waited for our messenger, who continued on, after the Hurons had come to a stand. Thus far every thing looked propitious.

"Do you bring us good news?" Herman Mordaunt eagerly asked. "Are our friends unhurt?"

"Got scalp — no hurt — take prisoner — jump on 'em, ten, two, six — cotch 'em then. Open eyes; you see."

"And the Hurons — do they seem inclined to accept the ransom? Rum, rifle, blanket and powder; you offered all, I hope, Susquesus?"

"Sartain. No forget; that bad. Say take all that; some more, too."

"And have they come to treat with us? What are we to do now, Susquesus?"

"Put down rifle — go near and talk. You go — priest go — young chief go — that t'ree. Then t'ree warrior lay down rifle, come talk too. Prisoner wait. All good."

This was sufficiently intelligible, and believing that any thing like hesitation might make the condition of Guert desperate, we prepared to comply. I could see that the Rev. Mr. Worden had no great relish for the business, but was ashamed to hang back when he saw Herman Mordaunt cheerfully advancing to the interview. We three were met by as many Hurons, among whom was Jaap's friend "Muss," who was evidently the leading person of the party. Guert and Jaap were held bound, about a hundred yards in the rear, but near enough to be spoken to, by raising the voice. Guert was in his shirt and breeches, with his head uncovered, his fine curly hair blowing about in the wind, and I thought I saw some signs of blood on his linen. This might be his own, or it might have come from an enemy. I called to him therefore, inquiring how he did, and whether he was hurt.

"Nothing to speak of, Corny, I thank you," was the cheerful answer; "these red gentlemen have had me tied to a tree, and have been seeing how near they could hurl their tomahawks without hitting. This is one of their customary amusements, and I have got a scratch or two in the sport. I hope the ladies are in good spirits, and do not let the business of last night distress them."

"There is blessed news for you, Guert — Susquesus, ask these chiefs if I may go near my friend to give him one word of consolation — on my honor no attempt to release him will be made by me, until I return here."

I spoke earnestly, and the Onondago interpreted what I had said into the language of the Hurons. I had made this somewhat hardy request, under an impulse that I found ungovernable, and was surprised as well as pleased to find it granted. These savages confided in my word, and trusted to my honor with a stately delicacy that might have done credit to the manners of civilized kings, giving themselves no apparent concern about my movements, although they occurred in their own rear. It was too late to retract, and leaving Herman Mordaunt endeavoring to drive a bargain with Muss and his two companions, I proceeded unconcerned myself, boldly toward the armed men who held Guert and Jaap prisoners. I thought my approach *did* cause a slight movement among these savages, and there was a question and answer passed between them and their leaders. The latter said but a word or two, but these were uttered authoritatively, and with a commanding toss of a hand. Brief as they were, they answered the purpose, and I was neither molested or spoken to during the short interview I had with my friend.

"God bless you, Corny, for this!" Guert cried with feeling, as I warmly shook his hand. "It requires a warm heart, and a bold one too, to lead a man into this 'lion's den.' Stay but a moment, lest some evil come of it, I beg of you. This squeeze of the hand is worth an estate to a man in my situation; but remember Anneke. Ah! Corny, my dear friend, I could be happy even here, did I know that Mary Wallace grieved for me."

"Then be happy, Guert. My sole object in venturing here was to tell you to hope every thing in that quarter. There will be no longer any coyness, any hesitation, any misgivings, when you shall be once restored to us."

"Mr. Littlepage, you would not trifle with the feelings of a miserable captive, hanging between torture and death, as is my present case! I can hardly credit my senses; yet you would not mock me!"

"Believe all I say—nay, all you *wish*, Guert. It is seldom that woman loves as *she* loves, and this I swear to you. I go now only to aid Herman Mordaunt in bringing you where your own ears shall hear such proofs of what I say, as have been uttered in mine."

Guert made no answer, but I could see he was profoundly affected. I squeezed his hand, and we parted in the full hope,

on my side at least, that the separation would be short. I have
reason to think Guert shed tears; for on looking back, I perceived his face turned away from those who were nearest to him.
I had but a single glance at Jaap. My fellow stood a little in
the rear, as became his color; but he watched my countenance
with the vigilance of a cat. I though it best not to speak to
him, though I gave him a secret sign of encouragement.

"These chiefs are not very amicably disposed, Corny," said
Herman Mordaunt, the instant I rejoined him. "They have
given me to understand that Jaap will be liberated on no terms
whatever. They must have his scalp, as Susquesus tells me, on
account of some severity he himself has shown to one of these
chiefs. To use their own language, they want it for a plaster
to this warrior's back. His fate it would seem, is sealed, and
he has only been brought out yonder to raise hopes in him that
are to be disappointed. The wretches do not scruple to avow
this in their own sententious manner. As for Guert, they say
he slew two of their warriors, and that their wives will miss
their husbands, and will not easily be quieted unless they see
his scalp, too. They offer to release him, however, on either
of two sets of terms. They will give up Guert for two of what
they call chiefs, or for four common men. If we do not like
those conditions, they will exchange him, on condition we give
two common men for him, and abandon the Nest to them, by
marching out with all my people, before the sun is up above
our heads."

"Conditions that you cannot accept under any circumstances,
I fear, sir?"

"Certainly not. The delivery of any two is out of the question — would be so, even to save my own life. As for the Nest
and all its contents, I would very willingly abandon all, a few
papers excepted had I the smallest faith in the chiefs' being able
to restrain their followers; but the dreadful massacre of William
Henry is still too recent to confide in any thing of the sort. My
answer is given already and we are about to part. Possibly,
when they see us determined, they may lower their demands a
little."

A grave parting wave of the hand was given by Muss, who
had conducted himself with great dignity in the interview, and
the three Hurons walked away in a body.

"Best go," said Susquesus, significantly. "Maybe want rifle.
Hurons in 'arnest."

On this hint, we returned to our friends, and resumed our
arms. What succeeded, I learned in part by the relations of
others, while a part was witnessed by my own eyes. It seemed
that Jaap, from the first, understood the desperate nature of his
own position. The remembrance of his misdeed in relation to
Muss, whose prisoner he had more especially become, most
probably increased his apprehensions, and his thoughts were constantly bent on obtaining his liberty, by means entirely independent of negotiations. From the instant he was brought
out of the ravine, he kept all his eyes about him, watching for
the smallest chance of effecting his purpose. It happened that
one of the savages so placed himself before the negro, who was
kept behind all near him, as to enable Jaap to draw the Huron's
knife from its sheath without being detected. He did this while
I was actually with the party, and all eyes were on me. Guert
and himself were bound, by having their arms fastened above
the elbows, behind the back; and when Guert turned aside to
shed tears, as mentioned, Jaap succeeded in cutting his fasten-
ings. This could be done, only while the savages were following my retreating form with their eyes. At the same time
Jaap gave the knife to Guert, who did him a similar service.
As the Indians did not take the alarm, the prisoners paused a
moment, holding their arms as if still bound, to look around
them. The Indian nearest Guert had two rifles, his own and
that of Muss, both leaning negligently against his shoulder, with
their breeches on the ground. To these weapons Guert pointed;
and when the three chiefs were on the point of rejoining their
friends, who were attentive to their movements in order to
ascertain the result, Guert seized this savage by his arm, which
he twisted until the Indian yelled with pain, then caught one rifle,
while Jaap laid hold of the other. Each fired and brought down
his man; then they made an onset with the butts of their pieces
on the rest of the party. This bold assault, though so desperate
in appearance, was the wisest thing they could do; as immediate flight would have left their enemies an opportunity of
sending the swift runners of their pieces in pursuit.

The first intimation we had of any movement of this sort was
in the reports of the rifles. Then, I not only saw, but I heard
the tremendous blow Jaap gave to the head of Muss; a blow
that demolished both the victim and the instrument of his destruction. Though the breech of the rifle was broken, the
heavy barrel still remained, and the negro flourished it with a

force that swept all before him. It is scarcely necessary to say Guert was not idle in such a fray. He fought for Mary Wallace, as well as for himself, and he overturned two more of the Indians, as it might be in the twinkling of an eye. Here Dirck did good service to our friends. His rifle was in his hands, and levelling it with coolness, he shot down a powerful savage who was on the point of seizing Guert from behind. This was the commencement of a general war, volleys now coming from both parties; from ourselves, and from the enemy, who were in the cover of the woods. Intimidated by the fury of the personal assault under which they were suffering, the remaining Indians near Guert and the negro leaped away toward their friends, yelling; leaving their late prisoners free, but more exposed to fire than they could have been when encircled, even by enemies.

Every thing passed with fearful rapidity. Guert seized the rifle of a fallen Indian, and Jaap obtained another, when they fell back toward us, like two lions at bay, with rifle-bullets whizzing around them at every step. Of course we fired, and we also advanced to meet them; an imprudent step, since the main body of the Hurons were covered, rendering the contest unequal. But there was no resisting the sympathetic impulses of such a moment, or the exultation we all felt at the exploits of Guert and Jaap, enacted, as they were, before our eyes. As we drew together, the former shouted and cried —

"Hurrah! Corny, my noble fellow — let us charge the woot — there'll not be a reat-skin left in it, in five minutes. Forwart, my friends — forwart, all!"

It certainly was an exciting moment. We all shouted in our turns, and all cried "forward," in common. Even Mr. Worden joined in the shout, and pressed forward. Jason, too, fought bravely; and we went at the wood like so many bulldogs. I fancy the pedagogue thought the fee-simple of his mills depended on the result. On we went, in open order, reserving our fire for the last moment, but receiving dropping shots, that did us no harm, until we dashed into the thicket.

The Hurons were discomfited and they fled. Though a panic is not usual among these wild warriors, they seldom rally on the field. If once driven against their will a close pursuit will usually disperse them for a time; and such was the case now. By the time I got fairly into the ravine I could see or hear of no enemy. My friends were on my right and left, shouting and pressing on, but there was no foe visible. Guert and Jaap were in advance, for we could not overtake them; and they had fired, for they had got the last glimpses of the enemy. But one more shot did come from the Hurons in that inroad. It was fired from some one of the retreating party who must have been lingering in its rear. The report sounded far up the ravine, and it came like a farewell and final gun. Distant as it was, however, it proved the most fatal shot to us that was fired in all that affair. I caught a glimpse of Guert through the trees, and saw him fall. In an instant I was at his side.

What a change is that from the triumph of victory to the sudden approach of death! I saw by the expression of Guert's countenance, as I raised him in my arms, that the blow was fatal. The ball, indeed, had passed directly through his body, missing the bones, but injuring the vitals. There is no mistaking the expression of a death-wound on the human countenance when the effect is direct and not remote. Nature appears to admonish the victim of his fate; so it was with Guert.

" This shot has done for me, Corny," he said, " and it seems to be the very last they intended to fire. I almost hope there can be no truth in what you told me of Mary Wallace! "

That was neither the time nor the place to speak on such a subject, and I made no answer. From the instant the fall of Guert became known, the pursuit ceased, and our whole party collected around the wounded man. The Indian alone seemed to retain any consciousness of the importance of knowing what the enemy was doing, for his philosophy was not easily disturbed by the sudden appearance of death among us. Still he liked Guert, as did every one who could get beyond the weaknesses of his outer character, and fairly at the noble traits of his manly nature. Susquesus looked at the sufferer a moment, gravely and not without concern; then he turned to Herman Mordaunt and said:

" This bad — save scalp, that good, though. Carry him in house. Susquesus follow trail and see what Injin mean."

As this was well, he was told to watch the enemy, while we bore our friend toward the Nest. Dirck consented to precede us and let the melancholy truth be known, while I continued with Guert, who held my hand the whole distance. We were a most melancholy procession for victors. Not a serious hurt had any of our party received in this last affair, the wound of Guert Ten Eyck excepted; yet I question if more real sorrow would have been felt over two or three other deaths. We had become ac-

customed to our situation; it is wonderful how soon the soldier
does; rendering death familiar and disarming him of half his
terrors; but calamities can and do occur, to bring back an army
to a sense of its true nature and its dependence on Providence.
Such had been the effect of the loss of Lord Howe, on the troops
before Ticonderoga, and such was the effect of the fall of Guert
Ten Eyck, on the small band that was collected to defend the
possessions and firesides of Ravensnest.

We entered the gate of the house and found most of its tenants
already in the court, collected like a congregation in a church
that await the entrance of the dead. Herman Mordaunt had
sent an order to have his own room prepared for the sufferer, and
thither we carried Guert. He was placed on the bed, then the
crowd silently withdrew. I observed that Guert's eyes turned
anxiously and inquiringly around, and I told him in a low voice,
I would go for the ladies myself. A smile, and a pressure of the
hand showed how well I had interpreted his thoughts.

Somewhat to my surprise, I found Mary Wallace, pale it is
true, but comparatively calm and mistress of herself. That instinct of propriety which seems to form a part of the nature of
a well-educated woman, had taught her the necessity of self-
command, that no outbreak of her feelings should affect the sufferer. As for Anneke, she was like herself, gentle, mourning, and
full of sympathy for her friend.

As soon as apprised of the object of my visit, the two girls
expressed their readiness to go to Guert. As they knew the way,
I did not attend them, purposely proceeding in another direction,
in order not to be a witness of the interview. Anneke has since
told me, however, that Mary's self-command did not altogether
desert her, while Guert's cheerful gratitude probably so far deceived her as to create a short-lived hope that the wound was
not mortal. For myself, I passed an hour in attending to the
state of things in and around the house, in order to make certain
that no negligence occurred, still to endanger our security. At
the end of that time I returned to Guert, meeting Herman Mordaunt near the door of his room.

" The little hope we had is vanished," said the last, in a sor-
rowful tone. " Poor Ten Eyck has, beyond a question, received
his death-wound, and has but a few hours to live. Were my
people safe, I would rather that every thing at Ravensnest, house
and estate, were destroyed, than had this happen! "

Prepared by this announcement, I was not as much surprised

as I might otherwise have been, at the great change that had occurred in my friend, since the time I quitted his room. It was evident he anticipated the result. Nevertheless, he was calm; nay, apparently happy. Nor was he so much enfeebled as to prevent his speaking quite distinctly, and with sufficient ease. When the machine of life is stopped by the sudden disruption of a vital ligament, the approaches of death, though more rapid than with disease, are seldom so apparent. The first evidences of a fatal termination are discovered rather through the nature of the violence, than by means of its apparent effects.

I have said that Guert seemed even happy, though death was so near. Anneke told me subsequently, that Mary Wallace had owned her love, in answer to an earnest appeal on his part, and from that moment he had expressed himself as one who was about to die contented. Poor Guert! It was little he thought of the dread future, or of the church on earth, except as the last was entitled to, and did receive on all occasions, his outward respect. It seemed that Mary Wallace, habitually so reserved and silent among her friends, had been accustomed to converse freely with Guert, and that she had made a serious effort, during her residence in Albany to enlighten his mind, or rather to arouse his feelings on this all-important subject, and that Guert, sensible of the pleasure of receiving instruction from such a source, always listened with attention. When I entered the room, some allusion had just been made to this theme.

" But for you, Mary, I should be little better than a heathen," said Guert, holding the hand of his beloved, and scarce averting his eyes from their idol a single instant. " If God has mercy on me, it will be on your account."

" Oh! no — no — no — Guert, say not, think not *thus!* " exclaimed Mary Wallace, shocked at the excess of his attachment even for herself at such a moment. " We all receive our pardons through the death and mediation of his blessed Son. Nothing else can save you, or any of us, my dear, dear Guert; and I implore you not to think otherwise."

Guert looked a little bewildered; still he looked pleased. The first expression was probably produced by his not exactly comprehending the nature of that mysterious explanation which baffles the unaided powers of man, and which, indeed, is to be felt, rather than understood. The look of pleasure had its origin in the " dear, dear Guert," and more than that, in the consciousness of possessing the affections of the woman he had so long loved, almost against hope. Guert Ten Eyck was a man of bold and reckless character in all that pertained to risks, frolic, and youthful adventure; but the meekest Christian could scarcely possess a more lowly opinion of his own frailties and sins, than this dashing young fellow possessed of his own claims to be valued by such a being as Mary Wallace. I often wondered how he ever presumed to love her, but suppose the apparent vanity must be ascribed to the resistless power of a passion that is known to be the strongest of our nature. It was also a sort of moral anomaly that two so opposed to each other in character — the one verging on extreme recklessness, the other pushing prudence almost to prudery; the one so gay as to seem to live for frolic, the other quiet and reserved — should conceive this strong predilection for each other; but so it was. I have heard persons say, however, that these varieties in temperament awaken interest, and that they who have commenced with such dissimilarities, but have assimilated by communion, attachment, and habits, after all make the happiest couples.

Mary Wallace lost all reserve, in the gush of tenderness and sympathy that now swept all before it. Throughout the whole of that morning she hung about Guert, as the mother watches the ailing infant. If his thirst was to be assuaged, her hand held the cup; if his pillow was to be replaced, her care suggested the alteration; if his brow was to be wiped, she performed that office for him, suffering no other to come between her and the object of her solicitude.

There were moments when the manner in which Mary Wallace hung over Guert, was infinitely touching. Anneke and I knew that her very soul yearned to lead his thoughts to dwell on the subject of the great change that was so near. Nevertheless, the tenderness of the woman was so much stronger than even the anxiety of the Christian, that we perceived she feared the influence on his wound. At length, happily for an anxiety that was beginning to be too painful for endurance, Guert spoke on the subject himself. Whether his mind naturally adverted to such a topic, or he perceived the solicitude of his gentle nurse, I could not say.

"I cannot stay with you long, Mary," he said, "and I should like to have Mr. Worden's prayers, united to yours, offered up in my behalf. Corny will seek the Dominie for an old friend?"

I vanished from the room, and was absent ten minutes. At the end of that time, Mr. Worden was ready in his surplice, and we went to the sick-room. Certainly our old pastor had not the way of manifesting the influence of religion, that is usual to the colonies, especially to those of the more northern and eastern portions of the country; yet there was a heartiness in his manner of praying, at times, that almost persuaded me he was a good man. I will own, however, that Mr. Worden was one of those clergymen who could pray much more sincerely for certain persons than for others. He was partial to poor Guert; and I really thought this was manifest in his accents on this melancholy occasion.

The dying man was relieved by this attention to the rites of the church. Guert was not a metaphysician; and at no period of his life, I believe, did he enter very closely into the consideration of those fearful questions which were connected with his existence, origin, destination, and position, in the long scale of animated beings. He had those general notions on these subjects that all civilized men imbibe by education and communion with their fellows, but nothing more. He understood it was a duty to pray; and I make no doubt he fancied there were times and seasons in which this duty was more imperative than at others; and times and seasons when it might be dispensed with.

How tenderly and how anxiously did Mary Wallace watch over her patient, during the whole of that sad day! She seemed to know neither weariness nor fatigue. Toward evening — it was just as the sun was tinging the summits of the trees with its parting light — she came toward Anneke and myself with a face that was slightly illuminated with something like a glow of pleasure, and whispered to us that Guert was better. Within ten minutes of that moment I approached the bed, and saw a slight movement of the patient's hand, as if he desired me to come nearer.

" Corny," said Guert, in a low, languid voice — " it is nearly all over. I wish I could see Mary Wallace once more, before I die."

Mary was not, *could* not be distant. She fell upon her knees, and clasped the yielding form of her lover to her heart. Nothing was said on either side; or if aught were said, it was whispered, and was of a nature too sacred to be communicated to others. In that attitude did this young woman, long so coy and difficult to decide, remain for near an hour, and in that quiet, cherishing, womanly embrace, did Guert Ten Eyck breathe his last.

I left the sufferer as much alone with the woman of his heart, as comported with prudence and a proper attention on my part; but it was my melancholy duty to close his eyes. Thus prematurely terminated the earthly career of as manly a spirit as ever dwelt in human form. That it had imperfections, my pen has not concealed; but the long years that have since passed away, have not served to obliterate the regard so noble a temperament could not fail to awaken.

CHAPTER XXX

" How slow the day slides on! When we desire
Time's haste, he seems to lose a match with lobsters:
And when we wish him stay, he imps his wings
With feathers plumed with thought."

ALBAMAZAR.

It is unnecessary to dwell on the grief that we all felt for our loss. That night was necessarily one of watchfulness, but few were inclined to sleep. The return of light found us unmolested, however; and an hour or two later, Susquesus came in, and reported that the enemy had retreated toward Ticonderoga. There was nothing more to fear from that quarter, and the settlers soon began to return to their dwellings, or to such as remained. In the course of a week the axe again rang in the forest, and rude habitations began to reappear, in the places of those that had been destroyed. As Bulstrode could not well be removed, Herman Mordaunt determined to pass the remainder of the season at Ravensnest, with the double view of accommodating his guest, and of encouraging his settlers. The danger was known to be over for that summer at least, and, ere the approach of another, it was hoped that the humiliated feelings of Great Britain would so far be aroused, as to drive the enemy from the province; as indeed was effectually done.

On consultation, it was decided that the body of Guert ought to be sent for interment among his friends, to Albany. Dirck and myself accompanied it, as the principal attendants, all that remained of our party going with us. Herman Mordaunt thought it necessary to remain at Ravensnest, and Anneke would not quit her father. The Rev. Mr. Worden's missionary zeal had, by this trial, effectually evaporated, and he profited by so favorable an occasion to withdraw into the safer and more peopled districts. I well remember as we marched after the horse-litter that carried the remains of poor Guert, the divine's making the following sensible remarks: —

" You see how it is, on this frontier, Corny," he said; " it is premature to think of introducing Christianity. Christianity is

410

essentially a civilized religion, and can only be of use among civilized beings. It is true, my young friend, that many of the early
apostles were not learned, after the fashion of this world, but
they were all thoroughly civilized. Palestine was a civilized
country, and the Hebrews were a great people; and I consider
the precedent set by our blessed Lord is a command to be followed in all time, and that his appearance in Judea is tantamount
to his saying to his apostles, ' go and preach me and my gospel
to all *civilized* people.' "

I ventured to remark that there was something like a direct
command to preach it to *all* nations, to be found in the Bible.

"Ay, that is true enough," answered Mr. Worden, "but it
clearly means all *civilized* nations. Then, this was before the
discovery of America, and it is fair enough to presume that the
command referred solely to *known* nations. The texts of scripture are not to be strained, but are to be construed naturally,
Corny, and this seems to me to be the natural reading of that
passage. No, I have been rash and imprudent in pushing duty
to exaggeration, and shall confine my labors to their proper
sphere, during the remainder of my days. Civilization is just
as much a means of Providence as religion itself; and it is clearly
intended that one should be built on the other. A clergyman
goes quite far enough from the centre of refinement, when he
quits home to come into these colonies to preach the gospel;
letting alone these scalping devils the Indians, who, I greatly fear,
were never born to be saved. It may do well enough to have
societies to keep them in view, but a meeting in London is quite
near enough ever to approach them."

Such, ever after, appeared to be the sentiments of the Rev.
Mr. Worden, and I took no pains to change them. I ought,
however, to have alluded to the parting with Anneke, before
I gave the foregoing extract from the parson's homily. Circumstances prevented my having much private communication with
my betrothed before quitting the Nest; for Anneke's sympathy
with Mary Wallace was too profound to permit her to think
much, just then, of aught but the latter's sorrows. As for Mary
herself, the strength and depth of her attachment and grief were
never fully appreciated, until time came to vindicate them. Her
seeming calm was soon restored, for it was only under a tempest
of feeling that Mary Wallace lost her self-command; and the
affliction that was inevitable and irremediable, one of her regulated
temperament and high principles, struggled to endure with Chris-

tian submission. It was only in after-life that I came to know how intense and absorbing had, in truth, been her passion for the gay, high-spirited, ill-educated, and impulsive young Albanian.

Anneke wept for a few minutes in my arms, a quarter of an hour before our melancholy procession quitted the Nest. The dear girl had no undue reserve with me; though I found her a little reluctant to converse on the subject of our own loves so soon after the fearful scenes we had just gone through. Still she left me in no doubt on the all-important point of my carrying away with me her whole and entirely undivided heart. Bulstrode she never had, never *could* love. This she assured me over and over again. He amused her, and she felt for him some of the affection and interest of kindred, but not the least of any other interest. Poor Bulstrode! now I was certain of success I had very magnanimous sentiments in his behalf, and could give him credit for various good qualities that had been previously obscured in my eyes. Herman Mordaunt had requested nothing might be said to the major of my engagement; though an early opportunity was to be taken by himself to let the suitor understand that Anneke declined the honor of his hand. It was thought the information would come best from him.

"I shall be frank with you, Littlepage, and confess I have been very anxious for the union of my daughter and Mr. Bulstrode," in the interview we had before I left the Nest; "and I trust to your own good sense to account for it. I knew Bulstrode before I had any knowledge of yourself; and there was already a connection between us, that was just of a nature to render one that was closer desirable. I shall not deny that I fancied Anneke fitted to adorn the station and circles to which Bulstrode could have carried her; and perhaps it is a natural parental weakness to wish to see one's child promoted. We talk of humility and contentment, Corny, though there is much of the *nolo episcopari* about it, after all. But you see that the preference of the child is so much stronger than that of the parent that it must prevail. I dare say, after all, you would much rather be Anneke's choice than be mine?"

"I can have no difficulty in admitting that, sir," I answered; "and I feel very sensible of the liberal manner in which you yield your own preferences to our wishes. Certainly, in the way of rank and fortune, I have little to offer, Mr. Mordaunt, as an offset to Mr. Bulstrode's claims; but, in love for your daughter, and in an ardent desire to make her happy, I shall not yield to him, or any other man, though he were a king."

"In the way of fortune, Littlepage, I have very few regrets. As you are to live in this country, the joint means of the two families, which some day must centre in you and Anneke, will prove all-sufficient; and as for posterity, Ravensnest and Mooseridge will supply ample provisions. As the colony grows, your descendants will increase, and your means will increase with both. No, no; I may have been a little disappointed, that much I will own; but I have not been at any time displeased. God bless you, then, my dear boy; write us from Albany, and come to us at Lilacsbush in September. Your reception will be that of a son."

It is needless to dwell on the melancholy procession we formed through the woods. Dirck and myself kept near the body, on foot, until we reached the highway, when vehicles were provided for the common transportation. On reaching Albany we delivered the remains of Guert to his relatives, and there was a suitable funeral given. The bricked closet behind the chimney was opened as usual, and the six dozen of Madeira that had been placed in it twenty-four years before, or the day the poor fellow was christened, was found to be very excellent. I remember it was said generally that better wine was drunk at the funeral of Guert Ten Eyck, than had been tasted at the obsequies of any individual who was not a Van Rensselaer, a Schuyler, or a Ten Broeck, within the memory of man. I now speak of funerals in Albany, for I do suppose the remark would scarcely apply to many other funerals lower down the river. As a rule, however, very good wine was given at all our funerals.

The Rev. Mr. Worden officiated, and was universally regarded with interest, as a pious minister of the gospel, who had barely escaped the fate of the person he was now committing " dust to dust," while devotedly and ardently employed in endeavoring to rescue the souls of the very savages who sought his life, from the fate of the heathen.

I remember there was a very well worded paragraph to this effect in the New York Gazette, and I had heard it said, but do not remember to have ever seen it myself, that in one of the reports of the Society for the Promulgation of the Gospel in Foreign Parts, the circumstances were alluded to in a very touching and edifying manner.

Poor Guert! I passed a few minutes at his grave before we

went south. It was all that was left of his fine person, his high spirit, his lion-hearted courage, his buoyant spirits, and his unextinguishable love of frolic. A finer physical man I never beheld, or one who better satisfied the eye, in all respects. That the noble tenement was not more intellectually occupied, was purely the consequence of a want of education. Notwithstanding, all the books in the world could not have converted Guert Ten Eyck into a Jason Newcome, or Jason Newcome into a Guert Ten Eyck. Each owed many of his peculiarities, doubtless, to the province in which he was bred and born, and to the training consequent on these accidents; but nature had also drawn broad distinctions between them. All the wildness of Guert's impulses could not altogether destroy his feelings, tone, and tact as a gentleman; while all the soaring, extravagant pretensions of Jason never could have ended in elevating him to that character. Alas! Poor Guert! I sincerely mourned his loss for years, nor has his memory yet ceased to have a deep interest with me.

Dirck Follock and I would have been a good deal caressed at Albany, on our return, both on account of what had happened, and on account of our Dutch connections, had we been in the mood to profit by the disposition of the people. But we were not. The sad events with which we had been connected were still too recent to indulge in gayeties or company; and, as soon as possible after the funeral, we seized the opportunity of embarking on board a sloop bound to New York. Our voyage was generally considered a prosperous one, lasting, indeed, only six days. We took the ground three times, it is true; but nothing was thought of that, such accidents being of frequent occurrence. Among the events of this sort, one occurred in the Overslaugh, and I passed a few hours there very pleasantly, as it was so near the scene of our adventure on the river. Anneke always occupied much of my thoughts, but pleasing pictures of her gentle decision, her implicit reliance on myself, her resignation, her spirit, and her intelligence, were now blended, without any alloy, in my recollections. The dear girl had confessed to me, that she loved me even on that fearful night, for her tenderness in my behalf dated much farther back. This was a great addition to the satisfaction with which I went over every incident and speech, in recollection, endeavoring to recall the most minute tone or expression, to see if I could *now* connect it with any sign of that passion, which I was authorized in believing did even then exist. Thus aided, equally by Anneke's gentle, blushing admissions, and my own wishes, I

had no difficulty in recalling pictures that were infinitely agreeable
to myself, though possibly not minutely accurate.

In the Tappaan Sea, Dirck left us; proceeding into Rockland,
to join his family. I continued on in the sloop, reaching port
next day. My uncle and aunt Legge were delighted to see me,
and I soon found I should be a lion, had I leisure to remain in
town, in order to enjoy the notoriety my connection with the
northern expedition had created. I found a deep mortification
pervading the capital, in consequence of our defeat, mingled with
a high determination to redeem our tarnished honor.

Satanstoe, with all its endearing ties, however, called me away;
and I left town, on horseback, leaving my effects to follow by
the first good opportunity, the morning of the day succeeding
that on which I had arrived. I shall not attempt to conceal one
weakness. As usual, I stopped at Kingsbridge to dine and bait;
and while the notable landlady was preparing my dinner, I ascended the heights to catch a distant view of Lilacsbush. There
lay the pretty cottage-like dwelling, placed beneath its hill, amid
a wilderness of shrubbery; but its lovely young mistress was far
away, and I found the pleasure with which I gazed at it blended
with regrets.

"You have been north, I hear, Mr. Littlepage," my landlady
observed, while I was discussing her lamb, and peas and aspara-
gus; "pray, sir, did you hear or see any thing of our honored
neighbors, Herman Mordaunt and his charming daughter?"

"Much of both, Mrs. Light; and that under trying circumstances. Mooseridge, my father's property in that part of the
province, is quite near to Ravensnest, Herman Mordaunt's
estate, and I have passed some time at it. Have no tidings of
the family reached you lately?"

"None, unless it be the report that Miss Anneke will never
return to us."

"Anneke not return! In the name of wonder, how do you
hear this?"

"Not as *Miss* Anneke, but as Lady Anneke, or something of
that sort. Isn't there a General Bulstrom, or some great officer
or other, who seeks her hand, and on whom she smiles, sir?"

"I presume I understand you, now. Well, what do you learn
of him?"

"Only that they are to be married next month — some say
they *are* married already, and that the old gentleman gives Lilacsbush out and out, and four thousand pounds currency down, in

order to purchase so high an honor for his child. I tell the neighbors it is too much, Miss Anneke being worth any lord in England, on her own, sole account."

This intelligence did not disturb me, of course, for it was tavern-tidings and neighbors' news. Neighbors! How much is that sacred word prostituted! You shall find people opening their ears with avidity to the gossip of a neighborhood, when nineteen times in twenty it is less entitled to credit than the intelligence which is obtained from a distance, provided the latter come from persons of the same class in life as the individuals in question, and are known to them. What means had this woman of knowing the secrets of Herman Mordaunt's family, that were one-half as good as those possessed by friends in Albany, for instance? This neighborhood testimony, as it is called, does a vast deal of mischief in the province, and most especially in those parts of it where our own people are brought in contact with their fellow subjects from the more eastern colonies. In my eyes, Jason Newcome's opinions of Herman Mordaunt and his acts would be nearly worthless, shrewd as I admit the man to be; for the two have not a distinctive opinion, custom, and I had almost said principle, in common. Just appreciation of motives and acts can only proceed from those who feel and think alike; and this is morally impossible where there exist broad distinctions in social classes. It is just for this reason that we attach so little importance to the ordinary reports, and even to the sworn evidence of servants.

Our reception at Satanstoe was just what might have been expected. My dear mother hugged me to her heart again and again, and seemed never to be satisfied with feasting her eyes on me. My father was affected at seeing me, too; and I thought there was a very decided moisture in his eyes. As for old Captain Hugh Roger, threescore-and-ten had exhausted his fluids pretty much; but he shook me heartily by the hand, and listened to my account of the movements before Ty with all a soldier's interest, and with somewhat of the fire of one who had served himself in more fortunate times. I had to fight my battles o'er and o'er again, as a matter of course, and to recount the tale of Ravensnest in all its details. We were at supper when I concluded my most labored narrative, and when I began to hope my duties in this respect were finally terminated. But my dear mother had heavier matters still on her mind; and it was necessary that I should give her a private conference, in her own little room.

" Corny, my beloved child," commenced this anxious and most

tender parent, " you have said nothing *particular* to me of the Mordaunts. It is now time to speak of that family."

" Have I not told you, mother, how we met at Albany, and of what occurred on the river? " I had not spoken of that adventure in my letters, because I was uncertain of the true state of Anneke's feelings, and did not wish to raise expectations that might never be realized. " And of our going to Ravensnest in company, and of all that happened at Ravensnest after our return from Ty? "

" What is all this to me, child! I wish to hear you speak of Anneke — is it true that she is going to be married? "

" It is true. I can affirm that much from her own mouth."

My dear mother's countenance fell, and I could hardly pursue my wicked *equivoque* any further.

" And she has even had the effrontery to own this to *you*, Corny."

" She has indeed; though truth compels me to add that she blushed a great deal while admitting it, and seemed only half disposed to be so frank; that is, at first; for in the end, she rather smiled than blushed."

" Well, this amazes me! It is only a proof that vanity, and worldly rank, and worldly riches stand higher in the estimation of Anneke Mordaunt, than excellence and modest merit."

" What riches and worldly rank have I, mother, to tempt any woman to forget the qualities you have mentioned? "

" I was not thinking of you, my son, in that sense at all. Of course, I mean Mr. Bulstrode."

" What has Mr. Bulstrode to do with my marriage with Anne Mordaunt? or any one else but her own sweet self, who has consented to become my wife; her father, who accepts me for a son; my father, who is about to imitate his example by taking Anneke to his heart as a daughter, and you, my dearest, dearest mother, who are the only person likely to raise obstacles, as you are now doing? "

This was a boyish mode of producing a most delightful surprise, I am very ready to acknowledge; and when I saw my mother burst into tears, I felt both regret and shame at having practised it. But youth is the season of folly, and happy is the man who can say he has never trifled more seriously with the feelings of a parent. I was soon pardoned — what offence would not that devoted mother have pardoned her only child! — when I was made to relate all that was proper to be told of what had passed between Anneke and myself. It is scarcely necessary to say I was assured of the cheerful acquiescence in my wishes, of all my own family, from Captain Hugh Roger down to the dear person who was speaking. They had set their minds on my becoming the husband of this very young lady; and I could not possibly have made any communication that would be more agreeable, as I was given to understand from each and all that very night.

My return to Satanstoe occurred in the last half of the month of July. The Mordaunts were not to be at Lilacsbush until the middle of September, and I had near two months to wait for that happy moment. The time was passed as well as it could be. I endeavored to interest myself in the old Neck, and to plan schemes of future happiness there, that were to be realized in Anneke's society. It was and is a noble farm; rich, beautifully placed, having water on three of its sides, in capital order, and well stocked with such apples, peaches, apricots, plums, and other fruits, as the world can scarcely equal. It is true that the provinces a little further south, such as New Jersey, Pennsylvania, Maryland and Virginia, think they can beat us in peaches; but I have never tasted any fruit that I thought would compare with that of Satanstoe. I love every tree, wall, knoll, swell, meadow and hummock about the old place. One thing distresses me. I love old names, such as my father knew the same places by; and I like to mispronounce a word when custom and association render the practice familiar. I would not call my friend, Dirck Follock, any thing else but Follock, unless it might be in a formal way, or when asking him to drink a glass of wine with me, for a great deal. So it is with Satanstoe; the name is homely, I am willing to allow; but it is strong and conveys an idea. It relates also to the usages and notions of the country; and names ought always to be preserved, except in those few instances in which there are good reasons for altering them. I regret to say, that ever since the appearance of Jason Newcome among us, there has been a disposition among the ignorant and vulgar to call the Neck, Dibbleton; under the pretence, I have already mentioned, that it once belonged to the family of Dibblees, or as some think, as a pious diminutive of Devil's-Town. I indignantly repel this supposition; though I do believe that Dibbleton is only a sneaking mode of pronouncing Devilton, as I admit I have heard the old people laughingly term the Neck. This belongs to the " Gaul darn ye " school, and it is not to my taste. I say the ignorant and vulgar, for this is just the class to be squeamish on such subjects. I have been told — though I cannot say that I have heard it myself — but I am told there have been people from the eastward among us of late years, who affect to call " Hell-gate," " Hurl-gate," or " Whirl-gate," or by some other such sentimental, whirl-a-gig name; and these are the gentry who would wish to alter " Satanstoe " into " Dibbleton! " Since the eastern troops have begun to come among us, indeed, they have commenced a desperate inroad on many of our old venerated Dutch names; names that the English, direct from home, have generally respected. Indeed, change — change in all things seems to be the besetting passion of these people. We of New York are content to do as our ancestors have done before us; and this they ridicule, making it matter of accusation against us that we follow the notions of our fathers. I shall never complain that they are deserting so many of *their* customs; for I regard the changes as improvements, but I beg that they may leave us ours.

That there is such a thing as improvement I am willing enough to admit, as well as that it not only compels, but excuses changes; but I am yet to learn it is matter of just reproach that a man follows in the footsteps of those who have gone before him. The apothegms of David, and the wisdom of Solomon, are just as much apothegms and wisdom, in our own time, as they were the day they were written, and for precisely the same reason — their truth. Where there is so much stability in morals, there must be permanent principles, and something surely is worthy to be saved from the wreck of the past. I doubt if all this craving for change has not more of selfishness in it than either of expediency or of philosophy; and I could wish, at least, that Satanstoe should never be frittered away into so sneaking a substitute as Dibbleton.

That was a joyful day, when a servant in Herman Mordaunt's livery rode in upon our lawn, and handed me a letter from his master, informing me of the safe arrival of the family, and inviting me to ride over next day in time to take a late breakfast at Lilacs-bush. Anneke had written to me twice previously to this; two beautifully expressed, feminine, yet spirited, affectionate letters, in which the tenderness and sensibility of her nature were barely restrained by the delicacy of her sex and situation. On the receipt of this welcome invitation, I was guilty of the only piece of romantic extravagance that I can remember having committed in the course of my life. Herman Mordaunt's black was well treated, and dismissed with a letter of acceptance. One hour after he left Satanstoe — I *do* love that venerable name, and hope all the

Yankees in Christendom will not be able to alter it to Dibbleton
— but one hour after the negro was off, I followed him myself,
intending to sleep at the well-known inn at Kingsbridge, and not
present myself at the Bush, until the proper hour next morning.

I had got to the house of the talkative landlady two hours
before sunset, put up my horse, secured my lodgings, and was
eating a bite myself, when the good housewife entered the room.

"Your servant, Mr. Littlepage," commenced this loquacious
person; "how are the venerable Captain Hugh Roger, and the
major, your honored father? Well, I see by your smile. Well, it
is a comfortable thing to have our friends enjoy good health —
my own poor man enjoyed most wretched health all last winter,
and is likely to enjoy very much the same, that which is coming.
I should think you had come to the wedding at Lilacsbush, Mr.
Corny, had you not stopped at my door, instead of going on direct
to that of Herman Mordaunt."

I started, but supposed that the news of what was to happen
had leaked out, and that this good woman, whose ears were always
open, had got hold of a neighborhood-*truth*, for once in her life.

"I am on no such errand, Mrs. Light, but hope to be married,
one of these days, to some one or other."

"I was not thinking of your marriage, sir, but that of Miss
Anneke, over at the Bush, to this Lord Bulstrom. It's a great
connection for the Mordaunts, after all, though Herman Mordaunt
is of good blood himself, they tell me. The knight's man often
comes here, to taste new cider, which he admits is as good as
English cider, and I believe it is the only thing which he has
found in the colonies that he thinks is one-half as good; but
Thomas tells me all is settled, and that the wedding must take
place right soon. It has only been put off on account of Miss
Wallace, who is in deep mourning for her own husband, having
lost him within the honey-moon, which is the reason she still bears
her own name. They tell me a widow who loses her husband in
the honey-moon is obliged to bear her maiden name; otherwise
Miss Mary would be Mrs. Van Goort, or something like that."

As it was very clear the neighborhood knew but little about
the true state of things in Herman Mordaunt's family, I took my
hat and proceeded to execute the intention with which I had left
home. I was sorry to hear that Bulstrode was at Lilacsbush, but
had no apprehensions of his ever marrying Anneke. I took my
way to the heights, and soon reached the field where I had once
met the ladies on horseback. There, seated under a tree, I saw

Bulstrode, alone, and apparently in deep contemplation. It was
no part of my plan to be seen, or to have my presence known,
and I was retiring, when I heard my name, discovered that I was
recognized, and joined him.

The first glance at Bustrode showed me that he knew the truth.
He colored, bit his lips, forced a smile, and came forward to meet
me, limping just enough to add interest to his gait, and offered
his hand to me with a frank manliness that gave him great merit
in my eyes. It was no trifle to lose Anne Mordaunt, and I am
afraid I could not have manifested half so much magnanimity.
But Bulstrode was a man of the world, and he knew how to command the exhibition of his feelings, if not to command the feelings
themselves.

"I told you once, Corny," he said, offering his hand, "that
we must remain friends, *coute qui coute* — you have been successful, and I have failed. Herman Mordaunt told me the melancholy
fact before we left Albany; and I can tell you, his regrets were
not so very flattering to you. Nevertheless, he admits you are a
capital fellow, and that if it were not for Alexander, he could wish
to be Diogenes. So you have only to provide yourself with a
lantern and a tub, marry Anneke, and set up housekeeping. As
for the honest man, I propose saving you some trouble, by offering
myself in that character, even before you light your wick. Come,
take a seat on this bench, and let us chat."

There was something a little forced in all this, it is true, but it
was manly. I took the seat, and Bulstrode went on.

"It was the river that made your fortune, Corny, and undid
me."

I smiled, but said nothing; though I knew better.

"There is fate in love, as in war. Well, I am as well off as
Abercrombie; we both expected to be victorious, while each is
conquered. I am more fortunate, indeed; for he can never expect
to get another army, while I may get another wife. I wish you
would be frank with me, and confess to what you particularly
ascribe your own success."

"It is natural, Mr. Bulstrode, that a young woman should
prefer to live in her own country, to living in a strange land, and
among strangers."

"Ay, Corny, that is both patriotic and modest; but it is not
the real reason. No, sir; it was Scrub and the theatricals, by
which I have been undone. With most provincials, Mr. Littlepage, it is a sufficient apology for any thing, that the metropolis

approves. So it is with you colonists in general; let England say yes, and you dare not say no. There is one thing that persons who live so far from home seldom learn; and it is this: there are two sorts of great worlds; the great vulgar world, which includes all but the very best in taste, principles, and manners, whether it be in a capital or in a country; and the great *respectable* world, which, infinitely less numerous, contains the judicious, the instructed, the intelligent, and on some questions, the good. Now the first form fashion; whereas the last produce something far better and more enduring than fashion. Fashion often stands rebuked in the presence of the last class, small as it ever is, numerically. Very high rank, very finished tastes, very strong judgments, and very correct principles, all unite more or less, to make up this class. One or more of these qualities may be wanting, perhaps, but the union of the whole forms the perfection of the character. We have daily examples of this at home, as well as elsewhere; though in our artificial state of society it requires more decided qualities to resist the influence of fashion, when there is not positive, social rank to sustain it, perhaps, than it would in one more natural. That which first struck me in Anneke, as is the case with most young men, was the delicacy of her appearance, and her beauty. This I will not deny. In this respect, your American women have quite taken me by surprise. In England we are so accustomed to associate a certain delicacy of person and air, with high rank, that I will confess, I landed in New York with no expectation of meeting a single female in the whole country, that was not comparatively coarse, and what we are accustomed to consider common, in physique; yet I must now say, that apart from mere conventional finish, I find quite as large a proportion of aristocratical looking females among you as if you had a full share of duchesses. The last thing I should think of calling an American woman, would be coarse. She may want manner, in one sense; she may want finish in a dozen things; she may, and often does, want utterance, as utterance is understood among the accomplished; but she is seldom, indeed, coarse or vulgar, according to our European understanding of the terms."

" And of what is all this *à propos*, Bulstrode? "

" Oh! of your success, and my defeat, of course, Corny," answered the major, smiling. " What I mean, is this — that Anneke is one of your second class, or is better than what fashion can make her; and Scrub has been the means of my undoing. She does not care for fashion, in a play, or a novel, or a dress even,

but looks for the proprieties. Yes, Scrub has proved my undoing! "

I did not exactly believe the last; but finding Bulstrode so well
disposed to give his rejection this turn, it was not my part to con-
tradict him. We talked together half an hour longer, in the most
amicable manner, when we parted; Bulstrode promising not to
betray the secret of my presence.

I lingered in sight of the house until evening, when I ventured
nearer, hoping to get a glimpse of Anneke as she passed some
window, or appeared, by the soft light of the moon, under the
piazza that skirted the south front of the building. Lilacsbush
deserved its name, being a perfect wilderness of shrubbery; and
favored by the last, I had got quite near the house, when I heard
light footsteps on the gravel of an adjacent walk. At the next
instant, soft, low voices met my ears, and I was a sort of compelled
auditor of what followed.

" No, Anne, my fate is sealed for this world," said Mary
Wallace, " and I shall live Guert's widow as faithfully and devotedly, as if the marriage-vow had been pronounced. This much
is due to his memory, on account of the heartless doubts I permitted to influence me, and which drove him into those terrible
scenes that destroyed him. When a woman really loves, Anneke,
it is vain to struggle against any thing but positive unworthiness,
I fear. Poor Guert was not unworthy in any sense; he was erring
and impulsive, but not unworthy. No — no — not unworthy!
I ought to have given him my hand, and he would have been
spared to us. As it is, I can only live his widow in secret, and
in love. You have done well, dearest Anneke, in being so frank
with Corny Littlepage, and in avowing that preference which you
have felt almost from the first day of your acquaintance."

Although this was music to my ears, honor would not suffer me
to hear more, and I moved swiftly away, stirring the bushes in a
way to apprise the speaker of the proximity of a stranger. It
was necessary to appear, and I endeavored so to do, without
creating any alarm.

" It must be Mr. Bulstrode," said the gentle voice of Anneke,
" who is probably looking for us — see, there he comes, and we
will meet —— "

The dear speaker became tongue-tied; for, by this time, I was
near enough to be recognized. At the next instant, I held her in
my arms, Mary Wallace disappeared, how or when, I cannot say.
I place a veil over the happy hour that succeeded, leaving the old

to draw on their experience for its pictures, and the young to live in hope. At the end of that time, by Anneke's persuasion, I entered the house, and had to brave Herman Mordaunt's disposition to rally me. I was not only mercifully, but hospitably treated, however, Anneke's father merely laughing at my little adventure, saying, that he looked upon it favorably, and as a sign that I was a youth of spirit.

Early in October we were married, the Rev. Mr. Worden performing the ceremony. Our home was to be Lilacsbush, which Herman Mordaunt conveyed to me the same day, leaving it, as it was furnished, entirely in my hands. He also gave me my wife's mother's fortune, a respectable independence; and the death of Captain Hugh Roger soon after, added considerably to my means. We made but one family, between town, Lilacsbush and Satanstoe — Anneke and my mother, in particular, conceiving a strong affection for each other.

As for Bulstrode, he went home before the marriage, but keeps up a correspondence with us to this hour. He is still single, and is a declared old bachelor. His letters, however, are too light-hearted to leave us any concern on the subject; though these are matters that may fall to the share of my son Mordaunt, should he ever have the grace to continue this family narrative.

A NOTE ON THE EDITOR

Robert L. Hough was born in 1924 in Los Angeles, California. His undergraduate years were interrupted by the war—he served from 1943 to 1946 with the United States Army Air Force, mostly in the South Pacific theatre. After graduating from Pomona College with highest honors (A.B., 1949), he studied at Columbia University (M.S. in journalism, 1950) and Stanford University (Ph.D., 1957). Now an associate professor of English at the University of Nebraska, Mr. Hough has contributed a number of studies to scholarly periodicals and is the author of *The Quiet Rebel: William Dean Howells as Social Commentator*, published by the University of Nebraska Press in 1960.